As All My Fathers Were

Other Books by James A. Misko

Fiction

The Most Expensive Mistress in Jefferson County

The Cut of Pride

For What He Could Become

Non Fiction

Creative Financing of Real Estate

How to Finance any Real Estate any Place any Time

How to Finance any Real Estate
any Place any Time – Strategies That Work

As All My
Fathers
Were

a novel

JAMES A. MISKO

For information regarding special discounts
for bulk purchases, please contact:
Northwest Ventures Press book sales at 907-562-2520.

Cover and interior design by Frame25 Productions

Library of Congress Cataloging-in-Publication Data
available upon request

ISBN: 978-0-9640826-4-9
eBook ISBN: 978-0-9640826-5-6

Manufactured in the United States of America

10 9 8 7 6 5 4 3 2 1

First Edition

*This book is a work of fiction. Names, characters, places, and incidents
either are products of the author's imagination or are used fictitiously.*

Dedicated to editors and authors alive and dead

When an author finishes a manuscript, a sense of elation and job well done surges through his entire being, Then it is submitted to editors who have no emotional attachment to its birthing. Their job is to offer suggestions and corrections to make it better.

When the author receives their critiques and starts to incorporate their suggestions pressing him to cut and revise, his attitude toward editors begins to change.

In the end, it is all for the better. Four excellent critique artists and editors edited this book: some for punctuation, some for story arc, and some for overall sense of novel construction. Any remaining mistakes are mine. I would like to thank them all, for without them many of my original literary offenses would have made it to the printing press.

Irena Praitis: Instructor of Creative Writing, UC State, Fullerton
Robert Masello: Instructor, speaker, author of *Romanov Cross*
Lisa Cron: Speaker, author of *Wired for Story*
Cathy Bromley: Copy Editor

An author tends to find other authors he enjoys both for style and content and their work guides him. They provide good reading and form a stable base. I owe a lot to the following.

Living Authors
James Alexander Thom, John Graves, Howard Frank Mosher, Kent Haruf, Pat Conroy, Nick Jans, Lynn Schooler, Herman Wouk, Richard Russo, Dick Couch and Andrew Neiderman.

Deceased Authors
Jessamyn West, A.J. Cronin, Erskine Caldwell, Robert Service, Robert Ruark, R.F. Delderfield, Vardis Fisher, Robert Penn Warren, Wallace Stegner, Rudyard Kipling, Ernest Hemingway, John Steinbeck, and Jack London.

Chapter 1

THE METALLIC RING OF the phone in the library bounced off the walls of books and sank into the heavy carpet. Shafts of afternoon sun that often lifted the spirits of Nebraska farmers in the spring filtered through the windows. Richard Barrett picked up the receiver. Startled from his peaceful contemplation of the coming crop season, he was not his friendliest.

Down the hall, his brother, Seth Barrett, scooped out the last spoonful of ice cream and threw the empty container in the trash. Spoon in mouth, he walked down the hall toward the library, his bare feet sticking to the bee's wax finish on the oak flooring.

"Who called?" Seth said.

"Craig Jamison," Richard replied. "Wants to read Mom's will this afternoon."

"Where—here?"

Richard nodded. "I will call Ginny."

"Why call her? She's not direct kin."

"I am sure she will be mentioned in it."

"She'd better not be getting any of the ranch."

An exasperated smile crept over Richard's face. My gawd, the brothers were nine and ten years old in the small town of Plattsmouth, Nebraska, when Mae and Andrew Barrett adopted Virginia and still the fence existed that Seth had built between them. Maybe Seth was going to tell him something he didn't know. With Seth, things seethed inside for some time before they surfaced. If something was going to surface now, Richard wanted to be fully aware of it.

Seth picked up the urn of cremains off the mantel and read the brass plate. "Mae Barrett. Born 1920: Died 2014." He looked up. "She lived a good long time, but she didn't give birth to Ginny."

"She is our legally adopted sister and has been for fifty years. She will be mentioned."

"Just isn't right, that's all." Seth pulled the spoon across his tongue and looked at the clock. "I'm gonna get a haircut."

"Be back by 5:00."

"Don't start without me."

Seth grabbed his Stetson off the hall tree, pulled his boots on, and opened the door.

With Seth gone the room was quiet as a cave. Richard let his eyes close, and relaxed in the chair that he had positioned to look out of expansive windows set in the stone house on a hill. He could see over most of the 8,000 acres of farm and rangeland down to the cottonwood trees just beginning to blossom along the banks of the Platte River. The cropland was ready for planting. He loved that time of year. Seeing the new growth split the soil with light green leaves and reach for the sun. It gave him a burst of energy and even at 65 years of age it never failed to excite him.

He could not imagine doing anything other than farming. Sitting on top of a giant piece of equipment plowing, harrowing, seeding— watching the land change from fallow to seeded to growing corn and soybeans and knowing that God had indeed treated the farmer well with returns of over 100 fold from each tiny seed stuck in its bosom, fertilized, watered, and harvested. It was truly a miracle.

On the other hand communicating with his brother had never been easy. Seth had lit out for Nevada after two years of college and ended up in Vietnam. The family heard from him once when he got back and two times when he needed money. He came up the driveway in a '55 Studebaker after twenty years and announced that he was sober, single, and wanted to work on the ranch. He had fathered a son who lived in Florida with his mother, but it wouldn't create any problem. It wasn't a hard decision to make. Mae Barrett and Richard and Ginny had sat at the dining table and talked it over. It was unanimous to let Seth become a full time family member again. The brothers split responsibility for the ranch work: Seth handled the animals and Richard the crops. They seldom crossed paths during the day unless there was a problem. There would be no problem here. He and Seth were the only direct relatives of Mae Barrett, the natural recipients of the proceeds of her estate.

SETH OPENED THE DOOR of the barbershop, grabbed the rim of his hat and spun it at the rack halfway down the wall. It caught a hook, twirled twice and stopped.

"Just like ropin' a calf," Seth said.

The barber put the scissors and comb in one hand and with his other hand took up a pen and marked a pad near the cash register. "That's five out of eight."

"I'll make it. I only need one more for my free haircut."

The customer in the barber chair smiled. "How do I get a free haircut?"

"You throw your hat on the rack six out of 12 tries from the threshold."

"Sounds easy."

"It is. Until you try it."

The barber trimmed the eyebrow hairs. "This is the first year he's close to it."

"I've been practicing for five years but I've got it down now. The secret is to use a hat you wear a lot and are familiar with, one with a big crown in it. You need the float and the space to catch a hook. I could teach you for $10."

"Hell," the customer said. "For ten bucks I can buy the haircut."

"It isn't the same. Winning one from Swede is worth way more than ten bucks. It gives you bragging rights all the way across Cass County."

"What if you don't make it six times?" the customer said.

"Then you pay just like regular, but he doesn't bet as high when you've got a good poker hand. It costs you either way."

Swede pulled the barber cloth off the customer, dusted him with the talcum brush and put the ten-dollar bill in the cash register. Then he swept the hair into a dustpan and dumped it in the trash. He brushed off the seat and smiled at Seth.

"Just a trim, Swede. I want to look good for the estate trustee."

"How good do you want to look?"

"I want to show a little age, enough for wisdom to set in. A care for my personal appearance so to speak."

"Do you want him to know you lost twenty-two dollars at poker Friday?"

"Hell no. That's too personal."

Swede pulled the barber cloth tight around his neck. "Someone said Klete Dixon was eyeing your place to add to his spread."

"I've heard that a hundred times."

"Maybe there's something you don't know."

"Like what?"

Swede shrugged. "Benny Johnson was in and said Klete had hired Craig Jamison to draw up an offer on your place."

"Swede…you know Craig is our attorney." Seth gestured with his hands to the ceiling. "Rumors are easy to start and hard to stop. If I had a dollar for every rumor I've heard about Klete Dixon buying our spread, Klete could have the ranch and I'd be living high on the hog in Florida."

"What do you want to do with these long hairs on the side?"

"Cut em."

VIRGINIA ALEXANDRIA MAE BARRETT HOUSTON, aka "Ginny," heard the phone ringing as she set the grocery bags on the counter. A mother of three, she knew how to multi-task and put butter, eggs and vegetables in the refrigerator as she picked up the phone.

"Hello. This is Ginny."

"Ginny. Richard. How is the family?"

"Great as far as I know."

"You short of knowledge on somebody?"

"Not that I know of. But Donavon is out looking at the Norstad Ranch and the kids are helping clean up the church for Easter services, so I'm not up to the minute on any of them."

"What have you got on your plate for 5:00 this afternoon? Could you come out to the ranch and hear Craig Jamison read Mae's will and testament?"

"That old pirate. How come Mom trusted him to handle the estate?"

Richard leaned back in his chair. "Well, you will remember he courted her after Dad died, and she had a soft spot for him. I am not aware that she knew any of his shortcomings. He can look awfully good in a suit and tie and fits in with the best of the community. Anyway, he wants us all here. Can you come alone?"

"I can arrange it. I'll pop a roast and some potatoes in the oven and be there."

"Good. See you then."

Ginny finished putting the groceries away, put a pork roast and half dozen potatoes in the oven, ground a wee bit of dark chocolate over an espresso, kicked her shoes off and sat down in the recliner.

She blew on the coffee while looking out over the back yard that looked like an outdoor gymnasium.

This was one of three times a day she loved and lived for. Before Donavon and the kids got home when she could think her thoughts, dream her dreams, and ingest either a stemmed glass of Sterling Chardonnay or an espresso—depending on what commitments she had made for the rest of the day.

She knew Craig Jamison as a local lawyer, card player, amateur politician, and widower long before he plied his courting skills to her mother. His attentions flattered Mae and provided her with a social life outside the family after Andrew Duncan Barrett broke his neck jumping his horse over a fence, leaving her in charge of the Barrett Ranch, two sons and an adopted daughter.

"Oh God, let me please be mentioned in the will," she prayed.

AT FIVE O'CLOCK, Richard opened the door for Jamison. "Hello Craig."

Craig nodded. "Richard. I see you haven't changed anything."

"No need to. We like it the way it is. Would you like coffee or whisky?"

"Coffee, thank you. Don't want to misread the will."

Richard pulled open the double doors leading into the library. Ginny and Seth stood up.

"Afternoon Ginny, Seth," Craig said. "Good to see you here."

"Hello, Craig," Seth said. "How was your luck Wednesday night?"

Craig smiled. "I came out ahead when I filled that full house on the last hand of the night. Early on I thought I'd have to borrow some money from you to finish the evening, but it worked out okay."

Seth sat down. "More'n likely we'd have had to borrow from you." He lifted his leg and brushed dust off the toe of the cowboy boot. "Rumor at Swede's this morning that you're drawing up an agreement for Dixon to buy our ranch."

Craig sat in a coach-leather love seat that Andrew Barrett had bought at auction when a neighbor had sold out to Klete Dixon over forty years ago. Klete never wanted personal property, just the land, the water, the fences, the barns and a good clear deed for his money.

Craig pursed his lips and shook his head. "First I've heard of it." He opened his briefcase. "You want to sell?"

"No," Seth said and looked at Richard sitting in his usual chair with his fingers steepled like some Supreme Court Judge. The room quieted.

Uneasy with the quiet, Craig cleared his throat and began. "I'm glad you're all here. The first of this is a lot of legal talk so let me just cut to the chase and read the will proper. Here's what she asked me to write.

"I wanted you all to be back into normal routine of running the family and the ranch before you heard my will. I had a long and enjoyable life and I want the same for each of you. Such a life needs purpose and goals and above all an understanding of history: history of your family, history of the land, and history of this place and people who make their lives here.

"As to the personal cars and money, I will $25,000 each to Dawson, Buchwald, and Valerie, my beloved grandchildren. There are three family cars in the garage and I would like each grandchild to have one. They must choose and settle ownership of the cars among themselves with no argument. The adults will respect whatever choices they make.

"Five hundred thousand dollars shall be kept as ranch operating cash and handled as in the past by Richard and Seth with the help of Craig Jamison, Attorney, and Bud Blaha, CPA. Any remaining surplus shall be determined and divided 1/3 each to Seth, Richard, and Ginny."

Seth's head snapped around. "A third?"

Craig nodded. "The Barrett Ranch"—Craig lifted his eyes from the document and scanned the three siblings sitting in chairs across from him—"shall be deeded 40% to Seth and 40% to Richard and 20% to Virginia, providing they jointly complete within sixty-one days, the task I set before them."

Craig smiled looking out over the document. He cleared his throat again.

"Starting May 1st the year of my death, or May 1st the following year, Seth and Richard will undertake a journey by foot and/or horseback, from the ranch to the junction of the North and South Platte River and canoe back. They are to stay on, or as close to the river as possible going into towns only for provisions or assistance. No motor or motorized vehicle may be used to speed up their journey, and they must complete the trip in sixty-one days. Along the way they are to look at other farms and ranches, soil conditions, rainfall, crops and animal condition. They are especially tasked to satisfy in their minds why my grandfather, Adolph Melzer, chose this property to homestead in 1845. They are to make special effort to act as brothers of good will and get along by learning the true meaning of brotherly love, which has been poorly demonstrated from time to time over the last forty years.

"I should have spent more time on our history and your forbearers while you were growing up and before Seth lit out for parts unknown. I fault myself for not making you more aware of the history and the hardships that have allowed the Melzer Ranch, now known as the Barrett Ranch, to be homesteaded, retained for 130 years, and passed on to you now.

"It always seemed there would be enough time to do that and I let it slide, which was not my intent. Klete Dixon and the Barretts evolved into industrial farmers at the same time, thinking we were being progressive after the drought of 1930s. We bought out Filoh Smith and divided his land between us, thinking we had done both Filoh and the land a favor. We should have sat down in the library and had some history lessons. As I got older, it was more difficult for me to put up an argument against your new-fangled farming and ranching methods. I had not studied them but I was innately opposed. I simply could not muster a formidable argument.

"I have expressed my displeasure about your continuation of industrial farming methods instead of returning to the sustainable system the ranch had thrived on in the early years. The Grange and Monsanto and the heavy use of the Ogallala aquifer have poisoned your thinking and it is your refusal to see my side of the argument that has caused me to set up these harsh stipulations. This ranch and the bequeathing of it is my last and only tool.

"Bear in mind while on the trip that Granddad Melzer could have chosen property on either side of the river anywhere between Plattsmouth and Ogallala. He chose this land on which my will is being read. It is my belief that a knowledge of, and a feeling for, the land and river and what it has provided to those who are giving it to you now, is essential in receiving it with a full heart and a mind that is receptive to the opportunities it provides.

"During Seth and Richard's journey, Virginia and the grandchildren are to operate the ranch on a daily basis as they would have done had Seth and Richard been drafted into the military, crippled or killed. It is a tough world but the Melzers and Barretts who preceded you have done the toughest part. You now have the land and all they built IF you succeed in this task I require of you.

"If the ranch is not operated and maintained well, or if the journey is not completed in sixty-one days, it is to be donated to Boys Town Nebraska directly from the estate.

"I expect you to complete it just as you have each done excellent work in your lives, on this ranch, and in this town. However, just to make sure I have appointed my good friend and attorney, Craig Jamison, as timekeeper for your journey. He is to record the date of leaving and return and certify that it is within the sixty-one days allotted. He is further tasked with certifying that the ranch is in substantially the same condition as it was when Richard and Seth left."

Craig laid the paper on the desk, removed his glasses, and put them in the breast pocket of his coat. "Mae concerned herself with this request for some time. In the end she felt it was necessary for the succeeding generations to understand what their families had gone through to be able to present them with these assets."

"They seem harsh to me," Seth said.

Richard stood up. "Would you care for a whiskey now?"

"Thank you, no, Richard. I better scoot on home, I want to catch the baseball game."

He stood and reached his hat. "Let's talk after you've had a chance to think about this. Maybe some time next week. I'll leave this copy here and you can go over it. I don't think the remaining items are of much concern, but you ought to read them. Good evening. I'll let myself out."

Richard patted him on the shoulder. "Talk to you next week, Craig."

RICHARD PULLED THE STOPPER out of the Laphroaig Whisky bottle and poured a double shot into a tulip shaped crystal glass. He swirled it around and brought it up to his nose. His hand trembled.

Seth looked out the window. "That could take all summer."

Ginny was shaking her head. "Every day, every day, every day. I can't do that. Two or three times a week is one thing, every day is entirely another."

"You'd have to move out here."

"I can't do that. The kids are in school until June. And Donavon…"

"Ginny—it's only for two months. It can't be more than 300 miles."

"And just how fast do you think you can travel by foot, horseback and canoe?"

Richard pointed at Seth who raised his head. "A decent horse can make ten miles a day; probably thirty on a trail."

"When's the last time you went thirty miles a day on a horse?" Richard said.

"And walking?" Ginny threw in.

"Well—if there aren't too many fences to cross we could make twelve, fifteen miles a day either afoot or canoe. I'm thinking we can do twelve any method, so that's about thirty days in all," Seth said.

Richard scoffed. "I don't think you know a damn thing about it. You've been riding back and forth between fence lines, not up river-banks crossing rivers and climbing over downed trees. We need to plan for the full sixty-one days."

"How long did it take Grandpa Melzer?" Ginny said.

Seth and Richard exchanged glances. "Don't know," Seth said. "Well—it doesn't make any difference. If we sign on to this thing we're gonna do it whether it takes us twenty days or twenty months. We've got no choice. What the hell would I do without the ranch? "

"Needs to be done in two months or less," Richard reminded him.

Seth nodded, his face reddening. "Hell—I know that, Richard."

"This is gonna shake my whole family up," Ginny said. "And just as we were getting ready for a nice summer too."

Richard tipped the glass to his lips and swallowed. "I'll need a mule to carry my Scotch."

"No sir—you'll carry it yourself. No more putting it in my pack."

Richard smiled. "You didn't even know you had it."

"What are you guys talking about?" Ginny asked.

"On our last elk hunt," Richard said, "some twenty-five years ago, I slipped a jar of peanut butter and a fifth of whisky in Seth's pack when he wasn't looking. He packed it up the mountain."

"I didn't know it until I got to the top. It damned near killed me," Seth said.

"But at night, you sure enjoyed your share of the Scotch."

"Well—I did. That's for sure."

"And the peanut butter too."

"And the peanut butter."

"Next time we'll take horses."

Seth frowned. "There ain't goin' to be a next time."

Ginny stood up. "Can you guys get off this and get some straight thinking done. I don't know what to do. My whole family is going to be in disarray over this. We've all counted on being set for life when we inherited the ranch and now it could go down the drain. I might have to go back to work."

Richard tossed back the Scotch, set the glass down on the table, leaned back and shoved his hands in his front pockets. "I think we need to take a day or two and work this out in our heads. It seems tough right now, but we haven't begun to detail it. What say we each think about it for a few days and get together first of the week?"

"Richard—you don't understand," Ginny said. "This is going to be a complete disruption to my life. Everything is going to go to pot while I'm out here kicking the cows and tending to the crops."

"Not to mention the hired hands," Seth threw in.

"That too," she said.

IF THERE WAS ONE thing Ginny could count on it was her daily schedule. She had organized it, and gotten it down to little squares on her Things to Do Today pad. There was room for twenty items. She seldom got past the fourth or fifth item, but the lesser important ones always hung around until they matured, moved up, got handled, and scratched off. She usually laid plans for thirty days in advance and would smile with self-satisfaction when she could complete and cross off each item.

To move to the ranch and run it was going to be a huge disruption. Maybe Donavon could work with it. He was up, breakfasted and gone early most every day. She would have a hundred things to do to get ready. And what about her commitments to the book club, the Friends of the Library, and the Fourth of July Extravaganza committee which she was chairman of this year?

The kids. What about them? Move out to the ranch? They enjoyed the times they spent there now, but if you made it an every day deal, would they like it? She had to figure a way to make it a living experiment: a challenge like camp or sports. It was a long ways back to her teen years, but she could try to reconstruct those times and avoid the arguments she had had with Mae and Andrew when she was a child living there. But think about it: pushing the warm, smelly cows into different pastures, watching the crops inch their way toward the sky, greening every day, and looking at the sky to check for rain for a good reason instead of the 'what to wear' reason. Oh God—it was at once troubling and thrilling.

And the brothers? Could they get along without killing one another, traveling up and down that sick river for two months? In her mind she pictured the time she heard the yelling in the barn, slid open the door and saw Seth on the concrete floor with Richard standing over him, fists clenched. She closed her eyes. Had they always fought like that?

She got out her Things To Do Today list and laid a pen beside it. "Tomorrow," she said. "That will be a good time to start working on this."

SETH BUILT A FIRE in the library fireplace and sat in the brown leather chair he used for thinking and stared into the flames. He could hear Richard coming down the hall.

"It's your turn to build supper," Richard said.

Seth, startled, popped his head around. "Is it Wednesday already?"

Richard nodded.

"We ought to get a cook out here. I'm not liking most of the food that crosses my plate lately. Some chief cook and bottle washer might make something that we'd enjoy eating instead of just tolerating it."

"We could do that," Richard said. "Did you want to share our house with a young girl, an old woman, or a male chief cook and bottle washer?"

"Don't think it makes any difference if they know how to cook and keep house."

"You think Ginny will want her or him if she moves out here?"

"Dunno," Seth said. He rolled his tongue around his lower teeth. "Are we really goin' on this trip—afoot or horseback, or are we gonna go to court and get it resolved?"

What's got you spooked about this little jaunt up the Platte and back?"

"I'm not spooked." He laced his fingers behind his head and leaned back. "I'm just trying to figure out why Mom would have put that in her will and never mentioned anything to us about it all her born days. She must have been thinking about it for some time before she had Craig write it down, don't you think?"

Richard nodded. "You know how she hated us implementing the new farming techniques? How she liked secrets—would keep things from us until they were ready to happen?"

"Yes, I do. But this is more than a surprise. It's our livelihood. Since Dad died we've been doing all the work and now we're to turn it over and go traipsing up the river."

"—And down," Richard put in.

"—And down, just to see why Grandpa Melzer picked this place."

"That's it." Richard poured a small Scotch and swirled it. "And understand the grip the new farming methods have imposed on the land. I can see her smiling as she told Craig to write that. Don't forget the rest of it: we're to get along."

Seth bit his lower lip. "Well—I hope she's enjoying it. All I can see is us getting arrested for trespassing, harassing cattle and game, and polluting river water." He adjusted his headrest. "And as for getting along, if we keep a little apart, like we are here and you don't tell me how to do my work, I think we can make it without killing one another." He threw a small pillow at Richard. "Don't you?"

Richard caught the pillow and squeezed it between his hands. "What's for supper, Seth?"

"Leave it alone, Richard." His fingers slid across his face and up beside his nose. "Macaroni and cheese."

Richard snorted. "And a salad?"

Seth nodded. "And a salad."

"Good balanced meal. We need to be thinking about what we'll cook on the river trip."

"Yeah. That'll be fun, won't it?"

Richard turned to look out the window at the setting sun. "You seem a bit upset."

"Well—Judas Priest, we're looking at the possibility of losing the ranch. What do we do then, wash dishes at Mom's Café?"

"There is the will money," Richard said.

"Yeah—and just how long do you think that will last me?"

Richard shook his head. "It could put us in a hell of a bind."

"And what about old age? No house, no land, no income—we could end up on welfare. Why the hell would Mom do this to us? She wasn't mean to us growing up."

"It gives us a clear purpose and that is always stimulating."

"If it's stimulation you're looking for, let me spell out some alternatives."

Richard chuckled. "No—I'll go with this one." He pitched the pillow at Seth and hit him in the back of the head as he lifted himself out of the chair.

~~~~~~

The Platte River

Fourmile Creek dribbled over a sodden sand and mud mouth where it dumped its water and chemicals and history into the Platte River a few miles northwest of Plattsmouth, Nebraska. Like an overfed snake, it slid sluggish and grey between its banks, seeking an escape from the plowed land it drained. It was a silent creek, hushed amid the rustling of leaves that whispered on the willows along its banks.

~~~~~~

Getting ready, Seth

SETH PULLED THE ANCIENT glass door open to the Riverside Grocery and walked down the aisle marked Prepared Foods.

"Where's your freeze-dried food, Doug?"

"It was on that third aisle, but it's all gone."

"When you getting some more?"

"Probably be a couple of weeks before they get back. They were just here."

"You didn't order much?"

"I did my usual order but Klete Dixon came in and bought it all. Said he was sending some of his men out to line shacks to do fence mending."

Seth plopped his hat back on his head. "Well, don't that beat all." He sifted through the jerky hanging on a metal strip. "You don't have any canoes, do you?"

"No. Probably get one at the Marina. What are you fixin' to do?"

"Just lookin', that's all. Have you got any Tang?"

"You goin' on a camping trip or something? Too early for hunting."

"Quit being so inquisitive and answer my question. Judas Priest— you'd think you were reporting for the Plattsmouth Journal. Have you got any Tang?"

"What size?"

"Oh for crying out loud. I'll come back when you can help me."

"Bring some money to the poker game next week. I'm tired of loaning you money to beat me with. Matter of fact, you owe me ten bucks."

Seth took out his billfold, pulled out a ten-dollar bill and laid it on the counter. "Call your freeze dried people and see if they can come back here, or I'll have to drive to Omaha and get a good price on it."

Getting ready, Richard

"CAN YOU DELIVER IT up around Ogallala?"

Jack Brown shook his head. "I can but you aren't going to like the price, Richard."

"How much?"

"With gas running three dollars a gallon and a day's time and a rig—probably double the price of the canoe."

"You know anybody up there that sells canoes?"

"None I know of." Jack put his right foot up on a bench and retied his shoelaces. "What in the world do you want a canoe up there for?"

"Seth and I need to come down the river."

"There won't be enough water to float that thing this summer with all the irrigation water being pumped out."

"Doesn't matter. I need to do it and a canoe seems the best thing to do it in. Don't you agree?"

"I do. But you'd better buy a pair of waders cause you're gonna be walking a lot of it." Jack crossed his arms. "Besides, walking is trespassing on that river so stay on the surface."

"You got any good news, Jack?"

"I do. Got in a case of .30-30 Winchester in the 170 grain soft point you were asking about a couple months ago."

"I'll take ten boxes. Add it to my bill."

"And the canoe?"

"I'll think about that."

"Ok. But it's the only one I've got and I'm not likely to be buying canoes to hang around here once that one's gone." Jack stacked the boxes of ammunition on the counter, evened the pile. "Tell you what. For $800 you can have the canoe delivered in Ogallala if you take it today."

"Throw in two paddles and a cooler and it's a deal."

"Can't you let a man have a little profit? Do you always have to have everything at my cost?"

"Don't start crying now, Jack. You know how I hate to see a grown man cry."

Jack punched in the figures on the cash register. "You and Seth should buy this place and I'll bargain with you."

"You'll win more than that back at the poker game and Barrett Ranch will be in debt again all winter."

"That'll be the day. OK. Bullets. Canoe, paddles and cooler delivered to Ogallala or North Platte or somewhere's close by...let's see... that comes to $1,000 plus tax."

"Send the bill to Blaha. I'll tell you where to drop off the canoe soon as I figure out myself. Enjoyed talking with you, Jack." Richard put a forearm against the door and swung it open without touching the handle.

"Come back tomorrow," Jack hollered. "I'm gonna mark everything up tonight."

Do we need a rifle?

RICHARD GOT THE KEY and unlocked the gun cabinet and placed the ten boxes of shells in the ammunition drawer. He looked at the day's mail on the hall table then walked into the kitchen. Thursday. His turn to cook supper.

Seth came down from the upstairs bedroom, his cowboy boots sounding like a chorus of hammers on the wooden steps, worn with 130 years of farmers' boots descending toward the pot bellied stove, and pushed the swinging door open into the kitchen.

"How about a snort before you set up supper?"

Richard pulled his head out of the refrigerator. "Good. Can't find what I'm looking for, anyway.

"You want to hear a good one? Klete Dixon bought all the freeze-dried foods in town. Now why would he do that?"

"Interesting," Richard said. He poured a Scotch and waved the bottle at Seth. "Think you can handle this stuff now?"

"No way. Alcohol and me have got to be just speaking acquaintances."

Richard stopped mid-pour. "Could be a coincidence."

"Could be. But I don't believe that—do you?"

"No." Richard sipped his drink. "We can get what we want in Omaha." He pulled out a kitchen chair and sat down. "I got a canoe off Jack Brown today. He'll deliver it to Ogallala. Also got ten boxes of .30-30 ammo."

"Are you thinking of taking a rifle with us?"

"Hell yes. Why not take the .30-30?"

"What are you gonna shoot with it?"

"I don't know yet. You always carry one on your saddle. Why do you do that?"

"Coyotes. Snakes. Buffalo running wild. Maybe a stampede."

"How long has it been since any of those happened to you?"

"Doesn't matter. I'll be ready if it does."

"Likewise."

"Humph." Seth pulled out a chair and straddled it. "What's for dinner?"

"Rabbit on a spit and fire baked potatoes."

"Sounds like trail food."

Conditions

RICHARD LOOKED UP FROM his plate. "I'm glad you got back before Mom died. I wasn't sure we could put a finger on your whereabouts."

"I was always close," Seth said. "Sometimes I felt too close. Especially when I was in rehab."

"I could have helped some. I know Mom cut you off from the money spigot, but I had a few dollars."

"There were times I needed more than a few dollars. I could have used $100,000, but it wouldn't have lasted long. Went through my hands like water." He shook his head. "Don't know what took hold of me like that."

"Addictions are hard to break. Where did the woman go?"

"Florida. She and the boy are down there."

"Do you hear from them?"

Seth shook his head. "Not much. I'm sending them some money each month. If we don't get the ranch I don't know what I'll do then."

Richard pushed back from the table, crossed his legs and clasped his hands behind his head. "Do you really think we can go up and back in sixty-one days?"

"Well, it ain't like when Adolph Melzer did it. He didn't have to contend with fences and other owners and farmers sucking so much irrigation water out of the river that you can't float a canoe."

"Jack Brown suggested we buy waders. He said we'd be walking half of it coming back down."

"Could be. At least it should be warm."

"And muddy."

"And muddy."

Richard shook his head. "I don't know. Ten years ago it wouldn't have bothered me much. But nearing sixty-five? Didn't sleep well last night and I don't know what it will be like sleeping on the ground for a month."

"We can go into town to a motel or something of a night, can't we?"

"The will said going into towns only for provisions or assistance. Makes it sound like we need to have a good reason for going into towns."

"Klete will probably have his boys there trying to lure us into town to break the terms of the will," Seth said.

"I doubt Klete is that much interested in how we perform the terms of the will."

Seth shook his head. "I'll bet he is. He's been wanting his hands on this place since before I lit out of here. He'd like nothing better than to buy it because we failed to meet the terms of the will."

"Craig wouldn't let him do that. There must be some legal stipulations that would protect us in that regard."

"I wouldn't bet on it." Seth stood up and stacked the dishes and started for the kitchen. At the end of the table he stopped, put the dishes down and put both hands on the table. "Whew. A little dizzy."

"You're not used to good food."

"That and I'm older."

"That's the truth. I'll help."

"I can do my own damn dishes," Seth said. He picked up the plates and carried them into the kitchen and set them down by the dishwasher. "That's the second time this week that's happened."

Ginny has problems too

"MOM—WHY CAN'T I wear this?"

"Bucky. It's Friday. School picture day. You want to look your best for the school pictures and that outfit doesn't cut it. Now go change before your breakfast gets cold. Go on—shoo."

Ginny took the toast out with her thumb and forefinger. "Yikes— that's hot." She buttered it and put it on a saucer on the table. "Dawson? Valerie? Breakfast's on."

Donavon took his coffee and the Omaha World Herald and moved over to the breakfast nook, a neat upholstered U-shaped bench and table built to accommodate the entire family for casual meals. He crossed his legs, spread out the paper, picked up the coffee and blew across it. "I see where Senator Clement is thinking of teaming up with Congressman Dworak to ask the Governor to pull out of the Platte River Recovery Implementation Program. That stinks."

"Donavon, don't let that stuff get to you. It's coming up election time for Dworak and most of it is just talk."

"It may be talk to you, but our bread is buttered by that project. That Hague ranch I just listed is counting on some of that money to improve the water system and habitat. The price differences can be a lot if a buyer can see that the restoration is going forward."

"It'll work out fine. It always does," Ginny said.

"Maybe, but if the Governor pulls Nebraska out of that program we stand to lose a bunch of federal funding for the Platte River. I think the federal share is over $300 million."

Dawson and Valerie plunged into the kitchen. Dawson poured a glass of milk and sat down. "Bucky's trying to wear my white shirt. Fits him like a tent."

"Oh for heaven's sake," Ginny said. She walked to the bottom of the stairs. "Bucky—wear that light blue shirt and the blue blazer. It won't make any difference with the pants cause the camera will only be shooting the top of you."

Valerie raised her head. "Mom—we're having our class picnic today. I can't go out to the ranch after school."

"Fine, honey. Are you taking clothes for the picnic?"

"You said I could wear my regular clothes."

"Not on a picnic. Why did they schedule the picnic the same day as class photos? Who's running that school—the inmates?"

"I'll take my jeans and boots in a bag and change at school."

Bucky slid down the banister and bounced into the room. "Ta da." He held his arms out like a showman seeking applause.

Ginny raised her chin and pointed at his breakfast sitting on the table. "Pour your milk and get to it, young man. School bus will be here before you get the raisins wet."

"I don't even like Raisin Bran. Don't we have—"

"No, we don't. I'll get some shredded wheat today—"

"— and Cheerios?"

"—and Cheerios and Lucky Charms and Grape Nuts. Does that satisfy everyone? Did I leave anyone out?"

Donavon lifted his head from the newspaper. "I'll be damned. Klete Dixon bought the Springer place and I didn't even hear about it. I'd have thought Ed Springer would have called me for an appraisal or to list it. I could have gotten him a better price than Dixon would've ever paid."

"Honey—you can't do every deal in town. Ed Springer is a smart man and he probably knows how to make the right kind of deal for himself."

"Maybe. But he was planning on going organic next year. Selling to Klete makes that go away. I don't like the sounds of it. If Klete turns that into an industrial farming operation, which he will, that means more runoff into the river. Besides, the Springer ranch abuts Barrett Ranch. Klete Dixon is our new neighbor and he could swallow up the Barrett Ranch next if things don't go right." He raised his arms toward the ceiling and rolled his eyes.

Ginny paused, as if flash frozen for an instant. "That won't make us happy."

"Not one little bit."

"Do you think Boy's Town would sell the ranch—not keep it and operate it?"

Donavon shrugged. "Who knows what they would do. You guys just better get the work done right and on time so there isn't a chance of that."

The school bus pulled up at the mailbox. The screen door slammed and the kids shouted goodbyes. Ginny poured a cup of coffee and sat down with Donavon. She turned her head around looking at the far wall and then the window. "I'm always amazed at how quiet it is just after they leave."

"It'll be like that in a few years. They'll be gone to college and we'll be here wondering if we've gone deaf." He folded the paper and set it beside her. "That reminds me—guess who I saw in town yesterday?"

"Twenty questions or hard guess?"

"Hard guess."

"I give up. Who?"

"Filoh Smith."

"He's still alive?"

"He seemed to be. He was walking and talking."

"My gosh. He must be 100 years old."

"Swede was giving him a haircut. He said Filoh was ninety and Filoh didn't deny it."

"What's he doing back in town?"

"Don't know. But I do know that I've got to get to work. Goodbye, honey." He picked up his briefcase and car keys and headed for the door.

"Brush your teeth, Donavon. You don't want to have bad breath all day."

He pulled a toothbrush out of his inside coat pocket and a smile spread across his face. "I'll brush on the way to work."

Ginny grimaced. "Without toothpaste—without water?"

"At the office," he said and the door closed behind him.

For several minutes Ginny sat on the upholstered bench seat that formed the inside of the bay window, both hands wrapped around her coffee cup, elbows on the table. She cherished this time of day. Peaceful. Quiet. Everyone fed, dressed correctly in clean clothes, healthy and smiling...and gone, another successful start of a day.

She looked through the window across the yard strewn with play equipment to the tops of the cottonwood trees at the end of their lot. A breeze just strong enough to carry the pungent smell of the wet earth drifted through the open window. A wild turkey cackled and she spotted him strolling across the far end, pecking at something near the fence line. She had heard them, but hadn't seen them until the leaves came back on the trees. She used to see pheasants, but the turkeys drove them out. Some say turkeys ate the young pheasants or ate the eggs or both. And then industrial farmers like Klete Dixon and Benjamin Fowler, and her brothers, bought equipment that would plow right to the fence line which eradicated the brush cover the pheasants used for protection and nesting.

When she was young, she could count on seeing a half dozen pheasants as she did her chores and on her way to school. Now it was turkeys. Her science teacher attributed it to global warming but Richard said, no, it was the loss of habitat and the carnivorous turkeys that spelled their doom. Who to believe? Didn't make any difference. The pheasants were gone and the turkeys were here. That was life as she saw it. Something always took over the land. If you didn't plant it to pasture or corn or wheat or soybeans, it grew weeds and native grasses. The pheasants were brought over from China in the late 1800s and once they got away from the eastern seacoast immediately prospered in Nebraska. Their call was as familiar to her as the bark of their dog.

She sat upright almost spilling her coffee. "Filoh Smith," she said. She thought he had died years ago. She liked him, although as a child she thought his odor offensive. That was before she was old enough to understand that he made his clothes from the wool of his own sheep. He sheared it, cleaned it, carded it, spun it, and wove it into shirts, pants, jackets, socks, and a stocking hat that went over his thinning hair in late September and didn't come off, as far as she knew, until May 15th. At which time, she and all the other kids in the neighborhood understood he took his annual bath near where Fourmile Creek emptied into the Platte.

They received this fantastical information from Eric Compton, a classmate, who claimed to have seen Filoh naked and in up to his bare bottom, scrubbing his white body with sand and silt while they were hunting animal footprints in the mud for a science project. He had left Cass County in disgust after Mae Barrett and Klete Dixon acquired more land and turned every farmhouse into an empty mausoleum and every acre into a well tuned productive investment tool. Now Filoh was back. Interesting.

She picked up the phone and dialed the ranch.

"Hi, Richard. Guess what? Filoh Smith is back in town."

"I'd like to talk with him. Where is he?"

"Donavon mentioned that he was getting a hair cut at Swede's. Town's not that big. Someone will know where he's staying."

"Thanks, Ginny. I'll do some checking around. If you hear anything, please let me know. "

"I will. How's the trip preparation going?"

"It's coming together. Seth is getting cold feet, I think."

"The actualities of it?"

"That's my take on it. He's hell for leather until the rubber meets the road."

"He'll do all right. He came back. He's been sober and hard working every day for the last few years, hasn't he?"

"Yup. So far so good."

"One day at a time, Richard. One day at a time."

"Amen to that. I did offer him a little bourbon last night. Kind of a celebration."

"For crying out loud, Richard. The man spent years being a drunk and you offer him some bourbon after he's sober. What's with you?"

"I wanted to see if he craved it. I think the rehab worked for him. He didn't take it and that makes me feel better about leaving it out in my office."

"I can't believe you guys. Well—I gotta get. Anything I can do to help you get ready, let me know. In the meantime, I'm trying to figure out how to juggle everything while you're both gone."

"I know, Ginny. Big task for all of us."

The conversation fell silent for a second and Richard listened to the line noises. "Richard—what's your take on why Mom did this?"

"Backup, I think. She wanted us to know that you have to work for things in life. They don't just get handed to you. Suppose she thought it would give us more respect for the land and livestock." He coughed. "Another thing—she moved hard toward sustainable farming the last ten years and we fought that transition. I believe she wants us to seriously see this whole thing like she did…a combination of land, water, air and people who are sustained by it year after year."

"Almost like getting religion late in life wasn't it?"

Richard set his water down and nodded to himself. "Exactly."

"Hmmm. Well—it's not such a big deal. You go up and come back and it's over."

"I hope it goes like that. I'm not so sure it will. I think there are a hundred things we're not seeing or even thinking about."

"You can handle it. You always have."

Richard coughed. "I believe I can, but I'm worried about Seth. He got dizzy getting up from the table last night. Almost dropped the dishes."

"For cryin' out loud. What's wrong with him?"

"I have no idea, but it will bear watching."

"I'd say so. Let me know if you find out anything. That doesn't bode well for a long trip like this."

"You got that right. Goodbye Ginny."

Chapter 2

RICHARD OPENED THE DOOR, walked in and sat down in the first of four red vinyl armchairs in Swede's Barber Shop.

"What's up, Richard?" Swede said.

"Morning, Swede. Looking for Filoh Smith. Ginny said you were cutting what was left of his hair yesterday. Probably charged him full price, too. Any idea of his whereabouts?"

"Takes just as long to trim 28 hairs as it does to cut a full head of hair, if you do it right. Then there's the powder and shave cream and head massage and wear and tear on the equipment."

"Plus the smell."

"Smell's not so bad anymore. I think the wool has outlived its odor. Anyway, the talcum powder drowned it out."

"Suppose you charged extra for that."

"No. Talcum is free. It's head lice we charge extra for. And smart talk. That gets expensive. Are you wanting a hair cut, I hope, 'cause the price just went up this morning?"

"Later. I'm trying to find Filoh."

"I'd look down at Brewster's B&B. They were friends."

EMMA BREWSTER LOVED MEETING new people. She also enjoyed old friends showing up in Plattsmouth and staying with her at Brewster's B&B. So when Filoh Smith stood on the top step and rang the doorbell, she slung her arms around him and kissed him on the cheek so hard he dropped the bag and held on to the banister with his free hand.

"Filoh Smith. As I live and breathe," she said. She held him at arm's length. "You've lost weight."

"Emma," he replied, the smile wide on his face. "You got a room?"

She grabbed his arm and guided him inside. "We've always got a room for you, any season, day or night. What brings you back to Plattsmouth?"

He took off his cap, the thin hairs sprouting off in divergent directions. "There is some work I need to get done before I'm done. I aim to make this my headquarters if you'll allow it."

"Of course we'll allow it."

"I want to pay in advance."

"There's no need for that, Filoh."

"At my age I don't want to leave any debts behind. How much for a week?

"Normally it would be $500—and that includes breakfast—but for you good friend, I'd think $450 would be good."

"How about $400?"

Emma scrunched up her face making slits of her eyes and curling up the ends of her mouth. "That's a little low," she hesitated. "But if you can get by on one set of sheets and towels, I'd do it. And if you don't eat too much at breakfast," she added, shoving him on the shoulder.

"Done. Show me the room." He picked up his bag. "I'm here to stay."

It felt good being back in Plattsmouth. The years he had spent living in B&Bs in Washington, D.C., pounding the congressional trail pleading for government intervention in food production had soured him on the big cities. Why man chose to bunch himself up into cities mystified him. And he surprised the sophisticated legislators whose first opinion of the wool clad gawky farmer was country bumpkin. But it was his understanding and direct questioning which led to the writing of the Organic Foods Production Act of 1990.

Richard spotted Filoh coming out of the No Frills grocery store, a half dozen plastic bags slapping against his bowed legs, his eyes on the blacktop in front of him.

"Let me carry that for you, Filoh."

"Obliged—but I can handle it." Filoh looked up. "That you, Richard?"

Richard nodded. "Yes, indeed."

"Been a good while."

"Goin' on twenty-five years I'd guess."

Filoh bobbed his head, his eyes darting. "More'n likely right."

"Can I buy you a cup of coffee?"

"I'm busy. Later."

"Now's as good as any, isn't it? You're retired."

Filoh kept walking, the plastic bags slapping his legs. "That's the truth. I am." He looked up at Richard. "You're talking store made coffee?"

"I am."

Filoh nodded. "What'll I do with these things?"

"Put 'em in my pickup and I'll drop you off at Brewster's after coffee."

"How'd you know I was at Brewster's?"

Richard chuckled. "It's not that big a town, Filoh."

"Well—dang-it—I don't like everybody know'n everything about me."

Richard held open the door to the Cozy Corner Café. They sat at a booth near the back where Filoh could see the front door, and ordered coffee.

"What brings you back to town?" Richard said.

"Unfinished work."

"Such as?"

"Barretts." He poured some coffee into a saucer and blew over it. "Klete Dixon, Ben Fowler, and a hundred other farmers on the Platte."

Richard arched his eyebrows. "Me?"

"You and your no-account brother. You're doing as much as anybody to kill the river. And the soil."

Richard sat back in the booth. "Whoa. Where'd that come from?"

Filoh pounded his fist against his chest twice. "Right here." He picked up the saucer with two hands, elbows on the table and tipped some coffee between his lips.

The sucking sound amused Richard. He could remember his father doing that and wondered why it had passed out of vogue. People had coffee delivered to them that was too hot to drink and everyone worked at cooling it down in some manner. No—he'd just stir his with cream and sugar until the steam quit coming up.

"Filoh, I'm too old to change now. Besides, I'm not killing anything. We've been farming like this for over fifty years. You need to talk to Ginny. One day she and the kids will be working the place and Seth and I'll be sitting on the porch in a rocking chair. I imagine you can convince her over time.

"The time is now. There won't be any Cuyahoga River Fire on the Platte, but it is being killed every day. The river, trees, plants, fish. Hell—even the ducks aren't going to land on it anymore if this keeps up."

Richard turned his cup around in circles on the Formica tabletop, pursed his lips. "I don't see that," he said.

"I'm sure you don't and that's why I'm here. You asked and that's why."

Richard leaned forward. "Let's say that I'm willing to hear you out. I'm not promising to do anything, but I am willing to listen."

"That's a start." Filoh put the empty saucer on the table. "Ok. First, stop with the chemical fertilizer. Stop plowing to the fence line. Stop using pesticides on the crops. Use drip irrigation. You think the Ogallala aquifer is gonna last forever?"

Richard sat back and dropped his hands in his lap. "Whoa. Just like that?"

"Amen. Just like that."

"The crops are already planted for this season. I've already used the fertilizer and I've contracted for the aerial pesticides."

"Well—stop the pesticides. It's always a good idea to stop doing the wrong thing."

"Filoh, the grasshoppers and corn borers would get most of it—"

"Would you rather have some or none?"

"It can't be that dire?"

"It is."

"What kind of campaign is this?"

"I'm gonna stop this chemical farming and feedlot crap. Here. Now." He pounded his fist on the table spilling coffee. He grabbed the cuff of his shirt and rubbed the sleeve over it.

Richard leaned forward and stared at his coffee cup.

"Why were you looking for me?" Filoh said.

Richard shook his head, lips pursed. "I don't remember anymore."

"Good." Filoh tipped his saucer.

"I remember now. I wanted to ask you if you had any inkling why, even though we're selling our crops for more each year, the net is coming down. Every year we get less per acre, yet we put more fertilizer on it. And more water, too."

Filoh nodded. "You've reached economic stagnation. You're spending more on fuel pumping up water from the aquifer and in chemicals than you did in the past and your yield is going down." He shook his finger. "Now you know that's not sustainable."

"We've been doing that for fifty years. The agricultural agent says we're doing it right."

"What do they know? They went to the same schools we all did."

Richard looked down. He took off his hat, set it on the table and smoothed his hair. "Do you agree with the Organic Foods Production Act of 1990?"

"I spent five years working with our congressmen to get votes for it. I guess I agree with it."

"But it's voluntary—right?"

"It's voluntary if you don't mind killing your grandchildren."

Richard stared at him. "You're serious?"

"I'm deadly serious."

"There was a guy talking about it at the Grange hall meeting last month and with Mom's death and all the changes going on, I didn't think about it until Ginny said someone had seen you in town. That set me to remembering you had tried that sort of thing before you sold out and skipped town."

"I didn't skip town. I was forced out."

Richard turned his face sideways, a skeptical look in his eyes. "Forced?"

"That's right. Forced."

"Who could force you to leave?"

"The two biggest farmers around. Klete Dixon and Mae Barrett."

"They did that?"

"They did. I was sixty-five. I'm ninety now. I don't move for nobody."

The waitress stopped by with coffee. "You boys want some fresh coffee?"

Filoh held out his cup and she filled it, the steam snaking over the table.

"No thanks," Richard said. He watched Filoh pour from the full cup into the saucer, tracked the coffee running off the edge spilling on the table and smiled when Filoh mopped it up with his sleeve. "You're going to need a clean shirt if you keep mopping up coffee with it."

"It's old like me. Wearin' out, but still serviceable. I reckon it'll last as long as I need it."

Richard pursed his lips. "More'n likely."

"You ever thought about the aquifer?" Filoh said.

"The Ogallala?"

Filoh nodded.

"Not much. Why?"

"You Barretts are helping ruin it. You're sucking water out of it. You're polluting it. You're taking care of today and not looking at tomorrow. You're inheriting a farm that's dying every day and you're standing there with your boot on its throat. The worst is that you and Seth think you're getting something real good. You're inheriting a corpse."

"Oh, I doubt that." Richard smiled, stood up and pulled out his wallet.

They walked to the pickup in silence. At Brewster's, Filoh lifted the plastic bags out of the truck bed and started for the front door.

"You gonna be around for a spell?" Richard said.

"I'll be here until my job's done."

Richard sucked on his teeth and nodded. "See ya."

Filoh started up the stairs, turned. "Forgot to thank you for the coffee."

Richard nodded as he stood at the bottom of the stairs, a frown traveling across his face and his hands jammed into his Levi pockets. "Inheriting a corpse? Huh."

Serena

"COULD HAVE BEEN WORSE," Seth said.

"Yup," Richard agreed. "He could have shot me."

"You don't want to let that old man get you down. He was weird when he lived up river from us and he probably hasn't changed. Used to bathe in Fourmile Creek once a year in the spring. Probably hasn't bathed since he left here. What's he been gone?"

"Twenty-five years."

"What'd he say he was doin' back in town?"

"Unfinished work."

"Unfinished work?"

Richard nodded. "Said it was with you and me and Klete and a hundred other farmers on the river."

"Wow. He spelled it right out, didn't he?"

"Said we were killing the land and the river."

Seth pulled a flare gun out of a sack. "Here," he said. "Put this in your pack. Yours is waterproof."

"How much do you think I can carry?"

"'Bout fifty-five pounds."

Richard hefted his pack and grunted. "Back when we were hunting, I could of handled this. Now I think we will take horses. I don't see lugging this thing up and down river."

"Hell—it's flat all the way."

"Well, I've been riding a pickup for the last twenty-five years with nothing heavier than a jacket on my back."

"Gonna change all that, aren't we?" Seth pulled the zipper closed, lifted the pack, stretched his arms through the straps and let it settle on his back. "Feels ok."

"If we're gonna walk it, let's at least take a pack horse. That's why man domesticated them in the first place."

The phone rang and Richard, unencumbered by a pack, walked across the room and picked it up. "Hi, Serena." He listened for a few minutes then sat down in a chair. His face drew tight and he stared at his boots. "I find that hard to believe, Serena. I'll see what I can find out before the meeting tomorrow night. Yes—I'll call you as soon as I hear anything. Don't worry about it for now. I'm sure it's a misunderstanding. Yes—goodbye." He cradled the receiver and rested his hand on it for a moment.

"What's up?" Seth said.

Richard looked up, took a deep breath. "Serena says Wily Creighton is going to recommend to the school board that they fire her."

"Fire Serena?"

"Yes."

"For what?"

"Insubordination, she says. Can't figure that." Richard shook his head. "Must be some mistake."

"Well—you've been on the school board since the first brick was laid. You can squash that, can't you?"

"Maybe. She's pretty upset."

"Well, I would be too. You gonna marry her now to keep her in town?"

"Hasn't gotten that far, Seth. Don't be putting spurs to the horse until you get to the fence."

"You've been pretty lovey-dovey since I've been home. I just thought that was a natural ending to such doin's."

"It was not for you."

"No. It wasn't. I took the King of Siam's advice and like a bee, went flower to flower. And look what it got me. I'm a recovering alcoholic.

I've got an illegitimate son in Florida, and I lost all my money. Great prospect, aren't I?"

"Someone will find something loveable about you."

"Well, I'll just wait around then. In the meantime, what are you going to do about Serena?"

Serena. Every time Richard looked at the family photo on top of the chest of drawers in his bedroom, looked at the smiling faces of him and his wife and their two children, he shrank a little in stature. Often, he and his wife had talked about growing old together and the joys they would have in retirement. But life has a way of working its own schedules and the quick discovery and rapid decline of his wife with non-smoker's lung cancer five years ago left him near retirement, wealthy, healthy, and missing her so much he could not consider a close relationship with any other woman. Until Serena. The urge to possess her, to squeeze her into the void left by his wife of twenty-seven years, was daunting. He could argue both sides of marriage and always, always ended up in the middle—a hung jury.

"I'm thinking. Don't push me, Seth."

"While you're thinking, make your hands work and finish the pack. I'm gonna check on a packsaddle. We used to have one in the haymow, but I haven't seen it for a while. We should balance up a horse with fifty-five pounds on each side. That wouldn't be too heavy for a horse."

"Don't forget water—"

"You can carry something besides the .30-30, can't you?"

The Platte River

The waters rose in the night and moved the sand bar in front of the mouth of Fourmile Creek. Carp and catfish found their way into the creek, but turned and hung in the eddy just east of the mouth where the churning current pushed their food toward the bottom. The water, darkened by debris from up-river flooding, ceased to burble and in a workmanlike manner cruised past the Barrett Ranch, tumbling and twisting, putting new patterns in old sand bars. A turtle climbed out on the bank and sat there.

The preparation

"WE STAY ON THE north bank up to Highway 50, then take the south bank to Highway 80. After that the left bank up to WQ Street…"

"What the hell are you talking about, Seth?"

"The Platte. I've been studying it on Google maps. I think we can do the trip up on horseback. There'll be some rough spots, but mostly everyone has built back from the river because of flooding. The banks are pretty clear."

"What's the footing like?"

"Can't tell. But it's bound to be silt from flooding, don't you reckon?"

Richard nodded. "I wonder if anyone has gone up and down that thing in recent times? Anyone we could query?"

"Likely," Seth said. "I don't see any problem with it."

"I know you don't—but I do."

"Richard—we walk or drive or ride along our bank every week and we've got ten miles of it. How's it going to be any different? It's not like we're going up the Grand Canyon or somethin'. It's flat as a griddle all the way."

"Last week I thought you were acting a little strange over this."

"Yeah—I was. But now I'm thinking it's gonna be a fun trip. Passing on that whiskey the other night gave me the notion that I've kicked that addiction. You know—" he looked Richard in the eyes— "when you can stare down liquor after what I've been through, a man can do most anything."

Richard clapped him on the back. A smile edged across his face. "I'm glad to hear that. Really glad."

The brothers stood, Richard's hand on Seth's back, closer than they had been for years, the closeness heating the air in the room. It was almost like when they were little kids and Richard was showing his brother how to swing on the rope out over the creek, or how to ride the bike, or how to drive the tractor. Then Richard's arm slid down in jerks and stops, like it didn't want to leave the warmth and strength of Seth's back. They looked at each other out of the corners of their eyes, then turned away and went back to their packing.

LUNCH WAS STEAK SANDWICHES, cheese, fruit, and raw spinach salad.

"We won't eat like this goin' up river," Seth said.

"No, we won't. You'll be doing most of the cooking," Richard said.

"Me? Why me?"

"Because you're better at it. I'm an excellent dish washer."

"There's a lot more to cooking than there is to dish washing."

"That's the truth. But I'll also be planning the next day's tactics."

"What tactics?"

"The tactics needed to get us up and down without mishap."

"As if I couldn't do that?"

Richard nodded. "That's right."

"Humph. I think I could plan it as well as anybody."

"That's your opinion and you're entitled to it. You read the maps and work out the strategy. I plan the tactics."

"What's for dessert?" Seth asked.

"Chocolate sundaes if you haven't used all the Hershey syrup. With chopped walnuts on top."

Seth pushed his plate aside and pulled the coffee cup closer.

"What's Serena feeling about the rumor?"

"She's troubled as anyone would be."

"You comforted her no doubt."

"I did what any gentleman would do."

"Did you ease her all the way?"

"Seth—when I want you to know everything about our relationship, I'll tell you. Until then, keep your juvenile requests to yourself. It is unseemly to pry into a man's personal life. I didn't pry into yours when you were off the wagon."

"Not that I knew of."

"And I didn't. Wanted to sometimes when I would hear stories about you."

"Why didn't you?"

"Respect. You're a grown man. That means you make decisions by yourself. If you had wanted anything from me, you could have asked. You didn't, and I didn't see any cause for butting into your life."

Richard set the ice cream down, moved around the table and sat at the other end. It was a long table for two people. Scars from thousands of meals eaten on it made dark patterns in the evening light and reminded them when it had served the family starting with two,

Grandpa and Grandma Melzer, up and through the highest at ten and now Richard and Seth held down the opposite ends, often feeling foolish for being so far apart. But Richard had eaten at that end all his adult life. After his children moved out and his wife died, he remained in that chair, the web seating having been replaced twice. Now with Seth back in the house it somehow seemed normal for him to sit at the opposite end.

Seth chewed and swallowed a bite. "When we leavin', you figure?"

Richard looked up. "Monday, May 1st. I like to start things on Monday. Gives sort of a push to the effort, don't you think?"

"Monday's fine with me. I'll be ready."

Seth licked the spoon and then the bowl. "There. Clean as being washed."

Richard smiled. "You remember that Springer that Dad had that he let lick his plate? And then he put it on the counter close to the clean dishes seeing if Mom would pick up on it?"

Seth chuckled. "I do."

"And how Mom would sniff the plates to see if she could find the one the dog had licked?"

"I do. Dad never got tired of that joke did he?"

"And then he'd let that dog under the covers on his side of the bed to warm it up while they were getting ready for bed."

"Yeah—and Mom said he smelled like the dog."

"Well—he probably did. Lying there in the bed where the dog had been. And that dog had ticks sometimes, too. I remember us picking some off him after we hiked up Fourmile."

"He was a good ol' dog. What was his name—do you recall?"

"Think it was Charlie."

"Yeah. That was it. Charlie."

Richard pushed back from the table. "I've got some thinking to do on this school board meeting tomorrow night. Think I'll get with my pad and pen and figure things out in the peace and quiet of the evening."

"You're not doing the dishes?"

"Let the dog lick 'em."

"We don't have a dog."

"Borrow one."

Seth piled the dishes on the counter. He sniffed the top plate. It smelled like steak. He wondered if you could smell dog lick.

SOMEHOW, IN THE MIDDLE of figuring out what points he wanted to bring up at the school board meeting tomorrow night, Richard had removed his reading glasses, set them on the table beside his chair and fallen asleep. It was the mantle clock striking three that forced his left eye to open which caused him to realize that he had been asleep and for a fleeting moment watch the disappearing stages of the dream he had been having of jumping his horse over a small water outlet. The horse, fully laden with gear, made a lot of noise as the loose stuff clattered against its ribs in making the jump.

He made a note to not have loose stuff hanging from the horse. He sat up, looked around at the quietness spilling over into every corner of the room. He'd miss this place for the time they were gone. They'd be back before fall, ready for the harvest and after that he could linger in front of the fireplace as the leaves fell and winds and snow froze the land for winter.

Chapter 3

FILOH THREW THE MATCH on the gasoline soaked dirt and ran as fast as he could. His footsteps sounded hollow, and the boots slipped on the plowed ground. He twisted his left ankle. He threw his arms out to balance as his body racked this way and that with each step. He'd made it fifty yards before the explosion ripped across the ground sprawling him face down and pelting him with dirt clods. He pushed up on his elbows and watched the dust cloud rise.

"Need a longer fuse," he said out loud. He stood up, his left ankle sore. He limped toward the end of the field. There was a dust trail rising off the county road. Every so often he glanced at the rising plume of dust but, head down arms swinging, he maintained a constant pace toward the gate where his rented pickup was parked between the fence line and the county road.

At the gate he struggled with the wire loop that held the gatepost, got it unhooked, stepped outside and re-hooked the gate. He could hear a vehicle approaching after turning the section corner, the engine whine telling him it was going all out. He got inside his pickup and put the key in the ignition as the vehicle—a white pickup with Dixon Agriworks painted on the driver door—skidded to a halt just inches from his front bumper. A lean young man wearing a belt knife left the driver door open, settled his hat on his head and sauntered up to Filoh's window. The stern look on his face was offset by the fact that he was chewing gum and his jaw revolved around it, sometimes open and sometimes closed.

"You're trespassing," he said. "Roll down your window."

Filoh looked around for the window crank.

"It's electric. Turn the ignition to the second position."

Filoh couldn't figure it out and the young man pulled the door open. "Come on out here."

"I'm not moving. You got something to say—say it."

"What the hell were you doing in our field?"

"Experimenting."

"Experimenting with what? I heard a blast. Saw a dust cloud."

"Soil testing."

"You say you were soil testing?"

Filoh nodded.

"Stay here. I'm gonna call the office."

The young man pulled a cell phone from a belt holster. His hard eyes stared at Filoh until he heard the phone picked up at the other end.

"This is Cort out on the river section. Found a guy just coming off our land after some sort of explosion. Says he is soil testing. You know anything about it?" He lowered his head and kicked at a ping-pong sized rock with his boot toe. "I don't either. Whaddaya think? Ok. Sure." He closed the phone. "They want to know your name and if you're from around here."

"Filoh Smith. Been here since before you were born. This used to be my place," he said pointing toward Fourmile Creek.

"Well—my orders are to tell you to get off and stay off. Anything you don't understand about that?"

"No, sir."

Cort nodded. "Ok—then git!"

A Dodge Ramcharger pulled up beside the two rigs facing each other on the county road. "What's goin' on?" Seth Barrett asked.

Cort gestured toward Filoh. "This old bugger settin' off fireworks. Can you get him out of here?"

"If he'll come, I can." He looked at Filoh like he was a juvenile delinquent. "You comin' peacefully or do I have to hog tie you?"

Filoh shook his head. "My gawd, what's this world come to? Two out of three people in this group is nuts."

"Will you follow me, or do you want to lead?" Seth said.

"Go ahead—I'll follow."

Filoh's plan

"JUDAS PRIEST, FILOH. You can't go blowing people's stuff up. Especially if it belongs to Dixon. He'll have you drawn and quartered and God help you if he buries you on his land. He's got about 7,000 acres and we wouldn't find you until hell freezes over." Seth paced the kitchen of the Barrett house, his stocking feet sliding over the polished walnut flooring. He looked at the rented pickup in the driveway, the driver's door still open and shook his head. "You want more coffee?"

Filoh raised the cup and Seth got the coffee pot and topped it off. Filoh sat erect in the cane bottom chair, his body supported by elbows on the table. The coffee in the saucer rippled as he blew over it.

"Richard and Ginny will be here shortly." Seth walked to the window, hands slanted into the rear pockets of his Levis. "Hell—I saw the dust cloud from clear over here. Had to find out what it was."

"Didn't work right," Filoh said.

"That's good that it didn't. You got spare money you don't mind paying Dixon for replacing his irrigation equipment? One of those ten tower pivots will cost about eighty thousand dollars. You got eighty thousand dollars you want to throw around; you might hire a lobbyist and talk to the legislature. That's the only way you're gonna get things changed around here. We're all farming the way we learned in school. We're using pesticides, fungicides, herbicides, and insecticides all over the place. Cass County Agri-spray hits us about every month during the season. Richard says we'd have lost most of the crop to corn borers if we hadn't sprayed last year."

"I never used all that stuff and I never lost a full crop." Filoh sipped the coffee. "Some short ones—that's true, but always had enough."

"But Filoh—what you need to see is that modern farming and ranching isn't built on enough. It's built on having some of the good stuff in life. A few luxuries—you know? This is the industrial age and farming has come along with it. Bigger farms. No backbreaking work; air-conditioned cabs with computers, stereo, and TV. It's a far cry from when you were farming in the 60s."

He could hear Filoh sucking the coffee from the saucer. He didn't want to turn around and see it. Actually he didn't want to see Filoh anymore. The old man had haunted him since his youth. Always intense, severe, full of thoughts and ideas that he was pursuing. He was not an adult for kids to be around.

Filoh ran the back of his sleeve across his mouth. "I'll wait until Richard and Ginny get here but I will say one thing here and now.

What you and Richard are doing is killing the land. And the air and the water. And mark my words, it's gonna take you down with it."

Seth wanted to scoff but he didn't. He held it back. Not bad for a guy who not so long ago would have said exactly what he thought when he thought it. That appears to be one of the benefits of being on the wagon but it was damn hard to hold in. It was like his tongue was going to force his mouth open and say it without any help.

A car door slammed and muted voices drifted in through the open kitchen window. Filoh looked up, saucer poised. Seth stood with his back to the stovetop, his hands jammed into his back pockets. Richard and Ginny came in the front door and made their way to the breakfast room.

"What's the story?" Richard said, looking at Seth.

Seth nodded toward Filoh. "It's his game. Let him tell you."

Filoh set the saucer down, tugged his sleeves to cover his wrists and, with his eyes just thin slits in his browned face, he looked hard at Richard. "First place I don't need to go through this scrutiny. I've got some things to do and I'm gonna do 'em until there is some recognition of the facts around here."

"Facts about what?" Ginny said.

"The death sentence you Barretts have put on this land and river. Those are facts."

Richard's head tilted down until his chin almost touched his chest. He took a deep breath and thought of all the changes he and Ginny had discussed coming over that would have to be made to run the kind of operation Filoh envisioned.

Ginny interrupted his thoughts. "We can't change it by ourselves. There must be hundreds of farmers along the Platte all doing the same thing."

Filoh shook his head. "That's true. But there's at least two dozen that are doing right by the land."

"Everyone around here is doing it the same way."

"Might be. But that don't make it right."

"Look," Ginny said. "Our mother just died. My brothers are set to complete the request of her will. I've got to run this place while they're gone and there is no way we can do anything about this at this time."

"You can start by stopping," Filoh said.

"Stopping what?"

"Stop spraying."

"Now?"

"You damn right. Stop it now. Stop killing the land—don't you understand that?"

Ginny exhaled, crossed her arms and leaned back against the windowsill.

Richard looked up. "What would you say if we agreed to look into it after we get back from the trip? Would you stop this destructive activity you seem bent on?"

"Tell you what. You take me with you. I'll show you what's happening to the land and the river and the aquifer and you decide. You weren't born dummies. I'll rest my case with your judgment."

Seth smiled. "You can't make it."

"I've made many a mile in my day."

"I'm talking about 600 miles up and back."

"I know."

"Well?"

Filoh nodded. "Tell me when and I'll be there."

"This is crazy. Hauling a ninety year old along. We'll have to put a coffin on the pack horse."

"You can get a coffin along the way but it will more'n likely be for one of you."

Richard smiled. "Let's see if we can make it work, Seth. At least for the first fifty miles or so. If what Filoh's saying has any validity, we should know in that distance, I'd think." He turned his gaze to Filoh. "How's that set with you, Filoh?"

"Just dandy. Give me a couple days notice so I can cook up some corn doggers."

"Seth?"

"I'm dead set against it. No way we're taking him with us. "

"Ginny?"

"I don't care. It doesn't change anything for me. The thing that bothers me is the logistics of making changes while you're gone."

Richard turned toward Filoh. "Looks like one for, one against, and one neutral."

Seth dropped his arms and pushed away from the stovetop. "Richard, I'm not letting him traipse along with us. I don't see anything that requires us to nursemaid him..."

"Nurse-maid? I've been doin' alright without your input for ninety years…"

"Damn right, nurse-maid. It's gonna take you longer to get ready, longer to do anything. No deal. You're not goin'."

Filoh looked to Richard. "Why don't ya vote on it?"

Seth sissored his arms in from of him. "No voting. The will says Richard and I go up the river. Not that we take a half-dead old man with us. We've got a schedule to keep and we can't keep it with you slowin' us down at every turn."

"Why I've…" Filoh began.

"Hold it." Richard held up his hands. "If Seth feels that strongly about it we can't do it. We can't have that kind of discord on the trip. There are too many unknowns in it as it is. No sense us making it harder than it needs to be."

"That's better," Seth said and crossed over to the sink.

"And what about me?" Ginny said.

"Don't make any changes. We'll keep an eye out for what Filoh's talking about and the three of us will confer on it when we get back. Ok?"

Ginny nodded. "Yeah—I'm ok with that."

Filoh snorted and crossed his fingers behind his back. The good thing about being ninety was you didn't give a damn what other people thought. He hadn't come back to stay behind.

The River

Between Fremont and Plattsmouth, the Platte River took on few contributors. It worked at keeping the spring water within the banks but fresh rains had sent it over into the low-lying fields. Carp had slid over the banks and into the drainage ditches alongside the road and now struggled to stay alive as the waters receded. The River had plenty of carp and like the farmers toiling on the banks, it could lose some stock and still maintain a balance.

Contemplation

RICHARD TOOK THE KEY from his wallet and opened Serena's front door. A quiet descended on him as he removed his boots and walked across the carpet in the darkened room to the kitchen to the coffee maker. Serena always left the coffee maker ready for action—exact amount of water standing by; filter in; coffee can out with the measure inside, but the lid on tight. Richard smiled at the thought of her efficiency. He looked around the kitchen. Everything in its place, counter clean, dishes put away, Regulator clock with consistency and conciseness, ticking the seconds of life away. He leaned back against the counter, legs crossed, arms folded across his chest, taking long breaths.

Maybe he was too old for this sort of thing: the farm, the provisions of the will, the school board, his feelings for Serena... and Filoh Smith. He'd heard it said that President Gerald Ford couldn't chew gum and walk across the street at the same time. He could relate to that; his plate was too full. In the cool dim light it was easier for him to categorize his problems—all needing some sort of resolution before he headed up the Platte for Ogallala. The coffee maker beeped. He took down a mug with a Burwell Rodeo logo on it, poured it full and sat down at the chrome and plastic table in one of the four red vinyl chairs. The regulator clock said 9:00 am.

What if Filoh was right? That he and Seth were helping kill the very thing that provided them their livelihood and they would find evidence of it all up and down the river? What would they—could they do about it? It hurt his head to think of changing everything over to what he thought Filoh was advocating. And was Filoh the ultimate answer on this? He'd been gone from farming for twenty-five years. There was a world of change during that time. The ranch's wheat was now selling in South Carolina, a thousand miles away, not in Omaha. His corn and soybeans were being marketed in South Korea, not North Platte. He ran his hands across his face, put his elbows on the table, and blew on the coffee.

He took a small pad and pen out of his shirt pocket and wrote SCHOOL BOARD in capital letters across the top and then wrote the number one on the left side. Pulling the phone across the table he lifted the receiver and dialed. Randy Cranston, President of the Cass County School Board, answered.

"Hello, Randy. Richard Barrett here. How are things at the elevator? Good. Nice to know my wheat is resting nicely. Is it getting any more valuable? No—I haven't seen the market today. Been kinda busy with stuff." He paused to set the right tone. "I'm hearing rumors about a move to fire Serena. You know anything about that?"

He sipped the coffee while making small noises to show that he was still there. Randy could talk a goodly bit without other people's input and he was not shy about his feelings, thoughts, or past actions.

"I don't know much," Randy said, "other than Mrs. Buell—the third grade teacher—she was in charge of the Christmas program you remember—says that Serena would not have her high school students learn all six verses to "O Come All Ye Faithful…"

"There's only four," Richard said.

"What?"

"Four verses."

"How do you know?"

"I learned them. There's only four. Actually there *are* only four. I misspoke using there *is* instead of there *are*. I apologize."

"For cryin' out loud, Richard. We're talking about Serena here, not how well you learned English in the Plattsmouth school system."

"I understand."

"Where was I? Oh yes—she wouldn't have her students learn all four verses. Said they'd learn the first and last and hum the middle verses. If the grade school kids needed to learn all verses, go ahead, but she wasn't going to spend their English period having them learn four verses of a Christmas Carol when there was a ton of other English they needed to learn to come out of high school able to get and hold a job."

"Hmm," Richard said. "Seems a bit harsh to fire her over that, doesn't it?"

"You know Wily. He gets a wild hair ever once in awhile and it takes some talking to get him to see another point of view. I thought we'd just take it under advisement at the board meeting and let it simmer down. Serena's a damn good teacher and I don't want to lose her."

There was a blank moment, then Randy said, "Course—you've got a vested interest. You might not get to vote."

"I suppose you could look at it that way." Richard said. He could feel Randy's eyebrows rising.

"I don't know how you could look at it any other way, do you? I mean—what's a fact is a fact."

"Humph. Doesn't mean I wouldn't take the community's interest to heart if I was to vote."

"Course not. Nobody's saying that. It's just that you are seen with her all the time and people will assume you're gonna take her side of any disagreement with Wily or anybody else for that matter."

"Sounds like this has escalated a little," Richard said.

"I don't mean to imply that. Just that I'd be hard pressed to allow you to vote if it came to a vote in the Board. You understand. The propriety of it and all."

"How much do you know that you're not saying, Randy?"

"Don't know anything more than what I've told you. Look—there's an eighteen-wheeler just came in wanting to unload some of last year's wheat. I gotta go. I'll see you tonight. Don't forget, board meeting starts at 7 o'clock sharp. New time, you know. Goodbye, Richard."

He let the receiver dangle in his extended fingers and looked out the kitchen window into the small back yard. It had been cleared of children's apparatus now that the children had grown and moved away. Even the worn out grass spots were grown over. It was clean, tranquil, even, and ahead of the curve. And that's where he needed to be. By whatever means necessary, he had to get ahead of the power curve in his life. He had to anticipate, be ready to act instead of reacting. Life was short enough and he had already lived more than two thirds of it; ten years longer than his dad. He cradled the phone and pulled the mug toward him, cupping his hands around it.

It was handy having Serena working in the school. Nice. They could see each other frequently. Neither had asked for a commitment. But if she was fired, or quit, the closest school she might find employment could be an hour's drive away—or more. Then what? Then bloody what?

Costs Escalate

"I'LL BE RIGHT OVER," Seth said. He wanted to do this face to face. It was getting too complicated trying to figure it out over the phone.

Seth parked in front of the hangar door with a big CASS COUNTY AGRI-SPRAY sign hanging above it. Scott Digney, the owner, was under the fuselage of the Grumman Ag Cat adjusting a cable to the tail wheel when Seth walked over and shook the wing struts.

"Get out from under there so I can talk to you," Seth said.

"I can hear you from here," Scott said.

"Naw. I wanta look you in the eyes when you quote that price again."

"It's not gonna change with me standing up."

"It might. We'll just have to see."

"Pour yourself some coffee. I'll be outta here in a minute."

Seth looked around the old hangar. Photos of WWII airplanes lined the walls. Spare wheels, tires, wings, tails, windshields, and cables of all sorts hung on pegs driven into a huge 12" x 24" beam that supported the roof structure. The coffee area was against one wall where a brown substance bubbled in a pot on a stained wooden counter next to a rack of mugs that looked like they hadn't been washed since they got out of the kiln. He wasn't sure, but Seth believed you took your life into your hands if you drank from one of those. He decided to risk it and poured a cup. Then he took a clean rag from the bin and spread it out over one of the chairs, sat down, crossed his right leg over the left and blew on his coffee.

The hollow hangar amplified every scrape and bang Scotty made in his under-the-fuselage work. Seth stared at him, blew on the boiling coffee and sat as still as a newborn calf.

When Scott slid out from under the plane and wiped his hands, he took down a mug, poured coffee, and sat in the remaining chair. His coveralls were ill fitting, spotted with grease, torn, and the cuffs sprouted ragged strings of material.

It was the saddest clothing Seth had seen in awhile. "When's the last time you laundered those coveralls?"

"Why?"

"Just wondered. I think I remember some of those spots from last year."

Scott shook his head. "No. I don't believe they're that old." He tipped his mug and sucked the surface of the coffee into his mouth in a maneuver he called carbureting. "What did'ja want to talk about?"

Seth looked at his coffee. "You boil your coffee all day long?"

"Until it's brown enough to suit me. You don't like it, quit drinking it."

Seth smelled it. "It'll do until some real coffee shows up." He uncrossed his legs and squared himself in the chair looking directly at Scotty. "Your spray quote. It's a lot higher than last year's. And last year's was higher than the year before. You aiming to retire early?"

"Have you noticed the price of gas? How about tires? And how about the wages of pilots willing to face death every day? How do you put a price on that?"

"You do most of the flying yourself."

"Not very good on the left rudder since my accident. Mostly it's young guys doing the flying. They're immortal, but they do like to get paid."

"You're not answering my question," Seth said.

"You're not making sense with it."

"Maybe I'll just drink your coffee and get another bid."

Scott carbureted another sip of coffee. "Flannigan's Ag-Air filed for Chapter 11 bankruptcy last Friday. They didn't raise their prices last year. I'm bidding on some of their surplus equipment. If I get it cheap enough I might be able to cut the price by a few cents an acre, but I doubt it. You remember Darrell Winslow, the old guy that used to live in Weatherby's farm house after Klete Dixon bought it?"

Seth nodded.

"He's in Lincoln in the hospital. Cancer. Doctors said it was from being an agri-spotter. He got wet with the chemicals too many times. That stuff gave him the cancer. Workman's comp is eatin' us alive on premiums and you want us to cut our prices." He raised his right foot to rest on top of his left knee exposing a hole in his coveralls that Seth had missed before. "Let me ask you this. How much have you lowered the price of your wheat or your corn or soybeans?" He nodded his head and raised the coffee to his lips.

"I deal with the cattle."

"Well—your cattle then. How much less?"

"They go up and down with the market, but your prices are always goin' up."

Scott shrugged. "That's the nature of this business. You keep your prices where you can make a decent profit until there is no more profit. Then you raise them a little—"

"—A lot."

"Not that much: pennies an acre. It just looks like a lot because you've got so much ground you want sprayed this year. Cut back on spraying and my bill goes down. As simple as that."

"Well—I don't know what this world is coming to. When I was a kid I could buy chocolate malts for seventeen cents. Now they want $3.50. Movies used to be a dime."

"Don't get started on that. Av-gas used to cost thirty cents a gallon. Now it's over three dollars. You're gonna have to find another argument, Seth, and even then it's not gonna work. I'll not go broke servicing the Barrett Ranch just to be a good guy."

Seth stared at the dirty coffee mug he held in his hand. Then he stood up, threw the remaining coffee into the sink, filthy from having had aircraft parts washed in it, and set the mug down on the counter.

"You can wash that if you don't mind," Scott said.

"Want me to wash yours, too?"

"No. I keep it running all day. I'll wash it tonight before I go home from this low paying job."

"Are you sure you wash it occasionally?"

Scott nodded. "Damn sure. Don't want to catch anything from any of my customers."

"Like common sense?"

"Could be."

"You coming to the poker game tomorrow night?"

"If I can scrape up the ante money."

"Two bucks?"

"I know, but times are tough. And you guys go hard for the big pots."

"It's the last game before we head up river. I need to build up a piggy bank for that so bring all your savings."

"Yeah—my wife'd like that."

"Bring her along as tradin' stock. She's a comely young lady."

"I'll be sure to tell her that. She'll be flattered."

Seth smiled. "Well—don't fly into some power lines and make her a widow or I'll be camping in your front yard as soon as your casket's lowered."

"That'd be mighty nice of you to support her past her prime. Her and the kids."

"I gotta take the kids too?"

"They're a package."

Seth dried the mug with a paper towel and hung it back on the rack. "Thanks for the coffee. I appreciate your business acumen and your willingness to reconsider your pricing strategy. I'll see you tomorrow night. Try and scrape up the two bucks."

Scott smiled. "See ya, Seth."

Seth did not turn on the radio nor open the windows as he drove back to the ranch. What Scotty had said about prices, the increased spraying required this year, and the cancer of ol' man Winslow irritated something in his brain. Prices were up for everything; production was down on the acreage; lots of wheat stored over for the next year's market—that cost money. Everything seemed all right. People seemed happy. Sun came up and went down and it rained when it was supposed to. What was that nagging feeling?

The River

Along its south bank the river allowed the runoff from Klete Dixon's spread and the Barrett Ranch to enter its flow. The ten tower pivot sprinklers each covered 40 acres of crops and each acre had a liberal sprinkling of herbicide to control the weeds, some pesticide to control the bugs, some fungicide to control the potential fungus, and a liberal dose of fertilizer to stimulate growth. Most of the water thrown out from overhead sprinklers would seep into the ground. But even on hot days, some found its way to the little ditches that water makes to rejoin its source and some days the surface water turned a yellow-green that feathered into the current and disappeared.

All in

"**DAMMIT, SETH, QUIT STUDYING** your cards and bet. They're not going to get any better," Scotty said.

"Seth thinks he can turn a deuce into an ace by staring at it," Swede put in.

"You knuckle heads wouldn't know a good hand if you got one," Seth said. "Ok—I'm raising Scotty a quarter."

Scotty put in a quarter and so did Swede and Doug and Jack Brown.

Seth smiled. "You guys think I'm bluffing, don't you?" He spread the cards on the table face up. "Read 'em and weep."

The other four hands were thrown face down into a pile. Seth scooted the coins toward him, smiling at the other players. "You guys are just up against a giant tonight. But don't let that keep you from betting."

"Where's Richard?" Jack Brown asked.

"He's seeing Serena, I guess," Seth said. "She got fired, you know."

"I bet she's taking it hard."

"I imagine she is. Nobody likes getting fired."

Swede put his elbows on the table and in a conspiratorial tone said, "I hear she's got offers from three schools around here."

"Wouldn't doubt it. She's a good teacher," Doug said. "She worked for me at the store last summer and I'll tell you, we made more while she was there than we did before or after. Usually summers aren't that good."

Seth shuffled the cards. "I wish he would marry her and get this resolved."

"They that serious?" Jack asked.

Seth nodded. "I think so. He doesn't talk to me much about it. But it's spring time and Richard being a farmer… that's when new life gets going."

Jack chuckled. "Richard's a bit past starting any new life, isn't he?"

"Who knows?" Seth said. "I have a seventeen-year-old bull that's still making calves."

"Yeah, but you're heading up river and gonna miss spring," Scotty said.

"True. Maybe when we get back," Seth said.

"If you get back," Jack said.

Seth turned to look at him. "What do you mean, if?"

"How many people you think have gone up and down the Platte in the last hundred years? By horseback?" Jack asked.

"So what?"

"You don't know what you'll find up that river. People drown in it every year. Hell—they just found Dustin Williams' body against the dam this spring. There's gotta be quick sand and rattlesnakes—"

"—And an alligator or two," Doug put in.

They laughed. "If there are any alligators, I'll bring you back one," Seth said.

"Deal," Doug said.

"I've flown over the river for the last fifteen years, but I never thought about walking it or riding a horse up it." Scotty said.

"Well—take some pictures, Seth, so you can show us IF you get back," Jack said.

Swede picked up his cards as they were dealt and placed them in his hand. "I've heard stories in my shop about some of the people living along the river. They're nuts."

"Like what?" Jack said.

"Like doin' illegal stuff on land fenced with barbed wire and willow trees and cottonwoods as thick as a log barricade. Don't like strangers stopping by river or by road or on foot."

"That's old time stuff. There aren't any of those anymore. That was in the '30s when North Platte was a roaring union town," Doug said.

"I don't know," Swede continued. "There's talk that the fish kills that are happening on the river from time to time are coming because of run-offs from those unseen places." He scratched the back of his head. "And you know—it's trespassing if you step on the bank anywhere on private property."

Seth picked up his cards. It was quiet for a moment, each participant studying his cards.

"I'll bet a dime," Jack said.

Swede called and so did Doug and Seth and Scotty. Seth raised it a nickel.

"Damn," Jack said. "I'm in. But I feel like a share cropper at a county fair goat roping contest."

The group laughed. Jack ran his sporting goods store like a pro. He played poker like an amateur. He bet like a nincompoop.

Seth, who was used to watching out for his cattle and fences and water tanks and the beef market, wasn't much on casting an eye at the river. If dead fish had drifted by the Barrett Ranch on the Platte River current, he had not seen them. A raft of dead fish would take some time to cover the ten miles of river frontage, but it was unlikely Seth Barrett would have spent more than a few brief seconds even looking that way. The river was the river. It rose and fell and ran downhill. That much he knew. But despite having 60+ years "on" the river, Seth barely acknowledged its existence. It wasn't that he didn't appreciate the river, and the water it provided, just that he didn't think about it. When he rode the banks, he was looking for stray cattle hanging out in the cottonwood breaks, or a lost calf or a broken fence. The river was there and he was sure it was wet and that it flowed every minute of every day and that the cloudy water it offered across the fields where Richard farmed was much appreciated, if not thoroughly understood.

The River

The river knew Seth and Richard Barrett. It knew the leaching from Fourmile River , the lesions on the frogs that dug into the mud on its bank, the one eyed fish that held in its eddies trying to get back to breed more of its kind, hopefully with two eyes. It knew as well the belching of bubbles from the contaminated mud and sand and the dead spots along its course where nothing lived because there was no oxygen. It was silent, but it had made a list and one day it would demand an accounting. The river had hosted the Oto and the Pawnee. It had altered its course to accommodate roaring waters emanating from Wyoming and Colorado and it remained stubborn. As stubborn as the white settlers that built sod houses and milked one cow and tried to push the land to support their meager existence. Now the Barrett men were going to get intimate with it and from here on it had a hand to play.

THE OTHERS CALLED AND Seth dealt himself two cards.

"Dealer takes two cards," Scotty said. "He's holding three of a kind, boys. Better bet high or clear out." He threw down one card.

The others took cards, fanned them out in their hands, held them close to their chests and tried to keep a poker face. Since Seth had dealt, it was up to Jack to make the first bet, hold or fold.

"I'll raise a nickel," Jack said. "I know you boys might need a loan and my interest rates hold for this game, same as a credit card—19%."

"Judas Priest," Scotty said. "What is 19% on a nickel?"

Everyone put in a nickel to call Seth and waited to see what he would show. He took one card from his hand and laid it face up on the table. "Ten of Hearts." He took a second card and turned it face up. "Jack of Hearts."

"He thinks he's got a straight flush," Swede said.

"He wouldn't know a straight flush if it stared him in the face," Jack said.

Another card up. "Queen of hearts."

"We can see the cards, Seth. Just lay 'em down." Doug was getting nervous.

"King of hearts." Seth clung to the last card in his hand and smiled at everyone around the table. All eyes were on the card. He laid it face down with his hand on top of it. "Anybody want to bet on this card?"

They looked at each other. None offered a bet. Seth turned it over and laughed. "Two of spades."

"You con artist."

"You'd try and bluff your mother, Seth."

"That's a tough hand to fill," Doug said. He had two pair, which took the hand, and he pulled the coins across the table.

"Boys," Scotty said. "I've got work in the morning and I need my beauty sleep. I'm outta here."

Doug rose from his chair. "Me too."

"Sure. You're leaving a winner. What am I gonna tell the Missus when I go home without the food money?" Swede said.

"You're not married, Swede," Jack said.

They all laughed. It was the common blather of an all male Friday night poker game where the loser lost a dollar or two and the winner made just enough to buy a hamburger with fries at the Dairy Queen on Saturday.

Jack Brown shoved the chairs in, drew his sleeve across the table and brushed it with his other hand, looked around and followed Seth out the back door turning out the lights in the "office" as he stepped out. He tugged on the handle testing the locked door. "Seth, you and Richard be careful now. There is more to this trip than you might be thinking. I sell a half dozen antivenin kits a year out of the pharmacy and most of them get used. Keep your eyes and ears open. There are times when you could be twenty—thirty miles from a town with a doc and a hospital. A horse throw you or you get rattlesnake bit and it could cost you. Know what I mean?"

"Yeah." Seth said. "Thanks for thinking of it. And caring about us. We'll be fine."

Jack nodded. "I hope so. See you when you get back." He stuck out his hand and Seth shook it. He looked in Jack's eyes and they both nodded.

Platte River, 2010

How it looks today.

Chapter 4

RICHARD SLID THE .30-30 Winchester into the saddle scabbard.

"You're bound to take that .30-30 with you?" Seth said.

"Yup. Like you never needing it on the ranch, I may not need it on the river. But in case I do—it'll be there. Rather have it and not need it, than need it and not have it."

"Oh, that's clever. That's from "*Lonesome Dove*," isn't it?"

Richard nodded. "You got the water purifier?"

"Left side of the pack horse. I arranged the packsaddle so that stuff we need often is on the left side. Stuff we need less than once a day on the right. Got a pretty good balance too, if I do say so myself."

"OK. Where we headed?"

Seth unfolded the map. "We'll take the side of the road out to Bay Hills Golf Course and hang around the river bank up toward Cedar Island."

Ginny stood beside the corral fence, arms crossed over her chest, her forehead wrinkled, eyebrows arched. Her feet made little short steps going nowhere, circling but staying in motion. "Stay in touch, you guys. Don't burn your battery up but call us."

Seth smiled. "It's gonna be fun, Ginny."

They said their goodbyes, waved to everyone and turned the horses west toward Fourmile Creek.

SETH TURNED IN THE saddle. "Did you bring their ashes?"

Richard patted his saddlebag. "Right here."

"Both of 'em?"

Richard nodded.

"Where do you think would be a good place to leave them?"

"We'll find a place that seems good to us."

"Yeah—reckon we will." Seth straightened in the saddle, pulled the pack horse even with his palomino, and gazed over the flat country where the rising sun, unimpeded by mountains or trees, beamed light that flashed green hints of new growth on all sides. He breathed in the wet earth scent of irrigated fields, the drying manure, the dusty hide smell slipping off the small bunches of cattle they passed, their eyes wide, new calves leaping and dancing on the edges.

He looked back at Richard, who, unused to riding, was adjusting stuff attached to his saddle bags, pulling his pants leg down so the wrinkles wouldn't bite into him, changing his seat on the saddle. Richard probably hadn't ridden a horse since they were kids. He was on a tractor, a combine, or a pickup seat half his life. They were soft, mounted on springs, and the cabs were air conditioned and had radios and computers.

"Hey—I'm hungry already," Seth said.

"You'll make it till noon."

"I don't know. I'm powerful hungry." Seth patted his stomach and as an after thought asked, "Did you bring toilet paper?"

Richard nodded. "Do you think Adolph Melzer had toilet paper?"

"I doubt he even knew what it was. Don't think it showed up before the Civil War. Came over from China about that time."

"Where'd you learn all this fascinating history of toilet paper?"

"Poker games mostly. There's a world of knowledge there if you tap into it. The thing is—you need to keep your mind open to grasp onto some of these intellectual straws that are floatin' in the breeze."

Richard smiled. Seth had a habit of talking continuously to cattle. He hoped he wasn't going to talk all the way to Ogallala and back.

The horses knew the field they were traveling over and headed for the gate that would let them cross into the Fourmile area.

"Dang horses know where we're goin'," Seth said.

"Appears that way. Don't want to run into Filoh anywhere."

Seth stood up in the stirrups. "No."

"Brady is approximately where Grandpa Melzer turned around," Seth said. "Shouldn't take us long."

"Seems long already." Richard held the saddle horn with both hands, tilted his head. He looked around and smiled. The lake and houses straight and even like soldiers on parade caught his eye at Bay

Hills Golf Club. The sun behind them shadowed everything above the surface giving a sifted grey background to the spring growth. "Pretty up here, isn't it?"

"Come on. We want to make it to Cedar Creek before we camp," Seth said.

"How far is that?"

"Give or take—some eight miles."

THE SADDLE FELT GOOD to Seth. He had felt a burning in his chest to do something unique after Mae died, but when the will was read and he stared the trip in the face it gave him quivers. He hadn't felt quivers since grade school. Now that he was sitting a horse and starting out, it gave him comfort. Something about the certainty of moving step-by-step up the Platte River soothed any anxious feelings he had buried within him about inheriting the Barrett Ranch. He was direct kin, he and Richard. He loved Ginny and it was okay to give her a piece, but he wanted control. Not that he had anybody to leave it to. He just hadn't planned anything else for his life except getting up every morning knowing what he was going to do and enjoy doing it. A cup of coffee in the morning and a drink at night—well, the drink part was out now. As a recovering alcoholic, he couldn't start running any whiskey across his tongue. Too tempting.

Nose to tail, the three horses moved up the unfamiliar riverbank, cutting clean hoof prints in the wet sand. Richard's gray, a settled horse under most circumstances, had his head up, ears forward and nostrils flared. He snorted several times causing horses in the pasture across the river to whinny and run, tails up, heads high, to the fence line and walk parallel with the travelers. Richard smiled. Animals greeting each other had always held a fascination for him and the farm provided lots of that. Sitting on a tractor seat plowing one field all day long, he pondered how much information they could pass to one another and if they retained it. How far away from human were they? They sure showed signs of old age just like he and Seth were doing.

They were moving along the south bank of the river near Treasure Island Road when Seth half turned in his saddle and motioned to Richard to come along side. They reined in their horses and Seth pointed to the far bank.

"I'll bet that's what Filoh is talkin' about. See that discoloration in the water over there? That runoff?"

Richard nodded. "But the river will swallow that up and spit it out. There are millions of gallons of water running down this river. A little discoloration won't last long. I remember Granddad Melzer used to throw the offal from butchering into the river. Said the catfish grew enormous on it."

A photo stream played in his head. Pictures of Granddad Melzer on his first tractor, close-ups of corn leaves shredded by hail or grasshoppers, corn higher than his head when he and Seth went barefoot all summer dressed in nothing but bib-overalls. Half the farm under river water; dead cattle lying in trampled pockets of deep snow in the winter of '48-'49. And Seth and I are killing this land? We are the land and the land is us. How can we be killing ourselves?

SETH FORDED THE RIVER at the east end of Cedar Island, barely getting his horse's belly wet. His horse, Pistol, not used to crossing rivers, moved across it without hesitation. It gave Seth a warm feeling, pushed him into a smile. He patted the horse's neck, "Atta boy, Pistol."

He had the packhorse unsaddled, halter on, and roped to a tree by the time Richard crossed.

Richard rode along side. "Help me off this thing."

Seth offered his arm and helped him slide off the saddle. Richard gimped around in a circle, straightening and stretching his arms to the sky. "Sure glad we went to tractors with soft seats. A man would be dead at one end if he had to do this all the time." He leaned over and looked down at his legs. "I hope they don't stay bowed like this all night."

"You get used to it," Seth said. "A saddle and a bicycle seat are about the same. The first few days you're dying and then something called a transformation occurs and it doesn't bother you again. Until next season."

"There isn't going to be a next season. Did you see that airboat? That's the way to see this river. We should have asked for a variance from the will. We could have seen all we needed to see from a soft seat in that boat."

"Mom had her reasons for us doing it this way. I'm not sure what, but I'm thinking it was to take us back to our roots. Seeing the land along the river at the same pace as Grandpa Melzer did. Scott could have flown us over it in half a day. This is the way to get intimate with the country." He nodded twice. "I'm sure of it."

RICHARD THREW A CUP of white gasoline on some sticks and tossed a lighted match at it. There was a whoosh of air and an explosion. Seth ducked.

"Tea?" Richard said.

Seth shook his head. "And I thought we were roughing it. You were goin' to break up little sticks, whittle fire catchers in 'em and build a little flame." He lowered his chin and squeezed his thighs with his calloused hands. "Then add larger sticks and suspend the tea pot over the fire while we set back and watched it. No." Seth shook his head and threw his arms in the air. "Boom! A gas starter and the tea pot boiling in a humongous fire."

"There were no conditions about how to start a fire in the will."

"I'll get the freeze-dried food," Seth said.

"Get the Scotch, too, will you?" Richard threw another stick on the fire. "I would like to imbibe in that great end of the day celebration which calls for whisky. Sorry you can't join me."

Filoh's intrusion

THE POPPING AND SIZZLE awakened him. Not only the sizzle but smoke too.

Seth peeked out the tent flap. "What in the hell are you doin' here?"

Filoh stood with his back to a small fire rubbing his butt with both hands as the morning light crept above the horizon.

"Thought you might need a chief cook and bottle washer."

"Judas H. Priest!" Seth ducked back into the tent. He emerged in a minute tucking the shirt into his jeans. "Now dammit, I said—we agreed—you weren't going along."

"I know. But sometimes a man just has to make up his mind and do it. And that's what I'm doin'. This is still a free country and a man can go where he wants."

"Yeah—but not into another man's camp."

"Didn't see no signs."

"Didn't put any out."

"Well, then—what says it's yours?"

Seth pointed his finger at the ground. "We're here."

"So am I."

Seth shook his head. "Richard. Come out here and back me up on this."

Richard, his voice muffled by the tent, muttered. "My gawd—I didn't think the ground could be this hard."

"You didn't blow up your mattress, Richard. No wonder," Seth said.

"Show me how to do that tonight before I become a permanent cripple."

Filoh handed Seth a cup of coffee. "Drink that and let's get goin'."

"Whoa," Seth held up his hand. "Just a minute. We're not goin' anywhere together. Especially with that mule you're riding."

"And we're not leaving with you, and we're not leaving without breakfast," Richard said.

"You got the rest of your life to eat breakfast," Filoh said.

"Oh no," Richard said. "I'm having bacon, eggs, and biscuits before I get back on that four legged grass processor."

"And you're heading back," Seth jammed a finger into Filoh's chest.

"You can't tell me what to do."

Seth shook his head.

No help from Richard. This gooney guy is stuck to us like a beggar-weed. I'm damned if I send him back and damned if I let him come with us. The pace will wear him out in a day or so. He took a deep breath. *Well—make the best of it.*

"Pretty small fire to warm ya," Seth said.

"Don't need warming," Filoh said. "Need a butt massage. The heat feels good on it." He poured coffee into his cup and blew on it. "Been some deer through here in the night."

Filoh moved through the area putting pots and pans on the sand near the fire. Seth, bent backwards to stretch, yawned, and put his hand to his head shielding his eyes. "Don't see much daylight."

Filoh stirred the fire with a stick. "Where's the flour?"

Seth set the box beside him. "Don't get sand in everything."

"Do you want to eat or bitch?"

Richard came out of the tent rubbing his eyes. "I'll make the biscuits. It's an old family recipe. Bisquick and water."

Filoh stirred up a half dozen eggs and dropped some bacon in the frying pan. "You guys bring butter and honey?"

Seth nodded.

Richard stirred the Bisquick, his eyes blinking from the fire's heat. "Reminds me of the Boy Scouts. I never much cared for those outings."

Seth looked at him and smiled. "No—you didn't. And you never passed Morse Code either. You weren't much of a scout."

Richard dropped dough in a pan, covered it, and shoved it into the side of the fire.

The three of them sat cross-legged, staring into the fire. Filoh, balancing the frying pan over the flame, scorched the bacon and eggs. He ladled some into each tin plate. A flame erupted when he poured the grease on the fire.

"Judas Priest, Filoh—don't kill us the second day out," Seth said.

"Won't kill ya and it makes the biscuits brown. Hand me the salt."

IT TOOK SETH LONGER to balance the packs on the horses in the half-light. A smile started on his lips. We are like Daniel Boone. Traveling up a river by horseback, cooking over an open fire; different river but same problems.

The River

For thousands of years from its base east of the Rocky Mountains the Platte has drained the flat country of the Central Great Plains. White settlers eventually named the areas Colorado, Wyoming, and Nebraska. The Oto and Pawnee came here many seasons past and the Sioux rode the land by its waters. Canoes laden with beaver, otter, mink, coyote and buffalo furs floated by and people found places to live beside the river and other people came and traded with them. The river rose in fall and spring when the rains came and often flooded the flat land through which it flowed. Like a giant licking his lips, the waters swept up everything it touched and carried it in its bosom to the Missouri. There were white men then and now. They moved on the river's currents and what little they put into it then was as nothing.

THE TRIO WAS ABLE to hug the bank on the right side after leaving Cedar Island. Neither Richard nor Filoh was talkative as they started out. Seth, ahead of them and leading the packhorse, turned in the saddle.

"We should be camping near the bridge on Highway 50 tonight. Think your butts can make it?"

Filoh rose up in the saddle and rubbed his buttocks. "When does the numbness start?"

The horses stepped up from the coyote willow and dogwood, up from the hard mud onto the grass. They snorted and shook, making early morning adjustments to the loads. Their equipment rattled, echoing through the cottonwoods. The sound of a truck working through the gears north of the river put a smile on Richard's face.

"Some other idiot up this early," he said.

He looked ahead at Seth who looked like a mountain man, reins in his left hand, his right settled on his thigh. Since pre-school days, Richard had known his younger brother longed to be a reincarnation of earlier kin. He had been on the edge for most of his life, not into this life but not out of it either. Richard had spent a lot of hours exploring the actions of his brother but had come to the conclusion that he could spend his life thinking about what drove Seth and it wouldn't change him one whit.

Before the will was read, Seth had wanted to charge up the Missouri like Daniel Boone just to be doing something to honor their mother. He had spent a good many years dishonoring the family, but since he got back he had turned his energies to the ranch and a life that had possibilities.

A doe and this year's fawn jumped up and bounded down the flat ground, jigged right, dug their hooves in and cleared a fence in one hop. Seth turned in the saddle and smiled.

"Coulda had the deer if we'd been hunting."

"You couldn't even have cleared leather," Richard said.

"She looked ok, didn't she, Filoh? No lesions on her hide. And the fawn was spry too."

Filoh stood in the stirrups. "Couldn't tell from here. We'll probably find a dead one sooner or later. Then we'll have something to talk about."

Richard shook his head. "Where we headed today?"

Seth turned. "I told you. The north bank near the bridge where Highway 50 crosses the river."

Filoh perked up. "Good. 'Cause I want to show you a little creek that comes by Diesel Lake and drains the fields to the south there. It'll curl your toes."

Seth tried to imagine his toes curling in the Tony Lama boots he had shoved into the stirrups. Not likely.

The horses, not being asked to exert themselves, walked their own pace, dodging the cottonwoods, and brushing sedge, bulrushes, and cattail. Opportunists always, they stretched out their necks to lengthen the reins and grabbed a bit of canary grass as they walked past.

The River

The land is watered where the river flows through, as long as it is healthy. When the glaciers receded they left the land mainly flat with little pitch, which made it hard for the river to find its course, but the river worked through the sand and mud and rocks the glacier left behind. From its start east of the Rocky Mountains, it flows across the even barren land into the big river men have called the Missouri, seldom changing course over a man's lifetime.

ON TOWARDS FOUR O'CLOCK, Filoh pointed across the river. "There it is, the little creek I mentioned. Locals call it Cedar creek. I call it Dead Man's Creek." He reined his mule toward the river and urged him into the water. The mule extended his neck pulling the reins through Filoh's fingers and drank. "Come on, mule." Filoh jabbed his heels into the soft flanks and they crossed through a narrow channel onto sandbars that stretched like a necklace of diamonds across the middle of the riverbed.

"Filoh," Seth hollered. "We want to camp on this side."

"Come on. This ain't gonna take long. We've got time to get to your precious campground. I want you to see what you're doing to this water.

The River

Where the water tumbled and ran over a chiseled sandbar a hollow burble rose from its bowels. It was late afternoon and the air had begun to cool in the lengthening shadows. Birds dove on the near backwater close to the bank where a small eddy twirled, a foam head dancing and circling. The river reached out and lapped over the stirrups to touch the heels of the man known as Filoh Smith, as if to say, "show them—show them—show them."

WATER FLOWED OVER THE mule's feet, pale green and sick over a muddy bottom. Filoh pointed at it. "Would you want to drink that?"

"Of course not," Richard said. "But…"

"…Neither does the river."

Seth shook his head. "We've been turning stuff loose in the river for hundreds of years and look at it." He waved his hand over the river. "It's still doin' its job."

"It ain't," Filoh said. "It's dying and you guys are helping kill it."

"Come on, Filoh," Richard said. "We're one of hundreds of ranches on the river."

"Yes—and you're each driving a stake in its heart."

"By gawd, Filoh, that's not fair. We've…"

"What the hell does fair have to do with it? You can see that dead catfish, can't ya? And the…"

Richard was shaking his head. "Don't put the hard sell on me for…"

"You're one of 'em. I could…"

"I'll take some responsibility for Fourmile Creek if that's what you want, but…"

"No sir," Filoh said. "I mean all up and down this river. There's only two or three that are practicing sustainable agriculture while the…"

"There are so many definitions of sustainable agri…"

"Yeah—but only one that counts for a damn."

Richard held up his hand. "Filoh—would you let me finish one sentence? Please?"

Seth sat easy in his saddle with a smile as wide as the river. "Boys, boys," he said. "This isn't a school board meeting. Take a deep breath and let's get 'er said and headed up to the camp site."

"Well sir," Filoh erupted. He pounded the saddle horn with his leather-gloved hand. "I don't intend that this will take long to educate you two dunces. Cedar Creek drains fields to the south of here and every blessed one of 'em has all kinds of chemicals on it. It don't take a genius to see that those chemicals mix with the irrigation water," he stirred the air with his hand. "And taking the course of least resistance, they pour into the creek and into the river. Let's say this creek is one of a hundred. And all the creeks bring along the pollutants and they all add together. Then what?"

Seth raised his eyebrows. "Then it's a hundred times more polluted."

"Now you're gettin' the picture."

"Ok," Richard said. "But the main purpose of us riding up the river is to earn the right to own the ranch. We must keep that foremost in our minds and not spend time and energy we don't have on your project. The river will be there whether we make it up and back or not."

The River

The river lives day to day on what is given to it. It was born with springs and creeks pouring bits of plants, bugs, and dung into it. Bearing them downstream or depositing them on the sandy bottom, it cleanses itself from moment to moment. Dead animals, fish, birds, and insects sail on the current as the river draws millions of gallons of water from mountains and prairies as it has since the beginning of time. It bends south into the Missouri, hell bent to join the Mississippi. That river is engorged and flows to the ocean, its destiny, day and night.

Education Begins

THEY CAMPED ON THE high ground east of the highway 50 bridge. Richard, saddle sore and irritated, stepped down off his horse, stabbed his finger at the ground and declared this camping site was good enough for him.

"Suits me," Seth said.

Filoh looked over the side of the horse. "Somebody help me down. I can't even see the ground from here."

Seth reached up, grasped the dry bony claw and tightened his gut as he took some of the weight while Filoh slipped off the saddle. He unsaddled Filoh's mule and placed the gear on a slight rise out of the traffic pattern. "Sit here for a spell," he said. "Watch how a mountain man sets up his night camp."

Seth untied the packs, staked out the horses, got the tent erected and the cooking gear spread out while Richard scrounged up firewood. The sun vanished from the prairie, and the coolness that set in always urged him to gather more wood than was needed. During his adult life Richard ate before he was hungry, rested before he was tired, and drank before he was thirsty. He applied that to every aspect of his life. He liked to have more laid aside than required and be ready to use it if necessary.

Filoh sat on the sand, his arms stretched over his pointed knees. "What's for supper?"

Richard pulled the .30-30 from the scabbard, pushed the lever half open and checked the cartridge in the chamber.

Seth snorted. "Daniel Boone here is gonna shoot you some supper. Do you have a taste for raccoon or possum?" He turned around to stare at Richard. "Did you have that gun loaded all day?" Seth said.

Richard nodded. "If I need it, I want it to be a gun not a club."

Seth shook his head as he stuck his hand into the food pack. "We have for your dining pleasure tonight, turkey tetrazzini, chili, or macaroni and cheese. Filoh, will you please pour the wine before the first course."

"Wine?" Filoh said. "Hell's bells—I thought we wuz campin'."

"Richard—napkins, please."

"Cut it out, Seth. I vote for chili. Good and hot chili. And you're not to be drinking anyway."

"I didn't say I was going to drink any. I know what I'm supposed to do and not do. Do you think I just got off a load of pumpkins?"

Richard turned his back. He hated an argument before eating anything. He closed his eyes and counted to ten. Alcohol is a poison, absolute and irrevocable, and Seth had gained the strength to erase it from his diet. Could they erase the chemicals from the soil they farmed? Would it be as beneficial? He sat and looked at the river. The surface rippled, then smoothed. He thought it had said something. He was sure of it. His lip curled into a smile. It was going to be a long trip.

"Chili it is then since the great white hunter didn't bag any edibles." Seth poured boiling water into the tinfoil container, stirred it with the long handled plastic spoon, rolled the top down to hold the heat in and set it beside a rock.

"Filoh—how'd you stay strong this late in life?" Seth said.

"Hell—I ain't strong. But I do have a secret if you promise not to tell anyone."

Richard smiled. "Ok. What?"

Filoh leaned back on his saddle. "Testosterone. I rub it on my chest every couple of days."

"What are you doing—trolling for the ladies?" Richard said.

"No. I could be a sugar daddy if I wanted to, but that's behind me. Testosterone gives a man some muscle definition and pep in his old age. I know a guy only sixty-three takes it once a week. Gives him the stamina to stay up with a twenty-two year old gal he fancies."

"You ever heard of HGH—human growth hormone?" Seth asked.

"Yeah, I've heard of it. My doc says that's for kids that are stunted. Says I should benefit plenty from the salve." He kicked a stick into the fire. "And I do."

"What if the seed manufacturers worked that into the corn and soy beans?" Richard said.

"I don't know," Filoh said. "That's way beyond me. I don't know how they do what they're doing now. They've got it so crazy you can't even save your own seed corn to grow. You plant it and it won't grow. You have to go begging to the seed companies every year for new seed corn that'll germinate. They've got you by the short hairs."

"Damn right they do," Seth said. "Get your bowls—the chili's ready."

They were seated on stumps around the fire, dodging and duck-ing as the air off the river danced along the shore pushing curls of acrid cottonwood smoke toward one then the other. A large cotton-wood limb lay across the fire, crackling and popping. When it burned in half, Richard kicked each piece onto the flames.

Seth swallowed and looked across the fire at Filoh. "Maybe Richard could benefit from some of that salve. He's courting that young schoolteacher. Wouldn't hurt him any to be stronger. Wouldn't hurt at school board meetings, either."

Richard snorted. "I'm not needing any salve."

"Maybe you should though, Richard. Perk you up a mite."

"My gawd...I don't need perking up."

Seth maneuvered the chili around with his tongue. "Just a little?"

"What would you know about it."

"Boys," Filoh butted in. "I've been thinking of where we need to go next."

"We're going up river," Seth said. "That's our mission. We go up and back and it's done."

"Yeah, but up around Fremont—"

"We'll get to Fremont, but we're not going there for your reason. We're going there for our reason."

Filoh set his metal bowl down and crossed his legs. "We've got a real problem at Fremont."

"Don't need to hear about Fremont right now," Richard said. Finished eating, he poured water into his bowl and added a squirt of liquid soap. "Pass me your dishes."

"Suppose I have to dry," Seth said.

"Unless you can talk Filoh into doing something."

"I'm along as an advisor. I don't do dishes. I need my time for thinking." He tossed a stick on the fire. "Thinking how I'm gonna convince you lunk heads to get back to sustainable agriculture."

"We don't want to go backwards. We want to go forward," Seth said.

"Dang it. That's what sustainable agriculture is all about. Going forward so you can preserve the environment for the future and not kill everything before the next generation can get a hold of it."

"We're not killing anything," Richard said. "If what you say is true, we should be seeing it all up and down the river, not just in certain spots."

"You're a stubborn man, Richard Barrett." Filoh leveraged on his arm, managed to get a leg under him and stood up. "Tell me two things. What has your crop and livestock yield done over the last three years? And—wait a minute"—Filoh held up his hand—"Don't interrupt me. And how much has your chemical bill gone up for the poisons you're putting on the land?"

Richard shook his head. "The chemicals that kill the miserable creatures that eat our crops are cheap compared to the losses."

"That's not what I asked," Filoh said. "I asked how much."

"I know what you asked."

"Then why don't you answer it?"

"Boys, boys," Seth put in. "Shall we have pistols from thirty paces at dawn?"

Richard took a deep breath then released it. "I suppose the yield has stayed the same or gone down. The chemical bill has increased."

"Now you're talking facts." Filoh stirred the fire with a green stick. "And what do you suppose is gonna happen as the yield continues down and the chemicals bill continues up?"

"I don't know for sure," Richard said. He stepped back from the fire.

"You sure as hell do," Filoh said drawing an X in the sand. "The two lines cross somewhere's out there in a few years where you're paying more and more for chemicals and gettin' less and less crops. And the chemicals go up in price. The land is producing less. And the land and water and air are ruined in the bargain. Now isn't that a fine kettle of fish?"

The three men sat silent. Like a friendly dog, the fire licked flames toward each of them before the top log collapsed on the bed of coals, exploding sparks into the night sky.

At last Richard lifted his head. He faced Filoh and with a faint smile on his face said his piece. "Filoh—I appreciate what you're saying and I understand it, I think. But I need you to remember Seth and I have a job to do. We need to get up the river and back before the end of July. Ginny is going to have her hands full while we're gone. We need to think about that right now—not about the ecology and the last fifty years of farming."

Filoh nodded his head. "I understand, but dammit you need to have your eyes open while we're traveling. Maybe when we get back, you will have picked up a thing or two."

"We're doing fine right now, Filoh. Let's leave it be at that."

"You can leave it be forever and you'll bequeath barren ground, dead water, and stinking air to the next owners who could just be Ginny."

"Or Klete Dixon," Seth threw in.

Richard smiled. "Look—this is only the second day. Let's not end every day with a preaching session from you and an argument before we go to bed. I like to have a pleasant thought in my head before I turn in. I might have a nightmare if I shut my eyes with this on my mind."

"We can leave it go until we get to Fremont," Filoh said. "Then it's starting again."

Seth shook his head and took a deep breath. "I'm turning in. Don't talk too loud and keep me awake."

"Yeah—might ruin your beauty sleep," Richard said. "Remember when Mom used to say that to us when we were kids?"

"Yes. She had a whole passel of things to say, didn't she?"

Richard nodded. "You remember the one about your chickens coming home to roost?"

"Yup. If all my chickens come home to roost, I'll have to build a new hen house."

The River

The water color changed where the channel deepened. Turning gray-green it hushed. Then rivulets woke up noisy where they rattled over the shallows, bantering back and forth with the river swallows turning and diving for the bugs that burst out at twilight. And then, holding its breath, the river calmed as it inhaled the water to swell its depths.

Filoh sat cross-legged on the bank of the river, arms across his knees, face lifted to the full moon.

"Old River," he shook his head. "I am old too, and yet I can hear you gurgle and sing. I see the tops of your waters as you roll toward the Missouri and I am with you. All day and all night you move, changing the sandbars, holding the fish, and watering this land. It could not live without you. You honor this land by flowing through it and it drinks from you. From the first springs in the mountains to the great Missouri River I love and revere you. Give us our needs as only you can. And help me get these people to understand your life and needs. From where we are today—let us get better."

Filoh rolled to one side, got on his hands and knees. He stayed there for a moment, then arched and stood up. "This being old ain't as good as it's cracked up to be."

He unzipped the tent and got into his sleeping bag.

"Kinda early to be takin' a whiz, isn't it?" Seth said.

"Wasn't takin' a whiz. Talkin' to the river."

"Talkin' to the river?"

"That's what I said."

"Well—don't that beat all."

Meanwhile, back at the ranch

GINNY AND DAWSON STRUGGLED with the small cow as they tied the halter rope to the post. It was their second day of working on the Barrett ranch they knew so well and their morning was about spent.

"Come around the other side, Dawson," Ginny said. "She might kick you from there."

"Mom—I'm not into this. Not at all." Dawson said.

"We've got to or she'll die. She's just a little girl heifer having her first calf and she's having problems. Stay close to her leg and touch her so she knows you're there."

Dawson started around the cow. "Can't we call the vet?"

"Too late. Put the glove on, Dawson."

The fourteen-year-old boy tugged the long glove until his fingers filled the pockets and the gauntlet reached up to his shoulder. He had seen a calf pulled from the mother in his time on the ranch, but he had never done the pulling or the holding of the cow or been any part of the process. He had been an onlooker as new life filled up the hen house, the hog pen, and the barns.

Ginny lifted the cow's tail. "Squirt the lubricant on and hurry. If she lays down on us it will be ten times harder."

Dawson's face tightened into a squeamish mask. He made his fist as small as he could and inserted it into the cow's birth canal, pushing until his arm was buried up to his shoulder.

"Feel around. Can you grab a hoof?" Ginny said.

"Something here."

"If you can grab a hoof see if you can get both together and pull them."

Dawson's face had not changed. He looked like he did when he was asked to clean the toilets at home.

"I've got 'em," he said.

"Good. Now pull them out together. Don't rush it."

Inch by inch, Dawson's arm emerged. The cow's head arched up and she bellowed. As his elbow then wrist reappeared, two small whitish hooves followed them. Ginny put a rope around the hooves and tightened the slipknot.

"Help me pull."

Dawson grabbed the rope end. Bit by bit the motionless calf appeared from the birth canal, white and slick with birthing fluids, then the head popped out. Both Ginny and Dawson caught it to keep it from hitting the ground. Wide-eyed and bellowing, the cow fought the rope holding her head. Dawson started to remove the birth sheath.

"Let the momma do that, Dawson," Ginny said.

She untied the heifer, which turned around and sniffed the newborn calf struggling in its enclosure. The cow licked it, freeing the membrane. Her tonguing nudged the calf. Struggle after struggle, topple after topple, the young life at last stood on legs as unsteady as a child on stilts and wavered there, head turning, taking in the surroundings.

"Great job, Dawson," Ginny said and raised her hand to high five him.

Dawson raised the gloved hand and for a moment both gave it a second thought, then their hands came together above their heads in a sloppy high five and they laughed.

"I'll be damned," Dawson said.

"Watch your language, Dawson Barrett Houston, or I'll wash your mouth out with soap."

"I'm sorry Mom. Just slipped out."

"That's the difference between gentlemen and bums. A gentleman knows when to hold his tongue."

She picked up some loose hay from the ground and scrubbed her hand with it. "Whew—what a mess. Let's go get cleaned up. I believe

this young lady has her priorities straight. Look at that baby nurse—
like it hadn't had a thing to eat for hours."

Bucky and Valerie walked out to meet them.

Valerie had the hint of a frown on her face. "Did it go ok, Mom?"

"Yup. Dawson will make a good veterinarian someday."

"He wants to be an astronaut," Bucky said.

"Once he's pulled a calf, he can do anything he wants in life."

Valerie winced. "That's so yucky."

Ginny smiled and moved toward the half bath. "You know what?
It washes off."

Bucky watched Dawson remove the long glove, throw it in the
trash barrel at the end of the barn and walk toward the water trough.
"You're not gonna wash off in that are you?"

Dawson looked at his younger brother and walked toward the
trough. When he was alongside, he jumped into the air and splashed
full length into the wide trough.

"Holy cow, Mom, Dawson jumped in the trough," Bucky yelled.

Valerie stood behind Bucky looking over his shoulder. "Euuu, I
wouldn't want to drink that water."

"Animals drink it, not humans," Bucky said.

"Just the same, it's yucky," she pouted and turned for the kitchen.

AFTER THE LUNCH DISHES were done, the four of them sat around
the kitchen table dividing up tasks that remained to be done.

"Bucky, do you think you can fix the fence down by the road?"
Ginny said.

Bucky nodded.

"And, Valerie—a couple of the hens have made their nest in the
hay mow. Will you get their eggs and the nests and get them set up in
the hen house where they belong?"

"They peck at me," she said.

"Well—take a broom with you and make sure they behave. Call
me if you need any help. And Dawson—"

"Aw Mom. I've done enough for today," Dawson said.

"Not by a long shot young man. I want you to open the number
five irrigation gate on ditch two. Think you can remember that or do
you want me to write it down?"

"I've got it. Number five on ditch two."

"And stay there until you're satisfied the flow is constant and nothing's hung up in the ditch or gate. Get back here around 4:00 o'clock so we can do some shopping and get home." Ginny looked around at her workers dressed in their farm clothes. They reminded her of when she and Richard and Seth had come to the dinner table so many years ago. Shoot. Where does time go?

"Ok. Off you go. I'll be paying bills in the den if you really need me. Try and do your work all by yourself. Someday I won't be around for advice, so get used to doing it now on your own."

"Mom—you're preaching again," Bucky said.

Ginny clenched her lips together. "Sorry."

After the kids had spread out to do their chores, Ginny sat at the old cedar desk that had been a fixture in that room since she could remember. The silence in the room was enveloping and she closed her eyes to absorb the ambiance. As her breathing slowed, the ticking of the clock eased into her consciousness and mental pictures of her childhood, stored in memory, played against the back of her eye lids. The smell of tobacco, always present from the meerschaum pipe that sat in a stand on the left hand corner, reminded her of Andrew Duncan Barrett. How he loved that pipe.

The phone rang. She opened her eyes, scattering the pleasant thoughts, and picked up the phone. "Hello. Barrett ranch."

A strong male voice on the other end replied. "Good afternoon. This is Klete Dixon, a neighbor. I'm looking for Richard, is he around?"

"Hello, Mr. Dixon, this is Ginny Houston."

"Hello, Ginny?"

"Richard's not around right now but I expect to talk to him soon."

There was a hesitation. "So you are the new owner of the ranch?"

Ginny searched her memory for what had been said. "I am not. Do you want me to have Richard call you?"

"That would be good. I'd appreciate that. An elderly gentleman has attempted to damage some of my equipment and I would like to ask him if he and Seth know anything current about Filoh Smith. Please tell him I called and he can call back at his convenience."

"He has your number?"

"Yes. Thank you."

"Good day, Mr. Dixon."

Ginny swallowed. She pondered whether to call Richard on his cell phone or wait until they called in. She picked up a pencil and added it to her list to talk to them about. They must be almost to Fremont by now. She opened the drawer and pulled out the map of Nebraska on which she had marked in yellow ink the path the North Platte River took from Ogallala to Plattsmouth. Fremont wasn't very far along.

Chapter 5

KLETE DIXON HELD THE phone in his hand a minute, then slammed it in the cradle.

"Dammit—she's acting like she isn't an owner." He punched in some numbers, sat back and looked over the map of his holdings that covered some of the wall to his left. The massive desk he sat at was made of timbers from the mast of the USS Maine that he had bought during a Sotheby's auction. There was only one such desk in existence. He took in the vision of the park he had built around his office casita. The peacefulness of it and the luxury of plants that had been imported from temperate climates around the world often eased his tension.

There had always been the grass—unless the drought killed it. As his fortune increased he found he preferred plantings to common grass, and giving way to an urge to be the only one in town to have a landscaped yard, he had engaged the horticulturist from the University of Nebraska to design, plant, and direct the maintenance of his garden. As a youngster the only green thing around their house besides the corn was the buffalo grass that grew wild in their lawn. "Good enough," his dad had said.

Now he enjoyed touring guests through the planned gardens as they sipped their drinks and listened to him explain the exotic plants from Hungary, Poland, and Scotland.

A female voice answered. "Craig Jamison's law office."

"Good afternoon, Melanie. Is Craig available?"

"He's always available for you, Mr. Dixon."

Klete smiled, leaned back in the chair and lifted his feet up on the desk.

Craig came on the line. "I thought you'd be out on the links this afternoon."

"I'm working how to acquire the Barrett Ranch while those two idiots are playing cowboy up the Platte. I just talked with Ginny and she says she isn't an owner. I thought you said Mae's will gave her a piece of it."

"It does, providing the terms are met. They aren't yet." Klete heard Craig open a drawer. Klete had seen him do it a hundred times in his office. He smiled. Knew Craig was looking for a cigarette and a lighter. A talk with Klete required a smoke.

"I'd like to work that ranch into my operation before planting season is over. Any way you can see to get that done?"

"Not this year, Klete. Be patient—Rome wasn't built in a day."

"Neither was my ranch."

"Of course not." Klete heard the lighter strike and the usual pause in the conversation while Craig sucked it to a red glow.

"I thought you quit smoking?"

"I did for three weeks. Almost made a month this time, but this election is getting to me."

"You'll make it, Craig. This state needs a senator of your stature in the legislature. I've sent another contribution to your campaign office. Take a look at the amount—I think it'll please you."

"You're very kind, Klete. I'll do my best to represent the interests of District 2."

"Be sure you have Cass County and Klete Dixon in mind."

"Foremost in my mind, Klete. You know that."

Klete dropped his feet on the floor. "Change of subjects. Can we make sure that the little school teacher Richard finds so interesting stays fired and maybe has to move before they get back?"

"I can find out who owns the house she's renting. I suppose it could be bought and during remodeling the tenant asked to leave. She's probably renting month to month."

"Good. Make the owners an offer and let's add that stick to the fire." He dropped his feet to the floor. "You know how I like to take little bites."

Craig bit his lip. He was crawling out on a limb. How far could he go and still be a fair representative to the Barrett Estate? "Who's buying it?"

"Grandview Properties. Keep my name out of it."

"I'll work on it the first of the week. I've got to get to court for a pleading now."

"Do it today, Craig."

There was a long pause. "Who's gonna sign for it?"

"You sign as my power of attorney."

"I don't like it."

"I didn't ask you to like it. I asked you to do it." Klete sat forward in his chair. "Call me when it's done."

The phone hung in Craig's hand, as if setting it in the cradle would sever his relationship with the Barretts and weld him to Dixon. He snuffed out the cigarette with his other hand as he set the receiver in the cradle.

KLETE PICKED UP A cell phone, punched a button and a scratchy voice replied.

"This is Cort."

"Cort—I want you to file a report with the sheriff on Filoh Smith. I'm beginning to see a conspiracy between Smith and the Barretts."

"He didn't do much damage."

Klete could picture his lean foreman. He had a quiet air about him, like all men he had known who worked with animals or on the land. Probably kicking a seeding dandelion head with his boot.

"When you file the report double the damage figure."

"Hell boss—we had our own replacement parts. We don't even have an invoice to put with the costs."

"Better yet. Make up your own list of damaged parts and make it high. Make sure the damaged materials are already recycled and unavailable for inspection. Bring me a copy of the report before you go home tonight. They can't trespass and blow up my irrigation equipment. I'll have their heads."

"Who's they?" Cort said. His voice had the timbre of water running over rocks.

"They. Them. The Barretts and Smith. You can see they're in this together."

Another silence. "Ok. I'll go into town."

"Don't forget. Bring me a copy of it."

Dixon plugged his phone into the charger. He opened the Edwardian Oak Tantalus and poured a tumbler of Macallan Gran

Reserva 1981. He admired the mahogany red color, sniffed the freshly cut wood and sawmill aromas and sipped it.

He took a deep breath. If he hadn't turned to farming he would have been a distiller. It was a lot the same: weather, grain, good water, waiting and waiting and waiting.

He eased off his boots and slung his stocking feet on top of the desk and leaned back in the chair. A slight smile curled his lips and he shook his head. From a lousy six-acre plot of poor soil where his daddy had tried to provide for the family, he now owned over 7,000 acres and was a whisker away from doubling that acreage. It had taken all of his life from tenth grade on, but it was worth it. It had to be priority. Friends, family, community, all had to be in the mix but numero uno was land. If you owned the land you lived like a king—not a peasant. Even Ginny Huston called him Mr. Dixon.

He had spent enough time on this for today. Whisky helped him sum things up. He thought about it and held up a finger up for each point: *file a complaint on Filoh Smith; get the teacher Serena out of town; figure out how to force the Barretts to fail or, in the alternative, have them miss the deadline and buy it from Boy's town. They wouldn't know what to do with the place. Hmmm. Which way would be better?*

What's enough?

THE TRAIL SOUNDED LIKE a hundred years of trails with men on horseback: horses grunting, equipment squeaking, and the soft syncopated beat of hooves on the sandy bank. Here and there they had to pick their way around thickets of sticks and leaves and mud mixed with sand that had been compressed by floodwaters into an adobe like substance as hard as mortar. Hundreds of bees they could hear through the foliage ten yards away raised a din as they crept around a bend of the river near Ashland but none ventured near.

Each man was content within himself: feet in the stirrups, reins in hand, mind and body drugged into silence by the gentle swaying of the horse beneath him, horses that had originated from those escaped from the Spanish Conquistadors hundreds of years ago. The Platte

River country was in their blood too. The Oto, Pawnee, and Sioux had caught them and ridden them there.

As Filoh liked to say when conversation drifted back to the good old days, those were the years before white man on the Platte. One of Filoh's uncles, who was somewhat more than half Pawnee, said the good old days were before horses, when it was too far for the young men of the tribe to reach another village on foot. Everyone had an opinion on what were the good old days. It wasn't so much a debate, as no one ever changed his mind on it, but it built a bench under the conversation and brought out smiles and chuckles when repeated.

Seth reined in his horse to allow Richard to come along side. "You know something? I've been thinking. Everything man does seems to get bigger and bigger. We're not content with leaving well enough alone—we've got to make it bigger and better."

Richard squeezed his knees to keep the horse alongside Seth. "What got you to thinking about that?"

"Well—just look at it. Every Melzer and Barrett has bought more land, more cattle, grew more crops. And look at Klete Dixon. He won't be happy until he corrals the whole Platte River Basin."

"And us with it," Richard said.

"And us with it. It's as plain as the nose on your face. Did you ever see a town that didn't want to get bigger? Taller buildings, better streetlights, enlarge and improve the park, build a new courthouse? And with that comes higher taxes taking away more of the money the people make to live there."

"You are on a run this morning, aren't you?"

Filoh nudged his mule up on the left. "Well, he's right. When I quit farming, I pretty much sold exactly what I had bought forty years earlier."

"Yeah—and we bulldozed your old buildings and built new ones. Bigger ones," Seth said. "Why can't man be content without making everything bigger all the time?"

"That's not the nature of man," Richard put in. "To survive you needed to store enough to cover bad times. So mankind started growing and building more than they needed so they could ride out those bad times. It just grew from there." Richard jabbed his horse to stay up with Seth. "Man starts out a child and grows and the things he plays with have to grow, too. Big things throw down a challenge. You recall when Dad got your first bike and you didn't want training wheels on

it? You thought that was sissy stuff. You were growing up from the tri-
cycle to the bike. You think about it—everything man does he intends
for it to be bigger and better."

"Well, that's not always true," Filoh said.

"Course not. Nothing's ever always true."

"Remember ole Doc Simmons? He and his missus sold off everything they had and squeezed into one of those motor homes. From a
big house into that bus no bigger than a milking shed. And they seem
mighty happy about it."

"And they are the exception that proves the rule," Richard said.

"How can you have a rule if there is an exception to it?" Seth asked.

"That's how it works. You have one that breaks from tradition
and it proves that most of the time most of the people do a certain
thing when confronted with life."

Seth rode on, his head tilted to the right. "What if we didn't get
bigger? What if we stay the size we are and just make it better?"

"That was your original argument. Bigger and better. Besides—we
don't have the ranch yet and at this pace we'll never get to Fremont."

"We'll get there," Seth said. "There's some good traveling clear up
past the Oto Memorial."

THE SUN WAS HIGH when the horsemen stopped on the west bank
under a group of cottonwood trees nudged up against a subdivision.
There was a three-strand barbed wire fence strung tight on cedar
posts enclosing the subdivision and a man-made lake. Filoh slid off
his horse like every bone in his body was broken and walked over to
the fence.

He peered through the low foliage. "There's houses over there a
piece."

Richard looked around. "Won't matter. We won't be bothering
them any."

Filoh jigged his head. "What if we do? This is private land."

"Big brother will draw down on them with his .30-30," Seth said.
He gathered up some dry branches and had a fire going in minutes
into which he shoved the coffee pot ladled with four cups of fresh
water and three heaping spoonfuls of Mayan Coffee. Then he lay back
on the ground, put his hat over his face and was asleep before the coffee pot eked out its first puff of steam.

AT FIRST IT SOUNDED in his dream. Then Richard was sure something was wrong.

Somebody was screaming at him. He jolted upright.

"Damn your hide. Get off my place. Get your shittin' horses off the grass and move on. Are you bums? Homeless bums? Get—before I call the police. You don't own this property. You can't stop here and build a fire and let your horses crap all over the place." The top fence wire reached to the man's chest, his long hair covered the straps to a pair of overalls hanging from his shoulders. He looked to be about thirty, had one hand knotted around the top wire while the other was balled in a fist that he was waving over his head as he yelled with no reservations.

Seth and Filoh were awake now.

"Go on—git." The man's grip on the wire caused his forearm to bulge showing cords of muscle. His eyes blinked so fast Filoh wondered if he could see through them. Next followed an outburst that was unintelligible to any of them.

"Git off my place. Ida noone forger ina wanafinnit inastta formen signar dammit."

Seth thought perhaps it was another language but he couldn't understand one word. He threw a glance at Richard to see if he could figure it out. Richard stood with his mouth agape, questioning but unafraid. The Platte riverbank was not public property. He had one hand on the saddle and the other close to the scabbard that held the .30-30.

"Lookee here, fella," Filoh started.

The man was not to be interrupted. "Id snyd fornatur damn werk!"

Richard moved his hand to the horse's hip. The animal's ears and eyes were fastened on the speaker, its muscles tense.

From the other end of the field a man was taking long strides through the harrowed ground toward them, his arms pumping like he was using ski poles.

Seth turned to the others. "Spread out," he said as he moved close to a large cottonwood.

The man crossing the field raised his arm and yelled, "Hold on there." When he reached the fence he looped an arm around the shorter man and pulled him close to his face. He was smiling. "Whoa now, Digger. These good people are just resting a spell." He looked up at Seth and Filoh. "Good day, gentlemen. Please excuse my son.

He suffers from Tourette's syndrome. He isn't always accountable for what he says. But he's a good son, aren't you, Digger?"

The man let go of the fence, gave a concentrated look at his hands and commenced scrubbing the palms up and down on his thighs. He looked at Seth, eyes blinking, his mouth part way open and silent.

Seth shook his head. "Sure put me to wonder."

"Yes," the man said. "But we don't let it get us down." He adjusted his arm around the man. "Where you folks headed?"

"We're bound for Brady or Ogallala. I believe the North and South Platte come together outside of Brady."

"Is that a fact?" the man said.

He turned to the short man under his arm. "Let's go back to the house now, Digger. These men are on their way up river. We don't want to delay them."

Richard stepped forward. "Why don't you and your son join us for some coffee? It won't compete favorably with what your Mrs. brews up but we've got plenty of it."

The man gave a brief nod of his head, his lips curled up at the corners, "There is something about campfire coffee."

Filoh pulled the cuff of his shirt over his hand to act as a hotpad and pulled the pot out of the fire. Steam belched out of the spout enriching the air with the fragrance of fresh coffee. The man extended his hand, "Name's Frank Watson," he nodded toward his son, "and this is Digger."

Richard shook his hand. "I'm Richard Barrett. This is my brother, Seth. We're farmers from Plattsmouth." He nodded at Filoh and added, "We dug up that chunk of buffalo jerky. His name is Filoh Smith."

After he climbed through the fence, Digger dragged over a downed cottonwood limb that was a foot thick and twenty feet long and sat down on it.

"Son," Frank said. "Did you check for snakes before you stuck your hand under that log?"

"No. Forgot."

Seth and Richard looked at each other. "You're pretty stout, Digger," Seth said.

Digger, blinking less now than he was, looked back and forth at the brothers unsmiling and then down at his feet. He seemed not to notice Filoh who had found three cups and two bowls and was measuring coffee into each of them like a sourdough weighing his partner's gold dust. He put a can of evaporated milk and a box of sugar cubes on the ground and sat cross-legged on the sand.

Richard blew on the coffee, which he held in both hands, a recipient of one of the bowls Filoh had distributed. "My brother was expounding on how man seems to want to build up and expand on anything he has. He was asking why a farmer can't stay with what he has and just make it better."

Frank Watson sucked in some coffee. "Whoa—that's steamy." He adjusted his seat on the log almost spilling the coffee. "I kind'a like that idea," he said. "Don't know that I could sell that idea to my banker or my heirs, but I get a pleasant feeling inside me when I hear you say that."

Seth scooted forward. "Why not? After you make enough to get by all you're looking to do is stack more up for the future generation."

"Well," Richard said. "It's the old ant and grasshopper story. The ant puts enough away to live through the winter and the grasshopper doesn't."

"The world is full of those stories," Filoh said. "The problem is that each man is different and what's right for one fella doesn't fit the other guy at all."

Digger straightened up. "You wouldn't want to pass any laws about what a man could do on a farm. Can you imagine a legislature telling us we couldn't buy out the neighbor when he wants to sell, or feed 1,000 head of cattle instead of 750? There'd be truckloads of farmers marching on the capital building."

Seth looked at Richard. He raised his eyebrows and nodded toward Digger. Richard nodded back. This was something they hadn't seen.

Frank smiled at his son. "Digger has a good grasp of this stuff. He's been doing the economic projections for us for a number of years now."

"He's stout as hell, too." Seth said.

"I work out three times a week," Digger said.

"Doing what?"

"Lifting. I lift bales over my head to warm up. Then I get to a keg of nails and a 12X12 timber twelve feet long."

It was silent a minute while Richard calculated. "My gawd," he said, "those are heavy pieces."

Digger chuckled. "I never got as tall as I should have but I grew out pretty well."

Filoh cleared his throat and edged into the conversation. "I've been trying to show these guys that the ways they've been following since the fifties on the farm and animal business has to stop. The practices are polluting everything. Get back to small, localized animal production and farming, keep it clean, and there will be higher profits along with a cleaner environment. Gotta be."

"That's the way I see it too," Frank said.

Digger nodded his head.

"Well—by golly, I've got me two converts right here," Filoh said.

Frank laid his cup on the sand. "Instead of getting bigger, we went to vegetables and row crops. Increased our net income per acre." He turned to Digger. "How much did we increase it?"

"Went from about $300 an acre to $6,000 an acre. More intense but smaller and easier to raise without all the chemicals."

"See," Filoh smiled. "I told you this could be done."

"Hell's fire, Filoh," Seth said. "What are we gonna do with the other thousands of acres?"

"I don't care so long as you don't pollute the air and water."

Richard stood up. "Gentlemen," he said, dusting off his pants. "Let's be on our way up river. Good to meet you Frank, Digger."

"If you come back down river, stop," Frank said. "Like to know how it went for you. Kind'a exciting beating your way up river on horseback, about a hundred years behind times."

Filoh rubbed his backside. "More like beating up your body."

Seth buried the coffee grounds and scrubbed the cups and bowls with river sand. They mounted and turned west. "Adios," he said.

Frank and Digger waved back. "Keep an eye out for rattlesnakes. We've had a few along the river this year. Usually don't get this far down but this is a different year for some reason."

"Got it. Thanks," Richard said.

Filoh, head down and hunched in the saddle, led the mounted group up a sandy bank and across a stream as clear as rainwater.

Seth, bringing up the rear, hollered ahead as they passed the bend, "What the hell is Tourette's?"

Richard turned in his saddle. "I don't think I can describe it to you."

"This is what happens when we get out of our little happy spot there on the ranch," Seth said.

"Takes all kinds of people. We should look it up when we get somewhere. He acted normal after that rant though, didn't he?"

Seth nodded. "Boy, I thought we were in trouble when that started. Seeing the muscles in his arms I thought he might just tear the fence apart and come over and upend the horses." He snickered into the back of his hand. "I was glad you had the .30-30 handy."

"I wouldn't have let him hurt the horses," Richard said.

"How about me?"

"I didn't consider that."

"Humph."

Filoh turned in the saddle. "What kind of snakes did he say was on the river?"

Richard said. "Rattlesnake."

"Yeah, but what kind?"

"Probably the prairie rattler."

"Why would a prairie rattler be on the river?" Filoh said.

"The river runs through the prairie, doesn't it? Hell—I don't know, Filoh. It's no big deal but doesn't hurt to be aware of it."

"I never seen no snake on my place," Filoh said.

"Your hogs ate them all," Seth said.

"That's why they tasted so good."

"They say that eating pork from the pig that has been eating rattlesnakes will make you immune to the snake bite."

"Don't that beat all. Well I'm not about to test that theory." Filoh said and shook his head. "Don't that beat all."

Richard glared at him. "You said that once, Filoh,"

"Yes, I did, but I wasn't sure you heard it since you're half deaf from that machinery you ride around in all day."

"Deaf?"

"Uh huh. At least half deaf."

"Well the other half works fine."

"Knock it off you guys. We're supposed to be having fun riding up this river. I can't abide you two arguing all the time," Seth said.

"We stopping at the Oto spot?" Filoh said.

"You just had a rest. Let's make it hard for Fremont. I do believe we can do that if you and Richard don't wind yourselves jawing all the time."

Richard stood in his stirrups. "How long does it take to get a saddle seat?"

"It should feel comfortable in a week or so. Grin and bear it."

"I might bear it but I doubt if I'll be grinning about it."

~~~~~~

The River

The river harbors snakes. Dens of them live along the high banks closer to the springs that are the beginning of the Platte. But some pioneers venture away from their birthplace and crawl over the banks and swim with the current to new places.

~~~~~~

Seth finds Martha

SETH REINED IN HIS HORSE. A boy was kneeling beside a chocolate Labrador retriever whose ears were hunched up, his eyes locked on Seth. Blood spurted from the dog's leg onto the sand.

"Got shot, did he?" Seth said.

"No, Sir."

"What then?"

"Don't know. He just hollered and came out of the river on the run."

"And he was bleeding like that?"

"Yes, Sir."

Richard took in the bloodied sand. "My gawd, boy—he doesn't have much more blood than that in him."

"I gotta get him to a vet."

Seth dismounted and handed the boy his neckerchief. "Here."

He tucked the kerchief around the dog's leg up under his chest, pulled tight and knotted it. The blood flow stopped. The big dog's head lolled to one side and his fading eyes looked at the man-smelling kerchief before his eyes closed.

"You afoot?"

"Yes, Sir."

"Git on board there with Richard. I'll bring the dog."

"Where is a vet?" Richard said.

The boy pointed. "In town—that way,"

They had come at least a mile, Seth figured, with stops to cross highways and roads while cars came to a halt and the astonished drivers gawked at the parade of three grown men on horseback towing a pack horse and a boy riding double with a guy that looked like it was his first time on a horse and another guy—a lean stretched out cowboy looking fella—with a chocolate Lab thrown across the saddle and him riding behind it. They hadn't gone more than two blocks into Fremont when a police car pulled alongside and motioned them to stop.

"Where's the vet?" Seth hollered.

"Just stop a minute," the policeman said.

"Can't. The dog is bleeding to death. Where's the vet?"

"Follow me." The red and blue lights burst on and the cruiser turned onto the blacktop in front of him.

They turned two corners and the police car pulled into the parking lot of a small building where a big sign read, Pet Meds.

The policeman caught the reins Seth threw to him, reached out and took the reins Richard handed him. He looked at them in dismay, then at the dog and the boy.

"Danny," the policeman said. "What's wrong with your dog?"

"I don't know, Mr. Jiles. He's bleeding something fierce."

Seth, cradling the dog in his arms, strode to the front door and hollered for the vet.

A woman attendant stuck her face around a corner. "What?"

"Got a dog here that needs immediate attention."

"The doctor's on a call. Just put him down."

"Where's your operating table?"

"Just put him on the floor."

Seth looked at the blood seeping from the wound, at the floor and back at the attendant.

"It's in there," the boy said, pointing to a room with a partially closed door.

Seth marched for it and shoved the door open with his foot. He slipped the dog onto the stainless steel table like a limp sack of wheat, eyes closed, the breathing short and labored.

The attendant sprang into the room. "What do you think you're doing?"

"Call the doctor now unless you want this dog to die in your clinic," Seth said.

The boy patted the dog's head.

Richard grabbed his brother's arm. "Seth, they'll take care of it."

Seth raised his voice. "We're taking care of it *now*."

They could hear the attendant on the phone. "They put the dog on the operating table...ok...please hurry." She looked in at the three men and a boy standing around the table. "The doctor is only two blocks away. He'll be right here."

The policeman edged in the doorway. "I'd like to talk to one of you."

Richard removed his hat and turned to him. "Let's go out here." The two of them went into the waiting room. "What'd you do with our horses?"

"I tied them to my car."

Richard nodded. "That's fine."

"What's this all about?" the Policeman said.

Richard described the events up to that point as they helped themselves to the coffee and Oreo cookies the vet provided for his customers.

"How'd the dog get that kind of wound?" the policeman said.

Richard shook his head. "Don't know."

The back door slammed and a spare man packing a Randall knife and a cell phone on opposite sides of his belt dropped a butt pack on the chair and looked through tinted glasses at the people collected in his operating room.

Doctor Brad Phillips set his hands on his bony hips, took a deep breath and said, "Well. What have we here?"

"Dog's bleeding to death," Seth said.

The doctor's eyes took in the blood on the floor, on the table, and the limp figure of the Labrador. In one step he reached out and grasped the dog's leg. "Martha, get me two units of blood and set up for a transfusion." He turned to the boy. "Danny—how old is he?"

"He's eight."

The doctor nodded. "How'd this happen?"

"Don't know. One minute he was romping in the river chasing his ball and the next minute he yelped and came running out without his ball."

Martha placed the blood on the counter and wheeled in the hanger. She moved in a direct and purposeful manner, in a sequence that had the blood ready just as the dog was eased into slumber by the drug the doctor administered.

"Martha—some sutures and chlorhexidine please."

While she tied an apron around the doctor, Seth noticed her meaningful method of doing the work. She knew what to do, when to do it, and anticipated the next need. She also looked familiar, like he had known her somewhere before.

"I'm thinking it was a turtle," the doctor said.

"A turtle?" Seth said, his eyes questioning the assumption.

"A big snapping turtle; they're in the Platte. Look at that bite and think how a turtle's beak looks—kinda like a small triangle," he drew a picture in the air with his finger.

"Well, don't that beat all," Filoh said as he sat in the only chair in the room.

"I heard last week that Billy Dunsmore caught a big turtle—thirty to forty pounds—on his cat fish line and cut him lose. A turtle that big could take that kind of a bite."

"Is he gonna live?" Danny asked.

The doc grinned. "You bet, Danny."

Martha chimed in. "We don't lose 'em, Danny. You got him here in time." She cast her eyes at Seth and for just a moment narrowed her eyelids.

Kansas City—I think it was Kansas City, she thought.

"These guys did it," he said, tears forming in his eyes.

"Yeah—glad we happened on to you," Seth said.

The doctor turned to the boy. "I'm going to keep him overnight, Danny. We'll see how he is in the morning."

"Can I come see him before I go to bed?"

"What time would that be?"

"Nine o'clock."

Martha came into the room with a bottle in one hand and wipes in the other. "I'll come back down and let him in," she volunteered.

"That'll be fine," the doctor said.

Martha sprayed some chlorhexidine on the operating table, following that with a clean swipe of the floor around it with hydrogen peroxide. She could feel eyes on her and looked up. Seth was staring at her while she squatted on her heels making circular motions with the sponge. The look in his eyes was of a tender nature—not at all commanding as it was when he laid the dog on the table. For a moment she didn't breathe.

He turned his hat in his hands. "We're goin' to have some supper and takin' Danny. You want to come with us?"

For a brief second she thought she would. "Like this?" She stood up and Seth saw the blood on her uniform.

He shrugged. "Well, maybe you'd like to change."

"Go ahead," the doctor said. "We're done with this day."

"Why don't I meet you there?" Her mind was in a tizzy. "Where are you going?"

"I don't know," Seth said. "This isn't my town. How about you pick a place?"

She ran her hands down her dress avoiding the blood spots. "The Whiskey Creek."

"Done," Seth said. He turned and reached for his wallet.

The doctor nodded at Richard. "He's already taken care of that."

Seth reached out his hand. "Thank you."

The doctor took it. "You're more than welcome. Your tourniquet saved his life; I just sewed up the hole."

THE SHARP SWEET TANGY smoke scent of charcoal BBQ beef hit them full in the face as they opened the front door. It was early but patrons were milling about at the entry waiting for supper companions to arrive.

Filoh, who hadn't drunk the coffee or eaten the cookies at the vet's office, got a booth and had a menu open, mouthing the words as he read down the items. Richard guided Danny in and then scooted in beside him. Seth sat alone on the other side.

"Kinda crowded over there isn't it?" Seth said.

"You'll need that room for Martha," Richard said before he wiped the smile off his face.

Seth tipped his head forward, a smile crinkling up his lips, his tongue between his teeth. "I did invite her, didn't I?"

Filoh lifted his gaze. "Fastest move I've seen in 20 years."

"So—let's see…so when you were seventy you saw moves like that?" Richard said.

"I heard about 'em—didn't see 'em."

Danny turned to Filoh. "You're ninety?"

Filoh nodded.

"My gosh that's old. My teacher is thirty-seven and I thought she was old."

"Old is a state of mind. If you've got something important to do it keeps you young."

Seth spotted her coming toward them but he couldn't bring himself to believe it. He slid out of the booth and stood up, pulling his hat off in the same move.

"Wow," he managed.

Martha smiled. She had done the best she could with a black leather skirt that ended above her knees and the white silk blouse, sleeves rolled up, neck open to show a hint of cleavage. "Found you guys."

"Yes you did," Seth said. "And we're glad you did." He stretched his arm to indicate his side of the booth and Martha, tossing her purse ahead of her, used one hand to hold each side of her skirt as she slid in. Her perfume lingered in the air.

Seth put his hat on the outside of the seat and moved closer to Martha. "So what's good to eat in this place?" he said.

"Do you like BBQ beef?" she said.

"Three times a day."

"Did you like the ribs in Kansas City?"

A smile crept over his face. Then he nodded. "So that's where it was—Kansas City."

"At the Sheraton Hotel before the Chief's game. You were with a blond from Independence."

"I was more interested in you."

"That's what my date told me."

"Why that big mouth. And to think I confided to him in the men's room."

She smiled. "I liked it."

He took her hand and shook it. "Martha, I'm Seth Barrett. I am going to be part owner of a ranch in Plattsmouth if my brother and that skeleton there beside him can make it to Ogallala and back, and

I'm mighty glad to meet you…again. May we consider this our first date?"

"Why not. I'm Martha Spelling from Fremont, Nebraska. I am fifty-five, single, and drive a Ford Focus. My IRA has tanked and I can't draw Social Security for another seven years and what I am wearing is my best outfit."

Seth did not release her hand. "I love this place," he said.

OUT IN THE PARKING LOT, Seth patted his stomach. "Two orders of ribs. Now I know what it feels like to be bloated."

Martha nudged him. "We treat bloated animals at the clinic."

"Think I'll just let my interior system take care of it, thank you."

"Of course that's best."

Richard pointed down the street. "There's a Hampton's Inn. How's that sound?"

"Way better than a sandy tent," Filoh said.

"It wouldn't be sandy if you wore some shoes when you went out at night," Seth said.

"I haven't got time to put on shoes."

"Plan ahead."

"I do. I go out barefoot."

"That's what brings in the sand."

Richard interrupted. "Ok guys, knock it off. I'll get a room. Seth— check the horses. Martha and Danny are going back to the clinic. We all meet for breakfast at eight o'clock at Hampton Inn."

"What about me?" Filoh said.

"I'm dragging you unless you think you can walk that far?"

"If I know there's a bath and a soft bed at the end I could walk clear across town. Might even wear off some of that key lime pie."

Richard looked at him. "You're not going to look suave with a belly."

"Don't need to look suave—just alive."

"Who says?"

"The ladies at the retirement home. There's got to be eight of them for every guy that makes it in there alive and single."

"Is that where you're heading after this is over?"

"I am. I'll be so tired of cooking my own meals and sleeping in a sandy tent, I just think I'll give those ladies a chance at me for the last ten years of my life."

Richard chuckled. "Let's see if we can make it to that bath and bed."

Chapter 6

TWELVE-YEAR-OLD BUCKY Houston grabbed the wood post with one arm, planted his feet together and swung around the corner into the milking parlor. "Holy shit!" he yelled. "Mom, come here."

Ginny burst through the doorway leading to the pasture with a corn stalk in her hand. "Buchwald Persington Houston, you know better than to use language like that, bend over." She took a swipe at his rear with the stalk but it was dry and broke when it hit his Levis. She looked around for something else to use and froze when she saw it.

Lying on the concrete parlor floor with its back against the wall, lay the carcass of what had been a Holstein heifer. It had been decapitated, the head crammed onto the 2x4 locking lever on a milking stanchion. It glared down at them with eyes dry and open, the eyelids removed. The body had five cuts from neck to rear; deep cuts through the skin baring muscle, fat and intestines. Blood covered the floor—some still wet.

Ginny clamped her hands to her mouth. In silent motion she moved her head back and forth. "Leave it," she said, and took Bucky by the arm. Together they ran to the house. "Get Dawson and Valerie in here," she said. She opened the kitchen cabinet, took down the Depression glass cream pitcher and poured out the key. Fumbling with getting the pitcher back on the shelf she left the glass door standing open and strode into Richard's office and unlocked the gun cabinet.

She withdrew a Ruger Mini-14, seated a magazine in the action, pulled back the bolt to chamber a round, closed the cabinet and walked back to the kitchen. Dawson and Valerie were there. "Sit down," she ordered.

"Why the gun, Mom?" Dawson asked.

"Shhh," she said as she dialed her cell phone.

After six rings, Richard's voice came through. "Good morning, Ginny."

"Richard—you have to come back. There is something going on here I can't explain. There is a ..."

"Ginny. Ginny, hold on and slow down. Start over. I don't have very good reception here."

She explained the dead cow in a voice that broadcast her anxiety.

He said: "Call the sheriff next thing you do. Don't touch the animal and lock the gates so none of the other animals can get in there. You'll have to milk Ester outside. Tie her to a corral rail and milk her there. She'll be all right with that. Just a minute.

"I just told Seth. He says to get a loaded gun and make sure the bolts are closed on all the doors."

"I've done that," she said. She held her hand over the phone; "Dawson, Bucky—go check the door bolts. Make sure they are closed and locked."

"Ginny," Richard said. "You got any idea who might have done this?"

"No. It's not like an ordinary person would do it. It looks too cruel and senseless."

"Well—get the sheriff out there and let us know what he thinks. We're leaving Fremont tomorrow. Filoh wants to show us some dangerous stuff today, something about hog and chicken farms, as if we didn't know about them. But we're humoring him on that point and it gives Filoh and me a chance to rest our saddle sores. Call me back when you know anything. We'll discuss it amongst ourselves and likely have a suspect when you call back."

"I thought Filoh wasn't going along?"

"Well—he kinda showed up and we couldn't get shed of him."

Ginny turned and looked out the window. "Richard, I don't mind telling you it's scary."

"I know. I'd likely be scared too. Call the sheriff now and get it rolling."

"Ok. You guys be careful."

"Sounds like you're the ones that need to be careful. Goodbye."

SHERIFF BUD PINSKY DIDN'T like calls on his cell phone. He preferred to use it to originate calls and he didn't like citizens to know his cell number. He frowned and looked at the screen that read Virginia Houston. For all the power the Barrett family had in Cass County they had not called on him often. He pulled over to the side of the road and thumbed the 'talk' button. "Good morning Ginny."

He listened staring out the windshield at the even cornrows trying to get a clear picture of what the caller was saying. "I understand," he said. "I'll be there in fifteen minutes. Don't mess with anything."

About time they found it. He closed the cell phone, stuck it in his pocket, turned on the roof lights and left a trail of rubber on the blacktop. He didn't really think this situation called for lights and burning rubber, but it was one of the things he liked about being sheriff—he could do it when he wanted to and nobody could argue with it. Besides, it would make an impression on Ginny Houston when he pulled into her driveway and he had been trying to make an impression on her since seventh grade math class when she had helped him with fractions and he noticed she had started wearing a bra.

Guests were expected to come down the long gravel driveway at a slow speed to avoid clouds of dust arriving just behind them, clouds that enveloped the yard and porch and clung to the windows on both floors. Sheriff Bud Pinsky was not an ordinary guest. And people sitting in his jail washed his patrol car anytime he wanted it. He got out and stood while the cloud enveloped the front of the house.

"I'll send some boys out to clean the windows," he said. "Wasn't thinking about the dust. Had my mind on other things." He removed his hat. "Hello, Ginny."

"Hello, Bud."

"Donavon or the brothers around?"

She shook her head, the Ruger mini-14 hanging by her side.

"You won't need that with me here, Ginny. Why don't you put it up and we can go about seeing what happened."

She turned and he admired the trim shape of her hips in the Levis. He hooked his thumbs on his gun belt and wondered what she was like in bed. Almost thirty years he had held his crush on her, even while dating others, getting married and fathering two children. He still looked upon her as his ultimate goal; something he had not mentioned to anybody, not even Father O'Doherty. He had told Father plenty, but not that. What he hadn't done, he didn't confess to anybody.

Sheriff Pinsky knelt down and touched the cuts on the heifer, put the back of his hand on its neck. "It hasn't been dead long," he said. He stood up and looked around the milking parlor. "This is the only one?"

Ginny nodded.

"Did you check around after you found this one?"

"No."

"Let's do that," he said and unsnapped the leather strap that retained his revolver in the holster. He tugged a skintight glove onto his right hand, pulled the brim of his Trooper hat to his eyebrows and walked out through the pasture doorway.

"Where do you keep the heifers?" he said.

Ginny pointed. Together they walked to the barbed wire enclosure. Bud walked close enough that he could accidentally bump shoulders with her as they moved over the uneven ground. He wanted to know if she would shy away from the accidental brushing. It didn't appear that she noticed it. He could feel his excitement rising.

They stood by the fence, cows looking at them and coming closer, raising their noses and darting away. "You keep the Holsteins in with the Herefords?" Bud said.

"When they're this young. Seth has always done that until they're ready to breed."

"So—I'm thinking whoever did this coaxed that animal through this gate and into the parlor where he killed it."

"He or they?" Ginny asked.

Bud nodded. "Could be more than one did it. It took a strong person to lift that head up and ram it on the stanchion lever. We'll check for tracks and stuff." He smashed the heel of his boot on a beetle. He looked at Ginny. "You and the kids gonna stay out here tonight?"

"No. We're leaving when you leave."

"You want me to hang around today and check things out?" He could hardly swallow, his mouth dry with expectation.

Ginny drew in a deep breath and shook her head. "I don't know, Bud. Either that or we're going back to town."

"I might could spend the day here. Let me check with my office." He flipped open his cell phone and punched in some numbers and waited. After a moment he said: "Larry, Bud here. I'm on a case out Barrett ranch; might be all day. Can you handle stuff there?" Pause. "Ok. I'll have my cell on. Check you later."

He nudged her with his shoulder. Her eyes lost their stare and she looked up at him. "What?"

"You and the kids go in the house. I'll check around here some more and then we'll sit down and work this thing out," he said.

"I'll make some lunch. How long will you be?"

He pushed his lower lip up over the top one and shook his head. "No more than thirty minutes."

She turned and walked back to the barn. He looked over his shoulder and took in her walk from behind.

Hot damn. Hot damn.

He studied the enclosure, the gate, the earth beneath the gate, the way the wire strap was replaced on the gatepost. That was how things usually worked for him. He piled all the information in his head and then let it brew until it codified into something that he could bank on. That's when Sheriff Bud Pinsky moved on it. He took the elk hide work gloves out of his uniform pocket, stretched them over each hand and grabbed the heifer's head by the lower jawbone and lifted it off the stanchion. He tossed the head beside the body. The whisper of a smile slipped over his lips.

This was how it is supposed to work.

At the metal garage Bud rolled back the high door and parked his car inside, closed the door and went to the house. He knocked on the back door. Ginny opened it.

"You don't have to knock, Bud."

He removed his hat, smoothed his hair and hung his gun belt on the back of a chair by the door. He looked trimmer with the belt off and if he got anywhere with Ginny he didn't want that to get in the way.

Dawson and Bucky stared at the gun belt. The rich black leather with two levels of silver cartridges, their gray leads sticking out below the bullet loop, handcuffs, and a mean looking can of Mace held their attention between bites of chicken sandwiches and apples. Valerie couldn't care less. She was interested in the dead cow.

"Put my patrol car in your garage so it wouldn't be noticed. Don't know enough about this caper yet but I suspect someone is watching the place. They've got to know Seth and Richard are gone. Wonder why the dogs didn't alert somebody?"

"There was nobody here, Bud."

"Oh—you come out from town every day?"

Ginny nodded.

Bud twisted up his lower lip again, squinted his eyes, and nodded like he was trying to understand how things worked around here with Seth and Richard on the trip.

"Have you looked around the house? Anything broken or disrupted—doors left ajar—anything suspicious?"

Ginny shook her head, a thoughtful look in her eyes.

"I'll check around if it's okay with you?"

"Sure, Bud."

"I think I'll keep my gun with me," Ginny said.

This wasn't working out the way he wanted. "Why don't you put it up and come with me to check things out? I'll show you what to look for."

Ginny nodded. She put the gun back in the cabinet, locked it and returned to the kitchen.

"Ginny—I'm certain there are no people in this house other than us. I'll just show you what to look for so when I'm not here you can check it out yourself."

He started at the side door. In his best teacher manner, he pointed to various things and spoke in a slow soft voice. "Now that door knob—don't touch it until you're satisfied it hasn't been opened. Could have prints on it." His eyes ran over the outline of the door. "Check to see that nothing is keeping the door from completely closing. Something sticking out near the bolt or latch. If someone's been here and wants to come back, often times they'll block the latch or bolt from closing." He looked to see if Ginny was taking it in.

She stood, arms crossed over her breasts, a slight frown working its way across her face. "We've never had any problem with anybody coming here."

"No," Bud said. "But Seth and Richard were here and they know the house and grounds. You're here all alone. 'Cept now you've got me."

"That's a comforting feeling."

That's what he wanted to hear. "Let's take a look at the other places."

They moved to the front door and then he suggested they look upstairs.

"Nobody would come in up there—," Ginny started.

"People have ladders." He looked at her like he was explaining it to a fifth grader.

Bud had never been in the upstairs and he painted a picture of it in his mind. There was a guest room at the far end of the hall that looked promising. "Let's take a gander in here."

He bent down and looked at the windowsill. "Take a look at this."

Ginny bent over and looked. He was close behind and waiting for her. When she straightened up she was completely in his arms. He leaned his face toward her lips, eyes closed. Her elbows, small and sharp, jammed under his collarbones on both sides of his chest. He couldn't quite make a connection.

"Bud—stop it! What do you think you're doing?"

He tightened his grasp and chased her lips, his heart pounding as the lust built up.

She was no match for his strength and her arms collapsed as he crushed her to him, his lips finding her cheek. She could smell the morning coffee on his breath as he panted. "Ginny—I've waited twenty years for this. Come on."

"No. Let me go."

"Ginny?"

"Let me go or I'll scream. The kids are downstairs."

"We'll be done before they get here."

"Let me go now!"

His grip relaxed and as she turned his hands closed on her breasts. She could feel his erection throbbing against her thigh.

She yelled: "Dawson, Bucky—up here!"

He released her and took a step back. She glared at him.

"Is this how to help the citizens of Cass County?"

He shook his head. "Now, Ginny. You know I've had a sweet spot for you for a long time. I thought you felt the same way."

"Well, I don't. I thought of you as a friend."

Bucky beat Dawson up the stairs and they stood in the doorway as they looked into the guest room. "What, Mom?"

Ginny took a deep breath. "Sheriff Pinsky was showing me how to tell if anyone has come in through an unlocked window. Come here."

She placed the boys between herself and Bud and pointed to the windowsill. "See the dust there? It hasn't been disturbed. Would you boys please check out the other windows upstairs and see if they are ok?"

They burst from the room and Ginny looked at Bud. "Don't ever try that again, Bud. In high school maybe, but not here and not now."

"Some other time—some other place?"

"No, no, no." She led the way downstairs. She could hear the boys racing from room to room upstairs and finally the plunk, plunk, plunk as they descended the stairs two at a time, ending up standing in front of her in the kitchen. "Nothing," they reported.

Sheriff Bud Pinsky was buckling on his gun belt, adjusting the height and positioning of the gun butt. As he buckled the belt and reached for his Smokey the Bear hat, he nodded to the two boys. "Thanks for checking it out. I'm going to my office now and write up a report on this crime scene. Think I'll mention you guys helped me in the investigation of it. OK?"

The boys looked at each other. "Awesome," Bucky said.

Bud nodded to Ginny. "Ginny."

"Goodbye, Sheriff."

Bud opened the garage door slid into the seat and put the key in the ignition. He sat for a minute before firing up the white Chevy SUV. He took a deep breath and exhaled.

Next time, I'll get her in this rig and lock the doors. No kids around. Night. Somewhere nobody can hear her yelling.

He was running locations through his mind as he started up the vehicle, backed out of the garage, and headed for the office. Halfway to town he pulled in at the Solid Waste Transfer Station and looked around. No cars. He drove close to the trailer that received all waste, got out, opened the rear door, pulled out a plastic bag and threw it over the top. Today was garbage day in Plattsmouth. A thousand loads of private garbage would be dumped on top of his today before it was hauled away to be burned at the state incinerator. Nobody would find, or even be looking for, a set of coveralls smeared with cow's blood and gauntlet vinyl gloves.

Filoh and the river

FILOH DRIED HIMSELF OFF and standing naked in the dark, pulled the top sheet and blanket off the bedroll. He slid onto the mattress and settled the bedclothes around and on top of him, loose like a tarp.

He couldn't stand tight bedding; made him think of a coffin and the confining borders it imposed.

When he closed his eyes, the last visual image he had of the Platte River impressed itself on the back of his eyelids. That was just before Seth spurred ahead to Danny and his dog and the rest of the day was a jumble of had-to-do's. It was tranquil and smooth flowing.

There was the color too. They crossed the river where pioneers and cattlemen had crossed for a hundred years, on sand hard packed by the rushing waters at the old Ferguson Crossing, the water, bluish on top, sliding toward brown where the sand was lifted by the current and moved down stream.

All of his life he had lived next to and on a river. When he was young, other kids were riding horses and trying to borrow their parent's car, Filoh built rafts from fallen trees, peeling them and tying them with bailing twine, sturdy enough to hold him up while he drifted downriver with the current to abandon the raft in some suitable place and walk home, satisfied with the afternoon's adventure and tranquil inside, the warm water having washed the river's knowledge into him and the sun, reflected off the river's face, tanned his body.

It seemed silly to lie here in a hotel bed with all the trappings of civilization bunched around him and try and communicate with the River a couple of miles away. He put himself into a listening mode, on his back, arms straight out, palms up and keeping his eyes closed.

He lay that way allowing the river to speak, suppressing all other thoughts that tried to run across his brain. He had to be there to interact with the River. His eyes popped open. That might be the key. The people who were ruining the River weren't connected with it. There were power lines and roads and buildings between them and the River and when they saw it at all, it was from the crest of a concrete bridge they were crossing at 50 miles an hour. They didn't hear, see, or smell the water, their senses immune. They weren't trying to kill the River—they just didn't know that what they were doing every day was taking its life.

By gawd—. He sat upright. "Richard," he said.

Richard rolled over. "What is it?"

"It isn't that you're trying to kill the River. It's just that you don't know you're doing it."

"Hmmm."

"I feel better now. That's curable—even with you nitwits."

A gentle half snoring greeted his remark.

Martha is green

MARTHA UNLOCKED THE DOOR to the clinic and turned to Seth. "You don't have to wait for us."

"I'd like to if you don't mind."

She smiled and stepped into the dark room. The stringent odor of antiseptic stung his eyes.

The three of them went to the back room. The dog lifted his head at the sound of Danny's voice.

"He looks worse…"

Martha put her arm on Danny's shoulder. "They always look worse just before they get better. Tomorrow morning, he'll be fit as a fiddle."

"Can I sleep with him in here?"

"No, Danny. It's not good to sleep with an injured dog. Let him heal and then you can be buddies again. He needs his sleep." She rubbed Danny's head, "Just like you do."

Seth stood, hands in his pockets, his mind racing with personal thoughts. He felt like a kid, like his brain had stopped growing in the ninth grade. The good night to the dog process was taking time away from sleep and an early start tomorrow. He nudged Martha.

"Can we go now?" he offered.

Martha stood up. "I'm going to take Danny home. You want to come with us?"

Seth nodded.

In the mild night they found Danny's house alight. His mother stepped out on the porch as soon as the car stopped in their driveway.

Martha waved and Danny got out and walked up the steps to get a hug from his mother. She waved back.

"Where are you staying?" Martha said.

"Hampton Inn, I guess," Seth offered. "It's somewhere downtown."

Martha backed out the driveway, both hands on the steering wheel and turned for the downtown section.

"Is there anywhere we can park overlooking the river and talk?" Seth said.

She looked at her watch. "I think I can find a place." Down a narrow dirt path heading due south they stopped on the bank of the Platte River. She rolled down the window and turned off the motor. "I sure hope Danny's dog is okay in the morning. I'd feel terrible if he got worse after the pep talk I delivered tonight."

"Aw, he'll be fine. That turtle just got some flesh, he didn't hit anything vital." He slid down on the seat. "Dogs are tough."

Martha leaned her back against the door. "What is it you want to talk about?"

"Well—I just thought we had stuff to talk about."

She let a smile emerge barely visible in the dark. "Oh. Why?"

Seth nodded, his lower lip clenched between his teeth. "We've had quite a day."

"Yes."

"I want to get to know you better." He looked down and picked at the dried grass clinging to his sock. "Our Kansas City meeting was kinda short."

She sat with arms crossed, her back against the car door, staring at him.

"You're making this kinda hard."

"You aren't used to sitting in a car with a girl, are you?"

"No—I'm not. It has been a spell."

She crossed her arms over her chest. "Ok—let's start with who I am and then you can tell me who you are."

Seth brightened up, smiled, and she started from kindergarten. She ended on a word Seth had not heard.

"You're an eco activist?"

She nodded.

"For cryin' out loud—I don't even know what that is."

"Have you heard of Friends of the Earth?"

"No."

"Do they have newspapers in Plattsmouth?"

"Of course. We get the Omaha World Herald."

"They've covered some of our stories. I'm on the committee to videotape the use of the 'cides around Fremont."

"'Cides?"

"All the 'cides: pesticides, fungicides, insecticides, etc."

Seth squinted his eyes, turned his head. "Why do you videotape that?"

"We want to prove what those chemicals are doing to our environment."

"How long have you been doing that?"

"Let's see—I'm fifty-five now and I started right after my divorce, so fourteen years."

"Made any difference?"

She nodded. "You betcha."

"You should spend some time with Filoh. He's harping on us the way we operate the ranch."

"Really. I thought you were all together."

"Together, yes. But he wanted to come on this trip to show us the problems. And he's saying we're killing ourselves with those things."

"No—you're killing all of us with poisons. Not only leeching into the river we all use, but the chemicals become part of the stuff you grow and sell or feed to animals that humans end up ingesting."

"The American farmer is the most advanced in the world. Produces more food per acre and per person working in agriculture than at any time in history. Couldn't do that without those things."

"That is true but you can't keep doing it because you're killing the creeks and the rivers and now the ocean."

"The ocean? Plattsmouth is a thousand miles from the ocean."

"Where do you think the water from the Platte River ends up? In the sky?"

"Of course not."

"It ends up in the Gulf of Mexico where the Mississippi dumps it. And there's a dead spot there where nothing grows. No fish, no sea life, no oxygen in the water—it is a dead zone."

Seth sat up. "I'm too tired to muscle through this conversation. I gotta catch some sleep."

Martha turned, put her hand on the steering wheel. "Look—the sky is getting light. It's almost dawn."

"Know a good place for breakfast?" Seth asked.

The River

The night currents whispered off the surface. The moon and stars provided a pale light over the water, warmer now in the longer days of summer. The river put out a good image at night, the moonlight not intense enough to pick up the problems that were visible during the day. If you didn't know better, it still sounded wet, cool, vital, and provided a highway through the territory.

Leaving town

FILOH WAS PULLING UP his pants. "Sure I remember ol' man Melzer. I was just a kid but I remember my Pap pointing him out to me. Said he'd run for congress but got thoroughly whumped."

"Yeah—great grandpa was not a good politician. Tended to speak his mind," Richard said. "Something I'd like to hear from our current crop." He pulled up his boots. "You about ready?"

"Why are we in such a gol-durned hurry? And where's Seth, anyhow?"

"Seth is wherever he is."

"Why'd you bring up old Melzer?"

"I thought you might remember him. That, and I've got nothing to do while I'm waiting for you to get dressed."

"I want to make sure we get a look at the creeks that come out of this town and hit the Platte. From the looks of things they've cleaned up the slaughterhouses and feed lots since I was here last. Used to have drainage from them right smack into the river. Guts, manure, chicken parts—the catfish loved it."

Beneath a raised chin and wrinkled brow, Richard appraised the older man. Why he had agreed to let Filoh come along was lost in his thinking. It hadn't been a week and he had forgotten it. The goal was to get to Ogallala and back and settle the estate. These sideshows were eating at the time limit and around the base of his neck there was an uneasiness that needed rubbing. It was interesting to talk with the old man who had known his great-grandfather, but he could do that in his comfortable office at the ranch. Didn't need to be sharing a room or a tent with someone who sounded like a sawmill when he snored.

"Your great-grand Pap made it to ninety-five so I figure I've got at least a few more years in me," Filoh said. He looked around the room. "Have you seen my other boot?"

Richard pointed at it half hidden under a discarded pillow. *No wonder there is sand in the tent. He doesn't think about it.* "Now that you are fully shod can we proceed with the day?" Richard said.

"Lead the way, pilgrim."

They walked down one flight of stairs and into the small breakfast room where guests of the motel were offered a buffet breakfast. Seth and Martha were seated at a table near the window and motioned them over.

Filoh snickered. "Lookee at the two early birds."

"The fruit is fresh," Seth said, spooning a piece of pineapple into his mouth.

"You don't look it," Richard said. "We ought to get a discount for you not showing up last night."

Seth smiled. "Martha and I had some talking to do."

Martha smiled at them. "Good morning Richard, Filoh."

"Hello, Martha. Good to see you again. Hope my wayward brother didn't ruin your night along with the rough day we all had yesterday."

"He was a perfect gentleman."

"Humph," Filoh said. "Doubt he knows the meaning of the word. He works with cows and horses all day long, doesn't take a gentleman to do that."

Seth pushed his dishes away. "I'll go find the horses and get this show ready for the road while you guys stuff yourselves. Martha and I will see you at the vet clinic. Don't be all day about it." He patted Filoh on the shoulder.

Richard nodded. "Seth—lend your watch to Filoh. He can't see the sun from inside this motel and doesn't realize it's moving across the sky while he hunts for his boots. I would lend him mine but some-one has to see that this outfit does things timely."

Filoh was mashing eggs into the pancakes with a fork. He looked up. "You two can try a man's spirit."

THERE WAS A NOTE scotch-taped to the front door at the vet's clinic addressed to Martha.

6:35 AM. Gone to a cow call at Stub Johnson's. Should be back around 11:00. Horses in recovery barn. —Doc

Seth slid the door open and heard the whinny of his horse. "That's a good sound to hear. I thought maybe he'd hate me after that ride into town yesterday."

"You couldn't help it," Martha said.

"How's Danny's dog?"

"Eyes clear, eating and drinking—feeling better."

She stroked the horse's neck as he looked at her and sniffed her hand. She took a packet of sugar out of her blouse pocket, tore it open and poured it into her palm. His rough tongue lapped across her hand, warming and wetting it at once. "He likes me."

"He likes sugar."

Their gear was in a corner, the load from each horse in a separate pile with the bridles draped over the saddle horn. "Somebody did a neat job."

Martha smiled. "Doc would have it no other way."

"How much do we owe you for boarding the horses?"

"I think we can charge it to the dust and let the rain settle it."

"I hope we can repay the favor."

Martha smiled. "I doubt we'll be riding down through Plattsmouth soon."

"There are other times and other ways to pay back a favor."

Her smile widened. "I'm sure there are."

"In fact, I've even thought of a few." He was bent over with one of the horse's hoofs between his knees. "How about I give you a kiss as a down payment and we'll work out the rest later?"

Martha blushed. "That's a good way to start a day."

Seth looked up. "Just a thought."

She started brushing the horse, combing the hay and straw out of his coat. The horse stood on three legs, ears up, and leaned into Seth who lifted each leg in turn to inspect the hoof.

Richard and Filoh came out of the sunlight into the dark of the barn.

"Can't see a durn thing in here," Filoh said.

"So it's true," Richard said. "Old people's eyes don't adjust to the dark very fast."

"We get there. Just takes longer."

Seth let the horses' leg down, put up the hoof pick and pulled the saddle blanket over his horse. "Big day today. We should make it to Columbus where the North Loop River runs into the Platte."

"This is a lot more boring than I thought it would be," Filoh said.

Richard smiled. "It wouldn't be if you weren't trying to run a school here."

Filoh put his hands on his hips, weaving a little. "You just don't understand. Word is that over 20,000 people die world wide from pesticide poisoning each year. What I've got to get across to you is that most of the ingredients in pesticides have been found to cause cancer in animals and humans."

"How'd you make it so long?" Seth said.

"Well I didn't spray it on my fields and I didn't stand on the fence line to show the pilot where to drop his load getting it all over me. That most likely kept me alive. That and then there's this mission I've got."

"Yeah—we're aware of that." Richard said.

Martha chimed in. "You don't disbelieve what Filoh is saying do you?"

Seth caught the girth swinging under the horse and cinched the saddle down. "The whole problem with Filoh's mission is that he uses phrases like, "the word is…" which doesn't give us anything to go by. Besides, our mission is to get up and back down the river. We're not in an investigative mode at the moment."

"You can learn while you're sitting on top of a horse, can't you?" Martha said, her frown and downturned eyebrows standing out. "Even Genghis Khan learned on horseback."

Richard turned to Seth. "My gawd—she's comparing us to Genghis Khan."

"We've cleaned this town up a lot since the seventies and eighties and the whole state and the whole nation needs to get on the program to quit poisoning our land and the air and water. That isn't so hard to understand is it?"

"Of course not," Richard said. "But we don't need to be compared to some murderous warlord to be educated. That's a put down, plain and simple."

Martha rubbed the palms of her hands together ridding them of the wet sugar grains stuck between her fingers. "A lot of what you're going to be riding through can't be seen. It is in the air and in the ground. But it's there. It's there and it's doing its work while you don't see it."

"What would you have us do?" Richard said. "We've got land, we've got people we're responsible for, we've got stock and crops, and all we hear from you and Filoh is to stop pronto. I mean just stop using the chemicals we've been using for years to control weeds and pests. Where do we go from there?"

"You clean it out and build it back up so your farming and ranching operations don't pollute the world. Is that so hard to understand?"

Seth was loading the packhorse, striving for a balanced load. His jaw muscles flexed beneath the sun darkened skin. "And just what do we do for income during that time frame?"

Martha stammered. "You sell off your stock and stored crops I guess."

"You guess?" Richard said. "You parade around the countryside with your friends of the earth, none of whom own one piece of land or productive asset and try to coerce farmers to take four or five years to change the way we've been doing our work for half a century." He took the reins in one hand and led his horse out of the barn.

Filoh stood in the aisle, hands on hips, a little stunned, his tongue off to one side between his teeth. "Well—I never...."

"Mount up Filoh."

"Can't we work this out?" Filoh said.

"Not here. Not now. You comin' or not?"

Seth threw a glance at Martha as he mounted. "We'll stop on the way back. In the meantime, we'll work on this. Both of us."

Martha stood with her legs spread, hands in her jacket pockets and watched the horses turn their backsides to her. "Think about it," she hollered.

Seth turned in the saddle. "Got nuthin' else to do."

Richard found the road back to the river. Folks along the way stopped and pointed at the three horsemen and the packhorse picking their way down the right side of the road. Cars slowed and drivers gawked. A few horns honked but mostly they were younger people who hoisted a thumb of approval and drove around them with a minimum of fuss.

The river had risen four or five inches during the night. It was a good morning, cool, with a dark line of clouds across the north, but the air had a damp clingy edge to it and a slight breeze that gave a hint of weather that was going to change.

Chapter 7

FILOH TWISTED IN THE saddle and squinted, crow's feet starting at his temples cratered around his eyes and deepened as he took in the shadowed river, the green fields beyond it and the clouds, a sagging gray mass building to the north. "Looks like heavy rain."

Seth pulled the poncho over his head. The thunder and lightning began at that moment. It came at them across the flat land from the northeast, rolling toward them like a stampede of horses.

"Richard—remember when we were kids how we used to count the seconds after a lightning flash to figure out the distance it was away?"

"You were mostly wrong. You counted too fast."

Seth threw a nod at the cloud. "How far do you think?"

Two and a half—three miles."

"Five miles if it's a foot."

"It looks big and strong. We should have stayed in the motel."

"Hells bells, Richard, we're on a quest here. Weather is part of it. Don't you have some snort and blow in your veins?"

"Same as you, but if I have to ride this horse in a rain storm I would rather be in the motel."

Seth shook his head.

"If I was on my tractor I could get the weather report on the radio and get the hell out of the way or run for the barn."

"A little rain isn't going to hurt you."

"No—not a little. But a lot could."

The River

From the canyons and draws water gathered to pour into the Loup River where it sought dominance, dumping higher and faster water

*into the Platte, taking it by surprise. The river had lived with surprise
for thousands of years, long before man turned it into a disposal system. It opened its banks and accepted the water and made it its own.
It was a testament to its majesty; one that had lived forever and would
live forever with a life given to it by the Creator.*

FILOH STUCK ONE HAND through the sleeve of his poncho and stood
up in the stirrups to pull it on. "I'd like not to get fried by a lightning bolt.
As I recall, folks on horses get hit more often than those lower down."

"Lightning strikes are one in a million," Seth said, "wherever you are."

"Don't feel like stretching my luck."

Seth pointed ahead. "See that island? Lets get to it and get hunkered down before this thing hits."

It wasn't a big island but it had trees higher up that had survived
minor flooding. The underbrush wasn't clotted with debris. It was a
fight to climb the bank. The horses gained the flat surface, ears up
and tails stiffened. Seth reined his horse back and forth over the least
disturbed area looking at the trees and the river, then at the mass of
clouds moving toward them. He picked a clear spot midway on the
island where several drifted trees had slammed up against large cottonwoods and had picked up debris that formed a barricade. "Here
she be," he said.

Filoh, sarcasm reeking in his voice, said, "Oh, don't this look nice."

"Let's go back to Fremont," Richard said as he looked around.
"We can beat the storm."

Seth tied his horse to a downed tree. "Grab some wood and we'll
build a fire. This shouldn't be tough."

"We're not gonna set up the tent?" Richard said.

"We've got ponchos. Should keep us dry enough."

"Hell's bells," Filoh said. He tugged at the unfamiliar poncho, trying to tuck it under his seat as the wind at the leading edge of the
storm whipped through the brush.

The dry cottonwood bark took the fire fast. Their backs to the
dirt and wood wall, they sat facing the fire cringing when lightning
and thunder ripped through the air around them. Filoh put his hands
over his ears and closed his eyes.

"I was about right on the distance," Richard said.

"Yeah—you were," Seth said. The wind whipped the poncho hood around his face. The rain added weight to the air; made it feel dense and gray. The burning smell of ozone crimped their nostrils.

The drops got larger, faster, punching divots in the sand. The roar of pellets hitting the wood, driving through the leaves, and distorting the surfaces of the sand and water cut their visibility and drowned out conversation. Huge raindrops, with light diffused through them, coursed through the air and shattered into hundreds of shards when they struck.

Lightning struck a tall cottonwood across the channel, splitting it in two. The near half fell into the river, the current swinging it in an arc attached by a scab of bark, its limbs torquing with the flow of water across the broad leaves. The other half stood upright, shorn of its previous height, a wisp of smoke emitting from the blackened trunk.

"Judas Priest," Filoh hollered. "I thought that one had our number on it."

Seth turned. "You won't hear the one that's got your number on it."

"Maybe we ought to spread out," Richard said. "What is that smell?"

"Ozone." Seth shook his head. "You pansies. This is just a good Nebraska thunderstorm. Enjoy it."

"Enjoy it!" Filoh said. "What's to enjoy?"

"You had a good night's sleep. You had breakfast. We're safe and sound, just sit and enjoy the majesty of it."

Richard stared at the lightning split tree. "The water is rising."

They followed his gaze. The water, darker and moving faster, had risen a foot to the base of the tree that was hit.

"Think we are in any trouble?" Richard said.

Filoh yelled above the sounds. "You dang right we're in trouble. This storm's coming from upriver. It's probably dumped tons of water on the Loup and it's rushing to get down here and sweep us off into this mess."

A faint cracking rolled over the prairie. Seth's nostrils flared. A blinding flash of lightning and an artillery of thunder crashed on the island. The horses jerked back, the bridle reins tied to the limb snapped like string. The horses gained their footing and pounded into the rising water across to the far bank.

Richard opened his mouth. Tried to clear his ears. He could see Seth's lips move but he couldn't hear. Filoh lay face down on the sand, hands over his head. Seth shook him. He stirred. Water was trickling in a small gulley to one side of their camp. Filoh got on his hands and knees, cast one foot out in front and stood up. He walked to the gulley, turned and followed it upriver. He was back in a minute.

"We best be gettin' out of here now," he said.

"Follow the horses," Seth said.

"How about we climb a tree?" Richard offered.

Filoh looked up. "There ain't no limbs for quite a ways. I couldn't do that."

Seth picked up a dead limb about wrist thick and started across the channel to the far bank following the horses' trail. He drove the stick into the bottom of the river upstream from his feet, creating a triangle out of the stick and his wide spread feet. The water tore at his knees. Richard looked for a stick. The water was smashing over the island now moving on a determined path, sweeping leaves and grasses and sticks atop of it.

Richard broke off two limbs, handed one to Filoh, and planted his left foot in the water. He shivered as the water rose against his leg. Behind them the fire emitted a sizzling sound and smoke rose into the air as the water crept under it and floated the burning sticks away.

Seth was across and trying to bunch the horses. Richard looked up, he saw it wasn't far to the bank but the water now gurgled around his thighs and was getting deeper and faster with each step. He looked at Filoh. He was in up to his knees. His face, usually hard to read, was an open book. Lips pulled tight, tongue stuck in one corner of his mouth, eyes squinted, he was committed and one hundred percent concentrated on the crossing.

Richard's next step brought the water to his crotch. He flinched and the force of the water against the flat of his stomach straightened him up.

You can't drown in crotch deep water, can you? Hell—just keep moving.

His next step was a mistake and in a split second he paid for it. Arms spread wide he flailed at the air, one leg above the surface as he toppled backwards, driving water up his nose. The force of the pounding water surprised him as he tumbled head over heels. He tried to gain footing, purge his nostrils and grab a breath of air. Tumbling and partly submerged, an underwater limb snagged the arm of his poncho. In an instant his body, pushed by the flood was fluttering underwater

like a leaf in a high wind. Richard, stunned and surprised by the roar
of the current had never expected that water could be so loud. He
let out air, struggled against the flexible root that held him on the
bottom. A mental picture of him on his tractor on a sunny day stuck
in his head. He thought of breathing but it was the noise that drilled
through him. In the midst of his pondering he was jerked from the
bottom and pulled upright almost against his will. He sneezed and
coughed. Filoh held him in a vise, arms locked around his middle.

"Can you go?" Filoh yelled in his ear.

Richard nodded, then sneezed and coughed.

Filoh clung to his belt and they plowed across the channel
together, the water getting shallower as they neared the far bank. It
took three tries but they got up the bank together and lay down on
the wet sand.

"What a start to the day," Filoh said. "I swear this river has a mind
of its own."

"I did not think a guy could drown in a couple feet of water but
I am about to change my mind on that," Richard said. He sat, legs
spread, water dripping from his nose and elbows, his arms pegged
behind him like a tripod. "I see Seth has found the horses."

"I do believe I'd as soon walk," Filoh said.

Richard turned to look at him. He looked older, his thin hair plas-
tered against his skull, whiter than he remembered. Filoh sat with his
mouth partially open, eyes wide, and Richard wondered where he had
found the strength to raise him from the river. *At ninety will I be able
to do that? Could I do that now?* "I doubt you want to be walking the
300 miles."

Filoh smiled. "I didn't say I was going all the way. I may have
taught you boys enough by now."

"We're not about to turn you loose and let you go back and blow
up Klete Dixon's stuff. You're stuck with us for the duration." Then he
smiled. "Come hell or high water."

Filoh chuckled. "And we've done the high water part, ain't we?"

"That we have." He clapped his hand on Filoh's thigh. "Thank
you for pulling me out of that mess."

Filoh nodded. "Couldn't let one of my pupils drown."

Seth and the horses stopped behind them. "The storm has passed. If you gentlemen are through with your synchronized swimming practice we should be getting on to Columbus."

"Just what this outfit needs," Filoh said. "A smart ass trail boss."

"By gawd, I will sure be glad when this is over. I truly will," Richard said. He turned the stirrup, stuck his wet boot in it and mounted up.

Drying out

DRYING OUT WAS SLOW. Richard could force water from his shirt by grabbing a handful and squeezing. River water seeped through his Levi's with every step the horse took. And steering the horse with broken reins was a stooped over, hard on the back kind of exercise. He wanted to stop and build a fire, dry out, but for several reasons, which seemed good enough to him— wood wet from the rain, Seth leading the way, every time he moved he was colder—he fixed it in his mind to sit in the saddle and dry out by wind and movement. Filoh had to be in the same fix and he was twenty-five years older. If Filoh started to complain, he would join in. Until then he would let nature take its course.

Somewhere on a bend in the Platte, between Fremont and Columbus, they came to a small creek, one of many that had risen with the influx of up-country water. Seth nudged his horse into the stream, leaning back in the saddle, a wary eye on the flow. The horse slid off the bank, front legs locked, ears forward and eyes wide. Seth turned and hollered above the sound of the water, "Cross here. Better going on the other side."

From the north a dirt road dead-ended in the river.

Seth thought it must be a boat launch but he couldn't envision a boat that could float in this shallow water. A canoe maybe, or a flat-bottomed riverboat.

Two boys, in their early teens, stood watching the three horsemen cross the river toward them. Each held a plastic garbage bag. Without any guidance from the riders the horses pulled up and stopped before the boys. Seth and Richard looked at each other.

"Morning," Seth offered.

The boys nodded and one said "hello."

"What's up?" Richard asked as he dismounted.

"Collecting cans," one said.

Richard pulled off his right boot and drained the water out of it. Seth smiled at the tractor rider turned cowboy.

"Movie money?" Seth asked.

"No sir. We wouldn't be wading through this muck for that. It's for money to bury my uncle."

"Your uncle?"

The boy shifted his feet. "Died yesterday."

The boy didn't look old enough to have an uncle of dying age. "What from?"

"Got crushed by a hay bale."

"One of those big ones I take it."

"Yes sir."

Seth shook his head as Richard removed his left boot and drained the water out of it. Filoh sat his horse like he was glued to it.

"Gathering cans is sort of a slow way of getting enough money, isn't it? How much do you need?" Seth said.

"Mom said twelve hundred." He looked out across the water, a frown starting to crease his forehead. "Your reins are awful short, aren't they?"

Seth took the lead rope off his horse's neck and tied him to a tree. "Horses broke them during the storm." He looked in the bottom of the sack one of the boys held. "Are you accepting donations?"

Richard looked up at the boys and back at Seth who was reaching for his wallet. Now what was Seth thinking? They had planned their money needs to cover expected expenses where credit cards couldn't be used. He turned to the boys.

"How much have you got so far?"

"Maybe seven dollar's worth."

"That many aluminum cans come down the river?" Filoh asked.

"That was yesterday afternoon and this morning. The flood will bring more of them down."

"Well don't that beat all," Filoh said. He shook his head. "And I didn't even figure in pollution from cans."

"Here," Seth said. He handed the boy a floppy wet twenty-dollar bill. "Wished I could help you more but we're on a tight cash budget at this point."

The boy looked at it, smiled, put it in his pocket. "Thanks, Mister."

"The name's, Seth Barrett. This is my brother, Richard and Filoh is the grandpa."

"I ain't a grandpa to you."

"You likely are to someone who will stay unmentioned."

The boy put his hand on the horse's neck. "Where you goin'?"

"We're heading for Ogallala."

"On horseback?"

"Yup."

"Why don't you drive there?"

"Gotta do it by horse."

The boys looked at each other. "Can we come along?" one asked.

"Nope. We need to get moving before Grandpa freezes up."

"You've got a funeral to attend to," Richard said.

Filoh bent forward, grabbed the saddle horn and swung down off the mule. "I'm freezing now. Here—hold my mule." He walked spraddle-legged over to a cottonwood trees, stuck one hand against it and balancing on one foot, took off a boot. He poured water out, peeled down his sock, sat down and squeezed it like a rag. "Boys—I need a fire. I'm cold to my core."

Richard slid off the horse. "We need to build a fire and get some coffee brewing."

Credit card refusal

IT WAS NOT DIFFICULT to locate the home of Everett Williams of Grange Hall fame. What was difficult was to understand the looks they got when they asked for directions.

At the home Richard slid off the horse, handed the stubs of reins and rope to Seth and walked across the sidewalk through the gate to the house. He knocked on the screen door and waited. Getting no response he opened the screen and knocked on the front door. It opened and a young man stood in the opening.

"Hello," Richard began, turning his hat in his hands. "I am Richard Barrett from Plattsmouth. We were told Everett Williams lived here. We talked with him at our Grange meeting and would like to say hello."

"He's dead."

The boy's tone struck Richard like a kick in the chest.

"He's dead?"

"Yes sir."

Richard stammered and half turned, his lower lip protruding. "My Gawd. When did that happen?"

"A week ago. The funeral's tomorrow."

Richard shook his head. "I am so sorry. What took him?"

"He stepped in front of a train. A hundred car wheat train."

"And you are burying him tomorrow?"

"What we could find of him, yes sir."

"My land…I don't know what to say. I was expecting to talk with him a bit about our crop situation but…"

The boy stood stock still, his eyes dull and face as drawn and plain and void of expression as a block wall.

"Well, I am very sorry to hear that. My condolences to the family." He looked back at Seth and Filoh and nodded. "We have a rigid time frame to meet or we would stay for the funeral tomorrow. Please tell the family we appreciated Everett's help and advice when we met him, and we will be praying for the family."

"Talk in town is that you are going clear up to Ogallala and back on horses," the boy said.

"Yes we are."

"Sounds kinda silly to me to do that with the highway right next to the river all the way."

"Well, our mother required it in the will so we are doing it."

The boy was silent a moment, then blurted, "Dad didn't leave a will."

"Pardon me for asking, but was he feeling poorly?"

The boy shook his head. "Not that any of us knew about." He looked out at the horses and men standing in the shade of the Dutch Elm tree. "I'd like to go with you. Get out of this town."

Richard snapped his head up, disturbed by the boy's demeanor. "Well—I thank you for the offer but we are on a schedule and we already have one more than we bargained for."

"I've got a horse and saddle and I know the river for a ways."

"I expect you do but I must say no at this time," Richard said, his head bobbing as the words tumbled out. He extended his hand. "Goodbye."

The boy took his hand. "My name's Ezra—After Ezra Taft Benson."

"You a Mormon?"

The boy nodded. "Does that matter?"

"No son, it does not. Good bye again." Richard stepped off the porch and walked like he was in a trance across the grass and sidewalk.

"What took you so long?" Seth said.

"Everett Williams is dead. Jumped in front of a hundred car wheat train."

Seth whistled. "That would do it."

"Apparently it did," Filoh said. "As much as I disliked what he talked about at the Grange meeting I don't like to think about a man ending his days in such a manner."

"You'd know about it for a minute or two before you did it, wouldn't you?" Seth said.

"Like most any other kind of suicide," Richard said. "You think about it, you plan it, and then you do it."

Seth cocked his chin, stuck his tongue between his teeth, "Yeah, but you'd have to wonder about the impact." He had wondered about alcohol poisoning when he saw the bottom of a bottle many times during his episodes. Another few drinks and he could erase the memory of a lifetime. Dying unconscious in an alcoholic coma seemed preferable to leaping in front of a twenty-ton locomotive.

"I've seen cows hit by trains," Filoh said. "It ain't a pretty sight,"

"The boy wants to come with us."

"What'd you tell him?"

Richard shook his head. "I told him we are on a schedule and need to get moving."

"We can't be pickin' up everybody's strays. We've already got one. Let's get some new reins and get on down the road."

"Humph," Filoh snorted. "I ain't no stray. I'm a educator."

THE SMELL OF LEATHER and gun oil greeted them when Seth opened the door of the Western Shop. "That's a good smell now, isn't it?"

Filoh closed the door and looked at the lock and hardware on it. "Isn't that the cat's meow," he said. "Keep out the whole durn Mexican Army."

"What makes you think the Mexican Army wants anything in here?" Seth said.

Filoh bobbed his head. "Don't know that they do. I'm just sayin'."

Seth spoke to the clerk. "Need some new reins."

"Back here, gentlemen. What kind do you want?"

"Kind?"

"We've got them all. Poly, laced, braided, split leather, flat cotton."

"Oh for cryin' out loud. Three for horses and one for a mule."

The clerk laid out three sets of reins. "What do you need them for?"

"Steering the horse is the first goal," Seth said. "Next we like to tie them to something in a hurry if we need to."

"I'd suggest the braided cotton reins. Tougher than a boot."

"Look at these," Richard said. "Royal King Braided Flat Cotton Split reins."

Seth picked up a pair, shook his head. "Next thing you know they'll be braiding gold and silver strands in 'em."

"How long has it been since you bought reins?" the clerk asked.

"Forever."

"Leather rots if not taken care of. These last forever."

"We don't need forever. A few years will do." He handed the split leather reins to the clerk. He had always handled leather and somehow cotton just didn't smack of real reins to him. "I'll take four sets of these."

"Good choice. What else do you need?"

Seth shook his head. "That's it."

They moved back to the front counter. "What are folks around here thinking about the Keystone pipeline?" Richard said.

The clerk looked up from writing on the receipt. "Boy—you can get an argument on either side of it."

"What's your opinion?"

"Me? I think it would be good for business. Give our young kids something to do besides farm. We're getting so good at farming we don't need much help anymore. The kids have to go to cities to get work. I think more would stay if we had it."

Filoh put his hand flat on the counter. "It'd kill everything in its path, including the Ogallala aquifer."

"And that's the other side of it."

"The farmers are killing the soil and water and air with their damn poisons and now a giant corporation wants to pump oil through the aquifer."

"You know, people use that argument, but before white men got here there were millions of buffalo and thousands of horses and other animals that left their shit and dead bodies all over the land and in the water. The Pawnee used to leave their river camps because the area got too full of crap. Nature took care of it. When they came back in a year or so, the place was green and ready for another beating. I don't see the chemicals and pipeline as anything different than what they used to do. It's just that we have reporters and organizations firing up the debate. Hell—the Pawnee's used to scalp 'em. That shut them up."

"So you are up for a scalping party?" Richard asked.

"No. I don't mean that. But I'd sure like to see some common sense about it and relate the pipeline to a modern way of life. We're not going to go back to burning cow chips and using candles."

Richard sucked in a deep breath, his forehead wrinkled; he straightened up and rolled his shoulders. "I am sure the debate will continue."

"You don't have to worry about it, you're traveling through."

"How'd you know that?"

"Word spreads in a small town. I'm surprised there isn't a crowd standin' around."

"There might be if we don't get outta here," Seth said. "Do you take credit cards?" He pulled out his wallet and handed the clerk a credit card, which he proceeded to swipe. The clerk looked at the machine and swiped it again. He looked up and smiled.

"It's rejected."

"What—the card?"

"Yes sir."

"I don't believe it."

"I can try it again. I've tried it twice."

"Try it again, please."

Seth stared at the screen. REJECTED. "Well I'll be damned. Richard…look at this."

Richard's eyes narrowed. "Something is wrong."

"You got that right. Get on the phone to Harvey at the bank and see what's goin' on."

Richard stepped outside to get enough bars on his cell phone to make the call. While he waited in the mid-morning sun for the connection, the sounds of a small town drifted across the parking lot. Cars starting, a horn honked, people shouting hellos and slamming car doors. Then Harvey Freeman, manager of Cass County Bank uttered his, "Hello, Richard."

"Morning, Harvey. Seth and I are in Columbus and our credit card has been rejected. Thought you could clear that up for us."

"I sure can. Give me a minute."

Richard let his eyes settle on two old men sitting on a bench in front of the courthouse. The Dutch Elm trees had let the morning sun seep through and the still air had heated up and now they pulled themselves forward on the bench and pushed with their arms to get upright. They stood, weaving for a moment, then shuffled to another bench in the shade, the Denim overalls flapping against their legs. Richard smiled.

Harvey came back on the line. "Richard? I see the problem here. The check from Houston Enterprises into your ranch account bounced so there was no payment on this account. I can't legally authorize the use until the system works it out."

"Harvey," Richard said. "You know we're good for it. We only brought the one credit card and we need it functioning."

"I know, I know. But I can't override the computer system for three days. They'll have my head if I do that."

"Why would Houston send in a bad check?"

"Can't answer that. I don't think they're having any problems."

"Their money pays a substantial part of our monthly operating expenses. I'll call them."

"I wouldn't do that, Richard. Give it another three days to regulate itself and then we can do something if it's warranted."

"Three days?"

"Yeah. That should do it."

Richard shoved his lower lip over his upper lip and stared at the sidewalk. "We should be in Central City or Grand Island by that time—if we don't run out of money. I'll call you from there. Get this resolved, Harvey, please."

"I'm sure this is just a computer glitch and it will solve itself shortly. Are you boys having a good trip?"

"Besides some short term disappointment, a couple of near disasters, and dragging Filoh Smith along with us, it has been interesting to say the least."

"Filoh Smith is with you?"

"He is."

"That's quite a trip for a ninety year old. How's he doing?"

"Other than hauling sand into the tent every trip he makes outside at night, it appears he's doing as well as I am."

"You're not used to the saddle, are you?"

"No. And I doubt I will ever be. Please take care of that card business and thanks for looking into it, Harvey."

"You boys take care now."

Richard found Seth looking at saddles when he came back inside. He looked up.

"Solved?"

Richard shook his head. "He said three days. How are you doing for cash money?"

"I've got a couple hundred I suppose."

"Pay for the reins with cash and we will call Harvey later when he gets this thing straightened out."

"What's to straighten?"

"Houston Enterprises' check bounced."

"Yikes. That's…

"…I know."

"Call Houston."

"Think I'll do that. Don't buy a new saddle."

Seth smiled. "I like this padded one. It would put me on a par with your padded tractor seat."

"You don't need par. You need incentive."

"Go call and quit botherin' me."

WHEN SETH SAW RICHARD'S face he knew something was wrong. "What is it?"

"Houston says their check did not bounce. They called operations at the bank and operations said the check was received and processed."

"Some damn bureaucratic screw-up then."

"Probably."

What'll we do if it doesn't clear up?"

Richard shrugged. Inside he could feel the tightening of his gut. Images of the years they had struggled to make ends meet paraded through his mind.

The plot thickens

THEY FOLLOWED 11TH ST. to the railroad tracks, turned down the frontage road out to the river road. The riders fell into the now familiar trail procedure of nose to tail, the sun washing them from behind, the dull clunk of equipment rattle mixed with the snorts and clops of horse strides as each man delved into his inner mind to eat up the time in the saddle.

Richard twisted in the saddle to move the sore spot to a new location. He was sure he had a blister on his butt. While he slumped in the saddle, the straight furrows the tractor travelled to plant corn imposed itself like a movie on his mind. He could feel the air conditioning of the cab and hear the satellite radio give out the information he needed to do a day's farming. Mae had to know it would be hard on him. He wished he could talk with her, figure out if there wasn't some other way to resolve her concerns about the Barrett ranch instead of this 100-year-old travel style. Endure it? Yes, he could but it was taking all he had so far and he couldn't even see the end of it.

Seth stood in the stirrups and pulled the new reins up to his nose. They smelled fresh from the tannery. *What is it about new leather that puts a sparkle in my eye?* He remembered his Cub Scout troop visiting a tannery where the smell of the chemicals gagged him. But the finished product—ah, that was different. And his first leather holster that held the Colt .45 single action revolver—same smell, same feeling. It was a ranch smell. Lifted his spirits a notch.

Filoh looked down at the ground passing by. He hadn't been atop a mule for more than fifty years. He didn't trust a horse much and carried some old wounds in his left leg and right arm from being kicked. They were big, strong, simple-minded animals and while he had harnessed and groomed them for work, he didn't trust them one minute. He hated being so distrustful of them, but by damn, experience either taught you or not and at his age he couldn't abide another kicking or biting.

HARVEY FREEMAN CLOSED THE door and shut the blinds on his private office at Cass County Bank. He looked at the clock and sat in the ox-blood red leather chair that had supported the backsides of seven bank presidents before him. He dialed the number from memory.

"Good morning, Harvey," Klete Dixon said.

"Hello, Klete. You should remove your caller ID so you can get some surprises some times."

"I don't like surprises. What's up?"

"The boys have bumped into the obstacle," he said, leaning forward to put his elbows on the desk. He brushed some paper lint onto the floor with his free hand.

"Where?"

"Columbus."

"How long can the obstacle be in place?"

"Could take several days to get through all the channels."

"But it will clear up?"

"Yes. Mistakes happen you know."

"How I know that." It was silent for a moment. "I have other diversions in the works. Don't let Houston get a black mark though, we need to keep our credit rating up there for the bond ratings."

Harvey nodded, distracted by a knock on his door. "Board meeting next Wednesday at 7:00 here at the bank. You'll be here won't you?"

The knock was repeated.

"Yeah," Klete said.

"Gotta go, Klete. Bye." He cradled the phone and said: "Come in."

Loretta Davidson entered wearing a skirt that was just a hint too high and a whisper too tight and he let his eyes remind him of the advantages of being president of the bank.

She turned the bolt lock on the door. "You asked to see these files?" She laid the files in front of him and stood a little bent with the fingers of each hand spread wide, the tips resting on the desk. A drift of perfume hung in the air while his eyes rested on the offered view of her cleavage.

He pushed his chair back and patted his thigh. She smiled, came around the desk and sat on his lap. Their first kiss of the day was always a turn on for him. With his left hand he reached up and under her skirt. No panties. This was a good sign.

KLETE DIXON WAS THE largest shareholder in Houston Enterprises. He foresaw the need to move large volumes of grain to distant points for manufacture and distribution before neighboring farmers knew the agricultural picture was changing from local production, manufacture, and consumption to a nation-wide and world-wide distribution system.

Houston Enterprises installed a grain crusher that allowed them to ship 25% more grain in a railroad car. The pyramid of profits from industrialized farming, to gigantic machine harvesting, to rapid distribution gave the stock, known as HED on Nasdaq, a huge advantage over the individual farmer. The profits from cash distributions and appreciation of the stock gave Klete Dixon a bank balance and financial statement that commanded attention in the statewide banking community and an element of control that was perceived or actual, depending on whom you talked to.

Cass County Bank, on whose board Dixon served as a director, held about half of its capitalization in a cash float and a speedy in and out cash distribution system that allowed its balance sheet to shine at any given audit moment. It seldom had more than 35% of its capital loaned out and made a good profit with the purchase of government securities and bonds with the remainder. It had re-entered the farm lending business after the crash of '86 to '91 but not before changing officers and bringing in Harvey Freeman, a classmate of Dixon's, to run it.

There was some local talk about the history of Freeman's association with First National Bank in York, Nebraska and why he had left there, but Cass County Bank had prospered under his leadership and guidance. Stockholders and board members were pleased quarterly when they opened the mail and looked at their cash distribution.

CORT ROCKED FROM ONE foot to the other as he stood before Klete Dixon's desk. Cort could hear what Klete was saying but his side of the talk made no sense to him. Klete motioned for him to sit down, then hung up the phone.

"I want you to run this check over to the First National Bank in York and deposit it. Be sure to get a deposit receipt and bring it back to me. Don't take a company car, use your own. Call me when you've deposited it."

Klete handed the check and deposit slip to Cort. "And don't tell anybody where you're going or when you'll be back. Got that?"

Cort nodded. "Yes sir."

THE TELLER RAISED HER eyebrows as she looked at the check she held in both hands. She pushed a button under the counter and smiled at Cort. "I need approval."

Cort nodded.

A middle-aged woman came out of an office and looked at the check. Then at Cort. Then back at the check. She nodded to the teller who smiled and ran the check through the processing machine and handed the deposit slip to Cort. "Anything else we can do for you today, Mr. Dixon?"

Cort started to put on his hat but stopped and smiled at her. "I'm not Mr. Dixon." He turned and walked out the swinging glass doors.

No sense letting her know who I am. I'm just running errands.

At Burger King he rolled down his window, ordered lunch and ate it on the way back to Plattsmouth. While chewing he stretched his neck from left to right. It sounded like popping corn. He pulled over at Beaver Lake, shut off the engine, reclined the seat, tipped his hat over his eyes, crossed his arms across his chest and was asleep in moments.

He didn't think he could run any faster when four knocks on the window glass pulled him out of his dream. Sheriff Bud Pinsky, one hand hooked in his equipment belt looked out over the lake, waiting for the window to roll down.

"Cort—what the hell you doin' down here?"

"Sleeping if you hadn't wakened me."

"Expect you were." Bud rubbed the side of his face. "You read the sign?"

"Bud—it isn't like the parking lot is crowded. I think the county can spare one parking space for a tired driver."

Bud moved his tongue around over his teeth and looked back and forth over the almost empty parking lot. "Where you been?"

"York."

"What the hell's in York, some honey?"

"Could be." Cort smiled.

"You headed back to the ranch?"

Cort nodded.

Bud nodded and clapped a hand over the top of the window frame. "She have a friend?"

"Something wrong with your wife?"

"No. You know how it is with us guys; we like to taste some forbidden fruit from time to time. Ask her if she has a friend." He tilted his head up. "What's her name? I might know her?"

"I doubt it."

Bud ran his tongue over his lips. "Try me."

Cort fumbled. "I was on an errand. No girl involved."

"Hmmm," Bud said, his head bobbing up and down. "What kind of errand?"

"What's with the fifth degree interrogation, Bud?"

"That's my job."

"I had an errand. I did it. I'm tired. I'm in a handicapped parking spot on a parking lot with 75 parking spaces in it and two other cars. If you're gonna ticket me do it and let me get back to sleep." He sat up. "I'll move the damn truck."

Bud smiled. "Won't be necessary. There are five other handicapped spots." He looked at the sky. "Doesn't look like many people will be coming out here today. Don't make a habit of parking in them. It irritates me."

Cort started the truck, backed out and put it in a regular parking space that read 12 hour parking allowed.

Bud, a faint smile on his face, waved when he left.

"The son-of-a-bitch," Cort said.

BUD REACHED FOR THE car radio, pushed the button. "Sheriff Pinsky."

"Did you find him?"

"Of course."

"Where is he?"

"Napping at Beaver Lake."

"How the hell did you find him there?"

"The GPS you stuck on his truck. Led me right to him."

"He tell you anything?"

"Nothing. Let on it was a girl he had gone to see."

"Did you pry any?"

"Some. He was close mouthed."

"Good. How about Ginny?"

"I'm gonna let the check and credit card thing work for a couple of days and then I'll go out there. Maybe she'll be more receptive."

"Keep your pants on. Our first job is getting the Barrett ranch before fall."

Bud nodded. He checked traffic both ways and pulled out on Highway 75. "I know the priorities."

"Just keep them in mind."

"You got it, Mr. Dixon."

The radio went dead.

Chapter 8

GINNY PICKED UP THE PHONE. "Ginny Houston."

"Hi Ginny. Serena. Got a minute?"

"Sure."

"My house is being sold and I have to be out of here by the end of June. I don't know what I'm going to do or where I'm going. I was wondering if I could stay out at the ranch while the men are gone until I get things settled."

"Oh my god, Serena. You're having to move?"

"Yeah. Things come in threes so I'm waiting for the other shoe to drop."

"Don't look too hard. You might find it."

"It'd only be for a month or so until I find another job."

"Oh, Serena, I'm sure you can come out there."

"I'd be eternally grateful, Ginny."

"I'm sure we can work it out. Can't let a future sister-in-law go wanting a place to put her head."

"Not close to that yet."

"You will. Richard's a farmer. He makes decisions based on the seasons."

"Well, so far, it's been no planting, no harvesting, no marketing."

"I know, but he loves you. I can see it in his eyes."

"He doesn't tell you?"

"Richard doesn't do that. Seth would tell me in a minute, but Richard holds on to those thoughts. You must have noticed he's pretty deliberate."

"Oh yes. And I love that about him, but it has been two years now and I'm not a spring chicken anymore."

"You're the prettiest girl in town..."

"Over fifty..."

"You could say that…"

"Unmarried…"

"That too.

"Ginny, I'm not asking to move out to the ranch to trap Richard. I hope you don't think that. It's just that I need a place in a week and I don't know how long I'll need it so I don't want to sign a lease on a place here in Plattsmouth and then find out I need to move to Fremont or Omaha for a job."

"We women need to stick together. I'm sure it won't bother anyone. But I've gotta tell you some weird things have gone on out there."

"Like what?"

SERENA KICKED THE DOOR shut on her Ford pickup and walked up the stairs of the porch without spilling a drop. She stuck her middle finger on the doorbell and stood back. Ginny opened the door.

"Wow—coffee."

"Mochas," Serena said.

"Better yet."

"I thought you could use a pick-me-up about this time of day with all the ranch work."

"The kids are out doing the work. I'm playing residential supervisor."

"Nice title."

"Title is good. Pay is lousy. Thanks for the mocha."

"Too early for wine."

"Let me show you the room."

"I don't need much. Just a couple of weeks or a month and I can locate somewhere."

Ginny put her hand on Serena's arm. "I hope you don't have to leave Plattsmouth."

"Me too. But I'm short for retirement. I need to teach another five years and if it can't be Plattsmouth, then it has to be somewhere in Nebraska."

"There are so many towns that would hire you but you'd be so far away."

Serena wrinkled her brow and nodded. "That's the way the cookie crumbles."

Ginny sucked on the straw. "Hmmm good. Thanks." She swung the door open. "Here's the guest room."

"This will be wonderful." She turned to Ginny. "You don't think the men would be upset if I camped in here for a little bit?"

"They left me in charge and I say it's just fine. Besides, they probably won't be back by the time you're gone."

"It would be great to have a little female companionship too."

Ginny smiled and nodded. "I don't stay out here all the time. Will you be okay staying here alone?"

"Been alone for the last eight years."

Ginny sipped her mocha, swallowed, and looked Serena in the eyes. "Can you handle a gun?"

"A gun? Judas—do I need a gun?"

"Just what if you did?"

"I've shot .22s but nothing big." Serena winced. "Would I need something big?"

"Maybe. I don't know." Ginny slid the mocha aside, put her elbows on the table and took a deep breath. "Let me tell you what's happened."

DAWSON SLAMMED THE DOOR and threw his hat on the couch.

"How many times do I need to remind you not to slam the door," Ginny said. "It is a solid door and it is heavy and it doesn't take a huge push like your hollow core doors at home. At fourteen that is something that should stick with you or God help you in later life."

"Mom. No big deal. I'll remember next time."

Bucky snorted. "How many next times?"

"Oh shut up." Dawson said. "The rendering plant guy came and picked up the dead cow."

"Good. I'm glad to get that out of there. Did he have any ideas about it?"

"The driver shook his head. He said he just drives the truck and picks up the dead animals. He don't solve problems."

"Doesn't."

"Yeah—doesn't."

"Did he take the head too?"

"Of course, Mom." Dawson looked at her out of the side of his eyes. He grabbed three Oreos from the cookie dish.

Ginny tilted her head and looked down at him. "Dawson, it's close to supper time. Serena is making chili for everyone tonight."

"Is Serena gonna live here with us?" Bucky said.

"Just till she finds a place."

Dawson pulled out a chair and sat in it backwards. "I like chili. Is she going to make sourdough pretzels too?"

"I don't know. But it's good to have a new cook for a change."

"Better than macaroni and cheese again," Bucky said.

"I thought you liked that?"

"I do Mom, but three nights in a row gets a little boring." He twisted in his chair. "It's neat having a teacher living with us. I can get all the answers to the tests for next year. It'll be a breeze."

"She doesn't teach your grade, crazy," Dawson said.

"Yeah, but she'll know the answers."

Ginny put bowls on the table. "Please put these at the places and get silverware for everyone, kids. And pick something to drink."

"Can I have one of Uncle Richard's beers?" Dawson said.

"Absolutely not. You have another four years to go before you even think of that young mister."

"Crap—then I'll have water."

"Dawson Houston!"

"I'm sorry, Mom. It just popped out."

"If you don't think of it, it won't pop out. Do you use that with your friends?"

Dawson looked at the floor. He nodded.

Bucky suddenly sat upright. "I wonder where Uncle Richard and Uncle Seth are now? They're getting to camp out every night. Cool."

Serena came into the kitchen dressed for cooking: old jeans and a Levi shirt with sleeves rolled up. "I'm ready."

Ginny smiled. "Ok. Dawson's going to cut the meat, Bucky the onions and tomatoes, and Valerie's going to measure out the spices. It's a team effort and you're the captain."

AFTER SUPPER AND AFTER the kids were in bed and the dishes done, Ginny and Serena sat in the living room, each with a glass of wine.

"The key to the gun safe is on top of the clock. You need to know where stuff is if you're going to be here with us. You never know when you might be the one that needs to get to it first."

"You're scaring the hell out of me, Ginny."

"Don't want to scare you. Just want you to be aware and alert to the possibility."

"Do you want to show me now?"

"No. Alcohol and firearms don't mix. Tomorrow." She lifted her glass. "Cheers."

"Cheers."

My gawd—have I jumped out of the frying pan into the fire?

Klete Dixon—Citizen of the Year

CRAIG JAMISON ADJUSTED THE microphone before addressing the crowd assembled in the school auditorium. He pulled out his notes, unfolded them, placed them on the lectern and pressed out the creases.

He looked out over the audience and smiled. "Good day to you folks. We're here today to honor a person as Citizen of the Year. This award used to be just for Plattsmouth but five years ago it was expanded to all of Cass County. Over the last seventy years, almost as old as the Korn Karnival, the citizens of this area have chosen a person of high integrity, of bountiful good will, and one dedicated to the preservation of our way of life who has donated time, talent and capital to the benefit of this county."

Craig droned on until he lifted his voice and made hand motions that signaled his intention to name the person they all knew he was going to announce.

"This year's recipient is none other than our good friend and neighbor, Mr. Klete Dixon. Please come up here, Klete."

As Klete strode to the platform Craig stepped aside and handed him a bronze statue of an old fashioned one bottom plow. It weighted ten pounds and Klete pretended he could hardly lift it when it landed in his hands. Smiles and applause burst out all around.

"Thank you, Mr. Jamison. May I call you Craig?" Klete said.

"You have for fifty years."

Klete Dixon nodded; his smile acknowledged their friendship.

"Fellow citizens of Cass County—I thank you for this honor bestowed on me today for past contributions." He hefted the statue and looked down at it. "This is not the end of my efforts for this county, nor the middle. It is the beginning. It is my intention to position Cass County as the premier corn-producing county in the state by introduction of enhanced farming methods and re-filling the Ogallala Aquifer so that future generations can benefit from this tremendous lake we have under our feet. Thank you and enjoy the rest of today. Remember to stop by our booth outside and get a free corn-dog, courtesy of Dixon Enterprises, and a free Coke courtesy of Coca-Cola."

Craig clasped Dixon's arm, smiled and shook his hand. "Klete Dixon, ladies and gentlemen." More applause. "My senatorial booth is right next to the corn-dog stand so stop by and register to vote and vote for Jamison in the primary. I intend to represent the good people of this county in Washington D.C. as your new senator come November." At that he turned off the microphone.

"How'd it go?" Klete said.

"Good. I'd say you cemented any cracks."

Klete nodded. "Heard anything from the Sheriff?"

Craig shook his head.

"Let me know as soon as you do, okay?"

"You bet. And thanks for your contribution to my campaign. I'm beholden to you."

Klete looked around. "I've got to get rid of this thing, it weighs a ton."

"What's next?" Craig said.

"The Barrett ranch."

"Of course."

Filoh has never died before

"BOYS," SETH SAID. "We've got ourselves about thirty miles to go today. I don't want to hear any complaining, saddle sores, hungry stuff—none of that."

Richard mounted his horse. "What's in thirty miles?"

"Central City will be nearby."

Filoh snorted. "And what's so good about that?"

"Central. Just could be the middle of the first half. How's that grab you?"

"I have been miserable before but nothing like this," Richard said. "My legs are going to separate in the middle."

Seth chuckled. "I'm sure Mom didn't expect it to be easy."

Richard turned in the saddle. "She knew how old we would be when she wrote that. Grandpa Melzer was a young man when he undertook this journey." He guided his horse around a puddle. "Plus—he was used to the saddle."

"What'd I say about complainin'?" Seth said.

Richard frowned. "I am just saying."

MID-MORNING SETH CALLED a halt to the caravan near a bridge that featured a bold sign stating 287th Avenue. He dismounted with ease and left Richard and Filoh contemplating how to get down from their horses with the least pain. Once on the ground they walked in small circles, hands on hips bending forward and backward and kicking their feet out from time to time to restore blood flow. The sound of an occasional truck passing on the bridge was all that disturbed the peace of the river.

Here the river narrowed and ran unbraided by sandbars and small islands, the dominant sound the gentle washing of the river against the bank. On horseback the sound of the four animals and equipment clanging was constant.

Seth had kindled a small fire, the coffee pot jammed into the side of it, steam bursting out of the spout. The horses nibbled grass and the three men sat on the south bank under a shade of trees on the sandy beach blowing on their coffee.

Filoh lifted his head and looked around. "I feel like my warranty is running out."

Seth chuckled. "You got it in writing?"

"What?"

"The warranty."

"Smart ass." He sucked in the cooled top layer of coffee. "I've been tired and I've been sore and I've been scared stiff. But this is getting to me. I am beginning to feel old."

"Hell—you are old. Any man past ninety is plain old."

Richard set his coffee on the sand. "You weren't old when you pulled me out of the river."

"No," Filoh pursed his lips, his smile shifting. "My only thought was to get your head up."

"That's what you need now. If it is any consolation to you I have pains I didn't know a human could have," Richard said.

Seth looked up at Filoh. "You think you're hurting, or are you dyin'?"

"Well—I'm not dyin'. Well—I could be. I ain't never died before so I don't know what it feels like comin' up on it."

"I've had friends die and there were so many different signs leadin' up to it and so many ways they either recognized them or shoved 'em off." He lifted his head and looked at the river. "I'm not sure anybody can know until they're right up against it. Rich, you remember Clarence Brown? I was talking with him on his cell phone in the hospital as he was dyin' and he was bitchin' because the nurse wanted to take his cell phone away from him."

Richard nodded. "Walt Gibbons was real calm about it. Said his daughters couldn't grasp it but death was just a part of life and he was ready to go."

Filoh worked his way to his feet, walked over to the river, threw his coffee grounds into the water. "Take that."

"You polluting the river on purpose?" Seth said.

"Given' it a shot of caffeine. It's already dyin'."

Richard turned on his side and with one hand on the ground pushed himself to a standing position. "How far along would you say it is?"

Filoh looked up and down the river. "It depends on where you're standin'. Right here it looks pretty healthy."

"So what's your point about coming on this trip? You worried about the whole river or just us?"

"My real goal," Filoh said straightening up, "is to get you boys to lead the campaign to quit poisoning the country. You gotta' re-evaluate this whole farming business to have farming survive. You can't castrate the bull and have any more calves." He shook his head. "If you'd promise me that I'll take leave of this outfit in Central City and let you go on in peace."

"Peace it would be, too," Seth said. "I'm not sure you can make it past Central City. You look like death on a cracker."

"What's that supposed to mean?"

"Just pullin' your leg. We can get you a bus ticket back to Plattsmouth."

"I'm not sayin' I'm goin' back. But I might be willin'."

"Duly noted." Seth looked at Richard. "You ok with that?"

Richard pushed his bottom lip up over his upper and nodded his head. "Yes."

The River

They sat on the bank and the river went by. It was making sounds to itself and now it made sounds to them. It was the first time they had divorced themselves from other things and listened and they understood what the river was saying. The Platte is an old river. It has seen many things, lived through many things, but remained constant in a real way. It incorporated them traveling along its banks and nestled them near its bosom. The river had a proprietary interest in them and a lesson to instill. It had done that with Grandpa Melzer and it would with his grandsons.

Silver Creek

"LOOKEE THEM COYOTES," Filoh said pointing into the brush. Two coyotes stood in the shadows, ears forward, alert. They were so still Richard had to blink twice to pick them out.

"They're followin' us, waitin' for Filoh to kick the bucket. Get some fresh meat," Seth said.

"Pshush," Filoh muttered.

"They do not look aggressive," Richard said.

"They ain't. Just curious."

"Or rabid," Seth threw in.

"If they was rabid they'd be comin' in now," Filoh said.

"Why aren't they movin' then?"

"Throw somethin' at 'em."

Seth picked up a bent cottonwood stick and threw it like a boomerang. The coyotes broke and disappeared.

"Real dangerous, ain't they?" Filoh said.

"That's why Richard brought the .30-30. To make sure we die of old age, not from rabies or turtle bites."

"Let's move this horse parade," Richard said. "I have enjoyed about as much of this as I can stand."

Holding to the north bank of the river they pushed on through small trees on trails barely wide enough to see let alone for horses to walk. Silver Creek was their destination for lunch but washed out banks, sweepers, and frequent river crossings hampered riverside travel.

Seth turned in the saddle. "Wonder if Grandpa Melzer had to cross this river so many times?"

Filoh straightened out. "He had nothin' but wilderness to ride in. No fences, no fields. He could ride anywhere he wanted to. "

"Let's go into Silver Creek for lunch," Richard said.

"We need to be careful of how many times we wander into the towns along the way. You recall we were only to go into towns when necessary, not for lunch or whiskey," Seth said.

"Or women," Richard added.

"Or women."

A faint smile worked its way over Richard's face. "You expect to ever see Martha again?"

Seth turned, returning the smile and nodded his head. "I do believe I will."

"I thought as much." Richard said and evened the reins in his hands. "We could go into town tonight and you could call her. We need to get some money anyway somewhere along the line."

"I'm getting concerned about our time frame, here," Seth said. "Might be we could spare an hour to get money and I could call. "He took out his cell phone, held it steady against the back and forth and side-to-side movement in the saddle. "No bars. No service here."

Clouds slipped in, covering up the sunlight and turning the blues to grays. Each man looked to the trail ahead of him immersed in his own thoughts. Richard thought about the advances in travel since Grandpa Melzer rode these banks: highways, cars, airboats, railroads, airplanes. Always travel became faster, more comfortable, more secure and more expensive. Once a good horse cost fifty dollars, now it cost that much for a tank of gas. And an airplane ticket would cost twice that to get you to the same place in a third of the time. What did the speed up cost and whom did it benefit? It certainly allowed a man to get more done in a day and it was more comfortable for the people involved, but did it make them happier or healthier or wealthier?

It was soul satisfying to pick his way along the bank of the river and feel akin to the country and the river without the asphalt, cars, noise, and smells of driving. Progress was measured in yards and short miles. Maybe the Barrett Ranch should promote horseback rides along the Platte River. Leave it to the kids. Seth and I have farming and cattle raising to do.

As they neared Silver Creek Filoh pulled up. "What's that horrible smell?"

Seth and Richard stopped their horses, sniffed the air.

"Something dead maybe?" Richard said.

Seth shook his head. "Smells like vegetation rotting, not an animal."

They could make out the buildings at Silver Creek, a little railroad and farming community and steered their horses on the north bank to come up to the town where the river almost touched it.

"Let's try for some money here," Richard said.

Seth nodded, and Filoh, eager to stretch his legs anywhere off the horse, bobbed his head.

As they came off the river two large rectangular ponds were in front of them.

"There's your smell," Seth said. "Sewage holding ponds. Lagoons they call them."

"That's better than in the river," Filoh said standing in the stirrups.

"What about when it floods?" Richard said.

"Pond floods, and in the river it goes."

"Look how green the banks are," Richard said.

"Anything turns green if you feed it sewage sludge. But when high water hits, those ponds are gonna be swamped."

"Well that isn't a farmer problem. That's a people and civilization problem."

"Dang right," Filoh said. "But when you add the farmer pollution you get a chemical mix that kills everything. The biggest problem is that once it enters the river it gets carried downstream and the original polluter don't see it anymore. He thinks the river is clean. His stuff is gone. The poor guy downstream and in the Gulf of Mexico—he's the recipient of everything dumped into it upstream."

"Nobody dumps it in—"

"Of course not. They let it seep or wash or slide or get caught in overflow but it's in the river either way. Do you see that?" Filoh said, his face twisted in a scowl.

"Get off your high horse, Filoh. We get the picture," Seth said.

"By golly, that's good. That's what I'm here for."

"You going to take up a collection after that sermon?" Richard said.

"Just enough to get me a ticket home. This mule is killing me little by little."

Seth picked up on the ticket home. "How about we go into Central City and get you a nice soft bus seat back to Plattsmouth?"

"If you promise me you'll keep vigilant on up the river. We gotta know how far up they're doing this stuff."

They tied their horses to a pipe rack around a commercial propane tank, stretched and walked into the service station.

"Howde," Seth said. "Where's the bank in town?"

"Those your horses?" the clerk said.

Seth turned and looked. He nodded. "They okay there for a few minutes?"

"If they don't pull the pipe apart, it's just plastic pipe."

"We don't intend to stay long. Looking for a bank."

The attendant pointed across the highway. "Farmers State Bank is down yonder a block. Can't miss it on the right hand side."

Richard looked at the restroom key hanging on a nail with a broken crescent wrench attached to it with a chain. "Anybody ever walk off with that in their pocket?"

"Not yet. Did before I rigged it that way, though."

"Can I borrow it?"

"You gonna buy something?"

"Well—" Richard said. "We don't need gas or oil, but we could take some gum and…"

"…And chewin' tobacco," Filoh threw in.

Richard opened his wallet. "My last ten dollar bill."

"Is there a restaurant open here?"

"Vine Street Café just down the block on the river side."

"Decent food?"

"You won't die from it."

"That's good enough for us."

The attendant handed the restroom key to Richard. He hefted it then slipped the wrench in his rear pocket and limped to the door.

Seth smiled. "Hang on to that thing when you flush or we'll pick you up down at the sewage pond."

Richard waved as he passed in front of the glass wall.

AT THE BANK, RICHARD was livid. "What do you mean the account is on hold?"

The bank teller shook his head. "I don't know why, the request just came back denied. Said the account was on hold."

"Would you please call the manager."

A tall man as spare as a willow sprout came out of a glass enclosed office and offered his hand. "Hello, I'm the bank president, may I help you?"

Richard explained his problem and the president looked to the teller with raised eyebrows. "You checked for sure on the hold?" he said. The teller nodded. "Some other bank has placed a hold on your account. It is a routine matter and could probably be cleared up with a couple of phone calls. Have you had this problem before with large checks?"

Richard shook his head. "No. We had our credit card refused in Fremont. Same kind of shadowy deal. Could you place a call or two on this? We're running short of cash and we have a scheduling problem for this trip."

"Sure. Please come into my office."

After several phone calls the president leaned back in his chair. "I don't have any quick good news for you. A bank in York has placed a hold on your account until they can clear a large check. Are you aware of that?"

"No. We didn't write any and I can't imagine why Ginny would have. Did they say the amount?"

"No, just the hold. I'm sure it is a short-term thing. Usually we clear a check in a day or two now. I wouldn't worry about it. When will you be where you can check again?"

"We should be in Columbus tonight and Grand Island tomorrow or the next day." And as an afterthought added, "If things go the way they're supposed to and of late they haven't been."

"I'm sure it will be cleared up by then."

"Can you give us a couple more minutes—let me call our sister who's managing the ranch in our absence—maybe get to the bottom of this?"

"Sure. Go ahead. I'll leave you to talk with her and just let me know when you're done and I'll see what we can do otherwise." He stood up, walked out of the office and closed the door behind him.

Richard dialed the ranch number. Ginny picked up on the third ring. "Ginny Houston."

"We're in a little village called Silver Creek at the Farmers State Bank. We've run short on cash and find the ranch account has a hold on it. Do you have any knowledge about that?"

"No. Don't even know what that is."

"A bank in York has put a hold on it for some large check is what they're telling us. Written any big ones lately?"

"I haven't. Did you authorize Bud Blaha to write any?"

"You would have had to sign them and I don't recall any. You don't recall signing any that either he wrote or you wrote?"

"No. Let me look at the checkbook. Hold on."

Richard put his hand over the receiver. "She's going to look in the check book."

Seth nodded and with a tilt of his head and a lift of his eyebrows noted Filoh in the chair. Filoh's head was tilted to one side, his jaw flopped open. He was asleep.

"Tough on the old timer," Richard said. He took his hand off the phone. "Yes Ginny, I'm here."

"No checks missing and no checks written since you guys left. Something's crazy."

"It does smell a little, doesn't it?"

"Smells a lot. Can you find out from there or do you want me to do some investigating here?"

"No—we'll do it when we get to Grand Island. We can squeak by until then." Richard paused. "Everything okay at the place?"

"Yeah. One new development I hope you can live with. Serena has moved out to the house until she gets a job somewhere and knows where she'll be going. The owner evicted her with short notice." Ginny held her breath. Richard was silent. She then heard him put his hand over the receiver and soft sounds in the background.

"Ginny—I just asked Seth if he was okay with that. He does not want me to make a habit of moving women into the house, but it is okay for now."

Ginny chuckled. "He should talk."

"Now Ginny. Let us not throw the first stone."

"You're right. How's it going other than short of money?"

"Filoh and I are sore to the bone and wishing it was over now. I am sure we have got enough left in us to make it but it gets harder every day. Camping out day after day is not that much fun at our age. Especially since Seth does not drink and Filoh drags enough sand into the tent to fill an hourglass every time he gets up at night."

"You poor guys. Out on a boy scout campout and itching to get home already."

"Anything more on that killed heifer?"

"No," Ginny said, her voice tentative. "Sheriff Pinsky calls every so often to assure me he's working on it but nothing so far. I'm leery of him. Have you ever heard anything bad about him?"

"No," Richard said. "Why?"

"He made a pass at me—actually more than a pass, and I don't like the feeling that our local law is not on our side."

"Can you handle it all right?"

"I think so. At least for now."

"Stay alert. We have got to go now. Thanks for your help on the money problem. We will handle it from this end. Goodbye for now."

"Goodbye Richard. Give Seth and Filoh my best."

Seth opened the office door and the president hurried over. "Thanks for the use of your office and phone. We'll let this sit a day and work it out in Columbus or Grand Island."

"Sorry I couldn't be of more help."

Outside they counted their money. "I think we can make it if Filoh doesn't use up the whisky and chewing tobacco before Columbus."

"I can pay for my own tobaccy," Filoh said. He pulled out five dollars.

"That gives us thirty bucks between us," Seth said. "Don't eat a big meal at the café."

Getting cash

"I DON'T KNOW HOW they make towns this small," Seth said. They ate their lunch sitting on the wooden seats in the Vine Street Café. "Don't seem like enough business to hold anyone here."

"They have a website," Richard said.

"Well, whoop-de-do. And that cures all does it?"

"Does give them a presence on the World Wide Web."

"Ok, but what does your graduating senior do for employment here?"

"Farms," Filoh said. "Or he might clerk in one of these stores."

Seth swallowed. "And how about the girls?"

"They go where the guys are."

"Speakin' of guys, there's the president of the bank sittin' there. I'm gonna have a talk with him." Seth slid out and sauntered over to the booth where the president was sitting with a man.

"S'cuse me," Seth said. "I'm Seth Barrett. You talked with my brother, Richard about gettin' some money a bit ago."

The president looked up. Seth continued. "We aren't poor. We've got lots of money and something fishy is goin' on between the banks and our accounts. Now—we've got a schedule to keep and places to go but I'd like to have some money in my pocket before I leave this berg."

"Mr. Barrett—you have me at a disadvantage. I have no knowledge of your situation and certainly am not participating in anything to do with your accounts." He adjusted the napkin and flatware to be square with the tabletop. "Why don't you come back over to the bank after you've eaten and we'll see if we can't take care of your needs."

Seth nodded. "We'll do that." He turned to go then turned back. "Thank you."

The president nodded. "You're welcome."

Back at his table, Seth slid in and stuck some pulled pork into his mouth. He chewed and looked at Filoh and Richard. Both looked at him expressionless.

"Well—don't that beat all," Filoh said and shook his head.

"Seth," Richard began. "Did it occur to you that you might mess up our goal of getting money in Central City or Grand Island?"

"It's our money. The banking system was put there to make money on our money but they can't hold it back from us. There's more than half a million in the operating account and you know it. I'm not gonna let these backdoor Johnnys make this trip any harder on us than it is already."

Richard looked at him like he was contemplating having him committed to an institution. He decided on silence. Let Seth get rid of the burr under his saddle.

After lunch they followed Sid Porter, President of Farmers State Bank back to his office. Filoh sat on a bench outside the office, arms crossed over his chest looking like an old-fashioned bank guard.

"Gentlemen," Mr. Porter said. "Let's start over."

Seth started. "There's something damn fishy about this bank account business. We haven't done anything of late to have a hold put on our account. There's over half a million dollars in our account and all we need is a few lousy hundred. We fully expect to get that here and now."

"I'm sure we can arrange that. What again is your account number and the name of your bank?"

After verifying the Barrett brothers were substantial members of the Plattsmouth community and carried an impressive monthly balance in their account, Sid Porter wrote out a check request for $500 and called in a teller to cash it.

"So," he began. "You two are brothers and running around camping on the river bank. There must be a story behind this."

"Oh, there is a story all right," Richard said.

Seth interrupted. "What keeps you in a backwater town like this?"

"Came here to prove a theory. I wrote my thesis on it in college." Sid took a sip of coffee. "Man, that's hot." He set the cup down. "I've been working on what I call the generational wealth escape."

Seth looked at Richard. Richard shrugged.

Sid picked up on that and went on. "It's like this. A couple living and working in Silver City raise a family, do well in business or a profession, buy a house, maybe a business location and invest locally. Their children go away to college and then go where there is work: new professions, new opportunities in larger towns. The small towns in Nebraska are losing population. But," he said, wagging his finger, "besides losing population, they are losing wealth. The wealth that the original inhabitants made goes away with the children and it doesn't come back."

Richard perked up. "I think that is what is happening in Plattsmouth. The young people are going to Lincoln or Omaha where the jobs are."

"That's true," Sid said. "Central City's population has gone down several hundred since the last census. It's a common problem of small towns in Nebraska—probably all over the country. The nation has been moving to the big cities and to both coasts in record numbers since 1950."

When Filoh heard that he came in and sat down. Hat in hand, he joined the conversation.

"I don't know what they find in big cities except crime, prejudice, and swindlers," Filoh said.

Sid laughed. "I can see, sir, that you are not a fan of cities."

"I am not. It's the demand of cities that is ruinin' the productive lands of the mid-west."

"How do you mean that?"

"It's as plain as day. Cities don't grow their own food. As they grow they put more demand on farms for crops and animals. The farmers respond by growin' more food faster, usin' chemicals that ruin the land and the water and the air. But everybody's gettin' rich so nobody makes a big enough noise to be heard. Meantime people, birds, fish, animals, everythin' is being destroyed to provide for the cities. They're bleedin' the countryside dry of people and killin' the earth. That's why I'm on this trip. To show these lunk-heads what they're contributin' to the problem."

Seth slid down in his chair. "Do you have an opinion about that, Filoh?"

Filoh glared at him.

Sid nodded. "I can agree with that point. It makes logical sense. And that leaves the small towns which used to be the backbone of America, political slaves to the cities and coastal states and all the while getting personally rich from sales of food products. And in doing so are killing the resources they need to do this work."

"That's it," Filoh nodded and stamped his foot. "By damn, he gets it!"

"Powerful conversation so early in the day," Richard said.

"Just as well have it now when you're fresh," Filoh said. "Maybe it'll stick in your thick head."

"First time for everything." Richard looked at Seth. "Let's get packed and get down the trail. We're burnin' daylight."

When they left the bank Seth counted out $250 and gave it to Richard. "Barretts don't take no for an answer."

"It's just enough for a short term," Richard said.

"It's money. That's what we were needin' wasn't it?"

"This is going to require more time in Grand Island though, isn't it?"

"It either is or it isn't, but right now we've got money and we need to get a move on. Where in the livin' hell did we park our horses?"

SETH CHECKED SADDLES AND packs and they headed the horses across the river to travel on the south bank, away from the "No Trespassing" signs posted on the north bank. The river was about 200 feet across and knee deep to a horse. The sounds of horses hooves plunging in and out of water was amusing to Seth and he marveled at the various sounds and pitches that came from the repeated steps. He tried to squeeze the sounds out of his lungs and mouth but couldn't imitate them."

"You trying for a vaudeville job?" Richard said.

"Can you make that sound?"

"Would not even try."

"Well that's the difference between you and me," Seth said. "I'm at least willing to try."

"What good is it to be able to make that sound?"

"I don't know. Opens a horizon for you, I guess. If you can imitate that sound it gives you another dimension. You've tried howling at a coyote or squawking at crow haven't you?"

"No."

"You serious? Never have?"

"No. It does not make sense to them and they do not make sense to me."

"Dad used to call in ducks and geese."

"Yes. I remember that."

"I just like to imitate sounds. Makes me a broader person."

"We'll all get broader in these saddles."

"I mean broader in a general sense."

"My gawd, Seth. I know what you mean. I'm just pulling your leg."

THERE WAS NO TRAIL OUT of Silver Creek up the Platte. The pioneers had wisely kept inland on flat ground away from the trees and brush that festered along the banks on both sides but Seth found numerous fences and irrigation ditches and pipes that dissuaded them from that course.

There was enough space between the cottonwoods and brush to maneuver and Seth was good at staying close without having to ford the river too often. The horses were now used to the placid shallow water and entered and exited it without trauma.

Atop a swaying horse, stomach full, and mid-day it was hard for Richard to stay alert. Filoh's dialogues had fallen off. He got tired of repeating that speech. After Fremont he had pretty much seemed to endure rather than preach. After all, there were just two listeners and now they had heard the same speech, seen the same results, and talked about it so much everyone was sick of it. After Fremont, Filoh started cooking and helping wash the dishes. They fell into a routine: Richard built the fire, Seth tended to the animals, and Filoh prepared the food. Nobody said, you do this or that. It just became a natural thing to do that took no conversation and no questions asked.

There were times when Richard just wanted to sell the horses, catch a bus, and go home. Get Craig Jamison to fight the terms of the will. He and Seth could mount a terrific fight against the conditions of the will, saying they had tried. They had gone far enough. Yes— they could see why Grandpa Melzer homesteaded this parcel of land and they—as direct kin of the deceased Mae Barrett—were in line to inherit the ranch. This plodding and plopping across the state, in and out of the river was boring as hell and the educational part of it was over as far as he was concerned.

He'd mention that to Seth in the morning when they were both fresh. Well—fresher than they were around the campfire at night cooking that freeze-dried food. If it weren't for the Scotch each evening he would throw the whole supper in the fire. Was he tracking Seth and bouncing around the edges of alcoholism? There was a string running through the Melzer and Barrett families that favored dependence on alcohol. If not dependence, at least the liberal use of it. And who's to point to where liberal use of it turns into dependence?

He'd ride closer to Seth tomorrow and they could discuss this if Seth could find a trail that allowed two horses to travel side by side anywhere in this bramble. In the meantime he'd think about how lucky he was to be alive, to be somewhat fit, to be able to make this trip, and know that at the end of it he could rest enough to cure the aches and pains that would be laid upon him between now and the end. That thought boosted his spirits and when Filoh pointed to a level clearing beside some trees, with dead wood for a fire, he felt a stroke of elation for the first time that day. The night camp was close to a bend in the river and the low murmur of the water dancing its way to the Missouri was soothing to man and beast.

RICHARD NUDGED THE sleeping Filoh.

"Huh," Filoh said.

"You're snoring like a gorilla. Turn over."

"How do you know what a gorilla sounds like?"

"I'm going to get a recorder and let you hear yourself some time."

"You do that. You'll find it ain't me snorin'."

"Who else could it be?"

"Seth."

"He's not here."

"What do you mean he's not here?"

"His bag is flat. He must be making breakfast."

"In the dark?"

"It's almost daylight. Seth likes dawn especially well."

Filoh felt the inside of the sleeping bag. "It's cold as a corpse. He's been gone for a spell."

Richard looked out the tent flap. There was no fire and no one in view. He could barely make out the four animals on a rope tied between two trees. "Well—where in the hell did he go?" He hollered a couple of times then dressed and looked for him. As the light grew he made out footprints leading toward Central City. He lost the trail at the roadway where he stood, hands on hips, looking toward the fading lights of the city in the distance and stars still hanging above it.

Confused, Richard ran options through his head as he retraced his steps. Filoh was up, had a fire crackling and boiled coffee for a starter.

"Whad'da think?" Filoh said.

Richard shook his head. "I have no good idea. None at all." He squatted by the fire. "Is that coffee drinkable?"

"If yer man enough. It ain't killed me yet."

Richard pulled a log over by the fire and the two men sat silent except for the occasional sucking sound as they carbureted the coffee through warming lips.

As Richard was finishing scrubbing the dishes with Platte River sand he looked up to see Seth walk into camp. He straightened up.

"Morning boys," Seth said. "What's for breakfast?"

"You missed it," Filoh said. "I ate your share."

A big smile set Seth's face. "Any coffee left?"

"A mite," Filoh said and poured the black remains into a porcelain cup.

Seth could see Richard deciding how to ask the question. He couldn't decide whether to wait him out or explain it to him now. "I went courting. The frogs were making so much courting noise I decided they were trying to tell me something."

"Courting where?"

"Fremont."

"Do I have to pull everything out of you or are you going to tell us?"

"I caught the evening bus to Fremont, saw Martha, and got back."

Richard shook his head. "You don't care a lick for our mission here? You did not think about the risk you were running for us completing the required journey? I do not understand you, Seth. There is time for courting and time for serious fulfillment."

"I'm back aren't I?"

For a moment the three men stood silent, unmoving. Seth dumped the coffee in the fire and broke the spell. Richard took a deep breath, let it out, and Filoh stuffed his sleeping bag into the sack. It would be a long day.

Chapter 9

"IT WOULD'VE BEEN KINDA nice to travel along Silver Creek wouldn't it?" Filoh said. "We could've checked it out—see what it looked like."

"From what I could see," Seth said. "It looked more like Muddy Creek."

"Wonder what's happened to make it so dirty?" Richard said.

Filoh turned his head. "Plowin' right up to the banks. Maybe cattle wallowin' in it."

"From what I saw in town," Seth said. "It looked like they had left a fair amount of undisturbed land on both sides."

"Well—their website said it was named after a clear and sparkling little brook that flows near the town," Richard said.

"Clear and sparkly it ain't. And where did you get so much information about such a small town?"

"While you were fetching supplies I was on the internet. I looked at every town we were going to go through or around. This whole country was laid out either by how far a horse would travel in a day or by the railroad. And you'll remember from your school days, the Oregon Trail came right along the Platte River and that is generally where Highway 30 is now."

"Richard, you should have been a school teacher," Seth said.

"And get fired like Serena?"

"You'd have been the principal."

"Who gets fired by the school board."

"Speaking of Serena, what are you going to do about her living out at the ranch?"

"What is there to do about it?"

Seth snorted. "You gonna live with her there?"

"She will be gone by the time we get back."

"But if she isn't?"

Richard pulled out a pack of gum and as the horse found the trail by himself, he unwrapped it and folded it into his mouth. He unsnapped his shirt pocket and put the wrapper in. Seth who was half a horse ahead watched the process.

"No pollution' no shootin' Barrett they called him."

Richard looked at him and lifted his head. Seth had words for everything. The occasion made no difference; Seth just had to fill it with words. Truth to tell, he had not thought about Serena at the ranch since the phone call. One thing he knew for sure, and that was he did not want her to move far out of Plattsmouth. What would he do if she was still there when they got back? There were enough bedrooms to live in separate rooms but then would he be thinking of sneaking down the hall at night? That did not set well. Hell—Ginny and Seth would figure that out right away.

OK. Marriage then. Was he there yet? If he married Serena would they live at the ranch and Seth be just down the hall? A couple of times he had been on the brink of proposing marriage but as he approached the line he could not bring himself to utter the words. He could hold her, kiss her lips and face and neck and think the words in his head but somewhere between his brain and his lips the message folded. There was never enough conviction behind the message to drive it through and make it audible. And what was it? Fear? Selfishness? Lack of confidence? He shook his head.

Seth spoke up. "What're you shakin' your head about, brother?"

"Just thinking."

"I quit thinking last night and went out to see her."

"How'd that go?"

Seth shook his head. "I'm likin' her a lot. She's gonna come see me at the ranch when we get home and get this stuff behind us."

"Love?"

Seth cocked his head. "I don't know, Richard. I've been around a few gals these last years but this is a totally different feeling."

"Even though she's a greenie?"

"I guess it would depend on how deep the green goes with her."

"You didn't discuss it last night?"

"Hell no, Richard. We only had a few hours and there were more important things on my mind than listening to her take on the environmental impact of farming and ranching in the modern era."

"OK. But could you live with that if she was adamant? I mean adamant enough to reject you if we didn't change?"

"I'll think on that. Let you know in a few days. Right now I'm savorin' the night's experience and I don't want to be pushed out of that memory to ponder things that may or may not come to pass."

The horses were on their own as each man abandoned steering and sat astraddle, absorbed in his thoughts.

"Look at that," Richard said pointing to Filoh.

"Well, don't that beat all," Seth said.

"Don't wake him. He might fall out of the saddle."

"Good. Then we could leave him here."

"He'd be sure to wake up if he fell."

"We could leave him on one of these islands and let high water take him."

Richard shook his head. "Where do you get such ideas?"

"Readin' westerns and crime novels."

Filoh's head popped up. "What high water?"

The brothers laughed. "Trying to figure out how to get rid of your body if you fell off the horse and died," Richard said.

"Oh. Well, I ain't dead yet."

"So we see."

"Will we make Central City tonight?" Filoh asked.

"Not with you sleeping in the saddle. That cuts our time in half," Seth said.

"Well, let's go then," Filoh said.

The mule's eyes were half closed, his head hanging low when the rowel of Filoh's spur dug into his flanks. He reared, bounced a couple of times on his back legs and then dove forward. Filoh's lean frame torqued like a noodle at the forward thrust but he stayed in the saddle while the mule sped off down the braided watercourse, wet sand and dried leaves rising in a plume behind him. At a bridge where a sign proclaimed Highway , he finally regained control.

Richard chuckled. "Sure woke Filoh up."

"It did that," Filoh said. "Could we take a minute off the horses?"

Seth looked at the sun coming through the trees. "Three minutes. That's it."

Filoh couldn't remember being more sore. Every joint from his ankles to the base of his neck popped and cracked when he got down.

That jolted spurt convinced him that he might have erred coming on this trip. The brothers seemed more concerned over their damn schedule then they did about the state of the river. He realized that not only the brothers, but also thousands of people living along the river had to be brought up to speed on what they were doing to the river.

Silver Creek—what the hell caused people to say they lived in a town named after a clear and sparkling little brook and not see that the brook had changed? It was a muddy dawdling stream the color of burned coffee. And it ran into the Platte right before their eyes, carrying topsoil and manure and anything else someone threw in it.

This was turning into a much larger project than he had thought when he returned to Plattsmouth with the goal of converting the Barrett brothers to sustainable farming methods. His little bout with Klete Dixon's sprinkling tower, in an effort to draw attention to the dwindling Ogallala Aquifer, had gone unnoticed. He had showed them a dozen streams that helped deteriorate the waters of the Platte.

The pioneers had reported it was too thick to drink and too thin to plow so historically it was carrying silt and surface junk 150 years ago, but not the chemicals. You could have bathed in it without burning. You could let it flood over your land, improving the topsoil, and not deposit a layer of black sludge that caused weird lumps on leaves of plants.

Judas, he hurt.

Seth mounted up and looked at Filoh. "You ready?"

"I need another minute." Filoh walked to the bank and sat down looking to the South.

The River

Then the wind came. The water roughened and lapped up into the bushes. The air along the river filled with the sweet scent of cottonwood and willow buds and the smell of mud, soaked and dried a thousand times. Then the air took the scent and disappeared.

AFTER FIVE MINUTES FILOH rolled to his side, got up and hobbled over to his horse. "I'm willing to go a little bit farther."

"You want to call it quits?" Seth asked.

"I'm not a quitter."

Seth's horse danced as he watched Filoh trying to mount up. Finally Seth dismounted, got behind the old man and boosted him into the saddle.

"Thankee," Filoh said.

"Welcome. We ready now?"

Filoh nodded. "Believe we are."

Seth stayed on the South bank and commented on the group of islands that sat midstream forcing the river into braided channels each with its own personality. "Do you reckon each of those little islands is polluted?"

Filoh shook his head. "The whole river is and the land and air around it. Tell me, would you take a drink of that water now?"

"Hell no. But the Indians and pioneers didn't either."

"No—but the creeks and streams that feed into it were clear long time ago. Central City used to be called Lone Tree. Several year-around streams were clear as vodka before the industrial farming started reforming their boundaries and washing chemicals into them. Some of the little streams plumb disappear. 'Course it was a bitch during the dust bowl days. Drought caused big problems too."

"You know," Richard said. "I kind of look at industrial farming as a rung on the ladder of feeding the world. Look how farming has changed from the dust bowl and depression days. We're moving ahead up each rung. We're getting four times the production out of the same piece of land as our parents were."

"And you're killin' it for your kids."

"The dust bowl did not kill it for us. We brought it back."

"The dust bowl didn't kill the air and water. It hurt it—but it didn't kill it. Once they turned to contour plowing the air and water healed right up."

"And you do not think it will this time?"

"Now you're talkin'."

"Filoh," Richard said. "Since 1945 our yields have gone up and we've gone from being poor farmers to wealthy farmers. The yield per acre has soared. We're feeding the world with our innovations in farming. Yes—organics is rearing its head but so far it is pretty much confined to farmer's markets and a few food elite. The bulk of the nation's farmers are doing it the way we are and we've lowered the cost of food in a family's budget percentage wise. I am just not ready to accede to what you are pushing. And besides that, my mind and body are committed to this trip first and foremost. If we don't get this done we don't need to worry about the Barrett Ranch."

"Dang, you're stubborn."

NOBODY TALKED FOR THE next hour. The horses, committed to the trail, lapsed into a dull pattern of foot drop, head sway, ears relaxed. Seth thought how much like merry-go-round horses they were: sullen, stiff, moving at the slow speed of the motor within them with no knowledge of a stopping place and completely dependent on the men riding them to make decisions.

The sun, taking advantage of the clear day, was reluctant to slip over the horizon as the small band came to another bridge. Seth rode up the bank and read the sign.

"What does it say?" Richard asked.

"Hord Lake Road." Seth rose up in the stirrups. "Looks like a park of some kind over beyond it."

"Let's take it. We are ready for evening," Richard said.

"Amen to that," Filoh put in.

There was good space for the tent, and while Seth removed the saddles and brushed the animals, Filoh and Richard set up camp, built a fire, and found a trickle of clear water leading into the Platte to add to Richard's Scotch.

"Now that's good enough to drink," Filoh said.

"To your health," Richard added lifting his glass. "This sure tastes better out here than in the living room. Why do you suppose that is?"

Seth smiled. "It means more here. Been there and know the feeling."

Sheriff helps sheriff

"I'M READY FOR THE next step. I want this clear and crisp and no screw-ups." Klete Dixon got out of the chair on the veranda, telephone to his ear, and moved toward the steps leading down to the lawn. "Do you have any questions?"

"No. Seems clear." An involuntary shudder ran through Sheriff Bud Pinsky. "Maybe it'll work," he muttered. "Worth a try."

"Good. Execute it and let me know when they get to Chapman." He clapped his phone shut as the smile started across his face. *It's like chess— moving pieces around to block and stymie the opposition. Damn, it's fun.*

IN THE MID AFTERNOON the three riders forded the Platte, thin, narrow and braided with small teardrop shaped islands bulging out from the north shore. They followed a dirt track for several miles to a bridge. Seth paused to read a sign.

"What's it say?" Richard said.

Seth turned in the saddle and hollered. "Come up here."

A police cruiser with Merrick County Sheriff painted on the side, pulled up beside Seth.

"Afternoon," the officer said, touching the brim of his Smokey Bear hat. "What brings you fellers to Chapman."

"We thought we were going into Grand Island. We're just to Chapman?"

The officer nodded and tightened up his lips. "I'd like to see some identification from each of you," he said.

Seth glanced at Richard. Richard nodded.

The policeman looked at each plastic identification card, lifted the flap on his breast pocket and put the ID's in and buttoned the flap. "Gentlemen," the officer said. "I'm Sheriff Russell Wolfe, Merrick County. I want you to go to my office. You can ride your horses in. It isn't but a couple of miles."

Richard pulled back on his reins. "What are you talking about, Sheriff? We're just riding up the river."

The officer reached across Richard's leg and lightning fast, pulled the .30-30 out of the saddle scabbard. He pushed the lever part way down, checked the cartridge.

"What do you think you're doing with a loaded rifle on a public road?"

"We weren't on a public road when you saw us." Seth said, lifting his left foot out of the stirrup.

"You are now."

"We don't intend to stay. Give us back the rifle and we're down the road."

The officer lifted the rifle, sighted down the barrel. "I think you'd better come with me. We'll find out what you're doing riding around this country out of hunting season loaded for bear."

"Bear hell," Richard said. "That gun would not stop a bear."

"Oh, so it's a man gun?"

"I did not say that."

"You implied it."

Richard looked at Seth. "Come on Seth. We are getting nowhere with this guy."

"That's right—you're not. Turn those horses up the road to my office. I'll be behind you in the patrol car." He lifted his upper lip and his eyes crinkled as his head tilted back, "And don't make a break for it. I believe this man gun could do a number on you."

In his office, the chief pulled out a pad and started to write. Seth, Richard, and Filoh stood before the desk. The scratching of a pencil on paper was the only sound in the room until Filoh coughed and asked if he could sit down. The Sheriff looked up. "Stand until I'm through with this. I don't like prisoners getting comfortable before jail time."

"Prisoners?" Seth said.

The Sheriff looked up. "Do you have a hearing problem?"

"There is no law against riding a horse along the river or in this two bit town."

"The law is what I say it is."

"I want to make a phone call."

"You can when I'm through here. If you keep pestering me this is going to take a lot longer."

"This shouldn't even be happening."

The Sheriff was silent as he filled in part of the form. He handed the form to Richard. "Fill in the rest of that and put your personal stuff in that box there."

"Personal stuff?"

"Wallet, watch, pocket knife, cell phones."

Richard shook his head. "I do not know what you are thinking but we have done nothing to receive this kind of treatment."

"That's interesting," the Sheriff said, rocking back in his chair. "I could add resisting arrest to those charges. That'd be about another two to three days."

Richard read the form and looked up. "We are not vagrants and we did not trespass. We are owners of the Barrett Ranch in Plattsmouth. What the hell are you talking about here?"

"Do you have the deed with you?"

"Of course not."

The Sheriff shrugged. "Then how do I know until I can make a few phone calls and see who you are and what you're doing loose in Merrick County."

"What does Merrick County got against people riding through?"

"You saw those no trespassing signs on the bank, didn't you?"

Seth looked at Richard. His eyes lifted toward the window as if he was trying to recall when he saw the signs and where. "We crossed over to avoid those areas."

"Yeah. Well, I gotta a call and a complaint and it's my job to clear these things up."

"Who called?" Seth said.

The Sheriff nodded toward the river. One of the farmers."

"This is bull-shit," Seth said.

"I'm not going to ask you again. Put your personal property in that box and go on in the cell."

"I'm damned if I will," Seth said.

He didn't see it coming. He'd had some hard knocks working with cows and horses but none of them cleared his mind like the whack of the gun barrel on the side of his head. He couldn't control his legs and he collapsed in a heap blinking his eyes and trying through the fog to hear what was being said.

Richard was tugging on his arms and he could hear sounds but nothing was in place. It was as though he was in a different world looking in but not focused. Then he felt himself being dragged across the floor and heard a sharp metal-to-metal clang. He could sense people beside him but everything was foggy. He heard a door slam and then no sound at all.

Sheriff Wolfe walked outside the building, dialed his cell phone and took out the three plastic identification pieces.

Sheriff Bud Pinsky of Cass County slid his cell phone out of the holster, flipped it open and put it to his ear. "Yes."

"The three wise men are in the manger."

"Any trouble?"

"Oh, not enough to speak of. A little resistance to arrest but a pistol whippin' solved that problem."

"Pistol whippin'?"

"Yeah. One of the cowboys didn't hear my instructions. I generally only give 'em once."

"Thanks, Russ. I owe you one."

"You've done some for me. Let me know when you want them loose. I doubt I can do more than three days unless it includes the weekend, then I might get five."

"Be back to you," Bud said.

"Yup. Well. Back to keeping the citizens of Merrick County safe and sound."

Jail Time

IT TOOK ABOUT TEN minutes for Seth to put things together in sequence and then the rest of the day to make sense of it.

"Is it bleeding?" Seth said.

Richard looked and spread Seth's hair. "No. It was the round side of the barrel. Probably a glancing blow."

"Throbs like hell."

Filoh stood up and swung his arms in a circle. "Feller don't take no sass, does he?" He pulled one knee up to his chest in a stretch. "Wonder what he did with our horses?"

"He damn well better take care of them," Seth said.

Richard walked around the perimeter of the cell. "We can not linger in here."

"How you figure to get out?" Seth said.

"Bail. A judge should grant us bail. We are easy to find."

"Give it a try."

"Sheriff?"

There was not a sound in reply. He tried two more times and it only echoed through the jail.

"Not a busy place," Filoh said. He sat down and retied his boot-laces. "Here I volunteered to come along and teach you fellers something about despoiling the country side and you get me in jail."

"Oh, shut-up," Seth said.

Richard stood up. "He will be back with some food and water sooner or later."

"Maybe. But I'll bet it will be later and not much."

"And likely not tasty," Filoh said.

IN THE MIDDLE OF the afternoon, Filoh's belly was growling. "I didn't have much breakfast."

Seth looked at the undershirt he had been pressing to the side of his head. There was no blood. "That'll teach you to eat when you got the chance."

"Humph," Filoh muttered. "If I starve to death on this trip it'll be on your conscience forever."

"Yeah—that'll cause me a serious loss of sleep."

Richard sat down. "Knock it off you guys. Listen to this. We have not had so much negative happen to us in our lifetime. Add it up: the dead heifer, then the problem with our credit card, then the hold on our funds. Serena gets fired and kicked out of her house. Now we are in jail. All in the short time we have been on the river. Does that sound fishy to you?"

Filoh made a small back and forth motion with his head, his tongue between his teeth.

"Coincidence," Seth said.

"How about delay? Delay us past our deadline and ranch goes to charity?"

"Still coincidence."

"And someone with money who wants it enough is behind it?"

Seth shook his head. "You've been reading too many Ayn Rand novels."

"Maybe someone who did not like Filoh blowing up his sprinkler tower?"

"Dixon? He's got too much to lose to mess around like that."

Richard stood at the cell door, one hand on the bar and shook it. "This is pretty stout."

"Were you figurin' on bustin' out?"

Sheriff Bud Pinsky checks up

SERENA WAS PUTTING ON the supper dishes. As the evening cooled she had gone upstairs to put on a sweater. She saw it then. The kids were outside finishing up evening chores. She glanced at Ginny a time or two while she cooked.

"Ginny," she said. "Any idea why a sheriff's car would be sitting down by the mail box?"

Ginny spun around. "Oh my gawd, Serena...anyone in it?"

Serena shook her head. "I couldn't see that well. It was just there facing the house. It gives me the creeps."

"Probably nothing. But let me know if you see it again. We had an incident here around the first of the month and Bud came to check it out. He might be making sure we're ok."

"That guy gives me the creeps. He's weird."

"What do you mean, weird?"

"He's so police like. Has his crisp uniform, big ole gun, hat just right. Makes you think he's protecting the President instead of being the Sheriff of Cass county.

Ginny took the lid off the stew, tasted it. "Done. Would you call the kids, please?"

SHERIFF BUD PINSKY WATCHED the three kids come from various places and walk to the back porch of the Barrett Ranch house. There were still a couple of hours of daylight left and it was Thursday. He'd just make a short appearance. Show the law was there to protect them. He started the car and let the cruiser glide into the parking area by the front door.

Always use the front door. Back doors are for peddlers and farm help. You didn't grow up to be Sheriff of Cass County and take a back seat to anybody.

He adjusted his hat, hefted his gun-belt and knocked on the door, stood back a respectful distance and waited.

Dawson Huston opened the door. At fourteen he was starting to fill out. Bud could see the pole vault potential in his shoulders and chest. Bud nodded. "Evening, Dawson. Just came to see how things were going. Ginny here?"

"Hello Sheriff. I'll get her."

Bud could hear discussion in the kitchen and soon Ginny appeared wiping her hands on an apron that accentuated her narrow waist.

He touched his hat. "Evening, Ginny. Just checking up on things. Anything unusual since the last time?"

"No," she said, the back of her neck starting to moisten. "Serena said you were parked at the mailbox." *Got to let him know we see him there.* "Anything wrong?"

"Oh no. I was on the phone with another sheriff helping to keep the peace. Not supposed to drive and talk on the phone anymore you know. Serious offense." He chuckled. "Smells good," he nodded toward the kitchen.

"I'd invite you to stay but I didn't make enough." *I'd rather invite the devil to dinner.* "I'm still trying to figure out how to cook for five people in these huge pots and pans."

"I appreciate the thought, but I'll git on back to town. I have some matters to attend to."

Thoughts whizzed through Ginny's mind. She settled on one. "Thanks for checking up, Bud. We're okay for now."

He touched the brim of his hat. "Okay." He nodded. "If you need anything give me a call."

She released her lower lip from between her teeth and holding the edge of the door with one hand she nodded. "We'll do that."

"Good night. Tell Serena hello from me."

She closed the door and turned the dead bolt, pulled on it twice to test it, then leaned her back against the wood feeling the cool hard surface press against her shoulder blades.

Serena was right behind her. "That's the way he acted when he evicted me from my house. Same polite, self-satisfied, priggy self."

Ginny looked her in the eyes. "I know." She said.

"What did the Sheriff want, Mom?" Valerie asked.

Ginny took a deep breath and released it. "Just checking. That's his job."

"Is he still chasing the guy who killed our cow?"

"Probably."

"Gross," Bucky said. "Don't remind me of that before supper."

"Aw you little wimp," Dawson said.

"Yeah—it wasn't you who found it. It was gross."

"Children," Ginny said. "Let's talk about something more appe-tizing. Where'd that big bag of Cheetos come from?"

Serena spoke up. "They were in the stuff from my kitchen. Thought we could eat them before they got stale,"

"I like it when Serena is here," Bucky said.

Hamburgers for breakfast

SETH LIFTED HIS HEAD. "What's the date you reckon?"

Richard pulled his lower lip between his teeth, sucked on it and frowned. "I would say it is around the 28th of May."

"And we're not even half way to Ogallala yet."

Richard shook his head. "Nope."

"You know," Seth said. "What you were thinkin' makes some sense. What easier way to get the ranch than to delay us from gettin' done. He can't just take it like he could've 150 years ago. But he's got money, power, cohorts in high places. And we're the only ones stand-ing in his way. We do this or else."

"I do not like to think ill of my fellow man and a neighbor to boot, but these events have a slight stink to them." Richard turned to Filoh. "What do you make of it?"

Filoh shook his head. "I told you when I come back to town, I was forced out. Your folks and Dixon was behind every step of it. This smells the same way. Step by step until they total up to more than you can stand."

The front door of the jail opened and a delivery boy stood in the opening. "Where are you?" he said.

Richard spoke up. "We are in the cell, son. Where would you expect us to be? Turn on the light there."

"I've never been in here before. Sheriff said to deliver this food to you and give you this." He held out a five-gallon can.

"And just how were you supposed to give us the can?"

The boy looked at the bars on the cell and back at the bucket. He smiled and shook his head. "I have no idea."

"Did he give you a key?"

"No." He set the can down and handed the food through the horizontal gap in the bars.

"Beats trail food," Filoh said. He unwrapped the sandwich, took a bite and reached for the drink handed him.

The boy nodded. "It all comes to twenty-seven dollars and fifty cents."

"Get it from the Sheriff," Richard said with his mouth full.

"He said to get it from you. Said you weren't vagrants and could pay for it."

Richard looked at Seth. "What do you think now?"

"Give him the money and tip him. We need one ally in this town."

Richard reached for his wallet. "Sheriff has our money. It is in his desk."

Seth looked up, winced and blinked hard. "Run us a tab and we'll catch you when we get out of this dump." He stood up. "You going to be around with breakfast?"

"Sheriff didn't mention breakfast."

"Good. Maybe we'll be out of here."

"I doubt it. He took off for Omaha. Some sort of conference."

Richard thought a moment. "Does your front door key fit the cell door here?"

The boy looked at it and shook his head. "Totally different key."

"Bring us a big bowl that will fit through this food passing slot and leave the bucket just there on the other side. Add five dollars to the tip."

"Ok. Thank you."

Seth sat down. "Hurry it up with that bowl."

"Please?" Richard said.

"Yes—please."

WHEN THE STREETLIGHTS CAME on the boy returned with a plastic bowl. "The Sheriff called and said the justice of the peace was also at the conference and they wouldn't be back until Monday morning and for me to keep bringing you food."

Richard's lips took on a wry grin and he snorted. "I guessed as much."

"Well then," Seth said. "We just as well order what we'd like."

The boy shook his head. "I've got orders to bring the same thing for each meal."

"Hamburgers for breakfast?"

The boy nodded.

"This wasn't intended to make us comfortable," Richard said.

"What if this damned place catches on fire?" Filoh said. "Who's to put it out?"

The question hung in the air. The boy left.

"Well, pass the bowl," Filoh said. "I'll be the first user."

Back on the Platte River trail

IT WAS MONDAY MORNING before Winthrop Farley, Justice of the Peace for the village of Chapman, Nebraska, set the Sheriff down and explained to him that keeping three men locked up in an old jail that hadn't been used in twenty years, was made of wood, and had a undergraduate high school McDonald's employee with the only key was tantamount to endangerment of life and limb and could be a cause of civil action by the occupants. However, given the unusual circumstances of the two of them being gone for the conference in Omaha at the same time, he could understand the situation.

A phone call to Sheriff Bud Pinsky of Cass County verified that the men were not vagrants and the local who had called in the trespassing could not be found to press charges so Richard and Seth and Filoh were released from the jail and, after rinsing out the bowl and the five gallon bucket, they were directed to where their horses were stabled.

"Don't this beat all?" Filoh said. "I ain't ever coming through Chapman again."

"We better be careful coming back down river. He might nail us as repeat offenders," Seth said. It wasn't his first time in jail but this time he was innocent and that put some starch in his 'get-even pouch'. "He's a no-good bastard."

Richard pulled the rifle out and pushed the lever part way down. "No bullets."

"Maybe they are in your saddlebag."

He looked. They all looked. Richard cocked his head. "Another delaying tactic. I've got a rifle that is now a club, we are short of cash, and now we have to look for ammo."

"Let it go, Richard," Seth said. "You won't be needing that damn rifle anyway."

"And that is why you keep it on your saddle at the ranch?"

"I just like the feel of it there. I've only used it a couple of times that I recall."

"What if I only need it once?"

Seth smiled wide and shrugged his shoulders. "Well—let's see if we can find some bullets in this little town."

"There's a feller," Filoh said. He hollered at him. "Excuse me. Is there a place in this town where a man can find some .30-30 bullets?"

The man rubbed his jaw with a gloved hand. "Have to go to Central City or Grand Island for that."

"Well. That's where we're headed." He nodded.

"Are you the fellas that were in our jail?"

"We were."

The man grinned. "How do you like our sheriff?"

"He's a rotten no good son-of-a-bitch," Filoh said.

"He keeps a tight rein on all 300 of us, just like we was chickens."

"He had us in there for nothin'."

"Be careful of him. He has a way of making his ideas work out. Ain't nobody here likes him but he gets re-elected every time and I don't know anybody who voted for him."

Richard mounted his horse and drew the reins up. Seth finished tightening the girth straps on the packhorse.

"We want to stop for lunch?" Richard said.

"We've got chow. Let's get out of this town," Seth said. "The back of my neck's itchin'."

They rode back to 8th Road and turned south to the river. When they reached Bader Park they followed the north bank of the Platte River staying in the low trees and out of sight of any roads or houses. They rode in silence for several miles before Filoh asked to stop.

He slid a leg over the saddle and stepped down. "How much further?"

"Filoh," Seth said and shook his head. "You're gettin' like a little kid always askin' how far it is."

"Besides needin' to take a whiz, I'm tryin' to figure out where the Wood River dumps into the Platte." He took a wide stance the other side of a cottonwood. "Once was a sizeable flow but I expeck its all bein' used up now." He shook himself. "I was hopin' to show you real destruction of water from what used to be a good flow. Keep your eyes out for it."

"Yeah—we'll know it by the dead animals floating in it and the frogs with three legs," Seth said.

Filoh shook his head. "They're trying a lot of new chemicals around there. Read about it in the *Farm Journal*. Chemical companies have a bunch of experimental plots and I'll bet you ten to one the Wood River is getting the run off from them and if it ever finds the Platte, into the river it goes."

Richard joined him. "Where do you think we would be safe to go into Grand Island? We need money and ammo."

"Sound like a revolutionary army don't we?" Seth said. "Money and ammo."

"And lunch," Filoh put in.

"Let's plan this out. We've gone to town too much so far and we get into trouble in these towns."

"Make a list," Filoh said.

"A list?" Seth threw in. "Hell, we only need two things. Let's get 'em and get the hell out of town." He took the map out of the saddlebag and unfolded it on the horse's neck. "After we come to the railroad bridge we want to cross over to the south side, stay on the river until we come to the Highway 34 Bridge. That's our best shot into town."

Filoh agreed to hold the horses while the brothers entered Platte Valley State Bank. He pondered the looks from strangers and let the thought come and go that here he stood at about 145 pounds holding more than a ton of horse flesh, his two feet against their sixteen, all of them planted on an asphalt parking lot a goodly distance from grass or water. It occurred to him that he and the horses resembled a bronze sculpture and if he stood stock still looking at the ground they might be taken for such. The horses adopted his dead-on-the-parking-lot stance and with the exception of an occasional tail sweep the horses, eyes half closed, stood side by side, their noses together, resting in the noon-day sun.

Richard approached the teller. "Is the manager available?"

"I'll see," the teller said.

"Tell him…" Seth said.

"I know what to say to him."

A well-dressed middle-aged woman emerged from a glass-walled office. She wore a black eye patch over her left eye and her smile was as broad as she was. "Good day to you gentlemen. How may I help you?"

"We have a strange request," Richard began. "Could we go into your office, please?"

"Certainly." She opened the half door and led them to her office. "May we get you some coffee?"

"I'd like that," Seth said. "Cream and sugar."

Richard nodded.

Seth's eyes followed the comely young teller who delivered the coffee until she left the office, a smile starting on his whiskered face.

"Now—about that strange request," the manager said.

THIRTY MINUTES LATER SETH handed Filoh a foam cup of coffee two-thirds full, loaded with cream and sugar.

"I figured you guys were in there lappin' up goodies while me and the horses starved to death out here."

"It'd take you thirty days to die of starvation," Seth said.

"Not at my age. It can come quick." He blew on the coffee. "Did you resolve it?"

Richard nodded. "Good enough for now."

"What's the deal?"

"We will fill you in at lunch. We have money. Now for bullets." The horse opened his eyes and snapped his head up when Richard stuck his boot into the stirrup.

"YOU FIGURE YOU CAN make it another four or five miles?" Seth said.

"Hell—my body is form fitted in this chunk of wood and leather. I'll probably have to be buried on it," Filoh said.

"Is that a yes or no?"

"It's as close to a yes as I can muster."

"Richard?" Seth said.

"I am good."

Seth nodded and shortened up the reins. "Let's find some bullets for that club and then we're off to the Mormon Recreation Area."

MIDAFTERNOON WAS GIVING WAY to early evening when they arrived at the Recreation Area. Swallows swooped and turned by the hundreds, a chorus of cheeps drowning out the gentle murmur of the Platte as the birds emerged from under the bridge, disturbed by people being that close. The sun, settling low in the sky, burned from the side casting shadows that reached almost across the river.

Filoh belched. "Feels more like supper than lunch."

Seth frowned and shook his head. "Damn but you sure can get testy."

"Wait until you're ninety and see how you like it."

"I'm getting to ninety fast listening to you. It's your turn to build a fire."

"I didn't sign on as a slave," Filoh said.

Seth blanched. "You foisted yourself off on us promising to cook and wash dishes. You want a hot meal, you gather firewood."

"I can't bend over so good."

"It'll loosen you up, all that bendin' and pickin'. How do you expect to cut your toe nails if you don't bend from time to time?"

"Got a woman who does that."

"Hope I don't get to where I need someone to cut my toe nails."

"You will."

"When's that come on?"

"Eighty four, eight five—"

"Well—that gives me another twenty years."

Richard had the tent erected and was preparing supper. When he stuck his head out of the tent he had an apron tied around his middle and a large skillet in his hand. "Where is the fire?"

Seth nodded toward Filoh. "Talk to Filoh. It's his turn to build it."

Filoh threw down an armload of small sticks. "I'm doin' it—I'm doin' it."

Richard arranged them by size, breaking some of the longer sticks into fire starters. He opened two cans of corned beef hash, dumped them into the skillet and cracked six eggs in it. He squatted on his haunches with his back to Filoh.

It was one of those times when Filoh thought there was enough time to get it done and do it right but as the event unfolded he found himself on the losing end of time.

All Richard heard was a clatter of sticks. He spun on his heels and saw Filoh spilling the firewood. Saw him take a step forward and bend, concentrating on the ground a step ahead of him. Filoh reached down and picked up something. In a quick motion he straightened and jerked his arm above his head. A long thick-bodied object rose out of the grass dangling from his hand. At the top of his reach, Filoh brought his arm down fast, and snapped it like a bullwhip. The object accelerated to the top of the arc and whipcracked in a flash. "Oh" Filoh muttered. It was an unusual sound. When the object descended, the other end stuck in Filoh's neck.

Richard stood up. It took a moment for his brain to organize what he saw. He recognized the object as a snake, with its fangs stuck in Filoh's throat.

Filoh's eyes widened. He staggered. The snake's head stuck to his neck; unable to get loose its tail thrashed his legs. He grabbed the snake around the middle and pulled. The weight of the snake and the angle of the fangs set in his throat bound them together.

Seth dropped the pack and started toward him but Richard got there first. He closed his fingers behind the snake's head, squeezed and lifted. The snake and Filoh separated. Venom ran down his neck, the two jagged holes already turning red around the edges.

"Jesus. Dear God!" Richard said. He threw the snake in a writhing arc toward the river and pushed Filoh down.

He struggled. "Hold still. Stop it!" Richard said.

Filoh fought back. "Onngh…"

"Stop!"

Richard and Seth pinned him to the ground. Seth pulled back the collar. The fang holes were oozing blood.

Seth ran for the antivenin kit.

Richard shook his head when Seth returned. "Hit the artery. No good now." His eyes narrowed.

Filoh convulsed, twisted and then lay still, his breathing stopped. Richard stood, went to the saddle and jerked the rifle from the scabbard, levered in a cartridge and marched toward the snake.

The coiled snake looked at him, his tongue flicking in and out.

"Kill the son-of-a-bitch," Seth said.

Richard hesitated, stood looking at the snake. His hands trembled. Seth kneeled nearby looking useless, impotent, unsure, expecting the explosion of the cartridge.

"Kill him," Seth said.

Richard's breath came in jagged spasms. His finger tightened on the trigger. Then he straightened, blinked several times and lowered the hammer, his eyes settled on the snake coiled in the grass. He swallowed. "Wasn't the snake's fault."

Seth looked up at him. "Richard—kill that snake. You know I'm scared of snakes. We don't want it around camp."

Richard watched the snake slip into the Platte—a V-shaped ripple trailing its body undulating from side to side in the water. He turned and took two steps in the high grass, thumbed back the hammer, raised the rifle and fired at a cottonwood stump across the channel. The shot echoed across the water, the sounds muffling against the bridge and the broad leaves of the cottonwoods. Hundreds of swallows erupted from under the bridge and joined the swarm in the air flitting above the water.

Kneeling beside Filoh, Seth stared down at him. "I've never seen a rattler on the Platte," he said.

Richard put his hand on his brother's shoulder. "I have heard of them but never seen one. It was a Prairie Rattler I believe. A pioneer snake."

Seth shook his head. "Don't make sense. Just a couple of minutes ago he was gathering firewood."

"No," Richard said. "He was protecting me. That snake was almost to me when he grabbed it."

"Why didn't he just throw it?"

"We'll never know."

The sun went down and the fire now cast the brothers' shadows across the corpse.

"God Almighty," Seth said. "What a way to die."

Richard nodded, took a deep breath. "It was fast."

"Should we pray or something?"

"We could. Do you feel like saying a few words?"

Seth shook his head. "I don't know about that stuff. Would you do it?"

"What if we each said something to ourselves…in our hearts. I would hate to have him gone to his death thinking poorly of us."

"Yeah—that works." Seth pulled off his hat and set it on the ground.

The fire popped and the first layer of sticks collapsed onto the coals that had built up on the sand. Each sat with his head bowed. Unknown words and thoughts filtered through the tiredness and pain. There was no prescribed end to the historical ritual of the loss of a companion on the trail and neither man was accomplished at the process. A loud pop from the fire triggered their release. Seth involuntarily said, "Amen."

Richard put the rifle back in the scabbard, measured some Scotch in his cup and sat on a log. Seth folded Filoh's hands over his chest and crawled into the tent. In a moment he came out with a toenail clipper. He pulled off a boot and sock and in a deliberate manner went about trimming his toenails.

Chapter 10

"I DON'T GUESS WE can bury him here," Seth said.

Richard's hand roved across his neck, tugging at the white hairs. "No, we'll need to go into town and resolve it."

"Where do you think we are?"

"You're the map keeper."

Seth stared at the ground as if the location would jump up at him. "Right. I'll look."

The wind picked up and was pushing leaves across the ground. Mud swallows dived, wheeled and glided in a swarm by the bridge. A raccoon scurried across the sand pausing to look at the camp, his dark inquisitive eyes seated in a black mask.

The river was respectfully quiet, the occasional burble shifting on the breeze running down river to where a small cottonwood tree, a third buried on a sandbar, split the overflow. A Sharp Shinned Hawk sat on the highest limb.

Seth looked up from his map. "Do you think we should load him tonight? He might be too stiff in the morning."

"He will be over the rigors by morning." Richard moved a burning stick back onto the fire. "We do not want the mule to stand all night with Filoh on him."

"Guess you're right." Seth crossed his arms over his knees. "I can't get that picture out of my brain. The snake hanging there—Filoh stumbling." He shook his head.

"Bad scene. I hate it."

"What a way to die. And him thinking he was going to have lots of lady friends in the retirement home."

Richard removed his hat. He stayed on one knee, eyes fixed on the silent corpse.

"You know," Seth said. "I'm gonna miss the old guy. I was dead set against him coming but I've kinda enjoyed the guy." He looked at Richard and nodded. "Didn't you?"

"Yes." He paused. "I did."

Night came in along the river until the firelight threw long shadows that danced with the flames.

Seth stood up. "Could we move him over away from camp?"

"Night animals might get to him."

"Oh—right."

Only the occasional crackling of the fire followed by a puff of smoke from a wet stick disturbed the quiet. Richard stood up. "Let's roll him in the tarp."

They placed Filoh on a tarp, rolled it up and folded the ends over his head and feet and tied a rope around it. Under a bower of cotton-wood limbs they laid him out straight.

"That will do for now," Richard said.

A FOG HUNG OVER the river in the morning, the damp air clinging to metal and leather. The brothers went about their chores in silence, each knowing now what the other would do.

Seth had both hands cupped around his coffee. "I don't look forward to what we have to do today."

"Needs to be done," Richard said.

Seth nodded. "I'm beginning to wonder if it's worth it." He was silent a moment. "Just sell the ranch and live the rest of our lives on the money."

"You are forgetting something. The ranch goes to Boy's Town if we don't complete it. I would like to look forward, Seth. It gives my life meaning."

"You can look forward all you want. You'll have some money."

A faint smile slipped over Richard's face. "I got the crops planted. You took care of the new crop of calves. Don't you look forward to the fall when the harvest is done and the buyers pick up the calves and we tidy up the place for the winter season?"

"Yeah, I do. But this trip's buggin' me. What if we just grabbed a bus in Grand Island and hustled back to the ranch, fought the will?"

"You are forgetting the terms. It all goes to Boy's Town. We would get only the operating capital."

"Hell—I've made it on a lot less."

"That is not the answer to my question."

"What would my share be?"

Richard grabbed a stick and cut figures in the sand. He pursed his lips. "Somewhere around $150,000… after taxes."

"Hell," Seth said. "That could last me ten years."

"If nothing went wrong, like you got real sick or had an accident or made some bad investments." He scuffed the figures in the sand with his boot and threw the stick on the fire.

The option of another course of action drifted through their conscious minds. It entailed calculations that neither of them had made the effort to confront.

"You know," Seth started. "Doin' that would sure reduce the problems Filoh pointed out. Leave it to the next guy."

Richard threw the remains of his coffee into the fire. "Man that is rotten coffee. Did you wash your socks in the water before you made it?"

"You made the coffee."

"Right. I forgot." He wiped out his cup, put it in the food sack and stood up. "Let's go find an undertaker."

RICHARD DIALED CRAIG Jamison's office number.

"Hello, Richard. I trust you are having a fine day on the river," Craig said.

"Good morning, Craig. The day is fine but the mood isn't. Filoh Smith, who forced his way on this trip, died last night."

"For heaven's sake, that's terrible. What now?"

"That's why we called, Craig. What are we required to do?"

"Hummm. I'll have to think on that. Been a spell since I dealt with something like this. Let me get back to you later today."

"Seth and I are taking him to the Curran Funeral home in Grand Island. It is the closest." Richard coughed. "Excuse me. We don't know what to do with him after that."

"I'll do some research and get back to you."

"What'd he say?" Seth said.

"He'll get back to us." Richard saw three people come out of a building and stand, hands on hips looking at them. "Are those people staring at us?"

"Wouldn't you stare at somebody with a body across a horse—in town?"

KLETE DIXON LEANED BACK in his chair. "Filoh Smith died?"

"That's what Richard said. Snake bite in the neck," Craig replied.

"That's bad luck for him. Good luck for me. Can you stretch this out for them?"

"I promised to call Richard back. I can take longer to do my research."

"Good. Do that. Put as much stretch into it as you can without raising suspicions."

Details, details, details

"Let's go around to the back end," Richard said. "I don't like the idea of leaving Filoh out front."

The back door was locked and Seth pushed the button on the wall below the sign that said, "ring bell for service." Bolts were turned, door-knobs twisted and a face appeared behind a screen door. "Good morning."

"Hello," Seth said. "We're in need of your services."

The man's gaze went from Seth to the corpse wrapped in a tarp on top of a mule.

"I'll get a gurney."

Inside, Filoh's body was laid on a marble slab, the mortician closed the door, and invited Richard and Seth into his office.

"We'll need a death certificate properly filled out and recorded. That comes from a physician or the county coroner. Then we record that and get a burial permit. What kind of service are you reqesting for him?"

Richard turned his hat in his hands. "That is not our decision to make. He may have next of kin?" He looked at Seth who returned his gaze and shook his head. "We don't know," Richard said. "We have our attorney looking into the procedure."

"And who is that?"

"Craig Jamison of Plattsmouth."

"May I contact him?"

"Of course."

"When we decide the details and costs involved we'll get it put together."

"We'll pay any costs involved," Richard said.

Seth turned his head in an instant. "We?"

"Yes," Richard nodded.

"Why us?"

"I don't believe Filoh has any living kin."

"Let the county bury him then."

"We are not going to do that."

"Humph. I'll be damned. First we don't want him on the trip; then we let him come along; and now we're paying for his burial."

Richard put his tongue over his upper teeth and sucked in his cheeks. "We will do what has to be done."

"Where will I be able to find you two?" the mortician asked.

Seth replied: "Guess we'll be at the Hampton Inn. We have cell phones."

"Fair enough. I'll call you when I get the burial permit. The family can then decide on cremation or burial. However, I doubt he can wait that long to be embalmed."

"Don't embalm him if you can help it," Seth said.

"I won't do anything until I get the burial permit. Probably tomorrow. I'll call you when a decision needs to be made."

Richard nodded. "We'll leave it in your hands then."

CRAIG JAMISON DIALED RICHARD'S cell phone before he sat in his high-backed leather chair. He lifted the crystal decanter filled with Macallan 18 year old single malt Scotch whisky and poured two ounces into a lead crystal glass.

This will do before dinner.

"Richard—Craig here. I've combed the records and find no living kin for Filoh Smith. This both helps and hinders the procedures. So far I have found no will so the court has to be brought into it." He sipped the Scotch then held the glass up to the light coming through the window as he swallowed. He admired the walnut color of the liquid and how the dab of water moved the oils in the liquor around in the glass.

Richard stroked his sideburns. "Have you tried Emma Brewster at the B&B? She knew him well."

"No. Good idea. I'll get on that." He took another sip. "In the meantime, stay available. I don't want to muck this up. A death out of my jurisdiction is not something I handle every day."

"Understood." Richard coughed. "We're getting tight on our schedule, so put as much speed into it as you can."

Craig nodded and let a smile creep over his face. "Yes—I'm keeping track per the terms of the will you know. I'll be back to you later. Be sure and charge your cell phone."

"We are aware of that. Talk with you later." Richard pushed the off button.

"Doesn't sound to me like he's in any hurry," Seth said.

Richard tightened his face. "Probably doing the best he can. Where would you start?"

"Hell—I wouldn't start at all. I'd leave him here and let them go through the process. Once he's off the mule he belongs to them, not us."

"That's an interesting point of view. He was our traveling companion."

"He was when he was alive."

"You have an interesting way of looking at this, Seth."

"It's the only damn way to look at it, Richard. I didn't want him with us in the first place. Ninety years old for gawd's sake, and us on a time frame to get up and back. Draggin' him up and down the river, into town, stoppin' when he's sore…"

"I'm sore as well." Richard said.

"…yes but you're kin and we're in this together."

"Did you learn anything from him?"

"Yes. I'll admit that." Seth nodded. "I did."

Richard bore down. "What did you think of Silver Creek?"

Seth twisted his head. "It was a mess. It was ugly. That brown foam settled on it almost made me sick."

"Can you imagine swimming in that?"

"Well, hell no."

"Did it remind you of Fourmile Creek?"

"Yes it did." Seth bobbed his head up and down. "Yes it did."

"We're the major contributors to Fourmile."

Seth nodded again. "Yes—I know."

"Would you swim in Fourmile?"

"What's this with me havin' to swim in everything? I'm not doing this alone."

"Of course not. Filoh's hope was that we would see the light he has seen and turn our operation into sustainable. Help get the creeks and river running clean again."

Seth looked away down the street through the trees at a huge clock. "You know, Richard, when the white people first got to the Platte they made a statement that it was too thick to drink and too thin to plow. Don't that kinda let you know it was full of stuff then?"

"Full of top soil and natural debris probably, but not chemically polluted. And not the land and air along with it."

Seth shook his head. "Let's find a place to eat where we can hitch our horses. This is makin' me hungry."

The curiosity of drivers caused several close calls. Two men on horses leading a horse and a mule in the middle of downtown Grand Island, Nebraska, appearing like they had emerged from some fantasy novel to roam amongst newer forms of transportation. Some stopped, rolled down windows and focused cell phone cameras on them, smiling and laughing.

Crossing Highway 30 took some doing. Finally to facilitate crossing, Seth held up his arm and steered his horse onto the shoulder and in a longer break of traffic he started across, one arm held high and waving, he led the pack horse and Filoh's mule over the asphalt. Cars from both directions stopped like he was a fire engine or ambulance.

At the Hampton Inn the clerk looked at their horse-carried luggage. "How long are you staying with us?"

"Can't say," Richard replied. "Could be a night or could be a week."

"Any place we can board our horses around here?" Seth said.

The clerk thought a moment. "Windchaser Acres would be the closest. My girl friend has her horse there. About ten miles."

"Could you give them a call and see if they'll come get our horses—need a trailer for four animals?"

"I'll do that. Will this be cash or credit?" He pushed the registration form across the granite counter with a smile to accompany it. "I haven't registered horsemen here before. Welcome to the Hampton Inn."

"Now," Richard said. "If you would just direct us to the Whiskey Creek Steakhouse please. My brother is hungry."

AFTER SUPPER THE BROTHERS lingered over coffee, surveyed the comings and goings of families and couples and the occasional single who slipped up to the bar and ordered some unusual drink from memory. Frequent visitors.

Hunger satisfied and sipping good coffee, Richard's mind cataloged events. "This is crazy. We are not even half way to Ogallala and look at what has happened to us. What we have learned and seen? And we know nothing about how the ranch is running."

"All we know is that Ginny hasn't called about much," Seth said.

"I suppose the kids are getting the work done. They probably hired out some of it."

Seth nodded. "I'd say so. Although the cattle can make it on the pasture this time of year."

"Farming needs more attention. How did you leave it with Scotty on spraying?"

Seth thought a moment. "You know, I don't remember that I left it any way with him." He thought back to the poker game. He shook his head. "I remember talking about his new prices and him bein' at the poker game but I don't recall settling anything with him."

It was silent for a moment, each man calculating what needed to be done next. "Well," Richard said. "I think we had better call Ginny—"

"Or Scotty."

Richard nodded. "Let's call her when we get back to the motel."

Filoh had a love child?

WHILE SETH SHOWERED, Richard put in a call to Ginny. She answered her cell phone at the ranch.

"What are you doing at the ranch this late?" Richard said.

"Hi Richard. The kids and I and Serena are out here."

"Serena?"

"Yes. You remember she got evicted and I am letting her stay out here until she firms up a contract with a school district?"

"You are right. I guess I do remember that. So much has taken place that it is getting hard for me to catalog everything. You heard Filoh died?"

"How would I hear that?" Ginny said. "That's so sad."

"Snake bite in the neck. Almost instant. We are in Grand Island getting him ready for burial. Craig is looking up relatives and advising us on what we need to do."

"I'm glad of that. What a shame. That poor old man."

"Ginny," Richard said. "Do you know if Filoh had any living relatives?"

The phone was silent a moment. "I don't know. I can ask around."

"Would you do that please? Craig might not be moving the fastest on this."

"I'll call some people who knew him when he farmed here. Should be able to find out something."

"Good. Let me know. "Anything from Scotty about spraying the crops?"

"No. Should there be?"

"We have it done every year—the combination spraying. Seth was supposed to have worked it out before we left but he doesn't recall settling it. Have you seen or heard anything?"

"No. Do you want me to call him?"

"I will do it or Seth will when he gets the trail sand out of his ears. How is Serena taking everything?"

"Good. Do you want to talk with her?"

"No, I'll call her on her cell as soon as we get the spraying taken care of. No more dead cows or suspicious stuff happening?"

"No, but Bud Pinsky is watching everything and getting awfully friendly."

"How friendly?"

"Friendly like hugs and squeezes and attempted kisses."

"You okay with that?"

"No, Richard, I'm not. I gave him a piece of my mind and it hasn't happened again although we've seen him a time or two parked out by the mailbox."

"We had a run in with a sheriff along the way. I wonder if there is any correlation between Pinsky and him? Sheriffs probably know each other—there are not that many in the state."

"I'm sure they do. So far we're okay. Cattle are good; crops are perking up, the field's turning green."

"How is the irrigation?"

"You know, it's good. The Platte is getting a little low. They must be pumping a lot out of it up river."

"We have got to canoe down it so I am hoping there is enough to float our boat when we get to Ogallala."

"You'll need some big rains I'm thinking."

"Gotta go, Seth is charging in here with a towel wrapped around him demanding to hear the rest of the Angel's game."

Ginny chuckled. "Tell my darling brother hello from me."

"SCOTTY? RICHARD BARRETT HERE. Seth cannot recall what sort of deal you two made on spraying this year."

"You mean that poker-cheatin'-lyin' son-of-a-bitch Seth out of Plattsmouth?"

"I think that would encompass his good qualities, yes."

"No deal, Richard. He left here thinkin' I was priced too high."

"Are you?"

"Not with fuel, tires, wages, taxes, and insurance all gone sky high…I'd say hell no."

"Can you work us in your schedule?"

"Same as before?"

"Yes."

"Let me figure it out and I'll get back to you."

"Thanks, Scotty."

"Thanks for calling, Richard. Good to work with an honest farmer."

Richard smiled. He didn't enjoy the banter as much as Seth did but the mental repartee did add an amusing background to doing business. The slandering and denigrating nature of these relationships showed the depth of affection each held for the other. You did not do that with strangers; only with friends you had a good understanding of and that you had known for years. Seth pulled that off like a champion.

Richard plugged his cell phone into the base and sat in the desk chair. "Scotty's going to spray at the new price."

"Hmmm," Seth muttered. He sat in the upholstered club chair with a towel wrapped around his middle, his eyes fastened to the TV. At a commercial break he turned toward his brother. "I'm sorry Richard. I should have taken care of that before we left."

"Well—none of us is perfect."

"I'm damn close."

Richard chuckled. "Ginny said to tell you hi and called you her darling brother."

"See?"

"I don't see how that brings you close to perfect."

"Did Scotty give you a final price?"

"No."

"What if he jacks it up?"

"Then we'll argue about it. But we have been working with him for twenty years. I think he'll cut us a proper deal."

"Could be." Seth rose part way out of the chair on his elbows. "No, no no, don't throw it to first base." He slammed the flat of his hand on the chair arm. "Where in the hell did you learn to play baseball?"

Richard glanced at the screen. "Bothers you when they do that, huh?"

Seth sat tight lipped, his arms folded across his chest.

DAWN BROKE ACROSS THE flat county east of Grand Island, the sun stretching past the horizon and building its full presence at 6:00 am. The leaves on nearby trees were hanging limp and a cardinal was singing close by. Heat was building on the asphalt and the sound and feel of the vehicles driving by pushed the rising sense of a hot day into the air. The local TV station blurted out that it was going to be 89 degrees, 55% humidity with a chance of thunderstorms. Whoopee!

Richard brought two cups of coffee back to the room. Seth's had a quart of cream and a pound of sugar in it, just like he liked it. "Here you go, cowboy."

"Thanks, Richard. It's good to have a personal servant again. I expect to have several now that we get all of the ranch's earnings."

"Don't forget Ginny?"

"Oh, I'm not. Just that Mom won't be needin' any. A third is more than a fourth."

"So you did learn your math?"

"I gathered up that much during that involuntary imprisonment."

"Was school that tough on you?"

"With you ahead of me and Ginny comin' up behind, I was caught between the brightest and the prettiest. I remember tryin' to carve out a spot. It wasn't in sports, wasn't in music." He shook his head. "Wasn't in debate or theatre or anything. But I could drink beer with the best of them. I remember the first time I chug-a-lugged a beer and fell off the fender of Blaha's Chevy. The guys put me on their shoulders and pranced around the park like I'd set a new world's record. That sealed it. I found out what I was good at and it didn't change until I damn near died from it."

Richard sat tight-lipped, imagining his brother's discomfort. Their silence made the TV louder, more intrusive. He stood up. "Let's get the hell out of here."

As they approached the mortuary a woman moved up and down the sidewalk with a sign. "Blessed is the nation who has God."

"Look at that. Wish I could believe in something so strong," Seth said.

"How strong?"

"You know. Carrying a sign like that. That takes guts."

"And belief."

"And belief," Seth echoed.

"Do you suppose she is making up for some sin?" Richard said.

"Like what?"

"Anything."

Seth smiled and shrugged. "Any particular sin you had in mind, dear brother?"

Richard shook his head. "Not today. You?"

Seth reached for the door handle. "I could quit one, I suppose."

"Which one?"

"Lying," he said as he pulled the mortuary door open. "I'm giving that up this year."

When Carrigan came through the door he destroyed all illusions they had about morticians. He was neither tall, thin, with a whiny voice, nor rotund, smiley and greedy sounding. He had an athlete's body, a half smile, and wore causal clothes. He extended his hand. "Stan Carrigan," he said. . "How may I help you?"

"We brought Filoh Smith in yesterday. We wanted to get things settled and get back on our way."

"Let me check my emails and last night's faxes. I'll be just a minute."

"What's that all about?" Seth said.

Richard shook his head.

In a couple of minutes Stan came back. "I see a response from Craig Jamison who informs me that a daughter of the deceased, living in Chicago, has requested cremation which could be done tomorrow, if things go right. She has also requested you to spread the ashes along the Platte River."

"Makes no sense," Seth said. "Filoh never married. He ain't got no kin living in Chicago."

Stan cocked his head and looked at the fax again. He nodded— "It says here he does and it's signed by an attorney, who you know is an officer of the court."

"May I see that?" Richard said.

Stan handed it over and Richard read it, tilting it to show Seth. The brothers looked at each other. "Maybe," Richard said.

Seth grimaced and took a deep breath, shook his head and said, "I guess we might not know everything about him. But if he has a daughter, I'll bet she was a love child and has no legitimate rights to do this."

"I have to go with what this fax says," Stan said spreading his arms in supplication, "unless I get other information or a judge changes it."

"When can we be ready?" Richard said.

"Tomorrow—late afternoon."

Richard shook his head. "No earlier?"

"I'm afraid not. To get things processed, the cremation done, the remains to you—it'll take that long."

THE WOMAN WITH THE sign was sitting on a folding chair eating a sandwich, the sign leaning against the light post. "Are you gentlemen saved?"

Seth pointed toward Richard. "He was saved and baptized in the Platte River."

"God's blessing on you," she said.

"Thank you, Ma'am," Seth said.

Across the street Richard asked, "What made you say that?

"I recall Filoh pulling you out of the river so that's the saved part. And I do believe I witnessed a complete immersion procedure. That be the baptized part." Seth was smiling, his long arms swinging beside him. "Let's find some breakfast before I steal her sandwich and lie about it."

"I'm going to call Ginny and get her on this."

Picking up the cremains

RICHARD'S CELL PHONE RANG just as he pushed away his breakfast dishes.

"Hello, Ginny."

"Richard. I found out Filoh Smith never married, never lived with anyone anybody knew about, there is no census record of him having had a wife or children at the farm and no marriage, birth, or death certificates filed in the county or the state."

He mulled his coffee. "Suppose he could have done this out of state. The mortician has a letter from Craig Jamison that says Filoh has a daughter living in Chicago. She wants him cremated and asks us to spread his ashes on the river. If we go by that we lose another two days here."

Ginny cleared her throat. "I can't tell you what to do, but there is no public record."

"I understand," Richard said. "Thank you. We will let you know. Good bye." He sat, elbows on the table, the cell phone in his hand like it was going to give him some important information, like it was a connection to life beyond the restaurant and today and the heat building up on the parking lot outside.

"Let's git," Seth said.

"To where?"

Seth looked around. "I don't know." He fidgeted, his index finger hooked through the handle on the coffee cup. "Waitress—more coffee please."

Richard took a pen out of his breast pocket, pulled a napkin over and started making notes. "We have been gone a month now and we are only about a quarter of the way."

"And we don't even know what's ahead," Seth added.

Richard nodded. The sound of coffee cups setting down on hard Formica echoed from their booth. The moment had come and gone when a gifted decision would jog them toward their goal. They stagnated in the quicksand of delay.

"I don't see we got a choice," Seth said. "If we just leave or fight it out, either way it's goin' to take two days. And you know what? I'm tired. I'm goin' back to the motel and take a nap."

"Ok," Richard said. But they both sat there, restaurant noises pushed into the background, stomachs full and minds stalled.

AT THE MOTEL RICHARD sat in the upholstered chair looking through the window to the rear of the building, out over a planted field. A youth with a trombone stood at the edge of the field playing to an audience of ankle high corn. Richard opened the window to listen. The notes came and went depending on the wind gusts and he smiled thinking of what the musician was saying to the corn between numbers.

Richard said. "I have been thinking. We—have not been thinking. The major part of our trip was to determine why Grandpa Mclzer chose the land he did. There is plenty of land on both sides of the Platte that he could have chosen. We have been so wrapped up in Filoh and his pollution theories that we have failed to make any notes or even lodge a guess as to why he chose the Barrett homestead."

Seth cocked his head from the pillow. "You wake me for that?"

"Needs to be said. And we need to start taking visual and written notes about it so we can complete this venture with our desired outcome."

"Fine. You do that." Seth turned his back to Richard and folded the pillow over his head.

"Needs to be done," Richard said in a whisper, his chin resting in his palm. He stood up and got the pen and pad from the writing desk and began outlining the trip. Where he had doubts about locations he put a question mark to ask Seth about later. It would not be good to wake him again. When he looked up the trombone player was bowing to the corn. He then turned, placed the instrument under his left arm and marched toward the backdoor of the motel. Richard smiled.

What scenes we concoct when we think no one is watching.

IT WAS TWO DAYS later when the mortician called. "Did either of you wish to view the cremation?"

"For what purpose?" Richard asked.

"Some people like to say their final goodbyes and see that the remains they receive are actually of their loved one."

"We wouldn't know one way or the other."

"I assure you sir, they will be the remains of Filoh Smith."

"That's good enough for me." Richard said. He poked Seth. "We will be there around 4:00 this afternoon." Seth nodded.

THE CURRAN FUNERAL HOME was not busy when they arrived by cab at 3:45. They entered the front door to a somber setting with celestial music playing from the four corners of the ceiling sounding like it was wrapped in down quilting. A chime announced their entry and a youngish woman with a half smile set on her face came from behind a curtain.

"We've come for Filoh Smith's remains," Seth said.

"Please wait here," she said and disappeared. She returned with a marble vessel that looked like something an ancient Egyptian would place in a tomb. "Here are his cremains," she said.

"Cremains?" Seth said.

"They are called cremains when they are in the urn."

Seth scanned it and turned it around. "Looks better than his house."

She continued smiling. "It is only $195."

"Do you have a container that isn't so spendy?" Seth said.

"Most people like to have an elegant container for their loved ones. If you display it on a table or mantle, you want it to look nice and reflect the elegance of their life."

"We had one urn on a mantle for more'n a year and this one's gonna get emptied in short order somewhere on the Platte River between here and Ogallala. We don't want to throw away this nice container." Seth looked around. "Do you have a cardboard box you can put these in?"

The lady looked back and forth between the two men and when Richard nodded she took the urn and disappeared behind the curtain. When she returned it was with a cedar box with a lock and key. "This is our special at $29.95."

"That'll do fine," Seth said. "Wrap him up."

Richard pulled out the credit card. The brothers looked at each other wondering if it would clear this time.

"Are you paying for everything?" she asked.

Richard nodded.

"The whole ball of wax," Seth said.

"That will be $1,250 total."

"That's the profit on about four steers," Seth said. "Is he worth it?"

A half smile lit Richard's face. "A bit late to consider that now."

Hefting the box of cremains, Seth held it with both hands in front of him, eyes forward, and marched in a funeral like procession out the front door to the cab.

THE OWNERS OF WINDCHASER Acres agreed to deliver the horses to the Highway 34 Bridge that crossed the Platte southeast of Grand Island. The cab beat them there and while the brothers felt sure their horses would get there they paid the cabbie to hang around until the horses showed up for sure.

Richard was surprised to find that his body slid into the saddle with a degree of comfort, like he was built for it. He checked the stirrup length, pulled the reins even and with a slight smile of satisfaction moved the horse in a westerly direction away from Grand Island headed for Wood River.

"Where did you put Filoh?" Richard said.

"He's right beside Mom and Dad."

Richard glanced at the protruding saddlebag. It struck him as odd somehow that the jostling of the horses on the trail would jiggle the cremains much as the saddle manipulated him. Now—where to dispose of them in a dignified yet meaningful way. Their cremains would be lost to the future, but it gave him a comfort to know that his parents would be on the river they loved and as they were neighbors with Filoh in life, so would they be neighbors in death.

Chapter 11

"IT'S SURE QUIET AROUND here without the kids," Ginny said.

Serena was spraying her hair prior to an appointment with the Douglas County School Superintendent. "Do you ever think of what it will be like when we're old and all the noise will be gone?"

"Occasionally," Ginny said. "It's far in the future for me."

"I've had it for some time but I don't look forward to it anymore."

"What time's your appointment?"

"Two o'clock. I need to get moving. How do I look?"

Ginny stood back. "Good enough to hire on the spot. Good luck."

Serena glanced both ways at the end of the driveway and pulled out on the county road. She didn't recognize the Sheriff's car until it had passed her going in the opposite direction. Then she followed it in her rear view mirror until it went out of sight. Coincidence? She wondered.

She looked at the dashboard clock—forty minutes until her interview. If she could nail a job in Douglas County, especially in the Southern part, she could still live in Plattsmouth and commute. Tales of the Omaha school district had been running around the education circuit for the last forty years and she wasn't interested in teaching in some of those schools, but she was anxious to see what options today's interview would present.

THE ROOM SMELLED OLD. Smelled used. The secretary looked at her over bifocal glasses that sat halfway down her nose and when she rose to go tell the Superintendent that Serena was there she resembled a barrel with a belt around the middle.

Obviously his wife hired her.

"Good morning Miss Baker. I'm Jason Boardwell. Would you care for coffee?"

"I would, thank you."

He held the door, ushered her in and directed her to a seat across from him at a conference table.

No looking down at me from across a big desk.

"I've gone over your application and I'm puzzled over one thing. What was the reason, in your opinion, for your dismissal from Plattsmouth?"

Serena lowered her head, fiddled with the strap on her purse. She had expected this question somewhere in the re-employment process but she had not formulated an answer to it. Try as she might, she found it difficult to lay the blame on any one person or any one thing. It seemed like trying to find a penny under a pile of leaves. She lifted her head, looked Mr. Boardwell in the eyes and gave her version.

She was amazed she got through it with little show of emotion. The final answer was a loose jab at insubordination but she had explained why and how it had come up. Boardwell sat back in the chair, pushed the aluminum framed glasses to the top of his head and smiled.

"I don't remember the middle verses to 'Come All Ye Faithful,'" he said shaking his head. "If I heard them I wouldn't remember them." He stared at the application in his hand, his shirtsleeves rolled up two turns to expose an inexpensive watch and a hairy wrist. "Have you looked at the conditions of employment on our website?"

Serena nodded. "Yes."

"And you agree with them?"

"Yes."

He laid the application down and removed the glasses from his head. "Then I would like to offer you a contract for the coming year."

"Which school are you thinking of?"

"Monroe Middle School."

"I'm not familiar with that one. Where is it?"

"That's on Bedford Avenue out near Gallagher Park. We've had a few issues lately but I think you can handle yourself and bring control to a reasonable level. The past teachers have been recent graduates whereas you have a good deal of experience."

"I didn't want to teach in a middle city school."

"Most applicants don't," he said nodding his head. "But I see in you someone who controls their destiny and one who can rise above minor issues to advance the greater good for the students and the school."

"Thank you, but I would really prefer a school on the southern out-skirts of Omaha if you have an opening. I will be living in Plattsmouth."

Boardwell heard her out, looking her in the eye and produced a gentle smile that cemented his eyes in an unaltered gaze. "Plattsmouth is but thirty minutes from the parking lot. You'll love the kids. Parents and graduates are involved and what they need this coming year is a teacher who can lift them to their natural levels. One who can inspire them to do their best. The job market has changed—is changing and high school graduates need to know our curriculum. Please let me put your name before the school board as a capable and willing applicant for Monroe." When he quit talking he leaned forward on both elbows, mouth open in the beginning of a questioning smile, his eyes sparkling with reflected light.

She nodded. "Ok."

He reached across the table, placed his hand on top of hers. "You'll enjoy it and I'll enjoy working with you, I can tell that now." His hand stayed on top of hers a little longer than a handshake would endure—a bit too long to be comfortable but she left it there feeling that it insured the position and granted her status.

What would Richard say? If he knew? That hadn't taken long. She had the rest of the day to shop, go visit the school or head back to the ranch. She would make that decision once she was in the car. Sort of let the rest of the day be a gypsy day, one that had been fully planned but now allowed freedom.

BUD PINSKY DROVE UP the driveway to the Barrett Ranch as if he owned it. He parked in the shade of the big elm tree partly to shield his cruiser from the blistering sun but also to obscure visibility from the road. Don't hide it but don't advertise it was his motto. He locked it and walked to the door where he removed his hat, held it in his left hand and punched the doorbell with his knuckle. He could hear Ginny coming down the stairs and when she opened the door he was struck, as he always had been, by her clean beauty and bouncy atti-tude. He struggled to remember that he was the sheriff and not a 9th grader asking her for a dance.

"Morning, Ginny."

"Why hello, Bud. What brings you out here this morning?"

He spun his hat in his hands. "Out this way and thought I'd stop in and see how everything was going."

"I'd invite you in but nobody's home and I wouldn't want anybody to think anything untoward."

"We could take a walk around the place."

"Ok. Let me change shoes."

Ginny came out in low-top hikers, locked the door and put the key on a nail in the far wall. "In case the kids get back before we do."

Bud nodded and placed his hat on his head setting it just the way they had taught him in the police academy. He stuck his arm out palm up and with a slight bow indicated that Ginny should precede him down the stairs.

"What a beautiful day," Ginny said.

"A grand day for this part of the year. The farmers are praying for some rain with the new plantings."

Ginny turned and smiled at him. "We're all that way. Loving what we've got but always asking for something else."

They walked toward the barn. "You haven't had any problems since the heifer killing?"

"No. We're more cautious than we were."

"That's good. That's good."

They walked into the garage portion and then out to the feed lot, all the time with Bud clasping his hands behind his back, leaning a bit forward as he picked his way over the hardened mud. They stopped at the fence and leaned on the top rail.

"How long the boys been gone now?" Bud asked.

Ginny cocked her head, looked at the sky. "Over a month."

"What have they got—two months to do it?"

Ginny nodded. "They've run into some unusual problems they hadn't figured on."

"Oh. Like what?"

"Banking problems. Then they got put in jail for a few days and then…" she turned to Bud. "…Filoh Smith died. Rattlesnake."

Bud shook his head. "I never heard of rattlesnakes on the Platte."

"This one apparently came down with a water spout. Just swam with the flood and ended up near Grand Island."

"Well—I feel mighty sorry about old Filoh. He was a strong voice in this community when we were growin' up." He shifted his gaze to Ginny. "What was he—90, 91?"

"I think he was 90."

"Ninety...hmmm. That's a ripe old age." He stayed a cool three feet from her on the rail making sure he didn't invade her territory. "I wonder if there is some conspiracy afoot to cause them those problems. They've never had issues around here."

"Makes you think so, doesn't it?"

"Why don't we go make a pot of coffee and outline this thing like we used to do in English class. See if there is anything to it."

Ginny felt a quick thump in her chest. Bud had already stood straight and was turning to go back to the house. She had to make a decision now. She was with the law. It was who she would call—and did call—when they had a problem. It would be ok. "Fine."

Bud made himself at home. Hung his gun belt over one end of the chair and plopped his campaign hat over the other.

"Cream and sugar, Bud?"

"Black, Ginny. I drink so much coffee that if I put cream and sugar in it every time I'd need three different sizes of uniforms."

"Is that a policeman's hazard?"

"You remember when Dunkin' Donuts opened up? I went from a thirty-two inch waist to thirty-six in about two months." He nodded once. "That cost me a new belt and pants." He patted his flat stomach. "But I got it under control."

"You like control don't you Bud?"

He looked at her. "What kind of control?"

"Oh—control over the city, your department, the things that go on around town."

He straightened up. "Ginny—that's my job."

"I know. But it fits you to a T. In school nobody would have predicted you would be a sheriff."

"No—probably not."

"You were a little shy for that."

"Is that what I was—shy?"

"We all thought so."

"We who?"

"The girls."

Bud smiled. "You guys talked about me?"

"Sometimes."

The smile stayed on his face. "And here I thought you were all talking about the big bad guys on the football team."

"Oh we did, but we got around to all the boys, including you."

"And I came out shy?"

"Oh Bud, don't take it seriously. It was just a bunch of girls spouting off in the locker room."

"You were talking about me in the locker room—that's sexy." His pants began to get tight around his groin. "Anybody talk about makin' a play for me?"

"Barbara Devers made several suggestive remarks as I recall."

"Barbara Devers? Cripes, I wouldn't have dated her."

"Well, you asked."

Bud put both palms on the table. "How about you, Ginny?" He sucked his lower lip between his teeth and waited.

"We all thought you were nice, but you weren't on my A list. And besides, you never asked me out."

"Didn't think you'd go." He leaned forward on his elbows and took the coffee cup in both hands. "Who was on your A list?"

"The guys I dated. Hank, Barry, Kenny."

"And then you married Donavon with the middle name of Glad. I almost died that day."

Ginny turned with a startled look on her face. "Died? About what?"

"It was my first full day on the force. I'd spent everything I had on my uniform and what was my first job? Directing traffic out of the church parking lot of your wedding guests on the way to the park for the BBQ and reception. I was on the outside looking in."

"It didn't occur to me."

"I'm sure it didn't. But it stung like hell. I spent three days in hell thinking about you being screwed on your honeymoon in Colorado Springs."

"Bud…"

He closed his fingers around her forearm and pulled her toward him. Her coffee spilled. He grabbed the front of her blouse with his other hand and jerked down hard. Blouse, bra and necklace gave way and his eyes feasted on her breasts for a moment as he pulled her toward him.

"Bud—no…"

He had talked last time. This time he would not talk. He would do what he had come out to do.

He closed his eyes to avoid her fingernails but he had her off balance and falling into him. He scooped her up with an arm under her knees, the passion in him swelling as he carried her up the stairs. He remembered the bedroom and could have reached it with his eyes closed.

The door was closed. He kicked it in and put his mouth over her breast. He put her on the bed and fell on top of her, one hand on her breast, the other searching to find the zipper on her jeans. She squirmed like a snake but his mouth on hers and his weight and strength held her.

He ripped the button and zipper out and was tugging on her pant legs and dry humping her like a machine. She struggled for air. His coffee breath pulsed into her nose. Whiskers burned her face.

The metallic click of a rifle bolt slamming shut echoed throughout the small room. Bud stiffened and turned his face toward the door.

"Get off!" Serena said. The rifle was pointed at his chest not more than eight feet away. He looked back at Ginny, debated with himself for a moment, then slid sideways off the bed. Serena backed up into the doorway keeping some distance between them. "Move into the corner." Keeping her eyes on Bud she said: "Ginny. Go behind me and get downstairs."

Ginny started to cover up.

"Forget about that. Just go."

Ginny pulled her pants up. "Don't shoot him."

"Go."

Ginny's feet on the stairway dissolved into silence.

"What now?" Bud said.

"I'm not sure. I'll shoot you if you move an inch, Bud Pinsky."

"So what's the crime about tryin' for a little kiss?"

"Huh. Let's try rape."

"That wasn't rape."

"Attempted rape."

Bud stood there unsure where to go with this. He started toward Serena.

The muzzle blast exploded in the closed room, the bullet tearing through the flooring between Bud's feet. A look of stunned surprise took over his face.

"Jesus Christ—this isn't a shooting offense," he said.

Serena kept her eye along the barrel, the muzzle aimed at Bud's groin. "It is for me."

"Well, you better think again. Shooting someone for this is murder one."

Serena shook her head.

"Let's just walk away and pretend it didn't happen."

"You pretend. I'm not going to."

"Look, Serena. I'm the law. Who are you going to report this to?"

"I'll work on that," she said. "I'm going to back up. I want you to walk to the head of the stairs and stop there."

"Why all this drama?"

"Because I'm the one with a loaded gun and that makes me the director."

Bud stopped at the top of the stairs, looking down. Ginny was not in sight. Serena pushed the gun barrel into his back.

"Walk down one step at a time in slow motion," Serena said. "Ginny—we're coming down. Have you got a gun?"

"No."

"Get one and cover him when he gets to the first floor."

There was a series of sounds. Wood, metal to metal, glass rattling followed by the sound of a bolt closing on a weapon. "Got it," Ginny yelled.

"Ok, Bud. One step at a time," Serena said.

Ginny had taken Bud's gun belt off the kitchen chair and Serena directed him to sit down with hands behind his back. He sat looking across the room and swallowing often.

"What now?" Serena said.

"We call someone."

"Who?"

"Call the city police."

"They won't come out here to his jurisdiction."

"Well, call his office then and see who answers."

"We could call the state troopers."

"Yes. Try that. Or 911."

Ginny dialed 911. The operator answered. "You dialed 911, is this an emergency?"

"Yes."

"Do you want fire, medics or police?"

"Police."

"I'll connect you."

After a moment: "Sheriff's office. Officer Clark speaking."

"Clark, this is Ginny Houston out at the Barrett Ranch. Could you arrest a member of the sheriff's office for a crime?"

"What?"

"I said could you arrest the sheriff for an attempted crime?"

It was silent for a moment. "I guess so," he said.

"Well—bring another officer with you to drive Bud's car back and get out here as fast as you can. We don't want to have to shoot him but we will if he moves and then you can stop and pick up the coroner on your way."

"Jesus, Ginny. What's goin' on out there?" Clark said.

"Clark, put on your funny little hat and hop in your black and white car and get out here on the double."

"We're on our way. And for God's sake, don't shoot him."

"I'm telling you—if he moves we'll shoot him."

Ginny cradled the phone. "Get the handcuffs from his gun belt."

Bud straightened up. "Now Ginny, there's no need for that."

"I didn't think so before but I've changed my thinking on that and you."

"Ginny," he tilted his head. "We can work this out before Clark gets here."

"Just how do you propose to 'work things out'"?

A frown creased his forehead. "I don't know." He shook his head. "My gawd we grew up together. Went to school together. You don't want to do this. This will ruin me."

Serena came in with the handcuffs. Ginny aimed her rifle at Bud's groin. "Cuff him to the chair, hands behind him."

"Damned if I'll stand for this," Bud said and started to rise.

Ginny tightened her grip, shoved the rifle forward. "Bud—you move one more inch and you will be in a wheelchair the rest of your life, if you live through it."

He stopped part way out of the chair, thought about it and sat down putting his hands behind the chair. Serena snapped the cuffs. Ginny lowered the rifle. "Now, we'll wait."

"Ginny—isn't there anything I can do or say that will let you change your mind on this?"

"Like what, Bud? Like what?"

He looked around the kitchen. "I don't know but there must be something."

"You keep saying that, but what? What would you do or say if you had finished what you started?" She carried the rifle in one hand and walked a circular path in the kitchen.

"I thought you were game for this sort of thing?"

"Game?" She squinted. "Game? What the hell gave you that impression?"

"I just thought."

"Well you did some stinkin' thinkin'."

"I didn't mean any harm."

"Is that what you call it—harm? Rape is no harm? What has happened in your lawman's outfit that a planned rape means no harm?"

A car door slammed and two sheriff's deputies came through the door with weapons drawn. Clark leveled his service pistol at Ginny. "Put the rifle down, Ginny."

She put the gun on the floor.

"You too, Serena, and step back from it."

Clark's eyes took in the situation. "Anyone else here?"

Ginny shook her head.

"Pick up the rifles Hank." He holstered his weapon. "Now—what have we got here?"

CLARK FINISHED WRITING IN a small blue notebook he carried in his breast pocket. "I think that does it for now."

"What are the charges then?" Ginny asked.

"Assault and sexual battery by a peace officer under the color of authority."

"Is that tough enough?" Serena said.

"Well," he cocked his head. "Depends on what the legal system does with it."

"I want him out of this jurisdiction and away from here," Ginny said.

"And that may happen," Clark said as he stood up. "I can still hardly believe it."

Ginny lowered her chin. "I believe it."

"Yeah—I know. I'm sure the DA will need to talk with you."

Ginny laid her hand on Clark's forearm. "Thank you for coming out. I know it has to be tough on you too."

He looked at her hand resting on his arm. "It's my job."

Bailing the sheriff out of jail

"**WHAT? SAY THAT AGAIN,**" Klete Dixon shouted into the phone. His mouth opened part way and his eyebrows arched. "No—let him sit there awhile. I'll think about it and get back to you." He slammed the phone down and spun his chair around to look out the back windows. His hand went to his chin and he rubbed it back and forth like it would bring a new idea to his head. He turned around and punched in a phone number.

"Craig. Klete here. Bud's been arrested for sexual assault on Ginny Houston. Yes, Clark brought him in and he called me for bail. We gotta be careful about this. Can't have him talking about anything. Can you come out here now? Good. Come in my office door and don't make a big show of leaving town."

Craig Jamison did not make a big show. He left his Mercedes in its usual parking space, walked out the rear entrance of his office across the street to the Chrysler dealership through the open bay of the service department to a rear parking lot enclosed by cyclone fencing with razor wire curled across the top. From his wallet he took out a key, inserted it in the lock and got in a tan PT Cruiser. Then touching a remote button that caused a sliding gate to open, he drove through it onto Main Street and out of town, the tinted glass masking his presence.

He knew that Klete would be infuriated. He also knew that they had been through tougher things than this so when he opened the door to Klete's office and felt the drama in the air it did not disturb him. He walked across the office to the coffee pot, poured a cup and sat in the leather-covered love seat, put the cup on a Spanish hand-carved leather disc and unbuttoned his coat. "Now—tell me the whole story."

When Klete finished, Craig sipped his coffee. "I don't see any connection between this incident and anything else that has occurred, Klete. I wouldn't put too much credence in anybody's thought processes to put events together. You and I and Bud know other things but this has nothing to do with those."

Klete spun his chair around. "We were doing pretty well with delay. Look where they are—about a third of the way and they've already used up half of the time. What bothers me is that Bud would risk the end goal for such a petty thing."

"Rape isn't a petty thing."

"I could have gotten his ashes hauled for a hundred bucks and it's going to cost more than that to bail him out."

Craig smiled. "Klete—you and I are old men. Forty years ago we were talking about our chances of getting laid. Now we're talking about our doctor appointments."

Klete leveled his finger at Craig. "But the risk was not a multi-million dollar deal."

"When your blood is hot..." Craig shook his head... "you don't think about that."

Klete crossed his arms and swung around in the chair. It was silent for a few moments while Craig sipped his coffee and waited for step two. It came soon.

"I want him bailed out and sent away. Get him in some damn school or training or something for at least two months. I don't want him in a position to be questioned by anyone with half a brain. They might ask a wrong question and he might answer it. Do you understand what I'm saying?"

Craig nodded. "How do you want me to handle the finances?"

"Pay for it out of your campaign funds. Put it under security. I'll donate a different amount but sufficient to cover it."

Craig had seldom seen him so glum. "Klete—I've been through many of these little blips in the road. This is just that—a blip. Not world war three. When we get to the other side of this we'll look back and smile at how serious we thought it was at the time."

"Yeah. Well—it's just money to you. It's empire to me. And that trumps money any time."

"I'll take care of it. See you at Rotary." He put the cup on the counter.

Klete sat not moving, arms crossed, feet on the floor, staring out the window. He rolled scenario after scenario through his mind. None of them reached the critical stage. All were containable even if some information got out. This blunder by Bud caused a number of other people to be brought into the picture and even if they couldn't connect the dots they could scratch for information. And that was dangerous.

Sometimes he wondered if it was worth it. Then he could picture the fence line changing if he owned the Barrett Ranch. See the rolling hills and river frontage making a gentle sweep before his eyes, his brand on the overhead above the gate announcing to all the world that everything you could see from that point belonged to him. A shudder ran through him. *My God, that will be the day.*

"**HOW DO YOU WANT** the check made out?" Craig asked.

"I'm sorry, Mr. Jamison. We only accept cash," Deputy Sheriff Clark said. He smiled as he watched the exasperation spread across Craig's face.

"Cash?"

Clark nodded. He pointed to a printed sign hung in a frame on the wall next to the counter CASH ONLY ACCEPTED FOR BAIL AMOUNTS.

Craig slammed his checkbook closed, capped his pen and stuck it in his coat pocket and walked through the door and down Main Street to the bank.

Ten minutes later he returned, pulled an envelope from his inner coat pocket and counted out twenty, one hundred dollar bills. "I trust that takes care of it."

"Yes, sir. Here is your receipt."

"Ask him to call me when he is released." He turned to go. "Please," he added.

Clark nodded. "I'll do that, Mr. Jamison."

BUD STOOD IN FRONT of Deputy Sheriff Clark's desk. "You lousy son-of-a-bitch."

Clark stiffened his neck. "What choice did I have?"

"Do you think I would have done that to you?" He put on his smoky-bear hat. "Where's my utility belt?"

"You're not supposed to carry a weapon while you're on bail, are you?"

"You damn turkey. I'm innocent until proven guilty. Now get my belt before I demote you to office jockey."

Clark handed him a note. "Mr. Jamison asked for you to call him when you got out."

Bud stared at him. His eyes squinted and he jerked the note out of Clark's hand. He adjusted his gun belt, checked his hat in the mirror and slammed the door as he left.

SHERIFF BUD PINSKY STOPPED in front of the glass window that in huge gold letters announced the law offices of Craig Jamison, Esquire. He had tried to control his breathing and his temper in the short walk but found neither had abated. He took six deep breaths and closed his eyes.

"Morning, Sheriff," a man said.

Bud nodded and touched his hat brim when he noticed a lady with the man. He turned and entered the office. The carpet was thick, the walls paneled, the lighting subdued and indirect, not glaring like his office where he got a headache everyday from the damned florescent lights. He looked at the smiling pretty face of the receptionist and when she called Craig on the intercom he took in the soft mounds of well displayed cleavage.

Why do they position bank tellers and receptionists so far below a standing customer? Is eye candy part of the establishment's perks to customers and clients?

Craig Jamison, who usually met his clients at the door to his office, was seated when Bud came into the room. He looked up but didn't get up.

The son-of-a-bitch. Thinks he's going to intimidate me.

Bud held his hat in his hand and stood between the two comfortable client chairs as Craig, unsmiling, looked up at him.

"Bud, there is a requirement in your contract with the county for you to obtain continuing education requirements in order to get to the next pay grade. An FBI school being held in El Paso, Texas fits the bill. It starts Monday." He reached into his right hand drawer and pulled out a ticket envelope. "Here are your tickets and hotel reservations. You'll be gone two weeks.."

"Bull shit. I'm not leaving town for two weeks."

Craig leaned back in his chair. He let his eyes wander over the man before him while he marshaled his thoughts. He had not expected this response. And yet he should have. A good attorney plans on all possible responses. It went back to law school where the instructors taught them to only ask questions they knew the answer to.

He lifted his head. "What do you have in mind?"

Bud was Sheriff, not a judge or a law professor or a DA. He had not thought beyond how to get out of jail. His basic tools were the law backed up by a billy club, handcuffs, a firearm, and a couple of deputies if need be.

"It'll quiet down."

Craig squinted his eyes. "It will quiet down faster if you are in El Paso. The Journal won't be sending any reporters to interview you and those classes are closed to phones for twelve hours a day."

"I'll leave when I'm damn good and ready."

"Bud, what would you do for a living if you went to prison for this? Have you thought about that? Think about what your family will do while you're earning twelve cents an hour in the prison craft shop. And when you come out and you're looking for a job with hard time on your resume." Craig cocked his chin up. "Why don't you go sit in the lobby, have a cup of coffee and think about this for thirty minutes. I won't cancel your reservations until you tell me to."

"Where are the little pricks now?"

"They left Grand Island on their way to Kearney."

Bud looked at the ceiling, his mind calculating time and distance. "What's my pay day if Dixon buys the ranch?"

"Ten bucks an acre—a nice round $80,000."

"I'll be out front."

Craig laid the ticket folder aside. "Have my receptionist call me when you're ready to talk."

Ashes in the Platte

"I think this looks good," Richard said.

Seth bit his lip, looked around and then at the rock embedded in the sand. He nodded. He handed one of the three urns to Richard. "Do you think we ought to dig a hole?"

"No. I kinda like the idea of high water taking them down river, don't you?"

Seth fidgeted a minute. "All right." He removed his hat. "Just pour them out on the bank?"

"I think so. I do not envision any of them wanting to be in the ground."

Seth swallowed and looked off across the river, his eyes catching the rise and fall of a sweeper as the current moved it. "You gonna say something?"

"Let's each say something in our hearts." Richard pulled the lid off the urn he held in his hands. "Is that ok with you?"

Seth nodded. "Who have you got?" He twisted the top off the urn and trailed the ashes around the base of the boulder.

"Mom."

"These are Dad's." He sprinkled the ashes on the sand in an even row and stood blinking back tears. "I hadn't thought about not seeing the urns again. Kinda final isn't it?" Ash dust rising from the sand caught the evening sunrays that penetrated the canopy of cottonwoods.

For all the time Mae and Andrew had to design their final resting place they didn't get beyond the cremation stage. With Andrew being gone so long and his cremains encamped in an urn under her bed, Mae thought often about setting up a family burial plot on the ranch but figured it wouldn't be perpetual. Something bothered her about a family claiming land after they were dead, their bodies in repose on the high point of a farm presiding over the working day and the people who performed it.

At any rate, she hadn't decided what to do when it was time to put her cremains in an urn so the brothers had placed it on the fireplace mantle thinking the daily vision of it would prompt them to come to a final conclusion on the matter. It did not. When the will was read and the brothers were about to start on the described journey, the family agreed on how to handle the cremains of Andrew Duncan Barrett and Rhonda Mae Barrett. Somewhere along the Platte River would do fine. Of course, none knew they would be adding Filoh Smith's deposit as well.

"You think it's ok to put Filoh's ashes with theirs?" Seth said.

Richard tilted his head. "I am okay with that."

Seth picked up the $29.95 cedar box, turned the key in the lock and took a deep breath. "Filoh, we commit you to the rise and fall of the Platte River you loved so much. You are here with Andrew and Mae. Neighbors in life, fellow passengers on the river in death." He turned to Richard. "God bless your afterlife."

Richard nodded. Seth handed him the box and he looked inside as if he expected to see something remaining. Seth crumpled the plastic bag that had held the cremains and the brothers stood shoulder to shoulder watching the occasional surges push up the low bank and wash over the ashes, watched them turn dark grey as they took on the water, watched in silence as the ashes separated and ran with the current freeing themselves from the land and riding the crest of the water as it journeyed toward the sea.

Seth held up the cedar box.

"Put it in the fire," Richard said.

The fire was obstinate. In between the bark and the wood, moisture, plant, and bug debris had made the cottonwood limbs so wet that Richard chopped off the bark before feeding a limb into the fire.

The River

Shadows built as the sun moved behind the trees across the river and crawled toward them building a bridge between the banks. They watched it come until it included them and the fire and the tent.

THEIR CAMP, SET ON a grassy bank about three feet above the river, was a nesting place for mosquitoes so after the meal they entered the tent, zipped the mosquito netting shut and lay on their bags, arms behind their heads. Firelight flickered against the tent walls, looking for all the world like dancing figures sanctifying the burial place.

"I kinda always thought we'd do this at the junction of the North and South Platte," Seth said.

"Probably would have if we had not lost Filoh."

Seth turned on his side. "You know—I can see each creek and little river coming into the Platte that Filoh pointed out. The foam and junk in Silver Creek. Wood River, those creeks he pointed out early on." He shook his head. "It's a damn wonder you can see the bottom of the river from the bank."

"You notice any difference in the air coming up river?"

"No. I hadn't thought about it."

"Keep sniffing. See if it changes any."

"Smells damper. Does that count?"

Richard chuckled. "I don't know. Just thought we would add that to our daily scientific tasks."

"We don't want to lose sight of our goal here."

"No—we will not do that."

"Let's see that we don't." Seth opened up his sleeping bag. "Man— it's getting warm in here. What time is it?"

"Nine. Good night Seth."

"Same to ya."

THE GOOSE WAS OBNOXIOUS. Sunrise was an hour away but he acted like he owned the river and the bank.

Seth rolled over. "Shut up!"

"Something is bothering him," Richard said.

"I don't care what it is. He shouldn't be bitchin' about it until dawn."

"Could be a coyote about to eat him, or her, or the kids."

"Yeah—well that's life."

Richard put his arms behind his head. "I wonder how things are going back home? The new hired hands and all?"

"They'll keep."

"No doubt. But I'm concerned anyway."

"Nothin' we can do about it from here."

"What could go wrong?"

"Everything."

"That's comforting."

"Well—you asked."

Dawn on the river spiked a hidden alertness in the people and birds and animals that were privileged to share another day near or on the rolling water. That portion of the water went by but once, recording what it saw, always taking with it whatever was offered.

Insects rode atop the water like watercraft, skipping across the eddies and drifting down to other places. Inanimate sticks and branches and whole trees, their roots having been undermined by the high water of spring, drifted by with seldom a murmur until a root spiked on a sand bar, then the whole upper structure bent down stream until it created a pocket of backwater at its base and it stayed there bidding goodbye to the floating items that it had consorted with coming downstream. Here it would stay, its green leaves curling and falling into the river as sand and mud built up around the roots, the foundation tree becoming part of a fortress the likes of which the river had produced forever.

"What do you say we call home?" Richard said.

"Too damn early. Go back to sleep."

"I have got an uncomfortable feeling about things."

"Yeah—well, it can wait until after breakfast, can't it?"

"Probably."

RICHARD CLIMBED UP THE bank and sat on the bridge railing hoping to get a good connection with a cell phone tower. He dialed the ranch home number.

"Good morning, Richard," Ginny said.

"Hi Ginny. Seth and I are just wondering how everything is going back home."

"Have you got an hour?"

IT DIDN'T TAKE A full hour but Seth was beginning to worry about how long the conversation was taking. He had the gear packed, the horses saddled and man and horses stood in the warming air warding off the occasional mosquito. Finally he saw Richard take the phone down from his ear, close it, and start back down the abutment.

"What the hell was that all about?" Seth said.

Richard shook his head and took in a big breath. "Don't know that I can remember it all but I think we better head to the airport and get back home."

"For cryin' out loud—at least start it."

The fixed base operator at the airport stood with hands on his hips, his aviator's sunglasses turning dark in the early sun. "We don't have any provisions for holding those horses."

"Anyone you know that can take them for a few days?"

He shook his head. "The slaughter house," he joked.

"That'll do," Seth said. "I'll take the saddles off first."

The pilot laughed. "I'll call my sister. She might know a place."

He pocketed his phone. "She says Elm Creek is about the closest. They've got a stock trailer. Don't have any idea what it'd cost."

"Cost isn't important to us at the moment," Richard said. "If you could please arrange it and then fly us to Plattsmouth it would be much appreciated and worth your trouble."

The pilot smiled. "I like that last part." He opened his phone and punched in numbers. Waiting for the ring he said: "Tie the nags to the flag pole and get whatever you're taking with you in a small bundle over by that open hanger door. We'll take the Cessna."

It only took one duffel bag for personal stuff and, by the time the Cessna was rolled out and flight checked and Seth and Richard had watched the fueling process, they got in the back seat and buckled their seatbelts.

"Plattsmouth you say?" the pilot said.

"Right," Richard said.

Seth said: "Did you ask Ginny to pick us up?"

"Yes."

"Okay. Now fill me in on why we're going back."

"Judas Priest," Seth said after Richard had finished the briefing. "We're heading into a buzz-saw."

"Maybe. We have help. Craig will be there. We can sort it out and then get back here and make time."

Seth nodded. "We'll need to do that; that's for sure."

AT PLATTSMOUTH THE PILOT circled the field once glancing out the left window as he banked to runway 16, and landed. Ginny got out of the car and greeted them at the fence. Her hug was tight and longer than usual.

"So how are you handling stuff, Sis?" Seth said.

Ginny smiled. "We can discuss that on the way."

She talked all the way into town where they stopped at Mom's Café for lunch. The usual lunch time group was there and several came by their table to welcome Seth and Richard home and were taken aback to learn that they were not finished with their travels. "It'll be a month or so yet," Seth said as a neighbor departed.

After lunch they went to Craig Jamison's office.

Craig appeared in the doorway to his office before his receptionist could announce them. He spread his arms wide. "What are you boys doing back in town?"

"We need to talk," Seth said.

"Come on in," Craig's uplifted palm directing them through the door. "Coffee?" Craig said.

Richard shook his head. "We just finished lunch, Craig. There is an urgency to this meeting." Richard sat down. "Craig—what is your take on the recent events?"

Craig leaned back in his chair, steepled his fingers and began.

When he finished it was quiet. Ginny looked at Richard and Seth. They were tanned, leaner than when they left, and looked tougher and more determined than she remembered ever seeing them.

Richard turned his hat on his knee several turns, looked at Seth and Ginny and then looked at Craig like he wasn't sure how to start his questioning. In fact he didn't know where to start. The circumstances didn't fit in his farming profile. He trusted people and ran his life in a manner that allowed that trust to dictate friendships, loyalty, and business associates. Plotting was not in him. It wasn't in Seth or Ginny either, but something was going on that bothered him, bothered Seth as well. And obviously Ginny had been caught in the events.

"You know," Craig began, "I can't explain these happenings. There just aren't enough facts to hang your hat on."

Seth took over. "I've got a feeling these incidents are bein' orchestrated and I'm hangin' my hat on that."

"Well…"

"There's no well about it, Craig. We need somebody who can work on the sly around here. Someone who can snoop around and find out what the hell is goin' on."

"I don't mean to be arbitrary or doubtful," Craig said, "but what would you ask this person to do?"

Richard said: "For starters, I would ask him to check out the attempted rape of our sister by our protective sheriff and the fact that someone bailed him out in a heartbeat. Then the bank errors, the credit card stuff, and our incarceration in Hall County. These processes have eaten up ten days of our trip so far and we're less than half way."

Craig spun his chair around, his index fingers poking against his chin. It was silent for a minute. He turned to Ginny and nodded. "What's your take on these events, Ginny?"

"To tell you the truth, Craig, I hadn't thought about the possible interaction of these events," she nodded, "but enumerating them has set up a pattern in my mind. I'm leaning toward what Seth said. There seems to be a conspiracy to prevent the completion of the stipulation of Mom's will."

Craig let a smile creep across his face. "Conspiracy may be too strong a word."

"Maybe," Seth said. "But suppose there is and we don't address it?"

Richard nodded. "What if we hire somebody and we find nothing? What has it hurt?"

"And what if we find something?" Seth said.

Craig slipped his arms off the chair. He tilted his head and looked at the family out the top of his eyes. "What do you want me to do?"

"Hire someone," Richard said. "Find someone who is good at this sort of thing, spell out the events, and turn him loose. See if he can find something or someone behind these events."

Craig nodded. "I'll need a thousand dollar retainer for that person. I'll get started on it first thing tomorrow morning."

Ginny took out her checkbook.

Chapter 12

THAD PERCY'S MIND DIDN'T work like other peoples. There was a section of it that simply held stuff. It held stuff until something like a shot of electricity pinned several of the facts together and pointed to an outcome that made good news. Even though his income as a reporter for the Plattsmouth Journal was not enough to afford him a lifestyle that he aspired to, he always turned down tips, fees, honorariums, and waited for bonuses that proved he had done something worthy of extra compensation. This made his life easy. He had no enemies, few friends, no girl friends, and no pets. His dry-cleaning bill was less than ten dollars a month and his bar bill, which covered dirty martinis as often as possible, was almost always picked up by someone who wanted to know something. Thad was two or three days ahead of the street information and always beat the *Journal*, which only went to print once a week.

The latest three things that had been deposited in his safe cell had no correlation. They resided there merely because they were interesting to Plattsmouth people who read the *Journal* and because he had no other place to store them.

Virginia Alexandria Mae Barrett Houston, aka Ginny, with whom he had gone to school, had filed a complaint against Sheriff Bud Pinsky. Her brothers, Richard and Seth Barrett had taken off on horseback to go up and down the Platte River to fulfill the conditions of their mother's will. And Filoh Smith, an old timer who had sold out to Barrett and Klete Dixon forty years ago had shown up in town, then disappeared, but his stuff was still in Brewster's B&N and his rent was paid for three months. All that stuff had drifted his way through casual conversations with the local populace.

None of that information weighed on Thad's mind or interfered with his daily work or evening play. It just sat there like a fence post standing in a hole waiting for the dirt to be dumped in and tamped so it could finish its job of holding up the fence.

It was accidental, but Thad started for the courthouse just as Craig Jamison strode into the Chrysler parking lot walking in a meaningful manner, which said to Thad that he wasn't stopping there, but going through. Thad changed direction and arrived at the corner of the building to see Craig get into a tan Chrysler Cruiser with tinted windows, close the door and drive off.

Everybody in town knew Craig's car—a black Mercedes with tinted windows. Everybody also knew Thad's car—a white 1990 Chevrolet with a dented left front fender.

Thad doubled back to the *Journal*, opened the rear door and shouted. "Evan—I'm borrowing your car for a bit. Be right back."

Evan always left the key in his car. Thad was out of the parking lot in a minute and caught Craig before he got to Washington Street. He followed him out Webster Blvd staying a half-mile behind, across Fourmile Creek and on to where he saw the Cruiser go up Dixon's driveway and continue behind the six-car garage.

Now why would he park back there? Thad turned around before getting to the Dixon driveway and drove back to town. He parked Evan's car in the parking lot behind the *Journal* and walked to the courthouse. He hesitated at the door to the Sheriff's office stringing together his thoughts and questions. His mind was a jumble and he wasn't getting a clear picture of why he was standing there and what he wanted to know or even ask about.

Thad pulled the door open to face the receptionist. "Do you have the Police Register?" He smiled and put his elbows on the counter, a little flustered.

The lady put the register on a table and he sat in the hard wooden chair and pulled the pages back to the citation of Bud Pinsky for attempted sexual assault. He read the complete item and leaned back. Witnesses were the person who filed the complaint, Virginia Houston and Serena Baker. Those were two people who would be hard to refute. He got up and walked to the headquarters of the Craig Jamison for Senate campaign.

Evelyn Lansky was a girl he had known all his life and she smiled when he came through the doors. "Ah—I see a big contribution coming this way."

Thad pulled his front pockets out and smiled back. "Empty as my gas tank."

"Then you're going to stay and help?"

"No. I'm here on official business for the *Plattsmouth Journal.* "

"Wow—that sounds ominous."

"Could be. I would very much like to see the records of contributions from companies and individuals and the list of people on the committee to elect Jamison, if you wouldn't mind."

"I don't even know where that stuff is," Evelyn said.

"Who does?" he asked.

Evelyn shrugged. "Maybe Connie knows. Come back tomorrow, I'll find out for you."

"Okey dokey. I'll call you after my nap."

"You get to nap on your job?"

"Absolutely. That's how I stay sharp 20 hours a day."

She smiled. "I'll trade ya."

IN THE SAME BUILDING Deputy Sheriff Clark was fulfilling the duties of Sheriff during Pinsky's temporary removal from his duties.

Clark strapped on his gun belt, grabbed the keys to the county SUV, and went to investigate a call about loose cattle running wild on Pioneer Trail. Barking dogs and loose cattle were numbers one and two on the Sheriff's weekly report. Impaired drivers were a distant third but presented more possible action.

After he found the owner of the rogue cattle having coffee at Mom's Café, Clark went back to the office to write the sheriff's report for the Plattsmouth Journal. He bit on the eraser as he pondered what and how much to say about Bud Pinsky's arrest for attempted sexual assault. It was in the police register, and thus available to the public but during the three years he had been in the sheriff's office, nobody but Plattsmouth Journal reporters had asked to see the register. The Journal accepted what the sheriff wrote. They would accept what he wrote.

He started to write. "Sheriff Bud Pinsky is attending a continuing education class out of state and in his absence, Deputy Sheriff Clark is managing the office." He held it up, looked at it and smiled. "Deputy Sheriff Clark is managing the office," he said out loud. "I like it."

The brothers at home

SERENA RAN INTO his arms. It was the first time either Ginny or Seth had witnessed their brother's affection for her. They stood in the entry holding on to each other like their very lives depended on it.

"Gosh, it's good to see you," Serena said.

Richard nodded. "I am feeling that way too."

Ginny put the groceries on the counter. "Don't let me disturb you but there will be seven for supper tonight and nothing is cooked."

Serena disentangled herself from Richard's arms and, looking up at him, smiled. "I need to help Martha Stewart here get supper ready."

Richard and Seth retired to the family room, each to his own chair. For a long moment both men sat shapeless in their comfortable chairs, heads straight ahead with only the clock advertising any activity in the room.

Richard broke the silence. "It is going to be difficult going back."

Seth smiled. "I was thinkin' the same damn thing." He turned a little. "Funny how easy it has been to go to work every morning here at the ranch but how hard it feels,"—he shook his fist in the air—"this very moment to go back to Grand Island, get on top that horse and keep goin' up river."

The smile that sneaked up on Richard's face was not visible to Seth. "Do you suppose Daniel Boone felt the same way?"

"I don't know but I gotta believe he did. We're a mite older than he was but we've had an easier life of it." Seth thought a minute. "Yeah—he had to wonder what the hell he'd gotten himself into somewhere along the trail."

Richard poured himself a Scotch and lifted the glass to Seth. "To your good health."

"Sure wish I could join you. Been there, done that, got the T-shirt." He touched his upper lip with the tip of his tongue. "Dang— it would taste good."

Richard sank back into his chair and set the drink on the humidor next to it. "I am proud of you, Seth, for being man enough to quit it when you saw it taking over your life."

"Yeah, well—when you've lost your girl, your money's gone, you've got a son living 1,000 miles away you've never met, and you can't remember where you live—it's time to quit doing what's causing those things." He glanced over at Richard sipping the drink. "But thanks. I appreciate your words."

Richard nodded. "It is nice here. Could we hire someone to finish the trip for us?"

Seth chuckled. "Not likely. Don't believe the will said Richard and Seth, or their authorized representatives, go up and down the Platte."

Richard shook his head. "No. You are right."

"Besides, think of the stories we can tell when we get back."

"Who are we going to tell them to?"

"Anybody who'll listen, I guess. Ought to be great fodder for poker night."

"And the barber shop."

"And the barber shop," Seth echoed.

Ginny popped her head into the room. "Would one of you guys call Donavon and the kids in? They're in the shop."

Seth straightened up. "What they doin' in the shop?"

"Hanging the tools on the wall in a nice orderly way."

"I liked them on the bench."

"If you don't like it you can change it—when you get back. In the meantime I want to know where the tools are and not have to guess which pile they're in."

"Seems fair to me," Richard said and tilted his glass toward Seth.

"Fair? What's fair got to do with it?" He stood up and walked to the back door. "Soup's on. Come and get it."

"Feels good to eat sitting in a chair instead of on a log fighting mosquitoes," Richard said.

Ginny stopped the fork halfway to her mouth. "Nice to have the whole family around the table again."

"Donavon," Richard said. "What is your position on what's been going on?"

Donavon stopped chewing, looked at Ginny, then finished his bite. "I'd like to kill the bastard. But I think proving anything is going to be very difficult. You've got Ginny and Serena against the law. And he is the law in Cass County."

"Yeah—but it's two against one," Seth said.

"I'm not sure it will come out that way. After he was charged I heard talk around town how hard it was to make that kind of thing stick."

"I think a court and a jury could not dismiss two eye witnesses," Richard said.

Donavon shrugged. "People are prone to think if it didn't really happen, it is hard to put a guy away. Most of the men hereabouts tried similar stuff in the back seats of their car when they were young. I've got to tell you, it's got my guts in a knot."

Serena looked pretty and natural sitting at the table. "I've had a good feeling. Holding a gun on a sheriff who evicted me—that has got to be the high of my life."

Richard nodded at Ginny. "How are you feeling, Sis?"

"I've gotten over most of it. The hardest part for me is why he thought he could attempt this and get away with it. It does put me at odds with the local law enforcement; I'd be nervous calling them for anything."

"Just keep your gun handy," Seth said. "He apparently understands that." He lifted his head and looked at the counter top. "What's for dessert?"

THE FAMILY GATHERED IN the big room after supper. Richard started it.

"Craig Jamison is hiring an investigator. The sheriff is out of state for a prolonged period of time. Our time is running down and Seth and I need to get back on the Platte and polish this trip off. As comfortable as it is here, we must go. Does anyone see any reason we should not leave in the morning?"

The kids looked at each other and smirked. It was the first time they had been involved in a family meeting. They had nothing to say. Finally Ginny spoke up.

"You guys go on back. We'll be okay now."

Seth slouched in his chair. "There is nothing else we can do right now anyway. We'll just tootle on back there and get going."

Ginny said: "Do you think you can make it in time?"

Seth nodded. "If I can get Richard to stay in the saddle longer."

Richard smiled. "We'll make it. If the canoe arrives in Ogallala we'll have a wonderful Boy Scout time paddling it down river.

What about the schedule?

THE EARLY MORNING AIR was cool and still. The Cessna slipped in from Kearney like a buzzard, touched both wheels and glided to the loading ramp. The brothers loaded, fastened seat belts, put on headsets and felt the pull in their stomachs as the plane broke ground contact, soaring into the blue sky tinged with soft grey clouds near the horizon. Seth let his eyes roam to the end of land. *You'd have to go a long ways to beat a Nebraska morning on a good day.*

Richard, lulled into quiet by the engine noise, tried to keep his mind on reconstructing the schedule. They were behind in their timing and some serious planning needed to be done to make sure they finished the trek with some margin for error. They had not planned on all the interruptions they had experienced so far and none could have been imagined. Consulting his calendar, he could see they had twenty-eight days left.

After they landed, the pilot gave them a ride down South 2nd Avenue to the river where the stable hands had delivered the animals. The horses were spirited. Having been standing in stalls for two days they had rested, eaten, and gotten interested in life again.

"Whoa, boy, whoa," Seth said, planting his left foot in the stirrup, throwing his right leg over the saddle and sliding into the seat with grace.

Richard held the stirrup with his left hand, struggled to get his foot into it. He grabbed the saddle horn, clamped his right hand on the cantle, and heaved himself into the saddle. Richard took the lead rope to the mule, Seth the packhorse. "Man was not born to ride a horse," he said to no one in particular.

"Let's get this show on the road," Seth hollered. His horse reared. Seth leaned forward, his head almost touching the horse's mane. He looked like the Lone Ranger on Silver bound on a lawful cause.

Richard shook his head and touched the horse's flanks with his boot heels. They were off.

At first the re-start was exhilarating and following the Platte River along the bank was a study in where to direct the horses. The water was low, and what little remained in the stream fought to find a way through the sandbars and early summer growth. A mile out from the

Second Street bridge much of the high water channel was dry, easy travel where the horses hung their heads and walked a studied pace.

The sandbars, smoothed off by high water, had been scrubbed of small growth, and dried by the sun into tan highways shifting from time to time as the channels changed. If the river had been a snake it would have left a similar trail.

"Is there a main channel anywhere around here," Richard said.

Seth shook his head and leaned toward him. "If there is I can't see it." He nodded toward the Southeast. "Looks like the weather is going to change."

"Lousy shelter around here," Richard said.

"Well—let's see what it portends before we make shelter. Could be nothing more than some droplets."

"Portends? That's a pretty big word for a cowboy."

"I use big words when the people I'm with can understand them. Otherwise I get a lot of questioned looks."

"Does Martha understand big words?"

"What the hell would you bring her up for?"

"Just wondering what size of words you use when you're smooching on the river bank," Richard said.

"Just don't sneak up on me some time tryin' to satisfy your curiosity. I might just shoot you."

"You would shoot a man who is trying to satisfy his curiosity?"

"Damn betcha. Probably twice for good measure."

Richard smiled and shook his head. "Looks like the weather is aimed right at us. You want to ride through it or shelter up?"

They rode for another hundred yards along the south bank while Seth, who was used to dealing with weather in the open, and Richard who simply rolled up the window on his equipment, debated the effects coming to them from the approaching dark clouds and occasional sheet lightning.

Seth said: "I don't think it's gonna amount to much. Let's keep rolling and make up for lost time." He applied a soft spur to his horse. The horse perked up his ears, bunched up, and increased his pace.

Although Richard had the squint and tanned face and arms of a farmer, he adjusted his living space most of the year by turning on the heater or air-conditioner. He was not used to adjusting to his environment by adding or taking off clothes. Seth either added shirts, jackets, gloves, galoshes, slicker, or took them off. When Richard saw Seth reach behind him and untie his slicker from the back of the saddle he did the same. It wasn't easy taking care of riding and getting into the slicker on the move but before the rain started driving pockmarks in the river in front of them he had it on, snapped, and adjusted.

A slight warning wind pushed ahead of the rain. First the treetops swayed and the breeze tumbled over the tops down to the river and ran along the surface making it opaque. Just before the first drops popped against their slickers there was the fresh smell of new vegetation and the musty pungent odor of dry, hard mud getting wet again. Swallows exploded from under the Highway 183 bridge, diving, mewing, and soaring back and forth in a defensive confrontation.

"Birds seem upset," Richard hollered.

"So what?"

"Just observing."

They rode about 100 yards before Seth spoke. "Their nests probably hold the bridges together. Seems like they've been under every one of them."

The rain was slow and spaced. The drops that did fall smacked their slickers and horses, splattering shards of water 360 degrees. It was the kind of rain that warned you rather than wet you. It advertised that it could do more if it wanted to, but for now it was content to search for a place to let loose the full force of its personality. Richard watched its course with interest. Thunder and lightning rolled over them from miles away, visible on the flat land but not over them.

"Not much river here. I think canoeing this thing is going to be a tough proposition," Richard said.

Seth looked down at the waters running alongside them. "Not much float in it, is there?"

"This is why Jack Brown said we would need waders."

"Yeah," Seth said. "But the water level can change with one rain."

The occasional sheet lightning and rumble of thunder put a damper on conversation. And in a way, the brothers were talked out. They both felt they had spent a lot of time talking, had explored about all there was to explore for the time being, and as solitary men by choice they opted for less rather than more.

In his years away from the ranch, Seth had talked more than listened. Liquor did that to a fella. But looking back on it, he had talked to strangers—not family. With family it was an area bordered by feelings. Nobody ventured into the personal feelings or doings of the other—except Ma. When Rhonda Mae Barrett wanted to know something she didn't ask somebody else—she asked the person who could tell her straight out. She did personal interventions whenever she damn well felt like it—in person or by phone. Nobody hung up on her, although afterward they wondered why they hadn't. She could ask a question so personal that even when grown, Seth would blush and stammer like he did in eighth grade.

Richard took advantage of a lull in the feeble storm. "I have been thinking about Overton. We could make it to the bridge at Overton if we keep up the pace."

Seth turned in the saddle. "You been making plans?"

"Well—we're behind…"

"I know we're behind, but it ain't my fault. The things that happened, happened. You're in charge of the schedule. We agreed on that before we left home."

"Don't get your dander up, I am just suggesting, not mandating."

"Let's don't go changin' the program while we're on the mission. We'll check it out when we stop for lunch…"

"…I was thinking maybe we could eat on the move…"

"…The horses need time off, too."

"That's true but they have had two days of sitting in a stall. Could be they would welcome the workout."

"Might be. We'll see."

Richard let it set for a mile or so then tried to draw Seth into a commitment. It had been easy when they started to see what they had to do over the sixty days but looking at the river level now, he thought they might be walking most of the way back dragging the canoe mile by mile. Walking and dragging could mean as little as five miles a day. If they could make time now they could use it on the return trip if conditions warranted. There was no telling what was going to happen with the issues hanging out there.

"It is only twenty-four miles by the map. Pony Express riders used to cover twice that distance in a day."

Seth bristled. "They weren't draggin' a mule and pack horse with them. Besides that," he threw in, "they were riders, not farmers."

"We should have sold Filoh's mule," Richard shook his head and drew up. "Don't know what we were thinking. But I know this—this outfit is moving too slow to get the first half done on time. I want to get there and give us some margin for error."

"Such as what? You gettin' bit by a rattlesnake?"

"Of course not. We didn't expect any of the other stoppages did we?"

Seth was silent a moment, choosing his way along a deer track, eyes intent on the trail but letting the horse have his head. "No, we sure didn't."

"I'm just saying that with fresh horses and two days off we could make that distance and give us a foot up on the timing."

Seth looked at the sky, looped the reins over the saddle horn and removed his slicker, shook it, rolled it into a tight bundle and tied it behind his saddle on the move.

"Might be we can. Let's decide around lunch time."

Richard nodded. "Ok. I'm for that."

Sometime around noon Seth reached into his saddlebag and pulled out a bag of jerky. He slowed to let Richard move alongside and passed him some dried beef and poured raisins in his hand. "Make sure you drink plenty of water with those or you'll bind up your guts."

"That is good to know," Richard said.

"Done it enough myself. It doesn't feel good."

RICHARD TUGGED BACK HIS sleeve and wound his wristwatch. "Four o'clock," he said.

"Did you notice that piddlin' stream coming in from the North?" Seth said.

"No."

"There wasn't enough water in it to float a hub cap. And dirty—it looked like it was coming from somebody's motorhome."

"Irrigation?"

"Probably. And look at this miserable river," he said directing his arm from shore to shore. "This is a mile wide all right but it's almost empty."

"We want to stop this side of the bridge on the north shore. Nice little lake there and no roads to it. We won't get hassled by anyone."

"Can we make it before dark?" Seth said.

"Oh, hell yeah. Dark comes around nine o'clock." Richard stood in the stirrups. "I am getting a bit saddle sore."

"Comes with the territory. Think of Grandpa Melzer. And he didn't have a padded saddle."

"Wonder how far I can ride standing up?"

"Not all the way to Ogallala; that's for sure."

Having not ridden long hours before, Richard pondered the progression of seat pain and if and how numbness took over. Of course, getting used to something took time and patience and while he now had the time he was running thin on patience. He let his mind wander to the Barrett Ranch problems.

There had to come a time when he and Seth would stop their daily work on the ranch and hand it over to the family or a new owner. He had a hard time seeing when that would be, but the time frame had been shaken when Filoh started pointing out all the problems they were contributing to. Was he up to making those changes, living through them, and coming out happy and successful on the other end? Was Seth?

And what if Filoh was on a tangent that would later prove unfounded? After all, miracles had occurred in agriculture, unthought-of in the 1940s, increasing the volume of produce. A crop increase of 1,000 percent per acre was not uncommon. And now processing corn to make gasoline and using the left overs from that process to feed hogs and cattle? Unheard of—undreamed of—magical.

That didn't take into account irrigation. The Ogallala aquifer was discovered in 1899 by a U.S. Geological Survey but was not thought to have much value for farmers on the dry plains. Now look at what it does: supplies water for every 160 acres of crops with a sprinkler system. What the projections of the 1940s had not taken into account were the innovations and discoveries that came along because of man's inventiveness. No one could have foreseen them.

What Filoh was seeing and had made him and Seth see now, was the degradation of the water. The degradation of air and land that Filoh had harped on was not visible, at least to him. But that didn't convince him. What if someone invented a "water cleaner" tomorrow that you stuck in every stream? It sucked in the fouled water, cleansed it, and shot it back into the streambed as clean as spring water?

What if day after tomorrow a company developed a spray to go on the upturned soil that would absorb all the chemicals that had been sprayed on it for the last fifty years—including the feed lots where nitrogen was imbedded in the soils?

Now the air; what do you do about the air? Well—as long as you are making hypothetical discoveries figure one out for the air, too. The biggest complaint was the accumulation of carbon dioxide. Some greenies even suggested going back to horses to do farm work. That was over. Besides, horses produced as much waste as they saved. If someone would invent something for air similar to the evaporation of water from tainted ponds, taken into the atmosphere and returned cleaned and distilled, that is what is needed. God took care of cleaning the water. Why wouldn't He figure out something for the air as well?

Seth interrupted his thoughts. "Now you see why the settlers put up a town about every 12 miles along here. That is a comfortable ride and a nice place for a new community."

"I have about had it, Seth," Richard said. "I need a break."

Seth pointed ahead to the right. "I can see the lake. Can you hang in there another few minutes?"

Richard nodded. He didn't trust himself to speak in a civilized manner.

The setting for a night camp was ideal. While Richard rehabilitated himself and got a fire going, Seth rode up to the house at the north end of the lake to ask permission to camp. Before he got off his horse a man pushed open a screen door and stood in his nightshirt on the porch with a shotgun hanging from one hand.

"Evening," Seth said.

The man nodded and raised his chin to look at Seth through glasses. "I heard you comin."

"I'm Seth Barrett from down Plattsmouth way. My brother and I are riding up the Platte. Wonder if we could get your permission to camp down by the lake for the evening?"

"Where'd you say you come from?"

"Plattsmouth. Down near Omaha."

"What'cha doin' up this far?"

Seth leaned one arm on the saddle horn and chuckled. "We're riding to Ogallala."

"We got roads you know."

"Yes sir," Seth nodded. "But we have to do it on horses and along the river."

The man hadn't moved since he got there, his nightshirt fluttering in what little breeze came up from the river. "Seems like a damn fool thing to do." He turned and reached for the screen door. "Don't burn up the place."

"No sir, we won't. Thank you."

"I heard you comin's why I got the gun. I wouldn'ta shot cha."

"That's comforting to know. We'll treat the place proper. Thank you."

The farmer let the screen door slam. "You be gone in the morning?" he said on the other side.

"Yes, we will. Thank you."

The man nodded and closed the door.

When Seth came back to camp, Richard was walking in a circle around the outside edge of light that danced from the fire. He smiled to see that his brother had cleared all flammable material away from the fire for five feet. Once a boy scout, always a boy scout. "Is it easing up some?"

Richard rubbed his butt. "I don't think I am permanently damaged."

"Which of our delightful freeze-dried meals have you chosen tonight?"

"That would be Turkey Tetrazzini. It is boiling now."

"Didn't we just have that?"

"I like it."

Seth joined him around the fire, the brightest stars now showing in the eastern sky, a few frogs around the lake starting their evening chorus and the always present murmur of the Platte River supplying the underlying harmony.

Historic Watson Ranch

"YOU KNOW," SETH SAID between bites. "We're probably camped on a chunk of the old Watson Ranch, truth be known."

Richard looked up. "The Watson Ranch?"

"I thought you'd know that, being a farmer and all."

Richard thought a moment and shook his head. "Doesn't ring a bell."

Seth enjoyed telling Richard something he didn't know but he wanted to establish that Richard didn't know it because he was likely to tarnish the tale around the edges some in the telling. "I worked on this place for a spell when I was gone from home. Fixed fences, checked cattle—horseback stuff. Rarely got down to the river but originally it was the southern boundary of the Watson Ranch. Eight thousand acres from the Platte up to those hill tops you can see from here.

"Watson and Granddaddy Melzer must have run into each other somewhere along the line. Watson started the ranch in 1888. They would have been selling stuff to the same buyers for twenty years or so."

Richard wiped his bowl with a paper towel. "I never heard him mentioned."

"Well," Seth said, scraping his bowl into the dwindling coals. "They didn't teach practical stuff in that college you went to."

"Yeah, they did."

Seth smiled. "It's fun to think of those old pioneers. And look at us now. We're still competing. Barrett Ranch is 7,000 acres. Watson had 8,000 at the height of his accumulation. And Klete Dixon is around 5,760 after he added his part of Filoh's farm to his home place."

"Do you suppose Dixon is looking to best the Watson acreage?"

"I don't know," Seth said. "But it bears thinkin' on. If he gets our place, look where that puts him in the history of the Platte—over 12,000 acres and miles of Platte frontage. He could suck so many acre feet of water from the river—hell, he could irrigate half of Nebraska."

"Somebody's sucking it out now," Richard said.

Seth cast his eyes over the slow water. "That dam up-river must be holding it back."

"How are we going to canoe in this dribble?"

"We'll walk it and push the canoe."

Richard squirted some liquid soap into the pan of heated water and washed the few utensils. They burned the burnables, cleaned up around the fire ring and sat holding their coffee cups, tired mentally and physically but unwilling to call it a day.

"What are you thinking?" Richard asked.

Seth squinted, took a swallow of coffee and shook his head. "I'm just havin' a hard time getting' my head around the things that have happened. I mean, we never had these kinds of problems until we started on this trip." He nodded. "There is something rotten in Denmark and I hope that investigator figures it out."

"Yes." Richard sighed. "Too much for me to consider at this moment. I'm headed to bed."

The night enveloped them along with the river.

The River

When the sun disappeared over the prairie, the fire shadows began their dance, evening spread until everything was ghostly in the twilight. Cottonwoods buried in the sand mumbled like things alive. It was soothing to awake in the night and hear the water moving what came to it between the sand and mud banks it had carved long ago. In the dawn the sun's rays speared through the shadows from the trees on the banks, the air scented with campfire smoke, pungent and invasive.

Saddle sore

THE MORNINGS WERE BECOMING monotonous. Unused to sleeping on the ground, they arose each morning out of sorts, still tired, joints and muscles rebelling at moving, reaching, lifting, and looking at a full day in the saddle without even the distraction of Filoh to juice up their remarks. Each was used to spending most of the day alone.

Seth didn't know when he had quit bringing up new subjects. In his mind they had discussed everything and the only goal now was to get up and back within the deadline. Richard could be quiet for long periods of time allowing his mind to run through scenarios and file them away. He had other things going—Serena and the school board business that Seth was not involved in. He would make up imaginary conversations with them, letting his horse nose the trail.

It was in these doldrums that the brothers became unresponsive to the signs that gave evidence of a split river ahead and they took the right hand channel after leaving camp.

Seth turned and yelled back. "I don't see how they can call this a river."

The sudden conversation jolted Richard back to reality. "Think we are lost?"

"No," Seth chuckled. "Can't get lost. But look at it."

Richard could see the bottom and nowhere was it wider than a hundred feet. "I'm sure Mom didn't think this canoe thing through."

"There was a lot less irrigation water being taken out when she wrote it, I'll betcha."

"I wonder how iron clad that part about canoeing back is?"

"Don't know. We could call Jamison and get his opinion."

"Could."

They rode until the main channel, which had been carrying the bulk of the water to the south of them, merged in and joined theirs.

Richard straightened in the saddle. "That's better."

"Yeah—now we can swim in it." Seth stopped to let his horse drink. "You hungry?"

"I could eat a bite."

"Lunch break," Seth declared and swung down from the saddle.

Richard pulled his cell phone out and looked at the screen. "Ginny's calling," he announced. "This is Richard." He listened and nodded his head several times. "We're near Lexington. I don't think we could come back and keep our time frame. You've got to handle it. Marshal our professionals there to put up a slate of competent, well-known people and get the judge to give us time to finish this damnable ride, then Seth and I can take them on." He nodded some more and then finished the call. "You're on the right track. Just keep the pressure on and protect yourselves. I can't believe they'd try anything stupid, but you never know. Yes—we will be careful. Goodbye, Ginny."

Seth had laid out some jerky, raisins, cashews, an apple apiece, and pumped water to fill their canteens. "What the hell is goin' on now?" he asked.

Richard shook his head. "Appears Bud is gathering up other law enforcement people to say he is a good guy and Ginny must have indicated her willingness to go through with the deal as a consenting adult, then changed her mind."

"Judas H. Priest," Seth said. He shook his head. "You know somebody for a long time and bingo—the next moment they do something completely out of character and you figure you haven't really known them at all."

"But you know—" Richard bit off some jerky and moved it around between his teeth—"it's his livelihood he is protecting. He is going to play it tough."

"We can do the same. We're not pansies."

Richard looked at his brother and a wry smile spread across his face. "Ah—finally the .30-30 comes into good use?"

"Could be. Batten down the hatches, bolt the gate, and keep the infidels at bay."

"Humph. I doubt we will be shooting at anybody."

"But what if it came to that? What if they showed up at the ranch and wanted to take Ginny and Serena to jail?"

"For what?"

"I don't know. Lying to an officer. Entrapment. He could make it up just like that Sheriff Wolfe did. It might not stick but it could be enough to get them damn scared and recant some of the charges against Bud."

"Might be," Richard agreed.

"You know," Seth said in a thoughtful mode, his elbows resting on his knees, "this whole thing is taking on a scary aspect. I'm thinking there is a conspiracy."

"I doubt it. Just circumstances finishing their sequence and ending up happening while we are gone. Think back, Seth, we have had issues before going back to when Dad died but they happened one at a time and spread out over several years. If they had happened during a short period we might have thought of them like this." He tossed some raisins in his mouth and shook his head. "No—I'm thinking there is some logical explanation for these events and they just happened to coincide with our trip." He brushed his hands together and stood up. "Doesn't that make more sense to you?"

"Sense—yes. But remember what Dad used to say about sense? 'If everything makes sense, something's wrong.'"

"Yes." Richard said as he stood, "Dad was not always right."

"That's the point."

"We aren't going into Lexington are we?" Richard said, weaving a bit and rubbing his butt with both hands.

"Hadn't planned on it."

"Good. Let's push on and get this horse riding over with."

"You thinkin' the canoe will be better?"

"I don't know, but I don't see how it could be worse than this saddle."

"You should've brought your tractor seat."

Sheriffs stand behind Pinsky

SHERIFF BUD PINSKY HELD the phone against his right ear, his elbows planted on the desktop and a single sheet of paper between them. He had returned from the Texas FBI School for two days, to hold a press conference while the brothers were on the river. Craig and Klete had said it wasn't a good idea, but Bud, being Bud and the by-gawd Sheriff of Cass County, had an idea that he thought would kill this thing at its birth. Like a majorette twirling a baton he ran a pen between his fingers. The action stopped the second someone answered the phone.

"Sheriff Wolfe—Bud Pinsky here. Have you got a minute?"

IT NEVER OCCURRED TO Sheriff Bud Pinsky that what he had attempted was a crime. It was high school all over again. He had seduced several women in his police cruiser since becoming a lawman. In his mind there was a giant separation between sexual activity and crime. Crime was where you robbed or beat or killed someone. In his years as a police officer he had apprehended seventy-six criminals, solved 242 robberies, investigated and prosecuted seven murders. Those were crimes. The detailed work on his part had put the bad guys away in the Nebraska State Penitentiary. He had plaques, photos of him with several governors and two presidential candidates, and Miss Nebraska, one of his back seat conquests in the police cruiser at the airport parking lot.

Having never arrested anyone for sexual assault he felt unsure of the perimeters of that charge. A broad definition was printed on the paper between his elbows:

> Sexual assault is any involuntary human sexual activity in which a person is threatened, coerced, or forced to engage against their will, or any sexual touching of a person who has not consented.

He rolled that around in his head. My gawd—he could recall a lot of those, but they eventually gave in. None had ever prosecuted it before. Who the hell did she think she was pulling a stunt like that? Little by little, like a glacier moving toward the sea, his remembrance of the encounter eroded with slight deviations and his retelling of the event to his law counterparts to gain their support, turned to more of a high school locker room discussion with chuckles and knowing comments being made by both parties.

Sheriff Bud Pinsky was smiling as he listened to another sheriff discussing an encounter he'd had when called to assist a woman on a county road. "I tell you, Bud, she as much as offered it when I showed up with five cans of motor oil. And it was so good. I stepped outside afterward and the night was bright with stars and I was smiling like a teenager. It's those occasional freebies that highlight this work, isn't it?"

"Listen, Dan. I'd like to have about a dozen county sheriffs standing behind me when I make my statement to the press. Could you do that for me?" Bud nodded his head twice. "I'd be beholden to you. And think up something you could give as a quip to the press if they ask you." He was quiet a moment. "Yeah—that's good, I like the tone of that. I'm gonna be meeting the press on Thursday. If you could come on down and be here before 11:00 we'll make quick work of this deal." Pinsky listened a moment. "And Dan," he said. "If there is ever anything I can do for you don't hesitate one second—call me, you hear?"

News of the event had traveled around town, through cafés, church meetings, poker games, barber shops, and gas stations so, Thursday at 11:30 am, Central Daylight Savings Time, there was a fair crowd outside the Cass County Courthouse when Sheriff Bud Pinsky, looking sharp as a tack in a well-tailored and pressed uniform, stood behind a portable podium the press had hauled in for the session.

Behind him with the shorter men on the outside, taller ones in the middle, stood eleven county sheriffs, their individual uniforms contrasting in the morning sunshine. All three press reporters, newspaper, radio, and TV shoved their recorders onto the podium and hunkered down in front.

"Good morning," Bud began. "As many of you know, I have been accused of a charge that I am innocent of. I know it makes for good gossip to have a lawman charged with a supposed crime, but the charge is false and I will prove it so. The plaintiff has twisted the story and I intend to give my full testimony at the arraignment. Until then I have the full support of my fellow lawmen—good men from counties near us—and will continue in my day-to-day duties to protect and defend the good citizens of Cass County." Several shutters clicked.

"Sheriff," one of the reporters asked. "We have 93 counties in Nebraska and only two female sheriffs. Why is neither one of them standing behind you?"

Bud turned and looked at the men in uniform behind him. "I don't know the two."

"So only your friends are here to help you?"

"They are not helping me. They are standing up for what they believe."

The reporter kneeled on a step. "There are 196 men and women in Sheriff's departments and members of the Nebraska Sheriff's Association. Did you ask any of the women law enforcement members to stand for you?"

"I just told you. I don't know any of them."

Suddenly a voice cried out from the edge of the crowd. "Why are you badgering the Sheriff? In America one is assumed innocent until proven guilty. Your questions are misleading."

The crowd turned toward the speaker. Klete Dixon waved his hands at Bud. "Personally, I think he is innocent and I would stand behind him anytime."

There was a slight murmur within the crowd.

Bud picked up the moment. "Being there are no more questions, I thank you for coming today and, last but not least, I want you to know that I and my department are available to you in your time of need."

He turned and shook hands with the three closest sheriffs behind him indicating the news conference was over. The lawmen returned to Pinsky's office and the people who had gathered on the courthouse steps stood with arms crossed, discussing the event. The reporters, fetching their recording devices, had a brief conversation and two of them left. The other, the one who had asked the questions, approached citizens asking the men their thoughts and the women, their feelings. He reported for the *Plattsmouth Journal*, the paper influential with the 6,000 people in the town by the river. Tomorrow the town would find out what he learned today.

Sheriff Bud Pinsky lifted the blind and watched out of a window as the reporter, Thad Percy, maneuvered his recorder from one person to the next.

"Something, Sheriff?" the clerk asked.

"Just another pissant." He let the blind close.

GINNY AND SERENA WATCHED the performance on the 5:00 o'clock news and sat stunned in the chairs usually occupied by Seth and Richard. Ginny sipped her gin and tonic, put the glass down and shook her head. "Twelve against two."

Serena tucked her feet under her on the big chair. "I don't see how any jury could discount what we say. And Deputy Clark can back us up."

"Except he didn't see it," Ginny said.

"No—but he's the one that got the call and made the arrest."

"What if Bud gets him to neutral—where he says he really doesn't know what happened? He got the call. He came out, took our word for it, and arrested Bud. Now we would have two sworn police officers against you and me."

"I'm not liking the sounds of that," Serena said.

Bookshelves of dark walnut lent the room a relaxing, scholarly atmosphere as evening sunlight filtered around the curtains lighting the corners as the TV sound faded.

"Wait," Serena said. "Turn the volume on. I want to hear what Thad has to say."

Thad Percy had few friends. He had been an employee of the *Journal* for three years but nobody really knew him. News stories and feature articles carried his byline but he remained an unknown and few people in Plattsmouth could name him or say what he did. His appearance on the nightly news was an anomaly.

When the newscaster asked him for his opinion on the story, he spoke into the camera. "This story is like a Baklava pastry—you peel back one layer and there is another. There is something ominous about Sheriff Pinsky bringing in eleven county sheriffs to stand behind him in a strictly local case without having any facts released to the public and the supposed victim being from one of the prominent families in the region."

"Thad—are you suggesting there is more to this than what the charges indicate?"

Thad looked away from the camera, the courthouse and old public library showing in the background. "I want to be careful of what I say here. What I'm saying is that there is a general underground feeling that the sheriff is working too hard to keep his good guy image on top. What people know and what they are willing to talk about seem to be two different things right now. And I..."

"...Thank you, Thad. You may view Thad's article in tomorrow's edition of the *Plattsmouth Journal*. Now to sports news with Bryce Peterson."

The newscaster shut off her mike and turned to the producer. "Cripes—I thought he was going to spill his guts."

"You stopped him just right. Let the *Journal* play with that one."

"Do you think Mr. Dixon will be displeased?"

The producer shook his head. "Don't see that there was enough to ruffle his feathers. We'll find out at the board meeting."

KLETE DIXON MOVED THROUGH the uniformed men smiling, and here and there shaking hands, and exchanging greetings. He jerked his head toward Pinsky's office as he got Bud's attention and together they entered and closed the door behind them.

"Thanks for your comments out there," Bud said.

Dixon nodded. "I'm going to help you fight this but don't ever pull a stunt like this again. And I mean ever." He walked over to the window and looked at the crowd as it separated. "I told you to stay in Texas and you didn't do it. I'll live with this once but finding another sheriff at the next election will not be that hard to do if you screw anything up again. Am I understood?"

"I know," Bud said.

"I asked am I understood?"

Bud's head nodded. "Yes—you are." He could not bring himself to apologize.

Dixon's eyes burned into him and in the silence Bud slipped back to his junior year in high school when he had been sent to the principal's office for discipline. He remembered being told to bend over and grab his ankles and the loud whap as a size twelve tennis shoe connected with his backside. The embarrassment far exceeded the pain. He was an elected Sheriff—why could Dixon instill such embarrassment in him at this stage of his life? Damn him anyway.

Dixon stood up. "I'm going back out to the ranch. Get these uniformed cowboys outta town before one of them starts telling stories out of school."

Chapter 13

LOOKING AT THE MAP, Richard said, "Looks like about six miles to the canal. A good place for supper."

"Which canal is that?" Seth asked.

"Thirty mile canal."

"Could be full of mosquitoes."

"Anything is possible but that is where we're headed anyway, mosquitoes or no."

Seth stood beside the horse, grabbed the saddle horn and shook it with both hands, slipped a foot into a stirrup and mounted. "Here we go."

Richard, stiff, sore, two years older than Seth, and carrying some twenty pounds more around the waist, got into the saddle but it was not a pretty sight.

The day, cool and cloudy, offered easy travel. The valley, carved out by the river long ago, was at least a mile wide West of the Plum Creek Parkway Bridge but the channel carrying water was narrow.

"I could throw a rock across it," Seth said.

Richard looked and calculated. "Not on your best day."

"Ten dollars on it?"

"I don't like to bet."

"You're the one that said I couldn't do it. Either bet or concede that I can."

Richard took a deep breath.

I know Seth—why do I put myself in these positions?

"Ok. Ten dollars."

Seth dismounted and handed the reins to Richard. "Hold this nag. I don't want to have to go chasin' him when he sees how strong I am."

"That will be the day."

Seth looked around the sand bar. He found a suitable rock and hefted it. "About right." He swung his arm in a circle forward ten times and backward ten, hunched his shoulders several times, squinted his eyes, threw his hat on the ground and took his stance. His approach to rock throwing was a cross between baseball and the javelin in that he ran forward four steps, cocked his arm and threw at a forty-degree angle.

The horses heads jerked up; Richard's eyes followed the rock; his body twisted as he strained to keep the flying rock in sight. There was no splash. The rock landed, bounced twice, and lay in plain sight on the far bank.

Seth turned, a big smile lighting his face. "Man, I feel good today. Pay up."

"Now?"

"Hell yes, now. When do you normally pay your debts?"

Richard took two turns of the reins around the saddle horn and reached for his wallet. "Here."

"No congratulations? Just 'here' and that's it?"

Richard nodded. "Good throw. What do you make it?"

Seth looked at the further bank. "About 200 feet."

"That is quite a distance."

"I get a lot of practice throwing my hat at Swede's."

Richard chuckled. "I'll bet."

"Remember that time I conked two grouse with rocks? Dad couldn't believe it?"

"Yes—and I remember Mom looking for pellets or damage to the birds when she skinned them and didn't find any."

"Head shots."

Richard smiled. Those were good days he recalled. Always a brotherly competition: Seth smaller, wiry and faster. Quick to grasp a concept and top of the class in subjects he liked; a pain in the ass in classes he didn't think he needed. A rebel at times and other times he led his classmates in excellence and clear determination to a goal that could not have been formulated by most of them, but which Seth saw with clarity and single-mindedness.

In the last of the afternoon they had the bridge in sight.

"Which side we want to be on?" Seth said.

"I believe the south side has a nice camping spot and no house nearby."

"We're supposed to get permission anyway, aren't we?"

"Yes. But how do you do that late in the day and no house in sight? There is a house about a mile down the road."

"Hell with it. We wouldn't care if someone camped on our bank would we?"

"I've never been asked," Richard said.

"Me neither. The hell with it."

"We might meet a new county sheriff."

"I doubt it."

They rode out of the river channel and up onto the south bank of the Platte River at Thirty Mile Canal Road. Tired and sore, they went about their evening chores without discussion: unpacking the horses, staking them out where they could get grass and water, unloading the packhorse, erecting the tent, gathering firewood and pumping water through the ceramic pump, building a fire and choosing the night's meal from their freeze-dried collection.

After the chores were done and before dinner, Richard liked pouring a whisky and sorting out a handful of cashews. He cherished the pleasure as much for the minutes of repose against the saddle on the ground, feet to the fire, as for the swift relaxation the spirits provided. Never had he had so many bodily locations to assuage.

Seth plopped down, pushed his hat back, crossed his legs and leaned against the saddle.

"Sorry you can't join me," Richard said.

Seth shook his head. "I've had my share—long ago and far away."

"Do you miss it?"

"You know—sometimes I do. I remember it more than miss it I think."

"That's strange."

"Yeah, it is but it isn't. By remembering I get the bad with the good that sure helps me from tryin' it again. When you wake up of a morning and don't know where you are or what you're doin' there and your whole body is sick, it's easy to vow to not touch it again. That's what I have to remember when I'm wantin' a snort again." He shook his head.

"What say we take a walk after supper?" Richard said.

"You got that much zip left?"

Richard nodded, a smile on his face. "I believe I do."

"Then we're not ridin' far enough."

"Walking doesn't use riding muscles."

"You got that right. Did you bring your walking shoes?"

"I believe I can make a mile or so in these boots."

Seth smiled and threw a stick into the fire. "Come on, fire—boil that water."

Richard sipped the Scotch while the sky turned from pink to crimson. The sun slid beyond the horizon fostering the arrival of mosquitoes and no-seeums and the evening chorus of frogs living in ponds nearby. Seth threw two soggy chunks of cottonwood bark on the fire. Smoke curled out at both ends as the flames went about drying the wood before it could burn.

"Mosquito repellent," he said.

"Don't know which is worse, the mosquitoes or the smoke."

"Smoke doesn't make you itch."

Richard smiled. Seth had an answer for everything. "Is that food ready?"

"As ready as it's gonna get."

"I do believe I am ready then. Do you have cloth napkins?"

"Yes—use your shirt."

"Fine." The chili filled his bowl and he turned to put his back against a tree. "Man I'm tired," he said shaking his head. "Real tired."

"Roger that." Seth took another biscuit. "You still want'a take a walk after supper?"

Richard looked up across the fire and studied the question for a minute. "Sometimes I say things in the spirit of the moment that lately I find difficult to back up. I do not know if it is age or that I have learned something I did not know earlier in my life. Right now, taking a walk is about a 2 on a scale of 1 to 10."

"I thought when you took your boots off the day was over for you."

"I believe you are right," Richard said.

Swine Flu

THE BANGING SOUND ECHOED through the trees and it was that moment between sleep and wakefulness where Richard could not determine the direction or source. He nudged Seth and reached for the .30-30 before he categorized the hollow metallic sound. Aluminum irrigation pipes. He released his grip on the rifle.

"What the hell is that?" Seth said.

"Pipe. Irrigation pipe."

"Tell him to shut up."

Richard lay on his back studying a mosquito trapped between the two layers of tenting. It would have a short life span. Spend 90% of its time looking for something to suck blood from, lay eggs and die, in anywhere from a week to a month. During his journey up and down the river, from two to eight generations of mosquitoes would be born, live, and die. What would happen to this one? Was it a male or female? Richard tried to generate sympathy for the living insect whose life was temporarily trapped between two layers of nylon but there was no response from his heart or mind. He felt comfortable with the visual image of a swallow, which nested under the bridge, taking it for breakfast. Or lunch or dinner—he didn't care which.

Seth turned over to lie on his back. He opened his eyes and stared at the canopy of nylon above his head. "Morning."

"Good morning, Seth."

The banging pipes echoed through the trees again.

Seth coughed and rolled over. "What's that guy think he is, the bell-ringer?"

Richard chuckled. "Do you want to go ask him?"

After a moment, Seth said. "Believe I will." He slid out of his sleeping bag, pulled on his boots, unzipped the tent door and stood spraddle legged, his shadow undulating over the tent. Richard relaxed.

Seth would now demonstrate why Seth was Seth. Just wait for it.

The source of the clanging was visible to Seth as soon as he walked out of the tree line. One man was assembling a series of aluminum pipes with sprinklers attached over an area of flat field. He was amazed at how far the sound carried in the dew-laden air. The man stopped work and stood with hands on hips as Seth approached.

"Morning," Seth said.

"Good morning."

"Couldn't help but hear you. You got something against sleep?"

"Not before the sun comes up."

Seth pursed his lips. "Not enough hours in the day for you?"

The man snickered. "Enough to wear me out."

Seth didn't know where to go with this. He was now confused as to why he had come over here in the first place. He indicated with a nod of his head, "We're camped on the river. Couldn't help but hear you."

The man stood looking at Seth. "It isn't illegal." He pulled his right hand glove off. "Camping without permission is though."

"You the owner?" Seth said.

The man shook his head.

"Well—we won't hurt it any and we'll be gone in thirty minutes anyway."

"You look kinda old to be camping out."

"Oh, yeah. How old you think I am?"

"Sixty—sixty five."

"Damn—that's close. Didn't know it showed that much."

"You gotta mirror?"

Seth chuckled. "No—we don't carry mirrors with us on important missions like this one."

"So what's your mission?"

"Don't know that I should tell you. It's kinda secret you know."

"Who would send a sixty-five year old man on a secret mission?"

"My mother."

"Does she hate you?"

"She's dead. Put it in her will that we go up and back the river to inherit the ranch."

"You must be one of the Barrett brothers."

Seth squinted his eyes. "How do you figure that?"

"Words out. Some say you might be carrying swine flu virus."

"Swine flu? That's a hot one. I'm as healthy as a horse."

"How about a pig?"

"A pig?" Seth chuckled. "We don't even have pigs. Haven't seen a pig since we left Fremont and I doubt we've eaten one either. I'd sure know about it if we switched from that freeze-dried cardboard." He looked the worker in the eye. "Who said we were carrying swine flu?"

"Didn't say you were. Said you might be and I think it was the sheriff's office put out a printed bulletin."

Seth shook his head. "Humph—another county, another sheriff." He paused a moment, then changed the subject. "You a hired hand?"

The man shook his head. "I work for free."

"Free? You a slave or something?"

"No. Just want to experience this kind of work once."

"Well—don't that beat all." Seth lifted his hat, smoothed his hair and set it back on his head. "When you're through here you can come down to our place and work for free."

"I'll be through here after harvest, then I'm going back home."

Seth looked at the man. "What's your name?"

"Bob Adair. I'm a real estate appraiser from Omaha."

Seth nodded. "Good place to be from."

It was quiet for a minute. Bob said: "So you're feeling ok—no swine flu?"

"I'm fine. So's my brother."

"You might want to go into Cozad and let 'em know cause there was a lot of unease when the word came out."

Seth looked at the ground. "Don't know that we have time for that."

"Might be well worth your time," Bob said. "They were marshaling up to quarantine the town when you came up river."

"Hmmm." Seth thought a moment. He took a deep breath and stuck out his hand. "Nice meeting you, Bob. We'll make a stop in Cozad. See what's goin' on there."

Richard had a small smokeless fire burning, eggs boiling in water, and grits thickening in a pan. Seth could smell the coffee twenty feet away.

What in the world could smell better than fresh coffee boiling on an open fire at the beginning of a spectacular day? He breathed in and let a faint smile crease his face.

"Caught him," Seth said.

"Did you tell him he was violating the law?"

"I threatened him with a bench warrant for disturbing the peace."

"What did he say?"

"Private matter between him and me. Can't let evidence out until just before we hang him."

"Get your cup and I'll pour you some coffee," Richard said.

Seth found his cup in the pack. He looked at it, lifted his shirttail and ran it around the inside twice before reaching it over to Richard. "I kinda like this playing lawman before breakfast. Something about power that builds a man's appetite."

"As if you needed an excuse."

Seth sipped the coffee. "Man, that's strong." He held up his left hand. "But good."

"Remember how Dad always wanted his coffee strong enough to float a double bitted axe?" Richard said.

"Yeah. Mom said it took the varnish off the table if he spilled any."

The brothers smiled as each recounted events around the table at home in their own way and in their own memory, often different from each other but distinct in their recollection file.

"What time you thinkin' about?" Seth said.

Richard bit his tongue between his teeth. "I was thinking about the first time I went duck hunting with him. Cold, dark, windy—he woke me up and I really did not want to go that morning but he had breakfast ready, his shotgun and bird jacket in the corner. That was the first time I drank coffee with him." He shook his head. "It was so strong I can taste it still. I poured milk and sugar in it and got it down. It sure did pick me up."

Seth chuckled. "Mine was pheasant hunting from a thermos jug. Cold enough to make steam rise when he took the cork out and poured it. No cream; no sugar, just black. Tasted like a rubber tire mark on asphalt."

When they finished cleaning up and re-packing, Seth made the announcement. "We're goin' into Cozad. Gotta dispel a rumor running ahead of us. According to the guy banging pipe over there, we are supposed to be carryin' swine flu virus. May be a quarantine developing."

"Is that something we can prove?" Richard said.

"I suppose we can drop into a clinic and get a quick exam. You feelin' ok?"

Richard nodded. "Except for a few travel pains, I am good."

"Yeah. Me too."

They mounted. Seth lifted the packhorse rope and took a dally around his saddle horn. The horsemen traveled along the southern side of the river where small trees planted repeatedly by floodwaters and just as often torn from their soil by the next flood, filled the broad channel from bank to bank. Behind them someone looking for clues would have been hard put to tell people had camped there. Horse droppings were scattered as well as the fire ashes and the area was sprinkled with winter-dried leaves. Hoof divots trailing toward Cozad were the only outward sign of trespass.

Sometime around noon the long bridge that spanned the river running north and south out of Cozad came into view. It was called several names on the map. South Meridian Avenue and Clayton Yeutter Highway.

"Must be a local boy cut down in his prime," Seth said.

"Actually," Richard began. "He was Secretary of Agriculture in the first Bush administration. I remember him giving talks around the country."

"You were good at history."

"It was current events—not history."

"Well—current events get to be history in a short time, don't they?"

"You are testy this morning."

Seth reined in his horse. "Look at that line of people up there. What the hell is that all about?"

From end to end on the low lying bridge, people in uniform were standing fifty feet apart, rifles over their shoulders.

Richard shook his head. "I have no idea."

"Well—let's go see." Seth nudged his horse. There was a tall man holding binoculars to his face who moved to a position in front of their line of travel. "Looks like we got us a new boogey-man."

"Seth," Richard said. "Wait a minute. Think this thing through."

"What's to think?" Seth said.

They reined in their horses.

"Do you want to John Wayne it?" Seth said.

"Of course not. But why so many? And armed?"

"We won't know until we ask them. Let's go—we're burnin' day-light."

"Wait. Are we in agreement here? There will be no trouble if we do what they ask us to do. Agreed?"

"Well—it depends on what they ask," Seth said. "I ain't in a mood to do anything they ask."

"No. Let's agree that we approach them, hear them out, and do what they ask. They outnumber us and we are not going to fight them. You and I need to agree on that right now."

Seth's horse turned a circle, pawed the sand. "Ok. I'll follow you. You've got the rifle."

"I won't be using the rifle," Richard said shaking his head.

The brothers approached the bridge abreast, stopping when they heard a shout from the tall man with the binoculars.

"That's far enough," he said. "Dismount and sit on the ground."

"Who are you and what do you want?" Richard said.

"I'll ask the questions. Are you the Barrett brothers?"

"Yes."

"Like I said before and I'm not going to say it again. Dismount and sit on the ground."

"We are not in the habit of taking orders from someone who doesn't identify himself," Richard said.

Seth turned and looked at him. This was a pretty feisty line for his brother to take after the fine talk they had agreed on not five minutes ago.

"Sheriff David Briggs of Dawson County. These fine citizens are members of the Dawson County Sheriff's Posse. Every one of them can shoot the eye out of a rattlesnake at 100 yards."

Richard looked at Seth and nodded. "Well," he said. "We will sit and parley."

"I don't think parley is what he's thinkin'."

As they dismounted, posse members came from both ends of the bridge and surrounded them. Most were smiling and laughing as they sat on their horses, ten to fifteen yards away, looking down at the brothers.

"Getting' your pants wet?" one asked.

Finally the tall man rode up on a horse as black and shiny as freshly mined coal. With the exception of an occasional horse snort the circle got as quiet as a mortuary. He leaned forward in the saddle, looked down on them, then settled himself with both hands affixed on the saddle horn.

"Which one of you is Richard?" he said.

"I am," Richard said, holding up his hand.

"Good. I was told you were the sensible one. Now—have you been in contact with anyone or anything that might have caused you to be infected with the swine flu?"

"Not to my knowledge."

"Did you stop in Fremont and visit a quarantined slaughter house or pig farm?"

Richard shook his head. "We stopped there but did not visit either."

"Do either of you have a fever or feel unease?"

"Just a little soreness from a night on the ground."

"Hmmm." Sheriff Briggs adjusted himself in the saddle. "Would you mind being tested at a clinic in town?"

Richard looked at Seth. "No."

"Your horses acting ok, too?"

"Yes. What's this about swine flu?"

"Message on my voice mail. I don't want our people exposed to something that could hurt kids or our older people. There is an occasional side affect of the swine flu called Reye's syndrome and we sure don't want that. You can understand that."

"Lead away," Richard said.

Deputies strung out in front and behind the brothers as the body of men moved from the banks of the Platte toward town drawing stares from passing cars. Bodies emerged out of rolled down car windows with shouts and jeers of wanted men—desperados, and other less flattering terms. The people in the cars recognized many of the men in the posse and greetings were exchanged all the way to town.

By the time the group arrived at the county health clinic, two dozen cars were gathered in the parking lot. One of the deputies held the Barretts' horses while Sheriff Briggs led them into the clinic.

"Doc," he said. "Check 'em out."

Sheriff Briggs' cell phone rang and he answered. "Sheriff Briggs."

He listened and looked around the office, pulled aside a blind, peered out the window at the parking lot, shoved his left hand in a front pocket and jingled some coins. "I could if it is warranted," he said into the phone. "Yes. I'll let you know." He holstered the cell phone. He opened the front door of the clinic and spoke to a man standing near the horses. "Randy—get me a cup of coffee—black—will you please?"

FORTY MINUTES LATER RICHARD and Seth Barrett stood on the front porch of the Dawson County Health Clinic with the sheriff beside them. "Gentlemen," he said. "I am sorry for this intrusion into your travels. The information I received does not appear to have been accurate but I hope you understand why I did what I did to protect our people."

"We were talkin' about that this morning," Seth said. "If we do what you want us to do—within reason—there won't be any trouble."

The Sheriff nodded. "Can I buy you lunch. The call came in before I had a chance to eat breakfast this morning and right now I could eat a small horse."

"We'd like that," Seth said.

"We'll just trot down to the Green Apple Café and put the tab on the Sheriff's budget. Right this way."

HALFWAY THROUGH LUNCH A young boy approached the table with a coffee can labeled BAND UNIFORMS. "Would you contribute to the Cozad band uniform fund?" he said.

Sheriff Briggs set down his spoon, wiped his lips and reached for his wallet. He studied the contents for a moment then pulled out a five-dollar bill, folded it and ran it through the slot in the lid.

Seth started for his wallet but Richard laid a hand on his arm. " How much do you need to get the uniforms?"

The boy looked at the Sheriff then back at Richard and shrugged his shoulders.

"Find out," Richard said.

The boy ran out to the parking lot and talked to someone in a car. A brief conversation and he burst through the door of the café and over to the table. "Five thousand dollars," he said. "They're used."

Seth looked at Richard as though he had guessed what Richard was going to do. He pushed his back against the booth and straightened his neck. Before he could say anything, Richard said, "Come back in half an hour. We'll have something for you then."

"Like how much?" he said.

Richard nodded. "Come back in half an hour. We will be here."

The boy went to other patrons in the café and as he was leaving he smiled and shook his can. "I'll be back."

Seth piled his silverware on his plate, swigged the last of his coffee, put the cup on top of the plate and pushed it toward the middle. He leaned forward on his elbows and looked the Sheriff straight in the eye. "Who was it exactly that called and said we were comin' up river carryin' swine flu?"

Sheriff Briggs put both hands on his coffee cup and thought a moment. "Don't know that that is of any importance."

"It is to us. You are the third sheriff that has trumped up reasons to hold us and delay us on this trip."

The sheriff's eyes cast around the room. To the left, to the ceiling, over toward the cash register until he said, "Do you know Bud Pinsky?"

"Hell yes." And for the first time that Richard could remember, Seth said only that and then kept quiet.

Sheriff Briggs nodded.

"You're saying Pinsky passed the rumor?"

"Not saying that at all. Just asked if you knew him."

"Ok. We know him. Now what?"

Briggs shook his head.

Seth looked at Richard whose eyes were locked on the sheriff. The sheriff cleared his throat, lifted the cup and swallowed the last of his coffee. He slid out of the booth, adjusted his gun belt and said, "Gentlemen, I need to get busy. Sorry for the delay." He touched the brim of his hat, "Good day." And he was gone. The heavy door swung shut as he left and little by little the restaurant noise began to fill the vacuum created by the absence of Sheriff Briggs.

"I'll be go to hell," Seth said.

Richard's eyes were vacant as he stared at the tabletop, his mind racing to put events in order. A sequence began to build until he had formed a calendar in his mind, had put events and timing and responsibility together. He slammed his fist on the table.

"Klete Dixon. He is behind this. He bought Pinsky the Sheriff's badge and Pinsky is paying him back. Dixon is after our ranch. The name of the game is delay. A few days here, a few days there and more as we come back and our time limit is gone."

"How much time do we have left?" Seth said.

Richard shook his head. "Not sure. Twenty-six days—maybe less."

"We better damn well find out, don't you think?"

Richard nodded. "It would be good to know for sure."

"I'm not likin' this. I'm not likin' this one damn bit," Seth said.

The boy with the coffee can stood beside the booth. "Sir—you said come back in thirty minutes."

"Yes I did," Richard said. He pulled a checkbook from his rear pocket and looked at Seth. "You ok with this?"

Seth pursed his lips and nodded.

Richard wrote on the check, signed it and handed it to the boy. "Good luck with your band."

"Thanks." He looked at the piece of paper he held in his hand and skipped out to the parking lot. A woman ran the window down and he handed her the check. She stared through the windshield as Richard and Seth crossed the parking lot of the Green Apple Café. The boy ran after them. "Thank you, thank you, thank you!" he shouted.

"You are welcome," Richard said, smiling. "Make some good sounds."

"That's more than this whole trip'll cost," Seth said.

"Probably. It makes you feel good though, doesn't it?"

Seth nodded. "Yeah—it does. Takes away the sour taste of Pinsky."

"Now to find our horses and get upriver."

The time dwindles

SETH THOUGHT A MOMENT. "Don't know... let's see. We started May 1st. We had what..."

"Sixty-one days, I recall. Same time frame as Granddad Melzer did."

"And today's what?"

"I thought you would know."

"Hell no." Seth un-holstered his cell phone and dialed. "Ginny? Seth and Richard here. What's the date today?"

"Hi, Guys. Let me look. Mine says June 5th."

"Do you remember how much time we had?"

"Time for what?"

"To complete the trip. The will. You remember..."

"Sixty-one days." There was a change in voice. "I just moved into the living room to hear you better. "Where are you?"

"Leavin' Cozad for Gothenburg, then Brady and swapping these nags for a canoe. How are things there?"

"Ok. No new surprises."

"What's Pinsky doing while he's on bail?"

"Sheriff's stuff, I guess. He came back for a press conference but then went back to Texas as far as we know."

"Ginny—Richard and I were wondering what you found out about the Pinsky and Dixon thing. We're thinking they're in cahoots."

"I'll check with Craig's office. See what he's found out."

"Let us know. We're not exactly on pins and needles but it's getting difficult to explain the things that are happenin'."

"Got it. You having more troubles?"

"Not that we can't handle." He paused. "There's gonna be a big check come through on the farm account to the Cozad Band. Richard dug deep."

"How deep?"

"Five grand worth."

"Holy cow."

"Yeah. Seemed good at the time. Get on the investigator, will you, and let us know what he found out."

"I'll do it. Everybody here says hello."

Seth leaned over to Richard. "Ginny and everyone says hello."

Richard smiled and nodded. The wrinkles in his face had tanned and when he worried they furrowed like high tide lines on a sandy beach. "I figure 25 more days. We need to get a move on."

"We need to do more than ten miles a day. Can your old horse do that?"

"He's staring at the glue factory if he doesn't."

Seth touched his spurs to the horse and yelled, "Hi-yaaaa." Pounding hoof beats, banging equipment, and Seth's voice disappearing into the stunted trees startled Richard. He reined in and listened as the sounds faded leaving him in a circle of silence, his horse's head lifted, ears pointed and alert. As Seth disappeared, the horse gathered himself up, flared his nostrils and shattered the silence with a whinny. The echo resounded until nothing but the gentle murmur of the river could be heard. Richard and the horse stood looking down the trail.

Wasn't that just like Seth? Spur a horse and dash across unknown terrain like the Charge of the Light Brigade. His mind open, unfettered, loving the wind in his face and the pulsing of the horses breathing without a finish line ahead—just the momentary thrill of being out front.

~~~~~~

The River

Where the shadows cut across the water the river played a different tune than where it spread out over shallow sand in full sunlight. In the shadows, where the bottom was not visible, the water burbled as it slid against the bank. When it spread out over the sand and mud it gossiped with quick sounds like young animals at play, laughing, stretching, until it tumbled into the channel and fell silent. Would they understand?

~~~~~~

Seth has a son in Florida

CLOUDS AROSE FROM THE southeast to shade the sun and erase the shadows that worked their way across the trail Seth had left: hoof divots planted in sand and mud that had been deposited amongst the scrub cedars and cottonwoods during high water. The Platte now was a thin ribbon of water like a sputtering length of cloth in a stiff breeze, turning and twisting through the carved bottoms, unsure of where to go or why. What little water was left after irrigation draw was aimlessly drifting in a narrow channel across the flat land— always downhill to the Missouri.

As much as Seth had tried to adhere to the south side of the river, Richard saw several crossings where he had decided travel was easier on the other side. Leave it to Seth to find an easy way.

He chuckled, thinking about the sounds of trucks and cars on Highway 80 less than half a mile to the south and Highway 30 half a mile to the north. And here they were travelling beside a river on horses that had been man's means of travel for several thousand years. It suddenly seemed like a strange world to him, that they would come from the ranch house with all the modern facilities and, in a heartbeat, transportion wise, be back a thousand years. How easy it was to go backwards in time and how difficult it was to go forward. How could you live in an advanced culture that you did not know anything about? You could only project, hypothesize, and make an attempt, using what you knew as a base for building the future.

But wasn't that what Filoh asked them to do? Was his suggestion to go forward into farming unknown to them or back to methods used by previous generations? The old-timers had made plenty of mistakes: plowed straight furrows and caused the dust bowl, washed lots of chemicals into the waterways, overgrazed. Seemed like farmers and ranchers were always experimenting. Wasn't that the way with men? Always seeking to increase yield from any asset. Whether it be farm, real estate, a business, or stock in some company, the people in charge were always trying to increase the yield so they could get more with the same amount of assets. That is what he and Seth were doing. Damnit! Filoh was asking them to go against the nature of man: to produce less and of questionable quality. The tradeoff? Hopefully clean land, water, and air. To get that they would need to convince every rancher on both sides of the Platte to follow suit. He shook his head. "My God, my God." The enormity of the proposed exercise overwhelmed him.

Seth was leaning against a tree, his horse tearing at clumps of spring grass that grew in the clearing. "Thought we'd set up camp here if you ever made it."

"I had some thinking to do. Could not do it running fast. But in low gear it seemed to come together and you will be happy to know the outcome."

"Oh yeah. I'm always excited when you figure somethin' out," Seth said. "This place suit you?"

"Sure," Richard said. "You sure polished off those miles."

"I did it in under two hours. You took most near three."

Richard lifted his chin. "I had a talk with my horse. We felt it would be fine to get here before supper time, both his and mine—and we did."

Seth nodded toward the river. "Lookin' at that river I'm thinkin' our trip back is gonna be more wadin' than canoeing."

"I agree." Richard pulled the saddle off his horse and set it on a fallen tree trunk. "How fast can we travel wading and pulling a canoe?"

Seth shook his head. "Not very damn fast. I'm thinkin' maybe two miles an hour if we've got some water to float occasionally."

"And we have 300 miles…"

"More or less, the way it twists and turns."

Each followed his practiced procedures with conversation relegated to grunts and the sounds of horses ending the workday. With the saddle removed, the horse shook. His whole body quivered having shucked the weight of man and saddle and the entrapment of equipment.

Richard eased himself to the ground, his arm leaning on the saddle. "Everywhere I can still feel anything, is sore."

"It's not tractor ridin,' is it?"

Richard let the comment pass and swirled the Scotch in his glass before passing it under his nose.

"Where do you think you are, Edinburgh?" Seth said.

"It is only fitting and proper to prepare to enjoy a drink of fine whisky in any location. One does not need to be in black tie and tux."

Seth shook his head. "You add ten minutes to gettin' a good feelin' goin'."

"Time is of little consequence to pleasure."

"I've told many a woman that."

The conversation stopped. Richard took a sip of his drink, his cheeks moving with the swallow. They had never talked about the period when Seth was gone from the ranch for personal reasons. He was welcomed back by the whole family and that was enough. He had been straight as an arrow since his return and nobody saw any benefit in probing the years he was absent—until now.

Richard looked at him over his whisky glass. "Were you pretty cozy with lots of women while you were out there?"

"I had my share."

"No health problems from it?"

Seth shucked his shoulders. "Couple times. Went to the clinics and got a prescription. Don't think I passed anything on."

"What did you think while you were living that life style?"

"Think? Hell—I wasn't thinkin,' I was busy doin'." He lifted the lid and stirred the chili.

"What do you think now with a son in Florida?"

"Well—it is what it is. I'm paying retroactively for past pleasures."

"Yes—but does the price equal the pleasure?"

Seth shook his head. "I don't know how to equate that, Richard. I can barely remember the gal, the night, or the incident. If I added them all together I guess you could say I was still lookin' for the right one and practicin' on everyone I could. Havin' a son is a good feeling but we're not close. Maybe when I'm old and crippled he'll be around. I won't end up like George Rogers Clark, a drunk sitting on the front porch watchin' the river go by and burn my leg off."

Richard dropped his head. "Hmmm. You think much about old age?"

"Once in a while. When I'm sore all over. I think about when we were kids and worked all day, slept all night, and were eager to do it again the next day. God—those were the days."

"Miss them myself," Richard said. He lifted the glass and let the last drop scroll down the inside until it gathered all it had left and dripped onto his tongue. "Good to the last drop. Let's eat."

"Wonder how many other people are campin' on the river tonight?" Seth said while lowering his spoon. "And how many had Scotch before Chili?"

"Damn few I'll bet," Richard said.

A Dairy Queen on the trail?

"WHAT DID THE MAP say?" Richard said.

"Quit worryin' about what the map says," Seth said. "Let's just get there."

Richard leaned and jigged his saddle a couple of times. It wasn't on squarely. "I like to know those things. You know that."

Seth let it drop. Answering Richard every time was a lifetime job. "Did you call to have the canoe delivered?"

"Not yet."

"When did you figure you'd do that?"

Richard looked at the thin surface of water riding over the sand bar. "I'm not anxious to swap methods of transportation."

"No choice." Seth turned in the saddle. "I thought you were tired of horses?"

"Tired—yes. But look at that water level. That is walking water, not boating water."

"It is what it is."

"Boy, I am tired of hearing you say that."

"Well, damnit—get a grip on reality then. We'll do what we have to do until it's done."

"Can't I simply express my displeasure without getting a lecture? Have I ever failed to do my work?"

Seth let thoughts rumble through his head. From childhood to high school, Richard had led the way, paving the path behind him for Seth to follow. He could have stopped, made his own path, or followed the one Richard had left for him. For years it was easier to follow. They shared teachers, friends, and activities. In fact they were like two peas in a pod until after college when Richard came home from the Vietnam War to find fault with the way the farm was being run. That was where the division began. Seth took the animals and

Richard the crops. No—looking back Richard had always done his work. Critical? Yes—but generally fair. Then the years he was "away."

Even today, he couldn't pinpoint the reason he left farm and family. The details were murky. If he tried to enumerate them he could get to two or three sometimes, but none of them seemed dominant enough to qualify as the "reason." Usually he simply let the facts speak for themselves: he left; he played fast and loose in the world; he came back. Enough said.

"No," Seth said. "You've never failed in that department."

"You are implying that I have failed in some other one?"

"Not necessarily."

"Well—out with it if you are thinking it."

"Damnit, Richard. Let it go."

They rode in silence as the horses, nose to tail, moved through the morning with no change in demeanor. *What wonderful beasts they are.* He thought about other beasts of burden: mules, camels, llamas, oxen. Of them all, horses seemed the best. He would miss the daily association with the horse. It was like a partnership between horse and rider. How can you thank an animal who carries you all day, sighs when you remove the saddle, and rolls in the sand with such satisfaction, expressing human-like grunts of relief and pleasure? Who gets tired and drags his hooves and lowers his head in the heat of the afternoon just like the rider? The deep desire to address them as human, kiss their nose while holding their head in your hands, and talking to them like they understood you, were traits he had observed with many horse people. Not Seth, but others.

Seth broke the silence. "How would you like an old fashioned hamburger, fries and chocolate malt?"

"That would be good."

"Turn left here." He put the map back in the saddlebag.

Seth led up the bank and onto a narrow grass lane beside a plowed field.

"Farmer isn't going to like this," Richard said.

"Hell—like he's going to be lookin' for horse tracks at the edge of his field."

"I would notice."

"Yeah—but you're not the average farmer."

"What is over here?"

"A Dairy Queen. Isn't that precious?"

Richard smiled. "I like it."

"Thought you would."

THEY LOOSENED THE SADDLES and tied the horses by halter ropes to trees behind the gas stop and Dairy Queen. They dusted themselves off, squared away their Stetsons and walked in the front door.

Food in hand they sat on a contoured plywood bench. "This is harder than my saddle," Richard said.

"The food's better though. Let your mouth do the thinkin'. Forget your butt."

A big man with a belly that touched the counter when he sat looked at them and with a smile asked, "Where you boys from?"

Seth smiled back. "Plattsmouth."

"Plattsmouth? How'd you get here? I don't see any rigs in the parking lot but mine."

"We rode horses," Richard said.

"Horses?" the big man said. He laughed. "That's quite a ride."

The door slammed shut and a thin man in bicycle clothes walked to the counter clicking with every step. He removed his helmet and sunglasses and stood looking at the menu posted above the cash register.

The big man shook his head. "I suppose you're on a bike?" he said.

The biker turned and nodded with a smile. "Yup. And I'm hungry as hell."

"Where you from?"

"Sterling, Colorado. Heading for Plattsmouth, Nebraska."

"Those guys are from Plattsmouth," the big man said pointing at the brothers. "They rode horses up here. You guys ought to get along well together. You're all nuts."

The biker nodded. "How long did it take you?"

Seth looked at Richard. "Around thirty-five days. But we were delayed several times."

"I don't doubt that," the big man said. He turned to the biker. "How long do you think it will take you to bike to the other side of Nebraska?"

"I've got double hip and knee replacements and I'm eighty years old so I'm not setting a time limit; just to get there will do."

"Eighty? My gawd, I'll be dead by eighty," the big man said. "I'd like to buy you guys lunch." He laughed. "I'd like to be able to say I bought lunch for two guys riding horses across Nebraska and a 80 year old with metal joints biking across it. That could win me some money in a betting contest." He pulled a wallet from his bib overalls and laid a bill down. The employee delivered the truck driver's order: two double cheeseburgers, a supersize French fries, and a container that held a half-gallon of Coke.

"Now there's a meal for you guys," he said as he tucked a paper napkin in his shirt. 'How far you goin' on the horses?"

"We're almost there," Seth said. "At Brady where the North Platte meets the South Platte, we're switching to a canoe and heading back."

The big man shook his head. "Ain't where they meet." He took a bite of his burger.

"Sure it is," Seth said. "Looked it up on my map."

"Roger," the big man said. "You got a Nebraska map handy?"

Roger pointed behind him. "It's on the wall by the cash register."

The big man stood up, his napkin flapping as we walked to the cash register. "Come 'ere. You see right there just south of the airport—that's where the two rivers meet. I've duck hunted there a hundred times. They come together like a wishbone."

Richard looked at Seth.

"Don't start," Seth said. "Can't be more'n a few miles."

"What's so important about being exactly there?" the big man asked.

"That's our turn around point. I thought we were there and celebrating it now," Richard said. "By the way," he addressed the server. "May I charge my cell phone?"

"Go ahead," the attendant said.

Richard plugged in the cord and stood looking out the clean glass window at the horses standing on three stiff legs, each with one crooked, heads down. So he would have to get back on a horse and go further. Further than he thought. Further than he had planned on. What would it take? Another half day—a day? A slow burn built in his chest.

Seth clapped him on the shoulder. "Just a few hours."

"Maybe to you, but I am through. If I never get on a horse again it will be too soon."

"I'm sorry. I should have looked closer. I would swear it was at Brady."

Richard stood with his arms crossed, legs spread. He worked at countering the rush of adrenalin that flamed from his guts to his skin. His breathing elevated. He could feel beads of sweat form and trickle down his forehead, just at the thought of getting back on the horse. He removed his hat, slid his arm across his face. "Let's just say we did it."

Seth didn't take the bite. He looked at his brother like he hadn't heard him.

Richard returned his steady gaze, his resolve flushing away with each tick of the clock. "I can do it."

"I know you can, brother—I know you can."

Finished with the meal and cell phone charged, Richard punched in the number for Jack Brown's cell phone.

"Jack Brown," the voice said.

"Hello Jack. This is Richard Barrett."

"I've heard of you."

"That's good because it is time for you to hop in your pickup and deliver my canoe to North Platte."

"I thought you wanted it in Ogallala?"

"My mistake. Can you make it tomorrow?"

"Probably. Where and what time? I don't want to be sitting around all day waiting for you and Seth to come trotting in. I've got a business to run here you know."

"I should never have paid for it early. You get surly after you're paid."

"That's because I lost my profit in the poker game to Seth the week after you paid for it."

"There is a freeway interchange called Newberry Access Highway just west of the airport on Highway 80. Meet us on the north side of that tomorrow at noon. Can you do that?"

"I can give it the old college try."

"You didn't go to college, Jack."

"Makes no difference—I try day in and day out."

"And Jack—don't forget the paddles and cooler."

"I remember. OK—noon tomorrow at Newberry Access off-ramp. You buying lunch when I get there?"

"I'll discuss it with the family treasurer. See if we can afford such extravagance. Oh, by the way, add two sets of hip waders to the bill. "

"Humph. See you at noon."

Richard unplugged the cord, wound it and put the cell phone in his pocket. "We need to make it to North Platte by noon tomorrow."

"No sweat," Seth said. "Git along little doggy, North Platte's your new home."

The big man turned from his meal. "What 'cha gonna do with the horses?"

"Shoot them," Richard said.

The big man laughed. "No—really."

"Sell them to somebody, I suppose," Seth said. "We've got plenty more at the ranch."

"Hell—I'll buy 'em. Horses that have come this far gotta be good horses."

"You buy the tack too?" Richard said. "Seth is going to ship his stuff back home but I'll never use mine again and I would not like to see it hanging in my barn for the rest of my life."

"I'll meet you at the off-ramp at noon tomorrow with my horse trailer. They used to loading?"

Seth nodded. "Load like a charm. Trained them myself."

The elderly biker rose from his booth. "Good luck, gentlemen. Maybe I'll meet you in Plattsmouth."

"Don't know who'll get there first," Seth said. "But you're welcome to stay at our ranch if we get there ahead of you. And—if you're still alive when you get there."

The guy laughed. "I get stronger every day."

"Even when you're biking into the wind?"

He nodded. "More then." He stuck out his bony hand. "Good luck and hope to see you in Plattsmouth."

"Look us up at the Barrett Ranch. Anybody knows where it is."

The horses perked up when they heard the brothers approaching. They whinnied. Seth's horse sniffed his vest. "You find something there, boy?" The horse nudged the pocket almost knocking Seth over. "Ok. You win." He took out a packet of sugar, poured it into his palm and the horse lapped it up with his tongue while Seth rubbed his ears and forehead. "I'm gonna miss you, Pistol."

Tightening the cinch, Richard looked over. "You could have him trailered back if you want."

"I thought of that. I really need a younger horse this fall and I'd just as well start breaking one into my work routine when we get back."

"We'll need to repack for canoe travel. Wonder how Grandpa Melzer did it?"

"He was travelin' a lot lighter than we are."

The horses stood still while the men mounted. Richard reached forward and patted the horse on the neck. "Just a few more miles and you will be shed of me." The horse bobbed his head up and down, rattling the gear.

"Seems like good news to him," Seth said. He gathered the lead ropes for the packhorse and Filoh's mule, giving the mule the longer rope to follow behind.

"We are both happy." Richard said. "Forward ho."

Chapter 14

"HARD TO TELL WHICH channel to follow," Richard said.

"The map…" Seth started.

"…We know how accurate the map is."

"Follow the middle branch." He looked around. "I can see why that guy hunted ducks here. Plenty of little ponds. Good flush and shoot chances."

Channels merged and some died out. They could see the airport and the east end of the town of North Platte and the map showed an intersection called Newberry Access Road and usually at an overpass there was a restaurant or motel. They would wait there.

The kid picking up wind-blown trash off the parking lot saw them first. He stood straight, broom and pan in hand, mouth agape as two horsemen leading a horse and a mule walked onto the hotel parking lot like they owned it.

"Afternoon," Richard said. "The manager in?"

The youth nodded. "In the office."

Richard dismounted, did a few partial squats to loosen his legs, set his hat and walked in a purposeful manner toward the entry.

The youth looked up at Seth who had cranked one leg around the saddle horn and looked like he was stitched to the saddle. "You come far?"

"Plattsmouth."

"Where's that?"

Seth looked him over. "You been to school?"

"Tenth grade. I'll be a junior next year."

"Don't they teach geography in there somewhere?"

"Yes, sir."

"Well, Plattsmouth—spell it out—Plattes mouth—that's the mouth of the Platte River."

"Oh."

"Where it runs into the Missouri. You've heard of the Missouri River, haven't you?"

"Yeah."

"That's good. I don't have to start back there."

"You rode horses clear from there."

"We did."

The youth looked at the horses standing still as bronze on the heated asphalt parking lot as evening customers began to arrive, park, and unload luggage. "Why would you do a fool thing like that?"

"It isn't a fool thing. It was required by an estate order—a legal document—that consigned me and my brother to ride up here to meet an ignoramus like you standing in a parking lot as the sun goes down."

"What's an ignoramus?"

Seth shook his head. "I was afraid of that."

Richard approached putting his hat back on his head. "We can stake the horses out back. I got us a room for the night."

THE BROTHERS WERE SAVORING coffee and cinnamon rolls when Jack walked through the lobby into the breakfast area. "What's for breakfast, boys?"

Richard looked at his watch. "What time did you leave, Jack?"

"Traffic's lighter in the morning," Jack Brown said. "I figured you'd be lounging around over a cup of coffee and sitting on an upholstered chair after a month in the saddle." He stared at Richard. "My gawd, Richard—you look like you were embalmed and it didn't take."

A smile creased Richard's face. Elbows on the table, holding his mug in both hands, he took a swig of coffee. "What kind of seats does the canoe have?"

"Soft as a cloud. You won't even notice, 'cause you'll be wading most of the time."

"You brought the waders?"

"Oh yes. I brought several pairs. Walking three hundred miles through the river will take the shine off them." Jack picked out a breakfast roll. "Pass the butter there, Seth."

Richard watched him dunk the roll in the coffee, lean forward and take the soaked bread into his mouth dripping all the way without getting any on his shirt. "We have not been in the saddle for a month. We received some legal hospitality along the way and other diversions that extended our journey."

"That's what we hear." Jack took a napkin to his chin. "A lot of buzz around town about Pinsky getting arrested."

"Man—I hate to be reminded of that," Seth said.

"Craig is taking care of that isn't he?" Richard said.

Jack straightened in the chair. "I suppose. But Bud's rope is snubbed close to Dixon's post, you know?"

Seth set his cup down. "How close is close?"

Jack swallowed his bite. "Dixon put up his bail."

The brothers looked at each other. "I wonder if Ginny is telling us the whole story?" Seth said.

Richard shook his head. "Look—we have a job to finish here. The ranch and politics cannot be a distraction. Ginny and Donavon will need to solve it."

"They're no match for Dixon and Pinsky," Jack said.

Seth leaned forward, elbows on the table. "Do you see this getting out of hand before we get back?"

"I don't know," Jack said. "Things have a way of happening that you can't predict. I'd say get in your boat and paddle like hell. The quicker you get back the better."

"What do you think's goin' on?" Seth said.

"Plain as the nose on your face. Your Mom's will is all over town. Dixon wants the Barrett Ranch and there isn't anybody who can stand in his way. He'll pay Boys Town what they ask and bingo—he's the largest land owner in the area." He lifted his head. "Besides, he's got Pinsky and Jamison in his pocket."

"Jamison?" Richard said.

"Hell yes. He doesn't make many moves without clearing it with Dixon first."

"How come you haven't told us this before?" Seth said.

"You guys live out there in the country. It's the town people that see the shenanigans."

"Like what?"

"Like when Jamison leaves his office out the back door and hops in a little tan PT Cruiser that always comes back dusty."

"That doesn't prove anything."

"Nope. You're right. Pass the coffee there, Richard, will you?" Jack filled his cup, stirred in cream and sugar and leaned back in the chair. "My delivery man saw the car going up Dixon's driveway and saw it being washed behind the dealership a couple of hours later. Delivery guys see a lot of stuff we don't see."

"So it would appear," Richard said. "What do you think, Seth?"

"Think, hell—there's no thinkin' to do. We count on Ginny and Donavon to hold down the fort and we scoot back down the river like our lives and fortunes depended on it."

"And they do," Jack said.

Richard looked at him. "You mean that, don't you?"

Jack nodded. "I do."

"IT'S BRIGHT RED," Seth said, looking at the canoe.

"I didn't want you to lose it," Jack said. "Here are the paddles, life jackets that you might need in the two feet of water, and the cooler."

"And the waders…" Richard said.

"Right here." Jack set the waders in the canoe. "What'cha gonna do with the nags?"

"There's a guy meeting us here who wants to buy them. Met him down the line."

"And the gear? I could take some back with me."

"Good," Seth said. "I'd like you to take my stuff back. Richard doesn't care to see his again—ever."

At that moment a pickup rolled in pulling a four-horse trailer. The big man waved from the window. "Let'er buck." He hollered.

Introductions were made, money changed hands, animals loaded, the big man drove off toward Highway 30 while Jack Brown, along with the Barrett brothers, canoe, paddles, waders, and cooler drove a couple of blocks to the river. Jack drew the launch duties. He pushed hard, the small keel carving a line in the sand. With Richard in the stern and Seth in the bow, the canoe settled on the Platte River. It bobbed for a moment before settling in, the displaced water moving aside as the river adjusted to the new thing it had to carry on its back. "Why do you get to steer?" Seth said.

"Lightest person is always in the bow. Your job is to keep us from grounding or hitting a rock or a tree. Keep your eyes peeled."

"Steer for that little channel right there," Seth said pointing his paddle.

In three seconds the bow grounded on a sand bar. Seth jammed his paddle in the sand and pushed backwards. The canoe stayed stuck as the stern started to swing around, the current pushing it sideways with the bow holding the point.

"Get us off there, Seth," Richard said.

Seth drove the paddle into the sand, put the handle in his armpit and shoved, pushing his body hard on the handle. With a grinding sound the canoe slid backwards off the sand bar, Richard straightened the stern, and they glided through a narrow channel a foot deep, the bottom visible through the green tinted water.

"It's going to be a long journey," Richard said.

"Stay left of that sandbar just ahead."

The morning cool had given way to mid-morning warmth as the sun shot across the water into their eyes. Seth put the paddle across the gunnels, removed his vest, unbuttoned his shirt and put on sunglasses. He flexed his shoulders, grabbed the paddle and dug in. The paddle struck the bottom. Half of the blade did not grab water.

"It will get deeper as we get close to the dam," Richard said.

"Hope so," Seth replied.

"Quiet, isn't it?"

"Yup. And no feedin', waterin', or saddling to mess with." He looked around. "Nice view from here too."

"What is the longest you have ever canoed?"

"Paul and I went down Fourmile couple of times."

Richard moved around on the seat. "Feels better than the saddle."

"Don't turn us over."

"You won't get more than your shoes wet if we do."

"Yeah. Take a left at the Y up ahead. That's deeper water to the dam."

"Aye, Aye, Sir."

"Now you're talkin'. Keep givin' me full power from the engine room."

Someone watching from the bank would have seen two muscular men with sleeves rolled above the elbows, shirts open, cowboy hats down low in front shading their eyes, engaged in an uncoordinated paddling effort. The canoe moved a bit faster than the current into water backed up by an irrigation dam.

"You know," Richard said. "We haven't put much effort into thinking about why Grandpa Melzer chose our ranch site. That was one of Mom's requirements."

"I know the answer to that."

"Such as?"

"It was there for the taking."

"So was the rest of this country."

"It was close to the Missouri?"

"Probably part of it."

Seth stretched the paddle out and shoved the bow away from a half-buried chunk of cottonwood. "It was close to a tavern?"

Richard chuckled. "Could be."

"How particular and precise do you think we have to be on that point?"

"I don't know how it would be challenged but it behooves us to have a good list of points leading to a conclusion of why he chose it."

"You got anything to write on?"

"We can remember it."

"Ok. Here's one. It had two sources of water—the Platte and Fourmile Creek."

"That's good."

"It was close to a tavern."

"I don't think that is going to fly, Seth."

"That would have been important for me." The slightest sound of the paddles stroking the water bounced back at them from the trees on the bank; otherwise it was like they were floating in a cloud. "How far do you figure we'll make a day?"

"I would think thirty to thirty-five miles."

"So—we could be home in ten days?"

"Might be."

"I recall we were to look at soils and crops and animals, too," Seth said.

"Yes. And with Filoh badgering us we didn't do any of that coming up river." He paused for two strokes. "I miss the old guy."

"I do too. But I don't miss that there's only two of us in this canoe."

"We could have sent him back on a bus."

"Bus driver would have killed him before they got home."

"Back to the point. I don't recall seeing anything other than corn and soy beans, do you?"

Seth was silent a minute. "Ya know, I just didn't pay enough attention to register that in my mind."

"How about soils and animals?"

"Same with those. I think Filoh had us lookin' at every damn creek that dumped into the Platte and we forgot the other stuff."

"Well then—that is our assignment as we ply these waters with the flotsam and jetsam."

The sounds of water going over the dam a half-mile away drifted up the river. Richard could see a thin veil of mist distorted by sunlight dancing in the air. "We want to hold left through the bend as we approach the dam. There is a road on the left side where we can get out and across."

"I thought we'd just drive over the dam, kinda like shootin' a rapids."

Richard let the remark pass and steered the canoe to the left bank at a small take-out beach 100 feet from the dam. Here the water noise was constant, burbling and pounding in a green wake over the concrete dam, splitting into an irrigation ditch going south with what was left of the Platte River, going east. The canoe slid into the backwater and Seth jumped out, bow rope in hand. The current began to swing the stern downstream but Seth held the bow against the bank.

They unloaded the canoe and carried the packs around the dam 500 feet to a low bank area, then both returned for the canoe. Packing it on their shoulders provided them shade from the noontime sun. "I kinda like it under here," Seth said. "We could carry this thing half way."

"My vote is no. Set it down here."

"You ready for some lunch?" Seth asked.

"I could eat something—yes."

"Just a moment while I find where I put the good stuff."

"Do we need a fire?"

"Not unless you want coffee?"

"I'm fine."

They sat on the bank, shoes off, dangling their feet in the water, chewing on beef jerky.

Richard cocked his head. "I would suppose that our requirement to delve into the soil and animals and crops would have to do with what was possible at the time and using only river front ranches for comparables."

"I agree. I don't think we're to go traipsing off away from the river collecting soil samples and weighing sheep and cattle."

"So—let's make it a priority to stop once a day at some convenient stopping place and check soils, crops, and animals."

"If we can do so without getting shot at."

Richard frowned. "I think that is unlikely"

"What would you do if some stranger dug a hole in your ground, walked around in your crop, and patted your animals?"

"Well—I sure would not shoot him."

"That's good. What we need to do is be careful and polite." Seth took a piece of jerky out of his mouth and threw it in the river. "You know we're supposed to ask permission from the landowner just to camp on the bank. Apparently everyone owns to the middle of the river."

"I'm not worried about that."

"Goodie. I'm happy to be with you. How do we divide these duties?"

"You take animals and I will take soil and crops. That is what we do, our specialties, and we should be able to make short work of it."

"Sounds good to me," Seth said. "When ya wanta start, now?"

"No. Our afternoon stop before dinner. Let's shove off."

Then the wind came. The water gathered near the bank, the white caps bursting up in the bushes. The air along the river filled with the sweet smell of cottonwood and willow buds and the smell of mud, soaked and dried a thousand times.

"Keep it straight, Richard," Seth said. "Keep the bow into the wind."

"That is your job."

"I can't do it all. You need to steer the damn thing."

"Keep the bow sharp into the wind."

Seth pulled on the paddle. "That's easier said than done. Push it—push it!"

The canoe bounced against the bank, sliding up on exposed roots, the right gunnel inches above the water. Richard drove his paddle into the bank and shoved them into the stream. Almost immediately the wind pushed them back.

"We're not making any progress on this. Let's hang it up for today," Seth said.

"Find a spot. If you can't keep it in line there is no use of fighting it all day.

"Well, it's not just me. There's two of us in this boat."

"But only one doing it the right way."

"When did you get to be a canoe expert?"

It was silent for a moment. "I'm heading for that break in the bank to our left. Get ready to hold us off. And don't tip the thing over."

Seth switched his paddle from one side to the other, paddling where the water was deep enough and shoving it into the sand and pushing where it was shallow. When the bow ground into the bank, Seth leaped out and pulled with the rope. The wind caught the canoe, lighter now in the front end, and as Richard stood to get out it turned and his left leg stepped into water up to his knee. He would have fallen but he jammed the paddle in the sand and got the other foot out—into the water. He stood there looking at Seth on the bank, dry and with the rope in his hands.

"I don't know whether to laugh or cry," Seth said.

"Oh, shut up and pull the canoe up."

AFTER SUPPER, THEY sat by the riverbank watching swallows filling the air, out and around in a circular pattern that seemed more exercise than feeding. Hundreds of the small black birds flew out from under the bridge, chirping and flying in an established pattern.

"What kinda birds are those?" Seth said.

"I think they are swallows." Richard said.

"Barn swallows?"

"Bridge swallows."

"Oh sure. Like that makes sense."

"No. They are cliff swallows. Notice the orange rump and white forehead patch?"

"Where did you learn stuff like that?"

"I took some ornithology in college. Something you avoided." Richard stretched out his legs, crossed them and leaned on one elbow. "They've been around for over 150 years building those clay nests under bridges."

"Where'd they build before we built bridges?"

"Cliffs. Hard for predators to get at them under a bridge. They keep the mosquito population down."

"Good for them." Seth turned his gaze to the river. "Did you ever think we'd be on the river this far away from home?"

Richard shook his head.

"This is something. Mom forces us to ride along side and then canoe down the river that makes our place what it is. We've been on it for what—sixty years—and we never looked at it like this. Never even gave it a thought except when it flooded and ran over the west quarter section."

"We used to swim it. Never thought about the junk that came along with it from Fremont."

"You remember those times one of us had to go upstream and pick off any guts from the slaughter house hung up on sweepers or sandbars?"

Seth grinned. "That was sure the time of out of sight, out of mind. I remember unhookin' a set of guts and sendin' em down the river thinkin' now the river's fit to swim in."

"And the water being so warm on those real long hot spells?"

"Hell yes. I remember one time we were hotter when we got out then we were when we got in."

"And Mom would have lemonade ready for us when we got home." Seth turned toward Richard shaking his head. "That was good, wasn't it?"

Richard nodded.

"Let's take a swim," Seth said.

"Now?"

"Hell yes, now. I'm hot and sweaty—aren't you?"

"Yes—guess I am. I'm just used to being hot and sweaty and smelling like a horse."

"Last one in is a mule." Seth pulled off his shoes—he wasn't wearing any socks—and in six seconds flat had shed his Levis and shirt. Naked, he took three steps to the water and jumped in landing in knee-deep water. " It's gonna be hard to get all wet." He looked up at Richard, just now shedding his pants. "You're the mule."

Richard stepped in and sat down on the river bottom, the water coming to his waist. In a clear baritone voice in synch with each swipe of the soap across his arm he sang: "There is no place like Nebraska, good old Nebraska U. Where the girls are the fairest…"

Learning time

"BOY, THAT WAS NOISY," Seth said as the canoe slid out under the bridge.

"We should wait until those trucks get over it next time."

"That and the damn birds showering us with poop. Did you get hit?"

"My hat got a couple of shots."

"You better clean it off or it'll eat holes right through."

"Seriously?"

Seth nodded. "Damn right. Had it happen to me."

Richard studied Seth's paddle action, took a deep breath and synchronized his stroke: lean forward, dip the paddle, pull back. At the end of Richard's stroke he added a modified "J" to keep the canoe in line. At summer camp as youngsters, Seth was always the first to get his canoe across the finish line. When they entered the race as a pair they won. But in this braided river, where the water traveled the course of least resistance, it was necessary to correct the direction all the time. High water had cut the bank at a bend in the river and a cottonwood tree, stubborn to the end, clung to the caved off soil like a clock's big hand stuck at two. A Piping Plover standing atop the exposed roots turned his head toward them, and screamed out, "peep-lo, peep-lo," before escaping downstream.

Ahead, the channel split, directed left and right by a large sand bar rivaling the river bank in height and armored with polished root systems and logs devoid of bark sitting half in and half out of the sand.

"Left," Seth yelled.

"Left it is," Richard replied and pressed his paddle like a rudder to turn the canoe into the current. As they rolled by the accumulated wood, Richard stared at the natural fortification that had been formed by water, sand, mud and wind. He poked his paddle at it. It felt like a concrete wall, as staunch as an iron peg in frozen soil.

The main channel split in two dividing the small flow, which put an end to regular dipping and paddling the canoe. Seth was mostly using his paddle as a pole to push the bow where he wanted it to go. They could hear the canoe bottom scraping the sand. Richard commented, "We are losing paint every time we do that."

"Can't help it. The water's thin here," Seth said.

They made about three hundred feet before Richard said: "This isn't good."

"No," Seth said. "Let's wade it."

They pulled over to a dry sandbar and swapped their tennis shoes for hip waders.

"I'm glad Jack threw these in," Richard said.

Seth hooked the waders to his belt, "He guessed it right."

Each man took a rope into his hand and they waded in ankle deep water that barely floated the canoe. Seth led the way the first hundred yards. The second hundred yards they could see the pace they were traveling was not going to get them thirty miles a day. If they got ten miles, with stops for meals, minor accidents, and portages around log-jams, it would be a good day.

The sun struck the water and bounced up under their hat brims burning their faces and necks. Eyes watered. Twice they stopped for short meals. Neither was hungry but both were weakened by the method of travel and discouraged by the slowness.

"Different bein' on the river rather than ridin' alongside it," Seth said.

Richard nodded. "Can't quite put my finger on it."

"More peaceful seems like."

"Maybe." Richard threw a piece of jerky back in the plastic bag. "Different sound than the horses. And we are lower down—that makes a difference."

"Yeah. Could be."

Richard had been casting his glances at the sky. "I believe there is some heavy weather coming our way. Should we get going and find a good place to stick it out?"

"Good idea." Seth bundled the food, stuffed it in the pack and they waded back into the river. "Hard to call this a river right here."

"When Grandpa Melzer traveled it, it was a full blown river."

"Yeah," Seth said as he pulled the bow away from a half-buried limb, "but it was shallow then too."

Richard took a deep breath. His ankles were sore from the rasping of the waders and the uneven footing. He took his mind off it. Off every damn step in the river, the rope chaffing his hands and sun burning his neck. Where he went now was not his choice. It was the will of others that had pulled him from the comfortable tractor seat and the cool pan-eled den and the restorative whisky and set him on this river. Ok. He would learn the river and sharpen his mind as to the crops and animals. He had it in him to set other considerations aside and bring the main topic to the fore, hold it as a single entity and not be distracted. There hadn't been anything yet in his life that he could not stand for a short period. He would simply change his attitude about it.

"Pretty setting with the dark clouds coming over those trees," Richard said.

Seth, who was looking for turtles, turned his head in that direction. "Yup. Let's find us a high and dry spot for camp."

Richard nosed the canoe into a low bank. Seth lifted one foot to plant it on the shore, wavered, and fell, momentarily punching a hole in the water, which then rushed back in to cover him completely. Richard watched as Seth's head disappeared below the surface, eyes clamped shut, a scowl etched on his face.

A hand and paddle lifted above the surface, then disappeared again. Seth drifted under the canoe and popped up on the other side, struggling against the limp current.

"Seth," Richard yelled. "Stand up."

Richard saw his hips rise, saw his belt and pants surface. Seth, being dragged along by the water-filled waders, fought to get his feet under him but his head stayed beneath the surface. Richard dropped his paddle, leaped toward Seth as he drifted on the current. He grabbed Seth and they sat up together, water parting around their chests. Seth shook his head and sputtered. He took a deep breath and vomited. Richard held him as he convulsed, remembering how as a sick child their mother had put her cool hand on his forehead while he emptied himself into the porcelain bowl.

Seth straightened up, looked at Richard holding him with both hands, and smiled. "Got kinda dizzy there. The shoreline moved and I tried to follow it with my foot. Bad choice."

"You ok?"

"I'll live."

Richard nodded. "Grab that paddle drifting away."

IT WAS NOT THE FASTEST, but probably the second fastest fire they had built while on this journey. Not that it was freezing cold, but the wet clothes and evening air along with the threat of injury had lowered each man's tolerance for discomfort. Getting the ingredients for a good fire took thought and effort. There was a tendency to short cut something and force it to be done over, which always took more time than if it was done right in the first place.

Seth was shivering by the time the fire was putting out heat and he could peel off his clothes and hang them on the bar Richard had built. Richard had driven two forked branches into the sand some three feet apart and rested a straight stick across the forks. The clothes were hung over that to dry. It took hours to dry clothes that way, but there was no other way unless you felt like running ten miles to dry them out.

"Dizzy you say?" Richard said.

Seth nodded. "I think it was standing up all of a sudden after sitting most of the afternoon. Everything started dancing before my eyes."

"And now?"

"Feel good. Cold, hungry, tired—but other than those minor items, I'm fine."

Richard looked at his brother out of the corner of his eye and tightened his jaw muscles. He'd have to keep closer watch on Seth. It was easy enough to do from the back seat of the canoe. He picked an envelope of freeze-dried food from the pack, scanning the product by light of the fire. He squinted to read it.

"Turkey Tetrazzini?"

Seth nodded. "I'm good with that." Then added, "Share your Scotch?"

Richard shook his head. "No way. Cuddle up to the fire."

"I was afraid of that."

"We are not going to plow the same ground again."

The two men sat naked before the fire. Seth shook involuntarily, his arms wrapped around his shoulders. "Warm on one side, cold on the other. Ain't you freezing?"

Richard shook his head. "I'm fine."

Chapter 15

THAD PERCY, BECAUSE OF his press credentials, had over the years been wined and dined by a gauntlet of American personalities. Few had enticed him to rise to his full potential for charm or conversation, preferring as he did to ask questions and solicit the other's feelings and thoughts about a subject while keeping his to himself. "An objective journalist," his professor had drilled into him at the University of Nebraska, "is as rare an object as a Pope Mobile and just as valuable."

However, when he started on his third martini, which had been purchased using *The Journal's* credit card, he observed as from a distance, a sudden clarity of thought and careful assemblage of information regarding various political allies within Cass County. That thought caused him to smile at Cort as he finished his statement with a question, and for the second time that night consider the outcome of the investigation he had started.

"Why do you ask?" he said.

Cort rubbed his index finger around the top of his glass. "I'm interested. We've heard about Old Mae Barrett's will."

"How would you hear about that?" He pulled Cort's card out of his shirt pocket and stared at it.

Cort looked him in the eyes and smiled. "Why would a sheriff, a well known lawyer, and a wealthy rancher form a secret group to throw obstacles in the path of another wealthy rancher?"

"Humph," Thad snorted. "Money and power. More of each."

"And you believe that?"

Thad nodded. "Doesn't make any difference if I believe it. Furthermore I think the sheriff is going to be blackened by the charges against him but I don't underestimate his ability to pull something off and avoid the charges or avoid the whole trial. He has been a good sheriff but he is a cagy guy, and Craig Jamison and Klete Dixon are formidable teammates."

Cort sipped his drink, his eyes welded with Thad's over the rim.

Interesting, Thad mused. He lifted his glass, "good stuff." Journalism 101 came back to Thad with a thump. "What's your play in this situation, Cort?"

"I work for Dixon." He pushed his lower lip up and turned his drink on the counter. "I've known the guy for the last twenty years."

"Who hired you for this caper?" Thad said.

Cort smiled. "Don't make a federal case out of this, Thad. I respect your work, but you're chargin' up the wrong chute on this ride." He crossed his legs. "That Filoh Smith character tried to blow up one of our sprinkler towers." He chuckled. "Didn't have any idea how to do it, but he gave it a good shot. This is not one-sided. The Barretts and Smith aren't getting washed clear by the Platte River, not by a long shot."

And then the third martini kicked in and Thad, for only the second time in his career, left objective journalism behind and opened up like a water gate on the Platte River spilling everything he could remember since high school. He was a classmate of Bud Pinsky and Ginny Houston, had lived in Plattsmouth his entire life, had served on the school board, the community council, and had put his feet on every inch of sidewalk and parking lot in town. He knew every business owner, every tradesman, all three librarians, and most of the municipal employees by their first names, knew where they went to dinner, what they drank, and whom they preferred for company. He knew 68,000 things that meant not one damn thing separately, but sat as ballast in his brain waiting to be attached to some other shard of information and become meaningful in his world.

His world had become lonelier two years ago when his wife packed up and left with a cowboy after Rodeo Days. He hated walking into the dark house and turning on one light at a time. He also drank more. He had thought about making a play for Serena but moving Richard Barrett out of the way was tough work. He and Serena had been on the same bowling team and occasionally, when they high-fived after a strike, he had thought he'd seen a glimmer of hope in her eye but offers to drive her home, suggestions of dinner out and a movie were always rejected with a smile and a "no thank you."

"How about Ginny Houston?" Cort asked. "Was she the typical high school cheerleader, spinning her skirt above her panties? She ever date Bud in high school? She ever leave town for an extended period of time, like eight or nine months? How about rumors...anything to chase there?"

Thad took them one at a time and flushed out his ballast tanks. What the hell, he thought. Everyone has heard this stuff in town. He asked for another martini to go with the filet mignon he ordered medium-rare with a side order of onion rings.

CORT LEANED IN THE cab driver's window. "Take him to this address and make sure the lights are on and his front door locked when you leave." He handed the cabbie a twenty-dollar bill. Then he dialed Klete Dixon's number and waited for the phone to ring.

DIXON ANSWERED. CORT SCRUNCHED up his lower lip and bobbed his head. "Newspapermen like him are tough as clams."

"Did he clam up?"

"No. I thought I'd have to get a tub to catch it all, the way he spilled his guts."

"Find out anything new?"

"Nothing," Cort said. "But the thing that bothers me is that Jamison has a foot on each side of the fence."

Dixon smiled. "So he gets his balls scratched on the barbed wire fence."

"Humph," Cort murmured. "Could be."

Ginny and Serena, heart to heart

"I'M SO EXCITED ABOUT your job, Serena," Ginny said. "And close too." She poured coffee into Serena's waiting cup.

Serena pursed her lips and swallowed. "I don't know if I took the job because it was close or because I think I can make a difference. I've always thought I didn't want to teach in a big city program."

"You can make a difference. How much different can middle school kids be in Omaha than here in Plattsmouth?"

Serena opened her eyes wide. "Oh my gawd, Ginny—you have to see it to believe it. They have small gangs. They dress like their older siblings and act like them. They don't grow up doing farm chores, having a schedule, and getting credit for performance."

"They can't all be like that," Ginny said.

"I'm sure that's true."

"Maybe you're just thinking it will be worse than it really is."

Serena let out her breath. "Maybe." She let her eyes drift to the yard out the window. "Now—to find a place to live and make sure my car is up to the everyday travel."

"What if you stayed here?" Ginny said.

"Are you crazy?" Serena set the coffee cup down. "You'll be in town with Donavon and I'll be here with Richard and Seth. Won't that look good?"

"If that farmer brother of mine would just make up his mind and marry you, you wouldn't be taking work or looking for housing. Clean sweep."

"If, if, if. Our world is not built on ifs, Ginny. Good old concrete facts lie beneath our rational decisions." Serena stood up, walked to the window and put her hands on her hips. "Do you know Thad Percy very well?"

"We were classmates in high school."

"He's asked me to coffee several times."

"Ooouuu…maybe wanting what?"

Serena turned to look at Ginny and shrugged. "Who knows? With him you never know anything except what he's wearing that day."

"Why don't you go and find out? What have you got to lose?"

"Because, dammit, I've always thought Richard was two minutes away from asking me to marry him." She crossed her arms over her chest. "Those have been the longest two minutes in my life."

"Richard is not a fast mover. He would prefer his mail to be delivered by Benjamin Franklin on a horse. We practically had to threaten him before he got a new baler. My guess is as long as you both are happy with the present arrangement it will continue."

"I don't like the sound of that."

Ginny shook her head. "Serena, I'm just saying what I feel I know."

"Oh, I know it too. I just don't like it sitting on the surface where I have to examine it. As long as we're putting a good face on it, then I feel warm and comfortable and save a place in my heart for the question and the answer. I've gone over it in a hundred places."

"Have you ever thought of asking him?" Ginny asked.

Serena dropped her arms. "He's too old fashioned to accept that."

"What have you got to lose? It's been three years now and this is a perfect time. Everything's lined up. New job, new town, new house, new people—people who don't know you're seeing Richard Barrett…"

"…Omaha is not that far away."

"It's a world apart from Plattsmouth, honey." Ginny washed out her coffee cup. "You started this conversation asking me about Thad Percy. I've known him for years. I think he is smart, discreet, capable, dedicated…"

"…Ginny—you're filling the air with adjectives. What kind of person is he and why is he divorced?"

"His wife took off with a rodeo cowboy and sued for divorce. Thad let her have it and appeared unfazed by the turn of events but you can't tell what he's thinking inside by looking at his outside. Outside he's the reporter: cynical, hard-eyed, flinty, and abrupt. Inside," She bobbed her head side to side, "I think he's probably soft and cushy but with humor and intelligence combined."

Serena took a deep breath and blew it out. "Maybe I'll give him a ring."

"Hey—it can't kill you."

"Speaking of killing you—what's that parasite Bud Pinsky doing?"

"Oh, Serena, haven't I told you?"

Klete pushes Pinsky's button

"I HOPE NO ONE saw you drive in," Klete said.

Sheriff Bud Pinsky shook his head. "Drove an unmarked car."

"Where are they now?"

"Latest word is they swapped their horses for a canoe and left North Platte several days ago. A farm hand on the Watson Ranch met them camped on the river bank."

"That's trespassing, isn't it?"

Pinsky nodded.

"Nail them for it."

Pinsky grimaced. "It's tough to get a conviction on it unless they did some damage and someone pressed charges."

"So—create some damage."

Bud lowered his head, looked down at his boot toes shining from the morning's application of mink oil. "I don't know if my guys could do that and get away with it—especially in another county."

Klete shoved his chair back and stood up. "For Christ's sake, Bud—if we wait for them to get to Cass County they're practically in their own back yard."

Pinsky nodded. He didn't mind shading the law where the results were minor even if figured out by someone—like Thad Percy. But trumping up a case by committing the misdemeanor himself or ordering someone to do it, added to the sexual assault case he was facing, could dislodge his career. Nothing had been mentioned about the slaughtered heifer at the Barrett Ranch for several weeks and he generally dismissed that as an incident. It hadn't had the riveting effect he thought it would have. It did open the pathway to Ginny Houston, however. Unfortunately he had over estimated her attraction for him and while he thought he could win at the coming trial, he didn't want other stains on his character prior to that. Yet Dixon was asking him to arrange an arrest that no county judge had issued a sentence on since the state had been incorporated providing title to the middle of the channel for riverside landowners. "Maybe there's another way," he said.

Dixon raised his head. "Find it. Now go on, I've got work to do."

Chapter 16

"WE'RE NOT GOING ANY further today," Richard said.

Seth shook his head. He was sitting on a half-buried log in his underwear, hands out to the fire, his clothes steaming on the make-shift drying rack. "Damn, that river can suck you in in a hurry."

"You disappeared like an empty bottle," Richard said.

"That was sure deeper than I expected. What do you think— three—four feet?"

"Enough to drown in."

Seth nodded. "That's for sure. That's for dang sure." He rubbed his hands together. "I couldn't get my feet under me. Kept feelin' like I was gonna somersault—never get my head up."

"Your waders were full of water and the current was pushing you down in that pocket. You would have come out of it in another thirty feet or so, it was just that deep channel hole."

"I don't want to try that trick again."

"Likely you won't have to. Would you mind moving your shoes so I could get the cook pot in there next to the fire?"

Seth felt his clothes on the limb. "You know," he started. "I wonder if Daniel Boone had these kind of problems when he went up the Missouri."

Richard shook his head. "You want your supper in a bowl or on a plate?"

"Does it matter?"

"Not to me."

"Well—do it any way you want then."

Richard took in a deep breath, let it out and looked down at the sand changing color as the fire played on it. He looked at his brother sitting on the log in his underwear and him completely naked and started to laugh. "If Mom could see us now," he shook his head.

"She sure put us in a spot."

"I am sick and tired of this trip but I am beginning to get it through my thick head what she was thinking. It is all starting to make sense. Maybe we need to be tired and dirty and sick of freeze-dried food and sunburned and mosquito-bit and half drowned to get her point."

Seth looked up. "What might that point be?"

"She did not come out and say it but she had to be thinking it would make us closer when we had to spend sixty days and nights together in a tent and canoe. You get to know someone quite well in this forced intimacy—even if that person is your brother."

"That's the truth."

Richard handed Seth a spoon. "You want to dress before I hand you this?"

"Naw. I'll eat it here. My clothes aren't dry yet, and neither are yours."

"The other thing is, we have seen wheat and corn and soybeans and alfalfa and oats, dry land, irrigated, big houses, little houses, small towns that used to be big towns, creeks that stink and rivers that look like they are hauling foam for a living. We've seen barns that look abandoned and barns that look like the pride of the farm."

"Yeah—well we coulda' seen those from the highway in a day."

"But this is different. You have got to feel it," Richard said shaking his head. "You can feel what Mom was thinking. Just put them together for two months, push them up the river and back on horses and canoes and when they come back to the Barrett Ranch they will have observed and absorbed what Grandpa Melzer learned when he laid claim to this land."

"I can see that," Seth said. "Makes more sense now than it did when Craig read the will. I thought, my gawd, what a thing to ask two busy guys."

Richard scraped his plate into the fire then dragged a long limb over and laid the middle of it on the hot coals.

Seth nodded toward the gathering darkness, his eyes dancing with expectation. Richard followed his gaze. A whitetail doe with a spring fawn was browsing at the edge of the firelight. They watched as the animal took a bite, jerked its head upright, and looked at them and the fire, checked where her fawn was, then took another bite.

"You want some fresh meat?" Seth said.

"I think not."

"The .30-30 would do it."

"Not interested. Probably some sheriff hanging around out there waiting to arrest us for taking game out of season."

"My, aren't we getting paranoid?"

Richard lifted his head. "Cautious."

Seth stopped eating, looked in the fire. "Wonder what tomorrow will bring?"

Serena and Thad

THE PHONE RANG AT Thad's elbow. He stopped typing and looked at the caller ID. He picked it up with a smile on his face. "Hello, Serena."

At 10:22 am, he closed the lid on his laptop, pushed back his chair and walked out of the Journal offices headed to Mom's Café. Serena was already at a table next to the big window, visible to anyone walking down the sidewalk. He smiled. He liked the visibility and started making up gossip that townspeople would manufacture when they saw them there and got to speculating. Let 'em. He rubbed both temples with his middle fingers, trying to push the effects of yesterday's martinis' someplace else on his body less painful. He picked up a heavy porcelain cup, poured it full and walked over to a smiling Serena Baker. It took more control than he thought it would to appear his usual self. He stirred his coffee for a moment, watched the cream move around, looked up and smiled. "Good morning, Serena."

"And a good morning to you. Did my phone call disturb your morning work?"

Thad stared at his coffee. "Not getting much done this morning. Feel like I fell off a county gravel truck."

"Hmm."

"Did you ever dump three martinis down at dinner and wake up in your own home with the lights on and your front door locked?"

She chuckled. "Not that I can remember."

"That's one of the criteria—remembering."

"Did you do this to yourself or were you forced to drink them?"

Thad smiled. "I don't recall any threats."

"Good. Then it is self-induced and easily remedied."

"Not entirely. Someone else paid for them so I didn't have to consider the economic ramifications of my actions. Something that always puts a newsman at a disadvantage."

Serena waved to someone going by on the sidewalk. "Who paid for them?"

Thad hesitated while he ran the possibilities, negative and positive, of revealing his dinner with Cort. He pushed his lower lip up and squinted. "A local news gathering organization you know. Also… Cort was there."

"Really?" Serena struggled to keep her increased heart rate from showing. "Why did you dine with him?"

Thad shrugged. "Said it had to do with my piece about the arrest and arraignment of Bud Pinsky. After that I lost track."

"Martinis will do that to a feller."

"Subject change. How have you been, what are you planning on doing, and what prompted you to call after my multitudinous messages? I'm flattered you accepted."

"Don't know that I can remember all of those. Let's see: I've been fine, although holding a rifle on Bud Pinsky has to rank high on the adrenalin scale of my life. I've accepted a teaching job in Omaha— an inner city middle school that both excites me and scares the hell out of me. And the last one—oh yes, I thought we'd enjoy a talk together over coffee. Something we haven't done for years and bring each other up to date."

"You're looking good, Serena. Course you always did except in 7th grade when you wore a pigtail on each side of your head."

"Mom's choice. It was easy to do in the dark and cold mornings." Serena accepted more coffee from the waitress. "How has bachelorhood treated you?"

Thad recognized the question from someone who did not want to delve any deeper into her personal feelings. He had dealt with it for years and he knew the way around it.

"It's been lonely, dark, quiet, littered with poor food, but a little less expensive. How did you find it after your divorce?" He put the shoe back on her foot.

Serena put on a half smile. "You used up all the adjectives. I might add cold to that list—especially in the winter." She stirred in cream and sugar. "You seeing anyone now, Thad?"

"I'm seeing lots of people but none of them qualify."

"Qualify how?"

"Start with looks, because that's what always motivates the male species, and then go to brains and body and life direction and children at home and car and house and finally finances."

"You have criteria for each of those?"

"You damn betcha," He said.

Serena glanced toward the kitchen where the employees were getting things ready for the lunch crowd. "What would Cort be looking for on Pinsky?"

"They were looking for info on Barretts, not Pinsky."

"Why would he do that?"

"Well—while I could still focus and remember stuff, it had to do with the relationship of Pinsky and Ginny Houston before the incident—going back even to school days." Thad felt a shiver run through his body, as if he had thrown something away that he could not retrieve and might need later.

Serena's brain whirled. "Any idea where he is headed with the info?"

Thad shook his head. "If I knew it left me."

She reached across the table and put her hand over his and shook her head from side to side. "You must have been a sight. I always thought of you as someone who was in control. It strikes me as funny that this 4H cowboy drained you so fast."

"You should've seen him. Knew where he was going and how to get there." He looked at her hand on his. No ring on her left hand, warm, soft, beyond friendly. "How about a pizza and movie Friday?"

"How nice." She nodded, "I'd love to do that."

"Good. I'll iron a clean shirt."

Serena smiled. "Do you think Cort reports back to Dixon?"

"Why?"

"I've got a bad feeling about that group."

"Woman's intuition?"

"Maybe. Tell me as much as you can remember."

For the second time that week and the third time in his life, Thad Percy emptied his memory bank while basking in the warm thoughts of a Friday night rendezvous with Serena Baker.

"MY GAWD, GINNY," SERENA said after entering the house shaking her head. "You won't believe what I found out. But first I've got to go to the bathroom. Three cups of coffee are about to be recycled."

It's routine now—and boring

THE CRACKLING OF THE fire and the aroma of steaming coffee broke his dream and Seth's eyes opened to the dim light of dawn. Richard's side of the tent was empty. Seth sat up and pulled his clothes toward him from the bottom of the tent. They reeked of cottonwood smoke. He smiled as he dressed.

At least they're clean.

When he unzipped the tent his eyes took in the neat small fire, steam pulsing from the coffeepot spout and the fact that Richard was not there. He looked around and saw Richard standing naked in the river scrubbing his armpits. He shook his head and smiled.

So that's how a farmer starts his day.

He got out the map, poured a cup of coffee and sat on the log. He could hear highway traffic. He guessed they were close to Highway 80 and within spitting distance of Gothenburg. The coffee had cooled enough that he could sip it as Richard, dried and dressed, walked up the bank.

"Feel better?" Seth said.

"Very much so. My clothes were stiff from last night and I felt grimy." Richard shook his head. "Now I feel chipper, as Granddad used to say."

"Yeah—I never figured out what chipper meant."

"Neither did I. But it does seem to fit this morning. How is the coffee?"

"Swell, Richard. If I'd have ordered it from Starbucks it couldn't be better."

"Good. It will go well with sourdough pancakes." Richard piled the ingredients on the blue tarp they used as a ground cover. "I was thinking of Serena down there."

"Really? Nothing like absence to make the heart grow fonder."

Richard nodded as he poured the flour in the pan and added water and the sourdough starter. "If we got married and we stayed in the house, would you be ok with living there?"

"Hell no."

"Why not?"

"I'm not going to be a spare tire in the house."

"What would you think we should do?"

"You move in and I'll build a cabin down by Fourmile Creek."

Richard stirred the batter. "How many bacon?"

"Four."

"You okay with that?"

"The bacon?"

"No. Building a cabin on Fourmile."

"Sure."

"How long do you think it would take to build?"

Seth looked at his brother. "Are you plannin' this thing soon?"

"When we get back."

While they ate, Seth seemed lost in thought. He chewed each bite until swallowing was no effort and he looked into the fire with an intensity that caused Richard to stare at the flames, as if they were revealing something that he ought to ponder too.

THE DAY STARTED WARM. It looked like every farmer in Wyoming, Colorado, and Nebraska, had taken his maximum allowable water from the river by 8:00 a.m. There were miserable little drizzles of channels that split every few yards on a sand island that had been constructed inch by inch from past flooding. Tree parts stuck out of them, some with leaves still clinging to limbs and one with a new bird nest.

By noon they had dipped their hands in the luke-warm water a hundred times to get a better grip on the dry slippery paddles. Shoulders sore from paddling, strained as every ten paddles the canoe bumped onto a sandbar and they had to get out and drag it. As far as they could see downriver, the channel bobbed and weaved, tied together like a ribbon amongst outcroppings of sand. The process of getting out of the canoe, dragging it forward, and getting back in deposited wet sand that clung to the bottom until it looked like a beach.

"Let's take a break," Seth said.

"I'm game. My shoulder is parting somewhere inside."

"Not like driving a power-steering tractor, huh?"

They beached the canoe on the headland where the Platte divided into three channels, none of which looked consistent or deep enough to support their canoe.

"Do you think Grandpa Melzer had an easier time of it coming back down?" Richard said.

"Hell yes. His load was lighter and there was more water in the river. Just figures."

Richard sighed. "Probably right."

Neither man moved to build a fire. Seth opened the food sack. "Jerky, raisins, nuts…"

Richard shook his head. "Fine with me. Add a little creek water…"

"That's a given. Don't know how I'd get these dry things down if it wasn't for some water." Seth lifted the water pump out. "I'll fetch some water from that creek back there if you get the stuff ready."

Richard nodded. He rotated his shoulders. His neck popped and a grating sound echoed in his ears. Maybe they could switch sides paddling. Everything was ganging up in a line across his body from shoulder to the opposite hip. He stood and stretched, touched his toes.

Methodically Richard opened the small sacks of food. He picked out a few raisins and cashews and popped them in his mouth, wishing he had waited for the water to wash them down. He sat on a log, took a deep breath, and tried to figure out what day it was, how much longer they had to complete this trip, and how he was going to stay in shape when he went back to his normal routine. Seth came through the scrub trees and handed him a water bottle. Richard held it up and looked at the sediment drifting through water.

"This drinkable?" he said.

"Hell yes. I've already had half a bottle. It tastes good."

"You are sure that ceramic filter picks up everything?"

Seth nodded. "All the info I could find on it said so. Even gets little tiny microorganisms out of it."

"Then what is this stuff drifting around in it," Richard said, holding up the bottle.

Seth shook his head. "Left overs, I guess." He shifted his seat to look at Richard.

"I figure it will take four months to build the house."

"What house?"

"The house on Fourmile that we were talking about last night. A month to get plans and permits, a month to get the foundation and utilities in and two months to polish off the house. How's that sound?"

"Pretty fast," Richard said.

"Can you hold off getting married that long?"

Richard smiled. "I believe it is possible. I have not asked her yet. It may take her that long to make up her mind."

"It'd be nice to see you two married and living in the homestead. Kinda fulfills the destiny of the Melzer-Barrett ranch. A level headed, hard working, wealthy farmer carrying on the tradition."

"Along with a hardworking, reformed cattle puncher keeping up the tradition of providing protein for the tables of America."

"Yeah—ain't that a hoot?"

"Nobody to hear us. I guess we can brag a little."

"That's for damn sure, brother."

Richard removed the cap and drank some of the water. He looked down the throat of the bottle after he swallowed. "It does taste ok." He stretched out his legs and lay resting his head on his hand. "I have been thinking about hiring that fellow with Tourette's to work on the farm. He is stout enough for two men and with the sizes of the new bales and equipment I am having trouble with a lot of it."

"I know we could use a hired hand, but you want a crazy fella like that?"

"He is not crazy."

"Well—he is from time to time. How would you work with that?"

"Same way his dad did."

"What makes you think he'd leave his family?"

Richard moved his head back and forth. "Just got the feeling he would."

"I'd be scared of him at night in the same house."

"He would be in the bunkhouse."

"Yeah, but he could tear the door off the house anytime he wanted in."

"Seth," Richard shook his head. "You are afraid of your shadow."

"Look who's carrying the .30-30."

"Has nothing to do with it."

Seth stood up, brushed off the sand, stretched and piled the snacks in the food sack, cinched the cord and looked at the river. "Not much of a river. More like a creek."

They waded into the river and Richard held the canoe while Seth climbed in the front seat. As Seth got in the canoe it settled into the water and lodged on the bottom.

"Too shallow here to paddle. We'll have to wade it for a spell."

Richard nodded, then, disgusted, threw his paddle in the boat. "We will never make twenty-five miles a day doing this." He grabbed the stern and together they walked through the shallow water. The canoe, without their weight in it, moved along on top of the water like a piece of driftwood, perfectly happy to serve as a water horse packing the daily needs of the travelers.

The River

The river had no choice. It ran high or low depending on conditions it could not control. Give something to the river and it would carry it or deposit it, but it was not autonomous. It did not differentiate between men in a canoe or a piece of a cottonwood tree that sought floatage down its path. The one goal—the sea; forever running from the mountains through the prairie to the sea. It could tolerate deflection and pollution and dams but it had its own life to live and every day it was what it was.

Klete is keeping track

KLETE DIXON HAD HIS feet up on the corner of the desk, leaning back in the chair listening to the ring tone as he waited for Craig Jamison to pick up.

"Legal genius and future U.S. Senator, Craig Jamison," he said.

Klete chuckled. "You're patting yourself on the back too early. You haven't even filed for the Senate seat yet."

"Just a matter of time, Mr. Dixon—just a matter of time."

"How much time do the lads have left to finish their little trip?"

"Well—they started May 1st and today is June, what…14th?"

"Get that sorted out to the week, day, and hour. I'm solidifying my cash assets and updating financials so I'll be in prime position to buy the ranch."

There was a shifting noise on the phone, then Craig spoke. "Those men are pretty resourceful fellas. They've done a yeoman's job of running the ranch and last time we checked on their current schedule and whereabouts they were running behind but not by much."

Klete lifted his feet from the desk and planted them with a thump on the walnut floor. "But we have further impediments in place to delay the trip..."

"We do, Klete. We do. It's just that I'm not current..."

"Get current and call me back." He cradled the phone and turned his chair to look out the French doors into the yard and beyond. "Damn it, damn it, damn it!" he slammed his fist on the desk and shook his head. "I'm dealing with nincompoops. Absolute nincompoops."

It's hard

DEATH CAME TO THE river at high noon. Silence engulfed the birds and frogs. The leaves hung limp and lifeless from the branches. Seth began to think he and Richard were the only living things on the river and his mind drifted to the origin of man theory where life crawled out of the water to live on dry land. His family had not. He and Richard drifted on the dead water only a foot from the warm wetness of the river. And the sun, directly overhead, bounced searing rays off the mirrored surface into his eyes. It was over 100 degrees.

Seth heard Richard twist the cap off the canteen. "Is it cool?"

"No," Richard said. "As warm as the river."

Seth reached his arm back. "At least it's wet. Pass it up, will ya?"

Richard closed his eyes. "The traffic noise is constant."

Seth nodded and took another swallow. "We're within spitting distance of Highway 80. Bound to hear it."

"So much for wilderness travel. Where do you reckon we are?"

"Cozad—or close by. You wanta swing into town and see if the new band uniforms have arrived yet? Get some pictures of your grand donation?"

"No. I want to put on clean clothes, jack my feet up, pour a Scotch and be at ease."

"Humph. That'll be a day or two yet."

"How much time do we have left?"

"Don't know. We'll figure that out tonight." He lifted his paddle and dipped it in the river where the blade struck the sand bottom half way in. "Let's do some paddling."

Richard let his mind drift to the monotony of plowing: up and down the field over and over but inside the cab it was air-conditioned, the radio played, and from his seat high above the ground he could see for a mile or more. From the canoe seat—maybe half a mile down river, but it was interrupted by sandbars, roots buried in the sand, and the constant flexing of Seth's back muscles. He watched as the skin on Seth's back went from pink to red to tan in several days and marveled at how a man could stay constant with paddle action for hours. Paddling was repetive, and boring, but demanding enough that you couldn't let your mind drift in the shallow water or you risked having the canoe shoved broadside and tipped.

Being dumped into a river that was only a foot deep and warm was no great threat, but it meant drying out stuff which meant more time on shore with a fire on a hot day and less time to get to their goal—return to the Barrett Ranch before the sixty-one days was up. The sun cooked his thighs; he scooped water with his hand and splashed it on his Levi's but it evaporated within minutes. He leaned forward and dug out his sunglasses. Maybe it wasn't kosher as far as Grandpa Melzer was concerned but wearing them gave great relief to his stinging eyes. Anyhow, there were a lot of upgrades since Melzer's day and none had been ruled out by the conditions of the will.

Seth shifted in his seat, the monotonous metronome of his paddling stopped. He put one hand on each gunwale and twisted halfway around. "Let's beach this thing. My butt is killing me."

"Steady as she goes, Sir. Preparing to beach," Richard shouted. He pushed the stern to the right, which swung the bow left and forward about six feet to a slight beach where the fiberglass ground against the sand. "Dismount."

Seth stood up, teetered a moment, gained his balance and jumped to the shore. He got on his hands and knees and kissed the ground. "I claim this land for the Barrett Ranch," he said and rammed his paddle into the mud like a flag. It quivered a moment then toppled to the ground. "Humph...I suppose my claim is no good if the flag doesn't stick."

Richard was walking down the shore with one hand settled over each kidney, stretching his head and shoulders sideways and backward. He didn't reply. The brothers walked up and down the shore, each in the opposite direction to turn and pass again going the other way.

"What're you thinkin'?" Seth said.

"Just pondering again," Richard said shaking his head," what Mom was trying to tell us by having us run up and down this river by horse and canoe." He pointed toward the highway. "We could have done it in several days by car."

"So, what do you think?"

Richard shook his head. "That pronouncement will have to wait until I am out of this damn canoe, showered, fed a decent meal preceded by a good single malt Scotch, and rested."

"You're showin' your age, brother."

"Might be," Richard nodded. "Might be."

Seth picked up the bow rope and threw it in the canoe. "Let's get a move on. We can make Lexington before nightfall."

Richard sighed. "Might as well. Nothing attractive about this spot."

Chapter 17

"MOM," VALERIE HOUSTON yelled, "Bucky's using a tennis rac-
quet on the birds again."

Ginny smiled and shook her head. How much different boys and
girls were. Valerie would pick up an injured bird, nurse it, put it in a
warm blanket and stroke its breast feathers. If it died she would hold a
full dress funeral for it, even giving it a name and a tombstone consist-
ing of a wooden shingle with the bird's name burned into it and the
date of death. Complete, compassionate, and ethereal.

Bucky was in the haymow in the height of the barn swatting at
the frightened sparrows with a tennis racket; Dawson on the other
side, swinging and chasing the birds back to Bucky. So far they had
swatted nine who fell to the floor of the barn where the cats grabbed
them, growling and flattening their ears if any other cat came toward
them as they dashed away to eat their prize under the old pickup
stored in the granary.

"We have too many sparrows, honey. It won't hurt to thin them
out some."

"Some of them aren't dead when the cats get them," Valerie pleaded.

"They are probably stunned and unconscious when they hit the floor."

"But, Mom, I might be able to save them."

Ginny hung the hand towel on the stove handle and cuddled her
daughter against her chest. "Honey, that's just the way it is on the
farm. If the sparrows didn't have the barn to shelter in and the scraps
from the granary and chicken feed to eat there would be far fewer of
them. But your uncles provide shelter and food and the birds take
advantage of the easy life and breed lots of babies who grow up and
do the same. Pretty soon we have too many for the cats to keep in

balance and in step Bucky and Dawson who act as a counter balance to the population boom."

Valerie looked up. "But, Mom, that's not fair. They're using rackets."

"Honey—life is not fair. Change clothes and let's get ready for evening chores. Call your brothers in, please."

Valerie changed clothes, went to the top shelf of the closet where Uncle Seth kept the fireworks and picked out a M80 firecracker. On her way through the kitchen she fetched two wood kitchen matches and skipped out the screen door headed to the barn. She leaned her weight into the sliding barn door and kept it moving until it was full open. Birds started streaming past as she struck a match and lit the fuse. She stared at the spitting fuse for a second then pulled back and flung it as hard as she could towards the roof.

The firecracker reached its apex and started down. At the hay-mow level it exploded with a concussion that thumped their ears. The birds, seeing the open door barreled out by the dozens, and Dawson and Bucky stood looking down at their little sister, mouths gaping open.

"What the hell do you think you're doing?" Bucky yelled.

"I'm gonna tell Mama that you're cursing," Valerie said.

"I'm gonna beat you to a pulp when I get down there."

Dawson laughed. "Beat you down," he said and pitched off in a somersault to land on his back in the loose hay stacked on the floor. He slid down the side to the cement. Bucky climbed down the ladder.

"Mom said to call you in," Valerie said.

"Did you mean to call us in or blow us up?" Bucky said.

"I was saving the birds."

"Big deal. We've got a million birds."

"How many did you kill today?"

"Nine before you blew us up."

"Serves you right for killing helpless birds."

"You're lucky you didn't set the barn on fire. Tell Mom we're comin'."

AFTER SUPPER, SERENA SLIPPED upstairs and reappeared in a cute outfit much more suited to a night on the town than lounging in front of the TV.

"Hmmm—date?" Ginny asked.

"Yes, indeed. Mr. Thad Percy is springing for a movie and popcorn."

"Serena, I don't feel comfortable with this—you dating Thad while my brother is somewhere on the river. I feel like a conspirator."

Serena took both of Ginny's shoulders in her hands and looked her in the face. "Ginny, you helped promote this. I love Richard, but we have no commitment to each other and I don't want to be a lonely irritable old woman waiting around for my knight to come back from the crusades. Thad is enjoyable and it gives me a break. I'm not sleeping with him or anything."

"Oh, I know that. It just makes me feel that I should be doing more to keep you primed for Richard."

"He's had three years of priming. It's time for the pump to flow."

They laughed. Serena grabbed her purse and opened the door. "Be back before midnight, Mom."

Ginny chuckled. "You see to it young lady or the door will be locked tight."

THAD PERCY AND SERENA parked in the Keno parking lot and walked to the restaurant entrance. Thad reached for her hand and she let him clasp it.

He smiled to himself. Hot damn—I'm on first base.

They took a booth and ordered.

"What did you think of *No Country for Old Men?*" Serena asked.

Thad shook his head. "A lot of gratuitous violence. And what was the point of it?"

Serena puckered her lips together. "I don't know and I don't know why they would consider it for a Pulitzer Prize either."

"Is it the Pulitzer or the Nobel?"

"I don't know. I get them mixed up."

"And you a school teacher."

"Well—I don't teach English or writing."

Thad smiled. "I know." He allowed his eyes to take her all in from the top of her head, the cascading hair, the classic collar of her form fitting suede jacket—to her hands clasped in front of her. He reached out and laid his hand on hers. The action brought their eyes together. He maintained his smile.

Serena cracked a wry smile, "What's that supposed to mean?"

"I don't know." Thad shrugged. "What do you want it to mean?"

His hands still overlaid hers. "Thad—we're friends. I enjoy being here with you but please don't think I'm making any sort of commit-ment," she shook her head, "because I'm not."

He nodded. "Understood." He bit his lower lip gently, picking at a piece of loose skin inside his mouth, then took a deep breath and let it out. "But it's good to be here with you."

Serena frowned. "I didn't lead you on, did I?"

"No. Just my optimistic approach to events." He sat back in the booth removing his hands from hers. "I thought after we had coffee that you were in the mood for further interaction."

"Interaction—yes. Romance—no."

Thad delayed his thought a minute. "You really hooked on Richard? He's twenty years older than you."

"Age doesn't play much of a part at this time of my life."

"I can't offer you the financial security he can, but you won't have to change my diapers or remind me where my keys are."

"Please change the subject," she said.

The waitress delivered their order with a banging of ceramic on wood and a clatter of flatware. "Anything else?"

Thad shook his head and sat with his hands in his lap, his eyes focused on the plate of food.

How do I get around this? I was on first base in the parking lot. She can't throw me out at second.

"Hmmm, smells good," he said. "We can go for a drive after supper."

Trespassing on the river

CRAIG JAMISON GOT UP and closed the door to his office. He didn't want this conversation going any further than the edges of his desk. He dialed Klete Dixon.

"Klete," Craig said. "We've come up with the implementation process."

"What about the timing?"

"That's part of the process. They left May 1st; they have sixty-one days, which brings them to June 30th." Craig doodled on a pad in front of him. "They are working on day 48 so they have thirteen days left.

Bud is willing to implement a little used law that won't harm them and is completely valid and defensible in any court in Nebraska."

"And it will buy us the time we need?"

"Bud and I agree on that."

"Do you need any funds?"

"Not yet. You can cover those if any appear."

"I'm counting on you, Craig. Or should I address you as Senator Jamison?"

"I like the sound of that."

"Keep me apprised."

Craig nodded. "Will do."

Craig pursed his lips and looked at the telephone receiver in his hand for a minute, his other hand drumming on his credenza. He punched in the numbers for Sheriff Bud Pinsky's private phone. He waited through three rings.

"Pinsky here," the voice said.

"Bud—time to implement the trespass issue."

"How much time do we need to erase?"

"Three days."

It was silent on the other end. Finally Bud said, "I'll get on it."

Craig turned his chair and looked out his office window to the parking lot. "No personal involvement this time. Make sure it's all legal."

"Will do."

He cradled the phone, crossed his feet on the desk and made a tepee of his fingers. *Let's see if he can follow through with this simple task.* Craig shook his head. *The boy hasn't garnered any intelligence awards so far.*

BUD GOT OUT PAPER and pen and wrote down the counties coming east along the Platte River: Dawson, Buffalo, Hall, Merrick, Platte, and Dodge County before they arrived in Cass County, where, until his trial came up, he ruled the roost. He chewed on the pen, pictured the sheriff in each county and what he could count on his doing at his request. Then he started making phone calls.

Thad doesn't get it

THAD SHOWERED, SHAVED, AND cleaned his fingernails. Then he put on a bathrobe and sat looking out his apartment window. An envelope of silence clung to him, which always put him in a reflective mood. Somewhere amongst the 68,000 free ranging items stored in his mind was the answer to what the hell was going on in this town. Such as, "Why would normally good and law abiding guys like the Barrett brothers be getting into trouble with the law on the river? And why would wealthy guys have banking problems? His last casual meeting with Serena brought that to his attention.

THAD SHOOK HIS HEAD. "I'm neutral. I report—not take sides."

"Why do your stories in the paper always seem to side with Pinsky?" Serena said.

"Don't think they do. I write what I find out. As new information becomes available I put it out so the public can make up its own mind."

"Public mind? I doubt that."

Thad moved forward from the hips. "Why are you asking this?"

Serena thought about it for a second. "Maybe it's just me but the *Journal* seems to come down on Pinsky's side every time there is a story about him in there."

"It has to be Pinsky or Barretts—maybe Dixon."

Serena shook her head. "You should go back and read your stories."

"I can," Thad offered. "But that won't change my mind."

"Thad, can't you see there is something sinister going on the way things are happening? It isn't just happenstance. It is a concerted effort to delay Seth and Richard with the ultimate goal of acquiring the Barrett Ranch."

He tilted his head to one side. "Could be. What do you know that I don't?"

"I'm just putting the puzzle together piece by piece. What do you know about Filoh Smith and how he works into this problem?"

Thad thought back to when he was a boy and Filoh had just sold out and moved out of town. "Not much. He returned to town just before the Barretts took off on their odyssey."

"That's it?"

His eyebrows lifted. "What do you know?"

"He had a list in his belongings at Brewster's B&B. Ten names, all big farmers along the Platte. Any idea why he made that list?"

Thad shrugged. "Any number of reasons." He leaned forward. "First of all, Filoh Smith was over ninety. Secondly, he had a case of environmental daydreams and no direct living kin—nobody to rein him in. Thirdly, he was angry at the way farming had developed, so much so that he was willing to commit his money and time to bringing about change. Fourthly—he had nothing else to do with the rest of his life. That makes a man dangerous."

"Dangerous? To whom?"

"Those ten farmers."

"Do you know he tried to blow up a sprinkler tower on Dixon's farm?"

Thad nodded. "I'd been told that."

"You never wrote about it?"

"Why would I write about something like that? No prosecution, no witnesses, no damage—no story."

"OK—what about Pinsky?"

"What about him?"

"Where do you come down on his indictment?"

"Look," Thad said. "I've known Bud Pinsky since middle school. He's an all right guy. He always had a crush on Ginny Barrett and maybe his groin got ahead of his brain in this case, but he's been a good enough sheriff and a good citizen for all the years I've known him."

"Is he involved with Klete Dixon?"

"Everybody's involved with Klete Dixon." He waved his hand in a broad sweep. "You couldn't go anywhere in this town and not find somebody that's involved with Klete Dixon. He's big, he's powerful, he's honored, and many people owe him a favor."

"Including Craig Jamison?" she said.

"Probably. Dixon has always contributed to his political funds."

"And Pinsky?"

Thad nodded. "Undoubtedly."

"Then we have a conspiracy."

Thad grimaced. "That's hard to prove. In a small town like this everyone works together for the good of the community. Factions develop from time to time, but nothing as strong as a conspiracy.

Everything is pretty much out in the open. Laundry is hung out on the line to dry—everyone can see what you're wearing."

"Try this on" Serena said. "Klete Dixon bought the house I was renting and kicked me out. He was behind my firing to get me out of town and throw a monkey wrench into my relationship with Richard Barrett, a delaying tactic. He bought up all the freeze-dried food in town forcing the Barretts to go to Omaha to get supplies for their trip, another delay. He pushed Pinsky to get the sheriffs of counties up the Platte to delay Barretts on their trip."

"Peanut items. How do you come by that information?" Thad said.

"I'm living out there. Information is coming in all the time."

"Sounds like you're working for Barretts."

Serena shook her head. "I'm just stating facts."

He looked up into her eyes. "Who are you trying to hoist on his petard?"

She didn't miss a beat. "Seems we have two factions here—the Barretts and the Dixons. Where Jamison and Pinsky and those who do their will fit in is still to be resolved."

Thad snorted. "You just picked all the main players and formed your own teams. Craig Jamison is the lawyer for Mae Barrett's estate. He courted her for years after her husband died. They were more than friends. And as for Pinsky and Dixon, they are in the public eye all the time. Sure the sheriff is indicted but nothing is proved and he is innocent until proven guilty—you know that. I think you're making a mountain out of a molehill."

Serena looked at her intertwined fingers resting on the tabletop. "Just when do you come down on one side or the other at the Journal?"

"That's editor's work," Thad said. "I just do the writing." He smiled.

THAD PERCY HEARD HIS editor on the phone when he passed the open door.

The editor turned his head. "What'd you find out?"

"Not much. A lot of loose information. Awful loose. Nobody seems incensed by stuff going on. In fact, most of the people I talked to wanted both organic farming and lower prices. They liked Pinsky but were against sexual assault. They liked Serena but didn't mind that her contract was not renewed. Nobody knew anything at all about the events of the Barretts on the river. I feel like I've been dropped into a blender."

"THAD IS PRETTY NEUTRAL," Serena said. Ginny put six potatoes in boiling water. "I can't tell if he has made up his mind or if he just has the sponge brain of a journalist and is taking in all the information he can before he has to write something."

"Nobody seems to be concerned. The thing that's bothering me is that Jamison hired some people from Omaha to investigate the circumstances but we can't find out who they are or what they are doing."

"You think we're the ping pong ball?"

Ginny nodded. "I'm getting that feeling."

"NOW," THAD SAID, TALKING to himself. "I don't know where to go from here. Ginny is clean as a whistle. Serena seems to have committed no big sin—other than sleeping with Richard Barrett. Richard has raised a few hackles on the school board but is generally thought of as a good guy by everyone else. Seth is a reformed alcoholic and a womanizer, but currently acting like he's cured of both. Pinsky gets re-elected by huge margins, Jamison is almost a shoo-in for the junior senator job, and Klete Dixon has more honors and awards for good citizenship and farming than he can hang on a large wall. I don't get it. I just don't get it."

Who gains from this activity? Always the place to look.

Bud Pinsky makes a request

LEXINGTON SITS ALONG THE Platte River in Dawson County. Dawson County elected Sheriff David Briggs to enforce its laws and ordinances and keep it safe from harm. For eighteen years Sheriff Briggs had done that. The call he received from Sheriff Bud Pinsky was different from the first call several weeks ago. This time, instead of swine flu, it had to do with trespassing. He had two reports of cattle out, a dog running loose near the intersection of Highway 30 and North Jackson Street, and an abandoned car at Plum Creek Park, which should be the city police's problem but had been bumped over to his department for reasons unknown by the caller.

"Morning, Dave. Pinsky here. Where did I catch you this morning?"

"Good morning, Bud. I'm in Lexington with a to-do list as long as my arm. What do you need?"

"I'm getting reports that the Barretts are doing some serious trespassing as they come down the Platte. Getting out of a canoe anytime they want, camping anywhere they want, no permission from landowners. I've talked with the sheriffs of five other counties and we're thinking this kind of disregard for common law has to be made an example of. You catch my drift?"

Sheriff Briggs nodded. "I see your point but I don't know that it is worth enforcing. Don't think we'd get a conviction on it. Juries here are more likely to give them a warning rather than convict."

"That's all right," Pinsky said. "But the sheriff's job is to enforce the law and trespassing is clearly against the law. These guys need to be stopped and taught a small gentle lesson. They just can't do as they damn please. A night or two in jail could remind them that sheriffs up and down the Platte are serious about complaints from their citizens."

"You're suggesting I jail them? They'll bail out in two hours…"

"…Yes, I know that, but not if you arrest them at night. But dammit, we—the sheriffs up and down the river—need to set an example that we're willing to enforce the laws on the books and protect our citizens from trespass. A good show like that could last all summer. Discourage others from flagrantly disregarding the trespass laws. You know—the hunters and the air boat people."

Sheriff Briggs was silent a moment. "Ok—so what?"

"Stop 'em; hole them up in your jail; fine 'em a few bucks, then let 'em make bail. Later you can drop the charges but everyone will hear about it and it should stop others from disregarding the law. Trespass is becoming an epidemic around here."

"This isn't another scam like the swine flu, is it?"

"Honest to God, Dave, that tip came from a prominent citizen and I thought you were the best man to get to the bottom of it. And I thank you for your response to that last call. If you would assist with this one, I'd be beholden to you."

"OK—I'll give it a shot. You have any time line for their arrival?"

"I'm told, again by a prominent river bank citizen, that they should show up close to Lexington tonight. And as dry as it is this year, don't let them build any damn fires on the banks."

Dave Briggs shook his head. Cows out, dogs loose, abandoned car, and now a real serious trespass potential. I thought, as sheriff, I would be chasing real honest to god criminals all day long and when I went home at night and took off my gun belt I could regale the wife with harrowing feats of courage, cunning deployment of my troops, and the jailing of serious offenders of the law. Hell—I could send the Boy Scouts down to the river to tell the Barrett brothers to quit trespassing. Likely they have been trespassed on at their spread. On the other hand, Pinsky and I raised a little hell at the 1990 convention and I'd not like what we did to be broadcast anywhere and Pinsky just might go public if he got pinched hard enough. Besides…I'm well within the law and it's only a delay. No big deal.

"Up we go," he said and stood, adjusted his gun belt and reached for his hat. "Smile, citizens of Dawson County, your sheriff is on patrol." As he walked through the front part of the office he spoke to the dispatcher. "Where is that fifty pound bag of doggy treats?"

She pointed at a closet. He opened the door and grabbed a handful, slid them by his nose. "They smell good. No wonder they work on stray dogs."

Another jail visit

THE LIGHT BLINDED SETH. He put his hand over his eyes and the pain stopped. "My gawd that's bright."

"Come out here…please," the voice said. "Sheriff David Briggs of Dawson County."

"You again?" Richard said. "What time is it?"

"Doesn't make any difference what time it is. Trespassing, plain and simple. Grab your personal items, we're going into town."

Richard roused out. "What kind of nonsense is this, Sheriff?

"You're breaking the law. The law of Dawson County and every other county on the Platte River. Now don't tell me you don't understand trespassing or I'll lock you up for ignorance."

"Who's going to look after our stuff?" Seth said.

Briggs nodded. "I'll leave one of my deputies to keep watch over it. Any liquor or firearms in there."

Richard said. "Scotch and a .30-30."

"Leroy," Briggs said. "Bring the whisky and rifle and follow us in. Darrell, you hang out here until we get back. And don't build the fire up too high, the country's drier than the dugs on a boar."

Briggs put the car in gear and started for town. "I need to drop by a place and tease a dog out. You gentlemen don't mind if I take a little detour?"

Seth looked at Briggs. "I guess there's not much we can say about that. You're drivin'."

"That's what I like. Nice compliant common trespassers."

He drove to Highway 30 and North Jackson Street, shut off the motor and looked around. "You boys see a dog, holler."

The headlights of an eighteen-wheeler headed West on Highway 30 lighted up a dog off to the side. Sheriff Briggs started up the car, turned on his flashing lights and slid over by the embankment. He opened the door and threw one of the doggy treats out.

He whistled. "Come here, fella."

The dog, part everything from each barnyard, sniffed the treat and snatched it. Briggs threw another piece, closer to the rig.

"Would one of you open the tail gate?" He pushed a button unlocking the rear door. Seth stepped out and lifted the SUV door. Briggs threw some doggy treats into the back of the vehicle. "Put them around back there. I want to lure him in."

"Am I employed by the county now?" Seth said.

"Yeah. Full benefits including board and room."

The dog was not wary. He followed the trail of the treats and when he got to the tailgate, his nose told him there were more inside. He made the leap and was into the second treat when the door closed. He watched it close then went back to the food.

"Cross that one off my list," Briggs said. He took a deep breath. "Now to resolve this trespass issue."

"SHERIFF," THE BAIL BONDSMAN said. "What's up this time of night?"

"Your ad says 24 hour service."

"I gotta change that thing. I'm too old to get up in the middle of the night."

"Hell, Jensen—it's only 11:30." He brushed dust off his pants. "Got a couple of trespassers needing a bond."

"How serious is this?"

"Not serious, but legal."

"Ok, but I can't get over there until tomorrow."

"What time?"

"Make it noon."

"I'll tell them." Briggs hung up the phone. He sat for a moment at his desk, his left foot perched on the top showing the tip of the ankle holster. He noticed that and pulled his pant leg down to cover it. In all his years as a lawman he had never had occasion to use the little Walther .380 but it gave him ease of mind when he put it on every morning over his calf high socks.

"Gentlemen. The bail bondsman will be here at noon tomorrow. I gotta get rid of that dog and we'll see you with a nice hot breakfast at 7:00 am sharp."

"Sheriff," Richard said. "What is the meaning of this?"

"Trespassing. Gotta make an example. People can't just trespass all year long and expect law enforcement to turn a blind eye."

"How many others have you cited for trespassing in oh…the last three years?" Richard said.

Briggs buckled up his lips and shook his head. "Not many."

"How many?"

"You know, I'm not the law breaker here. I ask the questions. I don't answer other people's questions."

Richard took another stab at it. "Is this another Pinsky call?"

Briggs snorted. "Good night, gentlemen. See you in the morning."

SHERIFF BRIGGS DID NOT see the dog when he got in his SUV. He called to him but got no response. A strange smell permeated the inside. He got out and opened the lift gate. The dog lay on his side, unresponsive. There was vomit on the carpet and leaking from the dog's mouth. He put his hand on the dog's chest and could feel no heartbeat. He pried the eyelid open but the exposed eye was non-seeing. Briggs shook his head. "I'll be damned. This doesn't bode well."

Thad tries again

SERENA OPENED THE SCREEN door and stepped onto the porch. Thad Percy almost swallowed his gum. He scooted around the back of the car and opened the passenger side door for her. His eyes rested on her legs as she slid onto the seat. "Good to see you," he said.

She smiled. "Did you see enough?"

"There is always the desire for more, isn't there?"

She looked at him, the smile infectious.

"That's an old journalistic question. When is enough—enough?"

"We'll have to decide that."

He got in the car, closed the door, started up and backed out of the driveway. "I've picked a nice quiet place where we can talk uninterrupted," he said. "Do you like Chinese food?"

AFTER SUPPER AND IN no hurry, they sipped hot sake from a small porcelain cup.

"I'm thinking of taking a teaching job in Omaha," Serena said.

"Did you get what you wanted?"

She nodded and set her cup down. "Almost everything. It's hard to tell what a school district can and can't do."

"You seem distracted...a little distant tonight."

She twirled her cup with both hands on the tabletop before answering. "These problems out at the ranch have us all distraught. There seems to be some connection between Klete Dixon, Jamison, and the sheriff, but we can't put a finger on it."

Thad chuckled. "That's the big question."

"Your opinion?" she said.

Thad sat back in the booth and stared at the steam rising from the sake. "My opinion doesn't count for much. My editor can and does edit most stuff I write. I'm not on a crusade but little bits and pieces float before me from time to time and when I try and put them together my editor says it is just conjecture and to stick to reporting facts and news. Well, dammit, conspiracy to commit a crime is news, but the paper isn't in the business of accusing people it doesn't have facts to collaborate."

"And you have no facts?"

Thad nodded. "I've got some but I can't connect the dots…yet."

"Like what?"

"Like the dead cow at the Barrett ranch—killed on purpose to intimidate? The indictment of Sheriff Pinsky on sexual assault—what was that about? The death of Filoh Smith on the river trip. The various miscellaneous arrests of the Barrett brothers on charges of trespassing that goes unnoticed the rest of the year. Seems too much to be coincidental, yet tying them together has been impossible."

"The sheriff doesn't care for you much, does he?"

"I suppose not. I ask a lot of questions and he doesn't answer many."

"I can tell you one thing we found."

Thad leaned forward. "Oh?"

"Two kids camped in that little pasture behind the solid waste station out by the ranch…you know the one…." He nodded "They saw the Sheriff's car stop and he threw something in. Turned out to be a pair of rubber gloves and blood covered overalls.

"Which kids?"

"The Clement kids."

Thad's eyes roamed over the room. That information still didn't close the circle.

"Ok," Serena said. "I told you one, now you tell me one."

Thad chuckled. "The *Lexington Clipper-Herald* called me this morning to ask if I knew anything about why the Barrett brothers were in jail in Lexington. The reporter doing the court house and police report found they were put in jail last night for trespassing." He snorted. "Their trip has become a state wide story. You know… the kind of thing where reporters write things like, "The aging Barrett brothers reliving the original homesteading trials of Great Grandfather Melzer…etc. etc. etc."

"For crying out loud. Trespassing? On what?"

Thad shrugged. "Private land. Technically you can't step foot on the river bed or banks because the owners on either side own to the middle of the traditional channel."

"That's kind of crazy," she said.

"Crazy, yes. But illegal just the same."

"So the Barretts are in jail. Who would have sprung that trap? I'm sure the sheriff wasn't standing around waiting for someone to step in six inches of water."

"I'm going to find out tomorrow, if I can. The brothers have less than two weeks to get back here or else the ranch goes bye bye. The river is drying up. They could be trespassing every day if they have to walk their canoe down the river. What if every sheriff along the way sticks them in jail for a day or two? They don't make it; the ranch goes away; somebody wins and somebody loses in that scenario. I'd like to find out who wins. I know who loses—the Barretts." He pulled the lobe of his ear. "How is Ginny doing running the ranch?"

"She's hired some extra people to work the farm and livestock along with her kids. They are a pretty productive group. I'm living there now and help out in the house."

"I saw you with her at Mom's the other day," Thad said, a brief smile on his face.

"We've become good friends."

Thad nodded and upended the sake cup in his mouth. "Let's take a drive."

Chapter 18

By 2:00 pm, Doug Jensen, bail bondsman for all of Dawson County, had accepted the pledge of security for his cash bond of $500 each from the Barretts and after a cup of coffee to keep him awake, headed to Kearney.

Richard called a cab to take them back to the river after receiving assurances from Sheriff Briggs that they would not be arrested again for setting the canoe into the water.

Sheriff Briggs pulled his Sheriff's report book from the shelf and began to record the activities of his office for the last twenty-four hours.

> 6/21/14—2014 loose dog. 2016 cows out at bridge; 2025 assisting other agency/Cass County.

> 6/22/14—0916 dead dog delivered to vet for autopsy; 1342 Barrett, Seth and Richard, bonded out of Dawson County. 1508 Ross Jakes collected loose cattle.

Darrell was sitting at the edge of their camp lobbing rocks at a tire half buried in the sand. He stood up as the cab doors opened.

"Afternoon, boys," he said.

Seth nodded as Richard paid the cab.

"Mind paying for me to go back with him?" Darrell said.

Richard looked up, and forked over another bill.

"Did you take care of everything?" Seth asked.

"Of course."

Richard brought the whisky and rifle from the cab trunk while Seth packed up their gear. "Let's get out of this county," he said.

The water was lower than they expected. They pulled on their hip waders, looped the snaps over their belts, secured their packs in the center of the canoe and found enough water to float the canoe.

Seth looked at the water level. "Seems like everybody's irrigating."

Seth's statement didn't need a response. Richard could see that. Where did this odyssey go from here? A low river, a tiresome trip for two guys in their 60s, and the likelihood of being arrested over and over for trespassing. For some reason Pinsky was working a delaying tactic. He didn't have the money to buy the ranch if they failed to get back in time. Jamison was their attorney. He was supposed to have client loyalty. Klete Dixon wanted the ranch—the whole town knew that. That wasn't new. But who else? Could Dixon be doing this alone, risking his reputation on the off chance of getting the Barrett ranch? What had the investigators that Jamison hired found out? Next time he had good phone service he would call Jamison and Ginny—and Serena. Hell—he had not called her since the turnaround at North Platte. What was he thinking, not to call?

"Ok, here's the deal," Seth said. "We only get out of the canoe at public parks and the like. Under bridge right of ways and public lands. That could eliminate the trespass issue, don't you think?"

Richard thought. The years of alcohol addiction had not hurt his brother's brain. That was a good resolution to the constant potential of trespass. If other sheriffs had been alerted they could spend half of their remaining time in local jails. "Good idea," he said.

"Steer right of that bunch of trees up there. I'm thinkin' the channel goes that way."

The silence was tangible. A clunk when Richard hit the canoe and the water gliding off Seth's paddle made the only sound there was. It was as if they had walked out into an empty football stadium.

Finally the canoe ground to a halt. Seth set his paddle across the gunwales and let his head drop to his chest. "I missed the channel," he muttered.

"Well—it can't be far. We will go back," Richard said.

"You wanta trespass right here and now?"

Richard thought about it a moment. "I don't see anybody."

"I didn't see Sheriff Briggs either until he stuck that flashlight in my face."

Richard took a deep breath. "Ok. What do you want to do?"

Seth looked around. "Back paddle. See if we can get off this sandbar."

After three strokes the canoe broke loose from the groove it had cut into the sandbar and floated, although both paddles struck bottom when they were used. There was not enough room to turn around so Richard looked over his shoulder while both back paddled. He headed for where the water split into two streams. Maybe the other one would float their boat.

He yearned for the horses now even though his butt was just healing from the ride and the trespass issue was staring them in the face. What a silly law to charge trespass against someone who steps out of a boat in the middle of a river. When they got home he would check to see how often the riverbank trespass law had been implemented. Right now he bet he and Seth were the only violators to be named in a year. The more he thought of it the crazier it became.

Seth pulled a map out of the pack and spread it out across his knees. He looked around the area and finally said: "That bridge leads to Overton, I do believe."

"Well—"

"We haven't done much today but in the four hours since our jail break, we've at least gotten this far. We can camp on the right of way. That's public ground."

"I am ready. Do it."

Seth pointed his paddle to the left. "Good spot over there."

Richard dug in, his shoulders sore from the hard surface of last night's sleep in the Lexington jail. The canoe nosed into the bank and as soon as it was unpacked, a fire built, and the tent set up, Richard poured a double Scotch and leaned back against a tree and looked at the setting sun. "Another day, another mile closer."

"That's about all we made today," Seth said.

"Cheers," Richard said, taking a swig of the brown whisky.

Can a river run dry?

KLETE DIXON PUT ONE foot on the running board of his Ram pickup, punched in a number and held the phone to his right ear as he looked out over the Platte River.

"Cort," the man said.

"Dixon, here. Get the rest of those farmers between here and Ogallala to take their irrigation water out as fast as they can. Store it in ponds or dump it on the fields, but dry that damn river up."

It was quiet on the other end.

"Did you understand me?"

"Yes."

"Well—get about it."

Klete could hear a deep breath being released.

"Ok."

Cort didn't know if he was committing a crime, abetting a criminal, or anything at all about it. He was a ranch foreman, not given to the fine points of the law. What he did know was who signed his paycheck every other week. He reckoned he was far enough down the food chain that if there was a big stir over this he wouldn't be dragged into it except as a witness. When he was driving he sometimes went over the conversation as he could imagine it on the witness stand. He seemed to do pretty well with it.

He went to lunch and plugged his cell phone into the charger. About 1:00 o'clock he got in his pickup and headed to the top of the small rise on the Dixon Ranch overlooking the Platte River. He pulled out a piece of paper, unfolded it, spread it out on the dashboard and took out a ballpoint pen. The first of thirty-two calls he made was to Orville Williams who was foreman/manager for the Rockford Cattle Company just outside Ogallala.

"Orville. This is Cort. Remember that talk we had about pulling your irrigation water when I called? Now's the time, good buddy. Open the gates."

He listened to the reply.

"No need to worry about that. Store all you can in your lake and then the stock ponds. If it overflows, my boss will pay the fine for you. What? Stretch it out over the next three or four days. Much obliged." Cort nodded unconsciously. "We're beholden to you."

Cort punched the off button and took a deep breath. That wasn't so bad. Not nearly as bad as he thought it would be. He put an X in front of Rockford Cattle Co. and punched in the next number.

It was six o'clock and the evening crowd was gathering at the Keno. Cort had showered and shaved and put on his best Levi's. The silver buckle he had won at the Burwell Rodeo was shined and stood out like a beacon in the inside light. He spotted Thad Percy sitting alone at a booth. That's strange, he thought and, removing his Stetson, slid in on the opposite side.

"Waiting for anybody in particular?" Cort said.

Thad nodded. "You'll do until she gets here."

Cort smiled. "Oh. A little action going outside the press room, huh?"

"Keeping my options open."

Cort ordered a beer, curled his arms around it on the table and sucked off the foam. "Who's the lucky lady?"

"You'll see."

"Hmmm," Cort said as he glanced around. "Not busy yet,"

"What have you been up to all day?" Thad asked.

"Ranch work. Cows, fence, gates—you know."

"How did you do that perched on the hill all afternoon?"

Cort straightened up. "I didn't see you there."

"I was down at the mouth of Fourmile Creek. You were in and out of your pickup all afternoon with a cell phone to your ear. Who you talkin' to?"

"What the hell were you doin' down at Fourmile?"

"Investigating. That's what I do."

"You were trespassing."

"I don't think so. I was on Barrett's land." He took a swallow of his beer. "How come you're so up on trespassing?" Thad lifted his head. "You been hearing anything about that?"

Cort picked up his beer in one hand, his hat in the other and slid out of the booth. "See you around," he said.

SERENA APPROACHED AND SLID in the booth beside Thad, "I've been at the library."

Thad nodded. "Figured you were up to something."

"You know anything about the US Bureau of Reclamation or the Central Nebraska Public Power and Irrigation District?" Serena said.

"It's been here all my life."

"I found out today that they will not be releasing any water into the Platte for the coming five days."

Thad shrugged. "So?"

"So," Serena smiled. "No water release means boating on the river is going to be slow or nil."

"Where did you get that information?"

The drinks were delivered. "I asked. It's the kind of thing investigators do."

"Ok, but who did you ask?" Thad said.

"The power authority."

Thad pondered that development. For thirty years the puzzle pieces had been as big as the farms around Plattsmouth, but this one had fragments of pieces. Clues led somewhere then drizzled into minute trails like the roots on a tree, each going to a dead end but alive enough to keep the main branch growing.

He shook his head. "I don't get it."

Serena brightened. "I don't either but I thought it was interesting. I just stumbled on to it and called them." She shook her head. "How is the chicken fried steak? Ginny and I are going to the movie so I have to eat and run."

AFTER SHE LEFT HIM sitting in the booth staring at his beer, he tried to think of the news story he needed for tomorrow. Several subjects crossed his mind. He wondered if he could find the Barrett brothers along the river at night—or early enough in the morning to get his story written, edited and printed? He pulled out his cell phone and punched in the number for Scott Digney, owner and pilot of Cass County Agri-spray.

"What the hell, Thad, I'm in the middle of supper," Scott answered.

"You shouldn't answer your phone then. Can you take me up first light of dawn tomorrow?"

"Where to and how long?"

"Somewhere between Lexington and Kearney?"

"The paper paying for it?"

Thad let his eyes close while he shook his head. "Yes."

"Just a minute."

"Dawn is 5:51 am at Kearney. Be at my shop at 3:30 sharp."

"See you then." Old Scott always needs to know who's gonna pay the bill. That's why he's still in business, but it sure gets under my skin sometimes.

Thad flies in

"I WAS JUST THINKIN'," Seth said. "We need to write down our impressions of the crops and stuff. Wasn't that what Mom put in the will?"

"Something like that," Richard said. He cut a hole out of the middle of each piece of fried bread and cracked an egg into it. He basted bacon grease over the top until the eggs turned a dirty brown.

"What have you written down?"

"Seth—don't bother me, I'm cooking."

"I can see that."

"Well—knock it off then." Richard looked up at the sound of the airplane.

"Some crop duster," Seth said.

"Looks like Scott's plane."

"Yeah—it does. Wonder what he's doing this far up river?"

The plane banked and the pilot cut the throttle letting the plane drift on the breeze down, down, down until Seth could see Scott's face in the window as it went by.

"I think Thad Percy's in there too," Richard said.

"It was Scott for sure."

On the second pass the window opened and a weighted bag trailing a bright red ribbon zinged down to land near the bridge. Seth walked over. "Looks like a May basket," he hollered. "It's from Thad Percy." He read the note. "Wants us to wait here."

Richard slid the toast and egg on to the plates and pulling his sleeve over his hand, grabbed the handle of the coffee pot. "Why should we do that?"

"Maybe he's doin' a story on us for the paper."

"Hummph." Richard cut his fried bread. "Why would they spend that kind of money flying him out here?"

Seth pushed the egg to one side of his mouth. "Don't know."

"Maybe something happened at the ranch."

"Let's call in."

Richard finished eating, wiped his hands on his Levi's and punched in a number.

A sleepy voice answered. "Hello."

"Ginny—this is Richard. Good morning."

"Is it morning already?"

"It is here. Listen, Ginny—is there anything wrong at the ranch, any problem or something?"

"Not that I'm aware of," she said. "But it's still early. Why you calling so early?"

"Scott just flew over and dropped a note from Thad Percy wanting us to wait here on the river for him to show up. Seth and I thought there might be a problem."

"Oh, Richard, there are many problems but we've been handling them. The big ones are in abeyance right now waiting for further action."

"The farm work getting done, irrigation going along…that sort of thing okay?"

"Yes. We're waiting for the calf buyer to show up and give us a bid on the yearlings."

"We will be back by that time. In fact, we will be there before the week is out."

"You'd better be. The time runs out Friday. We keep a calendar on the refrigerator and mark off every day."

"Serena is ok?"

"Sure. I'd let you talk to her but she got up early and drove to Omaha for some meeting about the coming school year. Everything ok with you and Seth?"

"Omaha?" Richard bellowed. "Why Omaha?"

"You probably haven't heard. She's been offered a position in Omaha."

"I don't like that a bit," he said. "Not one damn bit."

It was silent a moment. "Well," Ginny went on, "the poor girl has to find work somewhere."

"Yeah—but Omaha…"

Ginny brightened. "How is it on the river?"

"The river is low. Wading is hard but we will make it. This braided channel from Overton to Grand Island is the hardest. We will have a grand party when we get there."

"One other thing, Richard. Call Serena. She has been going out with Thad Percy from time to time. She says it's just for entertainment, but I'd hate to see her head turned."

"I thought absence made the heart grow fonder?"

"I don't know about that. But she mentioned something about her knight being gone on a crusade. You know—she's young, she's pretty, she's single, and that makes her prey for any guy in town with a car that runs. Thad has been pretty persistent."

"I'll call her today, I promise."

"Be safe and stay in touch."

"Goodbye, Ginny."

Richard pocketed the phone and stared into the fire. Seth knew to let him work it out in his mind and deliver the information in his own good time. You stood to irritate Richard if you pushed for information before he was ready to give it. Seth cleaned up their campsite and packed up the canoe as Richard stalked around the bank.

"Things are fine at the ranch. Something else must be on Thad's mind," Richard finally said.

At 6:57 a.m. they heard a door slam and Thad Percy came down to the campsite.

"Good morning, Richard, Seth," he said.

"Hello, Thad. Coffee?"

"Been drinkin' that since 3 o'clock. No thanks. Gotta ask you guys some questions." He opened a small notebook to a clean page and sat with pen poised. "Have either of you guys ever ticked off anybody at the Bureau of Reclamation or Public Power and Irrigation District?"

Moses parted the waters—Cort stopped them

CRAIG JAMISON TOOK THE easy chair and the cup of coffee offered to him by Klete Dixon. "Brandy?" Klete asked. Jamison nodded and Klete poured some in his coffee.

"Bud?"

Sheriff Bud Pinsky nodded and the three men sat in the study sipping coffee while awaiting the fourth person. Small talk ensued as each man sought to defend his information and involvement in the last major scheme.

When Cort walked in, Pinsky and Jamison sat upright and the skin on their faces tightened. They had each been crowded over the last three months, shoved beyond their comfort zone, willing, but at the same time reluctant, to participate in Dixon's plan.

"I believe you all know my foreman, Cort?" Dixon said. "Bring us up to date on the water."

Cort's eyes danced over the men before him. He stood like a lecturer. "The ranches on the western part of the river will start taking maximum water out today. As one stops up stream, another will start further down. I believe we can reduce the flow to less than half of what it is today."

Jamison moved to cross his legs. "How many of them know about this?"

"None. Only those of us in this room know what's happening." He looked at each person. "They each think they are accommodating me."

"And how about the Bureau of Reclamation?" Klete said.

Cort nodded. "The Grand Island office has agreed to hold back on the water they would normally release for five days, citing a potential shortage coming up in July and August."

"That ought to about dry it up then, right?" Klete said.

Cort nodded. "Should do it."

"Can they walk it in time?" Jamison asked.

Pinsky roused himself. "Not unless they abandon the canoe and travel 24/7. If they do that we've got the potential to charge trespassing."

"Anything we've missed?" Klete said.

They looked at each other and shook their heads.

"Thank you, gentlemen. This meeting was never held. Don't make any notes or talk to anyone about it. I believe that is clear?" Klete pushed his chair back.

"Isn't this something?" Cort said. "We dry up a whole damn river for a few days. Makes us look like Moses."

"Moses had the backing of God. I'm not sure He is on our side in this one," Jamison said. As they parted for their cars, Jamison added, "Don't forget to vote early and often in tomorrow's primary."

"Good luck in the election, Craig," Bud Pinsky said. "I'd be nice to call you Senator."

Probably be able to if Thad Percy doesn't connect the dots. Makes me nervous as a cat in a dog yard.

Chapter 19

TRAFFIC WAS LIGHT ON Highway 75 at six o'clock in the morning as Serena drove north toward Omaha. Her meeting today with the principal and new teachers was called on short notice and they were evasive with her on the reason. What would cause her to travel up there without a good reason or more timely notice? It couldn't be good.

An oncoming car slid across the centerline into her lane. She spun the wheel away from the headon collision. Her car zipped off the asphalt onto the grassy slope at seventy miles an hour aimed for a water ditch fifty yards away.

The car smacked the immature willow trees, the weight and speed bending the trunks and branches forward forcing the vehicle to a stop. It was poised, pointed at a forty-five degree angle toward the sky, like a ski jumper ready to leave the platform.

There was coffee on everything and just then her cell phone started ringing. She found it on the floor. Richard was calling.

"Oh, Richard. I've just had an accident."

"Are you alright?"

"I don't know." She looked around the inside of the car and moved her body parts. "I seem ok, but I'm aimed at the sky."

"Take a minute to calm down and we will take it from there."

"There's coffee over everything...the car, the windshield and my clothes. Oh no, I've got an appointment with the principal in Omaha too."

"Serena. Take a deep breath and sit still for a minute. You are fine and everything else can be cleaned up."

The first deep breath brought the tears. Slow at first and then as her mind wandered over the firing, the house, storing her belongings, going to work in a mid-town school, and sitting in a car pointed at the heavens like a rocket drenched in coffee, she let her body sink into the seat and cried. She heard Richard's voice but there was no stopping. Like a clock unwinding, the sobs slowed down with each heartbeat until it stopped. She could see flashing red lights in the rearview mirror and people walking across the grass toward her car.

"Shit," she said. "Shit, shit, shit."

Second thoughts

"WHAT KINDA CROPS DID you see flying in?" Richard asked.

Thad shook his head. "Miles and miles of corn and soy beans."

"Judas Priest," Seth bellowed. "We're on a push here and you're worryin' about crops?"

"Our mission—you recall," Richard said looking down at his brother.

"Right."

Seth poured another round of coffee.

"I gotta be getting' back," Scott said. "Time's a wasting."

Thad stood up, brushing the sand off his pants. "You get my drift though, don't you?" The bridge swallows swung out over them enveloping them with their chirping noise.

Richard nodded. "We need to be ahead of them."

"That's right," Thad said. He turned to Scott. "Let's get back." The two men walked to the plane. The brothers waved from the bank as the plane rose into the morning air.

THE SUN LIGHTED THE tops of the trees along the river promising a clear day with a tint of heat in it. The water level was up, and working with what Thad suspected, they moved quicker and launched in a decent channel that promised to add the river's speed in addition to what their paddles could produce.

Sore from paddling, hauling the canoe over shallow sands, and being jolted every time they smacked into a sandbar, the brothers were slowing. They had set their goal on making Kearney before they took a long break.

"There's a public area near Elm Creek where we can get out for a bit," Seth said. "Other than that, we're bound for Kearney. Keep paddlin'."

"My gawd, I am," Richard bellowed and, digging his paddle in, found the first full purchase on water since leaving their campsite.

They got to a stretch of water that allowed them to back off the fast paddling and drift for a bit. "So what'd she say?" Seth said.

"She had an accident. Not hurt but messed up."

Seth shook his head. "What's next?" he said. "What's next?"

The river was all confused water with a few protruding roots, sweepers from the last flood, some lying half out of the water. Where the water was deep enough and they could get a full pull on their paddles, they pushed their strokes up to sixty a minute.

The Voyagers, Seth recalled, often reached a continuous sixty-five to seventy strokes a minute, men accustomed to long canoe trips with heavy loads, men who sang French ditties as they powered their birch bark canoes through the lakes and rivers.

"What say we sing something?" Seth offered.

"Such as?"

"Row, row, row your boat, gently down the stream," he sang. "Merrily, merrily, merrily, merrily, life is but a dream."

"That is a children's song."

"No matter. It'll keep us up and together. Now sing it with me. "Row, row, row your boat gently down the stream." He stopped to see if he could hear Richard. And there it was, a clear baritone banging it out from the back seat of a fiberglass canoe zooming down the river halfway between Overton and Kearney. In that one instant he felt more love for his brother than he had felt in his memory. Always, Richard the older, the stronger, the more talented, but by the time Seth found he liked working with animals and was good at it, he had so much negative baggage he couldn't look up to anyone. He compared himself down instead of up. Up was where you had to go in life. Up was what people talked about. It was in all the obituaries and on the plaques and on the bronze plates attached to things.

Being out on the river in the cool of the morning, the sun beginning to dapple the river with light, filled his chest and Seth couldn't remember being this happy in years.

The climbing sun cast shadows that hid sandbars and the bow skimmed many of them but Seth was into it now. He forced his eyes to pick out the shallow spots and he moved the canoe by pushes and paddles with currents that kept them running and he measured their speed when the canoe passed islands of foam drifting on the river.

It was a familiar feeling. The stern of the canoe sinking into the water as the bow jammed into a sandbar. Seth fought it, shoved his paddle into the sand and pushed, but mostly lost and the boat's keel carved a neat trench in the wet sand, forcing the canoe to a stop.

"I need a minute," Richard said.

Seth turned in his seat to see his brother remove his cell phone and with a frown on his brow, punch in a number. "I'm calling Thad to help Serena out."

Seth shook his head. "For cryin' out loud, Richard. He's hot on her."

"I have to take the chance."

Richard held up his hand. "Thad? I had a call from Serena. She has had an accident on Highway 75 near Platteview Road. Could you take the time to help her? I would appreciate it so much." He gave him her cell phone number and hung up.

"Talk about shoving the fox into the hen house," Seth said.

"Oh, shut up, Seth. Who else is available?"

"Bud Pinsky."

"Grand idea. Get us off this reef."

Irrigation gates open

BENJAMIN COLLINS STARTED THE gas-powered engine that operated his irrigation gate and flicked the switch to open. It was a bit early to flood irrigate his fields of corn and soy beans but it was close enough, since the weather was never predictable this time of the year and it was a beautiful day to be out early and see the wild turkeys strutting through the fields.

Used to be pheasants, he mused, but now turkeys were ascendant. They were more destructive to his crops than pheasants but they tasted better on a platter. And the deer were all over. As a boy, he seldom saw deer. Now they were a daily sight.

Collins' ranch, just east down the Platte River from Brady, Nebraska, looked like an old time plantation with workmen's houses, foremen's houses, and the big house where the Collins family had lived for over 100 years. Even though they had had water rights since the late 1800s, getting flood irrigation and sprinklers to the crops waited until after WWII when fuel driven equipment could manage it. Now he sucked out 500 acre feet of Platte River water to flow across his fields. What didn't sink into the soil floated across the surface taking herbicides, pesticides, fertilizer, and fungicides with it as it followed the labyrinth of ditches through the fields and back into the Platte two and a half miles from where it came in.

Cort had asked him to irrigate early. A little earlier by a few days, but not a big deal. Benjamin would always do what he could to accommodate a friend and that was the context Cort put it in. Could have been Cort had a bet with somebody and the stakes were high enough to ask. Besides, Cort was Klete Dixon's right hand man and that could be good or bad for a rancher, depending on the situation. No—it didn't hurt to start irrigation today and look at what a wonderful day it was. Cort and Benjamin had partied together for twenty years, knew secrets about each other that would never be spoken and barely remembered. No—he was better off not knowing why the request was made.

The gate, as always, opened like a garage door, letting the cloudy water spill onto his field. He liked to follow the head of the splurge as it led the charge into the dry soil, rolling and pushing its own flotsam and jetsam like a miniature waterspout.

Pinsky tries again

SHERIFF BUD PINSKY, HIS face cracked, lined, and with a day's growth of beard puncturing through the tanned skin, almost shouted into the phone. "What do you mean, you can't find them? Hell— they're probably the only ones on the river." He stood up and walked toward the window. "They've got to be trespassing."

"Hold up, Bud," the sheriff of Buffalo County said. "What we've found is some signs of them stopping on public lands. No crime in that."

"Well, hold them anyway. I only need a day or two," Pinsky ranted.

It was quiet for a moment before a calm voice answered. "I'll see what I can do. But remember this. The election is only five months away and I don't need a false imprisonment suit filed against me."

"I understand. Don't arrest them then, just bring them in and question them, find out about them, hell—buy them lunch and turn 'em loose with a handshake, I don't care. I really need this, Warren—dammit, it means a lot to me."

"I'll see what I can do."

Pinsky let go of his breath. He didn't realize he had been holding it. "Thanks, Warren. I owe you one."

He hung up the phone. "Son-of-a-bitch," he yelled. "They've got to be trespassing somewhere." He stood at the window, hands on his hips, looking out at citizens going about their daily business.

If they only knew what I know.

Pinsky punched in another number, listened to it ring while he bit off the end of a plug of tobacco. He started chewing tobacco when he was fifteen and shocking wheat during a Nebraska summer that touched 105 degrees. It often made him dizzy.

Merrick County Sheriff Dan Wolfe answered the phone. "Sheriff Wolfe."

"Hi, Dan," Pinsky said. "How you makin' out today?"

"Good, Bud. How's yourself?"

"Hey—we're doin' okay here. Wanted you to be on the lookout for those same guys you nailed a month ago. They're coming down river in a canoe. They've been trespassing everywhere they go and my ranchers are fed up with it. Want 'em stopped and made an example of to keep the airboats and hunters from thinkin' they've got the right as well."

"We've got some events going on here, Bud. Don't know that I can spare someone to go looking for trespassers. What are they doing this time?"

"Camping. Building fires and makin' a mess of riverfront. They have little regard for other people's property. Think they own the place."

"I'll put a guy on it if I can spare him. When do you expect them through here?"

Bud looked at the calendar on the wall. "I'd say tomorrow. They left Kearney this morning before daylight or we'd of had them there. They're sneaky sons-a-bitches."

"They might get a little suspicious me hauling them in twice."

Bud could hear reluctance rising in Wolfe's tone of voice.

A sheriff had to be in control, run things his way, none of this questioning stuff. Better to protect your citizens too much than not enough.

"Dan," Pinsky started. "There isn't a court in the state that would doubt the legitimacy of your actions."

"I'll keep that in mind. I'll see what I can do."

"I'm beholden to you," Pinsky said. "Talk to you later."

Was the report ordered?

CRAIG JAMISON SLIPPED OUT the back door, across the street into the Chrysler dealer back lot and slid into the seat of his PT Cruiser. It took him 23 minutes at moderate speed before he drove up the long driveway to the Dixon Ranch main house. On his mind was the report he had supposedly hired a private investigator to produce. As soon as he closed the car door he saw Klete Dixon motion him to his office door instead of through the main entrance.

"Morning, Klete," Craig said and nodded.

"Hello, Craig. Coffee?"

"Yes—thanks."

"You know," Craig said while he blew on the surface of his coffee. "I never got around to ordering that investigation the Barretts wanted."

"And it's a damn good thing you didn't."

Craig pulled a rumpled paper out of his coat pocket and set it on the desk.

"What's this?" Klete said.

"I wrote down a couple of points Thad Percy called about. There is a story planned for this week's paper." He set his cup down. "The editor didn't want to okay it until I verified it."

Dixon stood spread-legged behind the desk, fists cocked on his hips, looking out the picture window across the greening fields of soybeans and corn. "Has anyone else seen this?"

Jamison shook his head and nodded toward Klete. "Just you and me."

"How long have you got?"

"Until the Barretts ask for their report, which could be today, tomorrow, or a week from now. They paid for it, so I've got to find one for them sooner or later."

Dixon nodded, his head bobbing for what seemed like minutes. "Or just tell them you forgot to order it." He took a deep breath. "When are they due back?"

"Sunday."

"Can they make it?"

"Probably not. Pinsky's got them tied up for trespassing and Cort is drying up the river as we speak. They should miss it a day or two at the minimum, maybe as much as a week."

"If they miss it that far they'll just scoot in and go to court and argue about it, won't they?"

Craig nodded. "I suppose."

"Let's hope you're right on the timing. Now be gone—I've got work to do."

The story starts

THAD PERCY SET THE 16-ounce container of Mocha on a paper napkin to the left side of his desk, turned on the computer and adjusted the chair. He sat looking out through the narrow window at Main Street traffic. He smiled and let the flush of the hug Serena had delivered to him roll over him for the tenth time since he plucked her from Highway 75, frightened and coffee soaked. He chuckled. Richard had felt secure enough in his relationship to ask him to help her. Why not? He had it all. And what did he have to put up against it? A low paying journalist's job, a fifteen-year-old car, a rental house, and one failed marriage. Hell of a deal.

He punched the first keys for the lead to his story.

Cass County citizens are not used to conspiracies. Hardworking, loyal, friendly people look on the positive side of events and seldom are required to delve into the undercurrent of happenings in Plattsmouth and its surrounds. But there comes a time when actions by elected officials and prominent citizens in concert toward a united illegal goal must be exposed and must be prosecuted.

He read it over. Then read it again and smiled. He liked it. Now to the facts of the story: *The Journal has learned…*

Repose

GINNY SHOOK HER HEAD. "Just climb out of those clothes, Serena, and throw them in the wash. I'll fix you a snack and you'll be back on top of this day in a heartbeat."

Ginny pushed the toast down, got out the cinnamon, butter, sugar, and tea bags.

"This has been a bummer of a day for you."

Serena answered from the hallway. "You can say that again." She came into the kitchen in a sweat suit, looking fixed for a run.

"Did you find out what they wanted you to come to Omaha for, anyway?" Ginny said.

Serena shook her head. "Not yet."

"Well, I hope it isn't important." She set the boiling water on a cruet. "But I guess it has to be important for them to just call you up and ask you to be there."

"I suppose. I'll call them when I settle down."

"Cinnamon toast and tea always works for me. That's what we had after we found the murdered heifer and it calmed us all down."

Serena looked out of the tops of her eyes at Ginny.

"Oops. Sorry. Didn't mean to add to it." She poured herself a cup. "How did Thad find out about it so fast?"

"Richard called him and asked him to fetch me, like I was sitting in a tree somewhere needing to be plucked off."

"Close enough description," Ginny said. "Better than sending Bud Pinsky."

"I don't know what I would have done if it had been him."

"Thad went to the office to write the story he has been gathering. I sure hope he knows what he's doing."

Ginny's face twisted into a grimace, lips tight, eyes partially shut with a slight cant to her head. "We'll soon know."

Serena nodded. "This is good stuff. It does relax one, doesn't it?"

"Do you want to call Omaha now?"

"Just as well."

Serena went into the office and called. In fifteen minutes she was back and sat down holding her head in her hands. "Budget crisis," she said.

Ginny straightened up. "What's that mean?"

"The school district has had a reduction in monies to be received from the state this coming year and all newly hired teachers are sort of in abeyance. Hired but not hired until this is straightened out."

Ginny sat down beside her. "Well, what the hell else could go wrong?"

Chapter 20

CHARLIE WOZNIACK PICKED UP the day's flows and instructions for the Dam, which were clipped to a chart, hung on a hook near the entry door. At first Charlie didn't think anything about it. He saw it, he read it, and he dropped it in his mental box like he did every day at 3:00 pm when he came to work at the Columbus Dam. Halfway to the generator floor overlooking the spillway, he did a 180 and walked back to the control room, picked up the chart and read it again. He frowned and dialed the phone number of the superintendent's office. On the third ring, David O'Brian picked up.

"David, this is Charlie. I'm reading the chart for release today signed by you. Is it legit?"

"What makes you think it isn't?"

"Too damn much."

"The Platte needs some help. We'll put some water in it from the lake."

"I can understand that but this release will have our lake fish gasping for water."

"It's just temporary. If you run into any problems with the turbines let me know, but they should take the constant flow easily."

"Not the turbines I'm worried about. It's the rest of the summer. We could run low on water."

"Don't worry your pretty head about it, Charlie. It's all been worked out."

Charlie fidgeted with the end of his belt, letting the silver enclosed tip slap over and over against the harness leather. "If I came over to your place right now, would you mind initialing this release sheet?"

Charlie heard the release of air from his Super's nose as he contemplated the why of this request. "Naw—I'm okay with it. Bring it over if you feel you have to. I'll be here for another thirty minutes."

Charlie sat down, got out paper and pencil and a calculator. The order asked for a constant flow. That meant opening all three gates and dropping 4,800 cubic feet of water a second, 115 feet down to the turbines. That would fill the tailrace, run over the top of the weir where the spillway entered the Platte, and raise the Platte River main channel a foot. And it would be rushing along at 2.05 miles per hour. Anything that couldn't run that fast or get out of the way was dead meat. He stood up and walked to the window. Hands on hips he stood looking at the water rushing into the spillway headed for the Platte River.

He pursed his lips. "Son-of-a-bitch," he said. He shook his head. "Son-of-a-bitch." He gave himself five minutes to think about it. Then he argued with himself some more. He figured it one more time on a clean sheet of paper, hung the clipboard back on the hook and crossed his arms over his chest. If the Super says it's ok, then I'm just following instructions.

At 3:15 pm Charlie dashed back into the control room to pick up the ringing phone. "Wozniack here."

"Charlie," Superintendent David O'Brian said. "We're cancelling the release this afternoon."

Charlie let out his breath. "That's good news."

"Yeah. Got a temporary restraining order from a lawyer in Plattsmouth that our legal eagles need to respond to so our release is on hold until that's handled. Stay with the normal release volume. If anything changes it will be on your clipboard tomorrow."

"Got it. I'm glad that's over. I wasn't sure how the spillway could stand that."

"Oh," O'Brian said. "I'm not worried about the spillway, I was a little concerned where it hits the Platte." He coughed. "But that's just water under the bridge."

Charlie snorted. The Super used that analogy every day and twice on Sundays.

The otter

NOW WASN'T THE TIME to criticize. Richard knew that, but he didn't always get it settled in his head before he let it go. And it was hot. What breeze there had been in the early morning had died along with the river. There were ATV tracks and even some Jeep tracks in and among the sandbars that Seth claimed to be the main channel. He wondered how many of them had been arrested or detained for trespassing.

If this is the main channel, I am a monkey's uncle.

They hadn't seen another living thing since Scott and Thad left. How nice it would be to fly the last 100 miles, shower, relax in his den, pour a Scotch and relive the trip looking out at the Platte.

"Can you not see the sandbars, Seth? If you are aware, they are a different color and are above water."

"Easy for you to say. Some are under water for your information." Seth dug his paddle hard and fast to shove the bow away.

"There isn't enough water here to float a cork," Richard shot back.

"Well—you skip lunch then and lighten this thing up."

Richard shook his head. When he took his eyes off the river, letting them cruise along the shoreline to relieve his nervousness about grounding every few seconds, he saw something move. He kept his eyes on it. When they got closer two black beads of eyes stared at him as the canoe slipped by.

"Seth—to your left—an otter."

Seth, used to large animals, turned too fast and the otter pulled back into the brush.

Seth snorted. "Otters have been outta here for a hundred years."

"By gawd, that was an otter."

"If you haven't seen an otter for a hundred years what makes you think you'd recognize one now?"

Richard nodded and rammed his paddle into the cut bank to keep the stern from pushing up against it. "Because I know an otter when I see one."

"If you start seein' mermaids let me know. I'd like that."

"It was an otter."

"Of course it was. Just cause no one's seen one in a hundred years doesn't mean that Richard Barrett didn't see one at 11:30 am on June 26th, 2014, while canoeing the Platte River with his beloved brother on an important errand."

Richard sat on the canoe seat trying to forget the otter. Trying to forget the otter and forget Filoh and the trip and Serena. Head down, hands clutching the paddle, he forgot until there was just the silence, the river, and him. On the river, waves of heated air fused with the smell of fresh vegetation skimmed across the surface bouncing against the canoe. He released one hand from the paddle and lowered it into the water, warm, wet, and like life blood itself.

In the next two hours the canoe ground to a halt on sandbars—some above water and some below. They seldom got more than three or four paddles in before a sudden stop jolted them. Each time, Richard formed some oath, bit his tongue and swallowed it. He had not canoed since Scout camp and that was on a lake. What did he know about a drying river? It just seemed to him like Seth should be able to make out the sandbars and end this dismal stop and go, stop and go that was wearing him down to a frazzle.

Seth thought he had it figured out. The bow made just enough wake, going faster than the current, to camouflage the sandbars. The sandbars did their best to construct ripples almost the same color as the water to fool the paddlers. The sandbars gained points by capturing the canoe—it was a game. Seth played it like he played poker. Bet high all the time and hope you either bluff your opponent or win more often than you lose. Today, Seth was losing.

Ever since leaving Silver Creek, it seemed the canoe was snagging on a sandbar more often.

"Does it seem to you," he said. "That the river is dryin' up?"

"Does it seem to you that we are not on a river?" Richard shot back.

"Well, hell—I'm doin' the best I can."

"I see ATV tracks all over. More like a highway. They would not be able to do that if the river was running anywhere near full."

"Well—it's not full, that's for sure. I've never seen it this low. At least running by the ranch."

Richard shook his head. "No." He thought a moment. "Something is going on. I am going to call Craig and see if the PI report is in yet. Might give us a clue."

"Good idea."

Seth let the canoe beach on a large sandbar in mid channel. It had an entombed cottonwood tree that provided good seats. The breeze that had come to them after the otter sighting had died along with the river flow. He picked through his pack and brought out the lunch makings and stood for a while, legs spread, looking back up river.

Richard had his phone out and was pacing across the end of the sandbar. "This is Richard Barrett, is Craig in?"

In a moment, Craig Jamison picked up. "Hello Richard. How is it on the river?"

"It is hot. It is tiresome. It is uncomfortable…"

"I suppose," Craig interrupted, "Your granddaddy wasn't used to a life of luxury so it went better for him."

"That and I hope he had more water than we have. Craig, the river is drying up and it does not make sense. We hardly have enough water to paddle in."

"It's the time of the year, Richard. Irrigation and power needs you know."

"Seth and I are thinking there is more to it. Have you received the investigator's report yet?"

Craig frowned. "Not sure. I'll check with my secretary."

"If not," Richard offered. "I'll call the investigator and see what is holding him up."

"Give me a minute." Craig pushed the hold button and stared at the top of his desk. After a minute he came back on the line. "Richard—it's here but I haven't read it yet. I'll read it and get back to you. Where do you think you'll be tonight?"

"We should be somewhere near Columbus."

"I'll call you as soon as I've read it."

Richard balked. "Could you just scan it now and see what it purports?"

"I'd like to do that, Richard, but I've got a client coming in and I need to get ready for him. I'll do it pronto and get back to you."

"Ok. I am counting on that. I am too sore and tired to put up with this nonsense."

"I understand. I'll call you soon."

After hanging up Craig checked that his secretary had gone to lunch and locked the front door. He closed his office door and dialed Klete Dixon.

"Dixon," a clear voice said.

"Klete—this is Craig. The boys are calling in wanting the PI report. I stalled them for now but they want it today. Are you sure everything is set and that it's going to work?"

"Well—you don't have a report."

"Richard will call them direct."

"He doesn't know who they are or what they wrote. Let him dink around with his cell phone from the river. He can't find out anything before the trip is over."

Craig shook his head and doodled on a legal pad. "I'm not so sure about that."

"I am," Klete said. "Tell them you lost it. Make up a good story. We only need three more days."

The doodle grew larger and ended up looking like a hangman's noose.

Klete sensed the indecision, the fear that was creeping up Craig Jamison's back and into his legal brain. It's too late for that.

"Craig—did you hear me!"

"Yes—yes I did."

"Does your secretary know anything about it?"

"No."

"Tell her you ordered it. Have her help you try and find it. You've got a thousand files in your shelves, it could have been mislaid in any of them."

Craig let out the breath he had been holding. "I've got $1,000 of their money."

"Give it back to them. Tell them you can't find the report. What the hell's the matter with you? You coming apart like Pinsky?"

"Klete...I"

"...Remember the payoff. A seat in the Senate, a lifetime pension, a good chunk of money after it settles down. You can live anywhere after you retire from the Senate. Three more days, Craig. We've made it this far and this is the payoff—the last ten yards. There is no report."

Craig nodded. "Ok."

"Good. Call me before you leave the office this afternoon."

"I'll do that." Craig put the phone in the cradle. He didn't know if he had planted the master seed or harvested a wasted carcass. In law school, everything was black and white. No shades of gray allowed. Now, here, and confronted with a loss of sponsorship for his life's dream, he could paint gray all over it.

The river environment being manipulated

ON THURSDAY, JUNE 29TH, the article written by Thad Percy would be published in the *Plattsmouth Journal* and by noon it would be in every newspaper stand in town and the surrounding area. Ginny's copy would be mailed to the ranch and arrive on Friday. Three lines down in Community Notes, would be a statement reporting Columbus Dam has cancelled its planned Constant Flow check for this week, which originally had been scheduled for June 26th. No reason is given.

Midway through lunch, Craig Jamison remembered the bill for the report he was supposed to order. He put down his fork and called Ginny Houston. When she answered he swallowed.

"Hello, Ginny. This is Craig." He coughed. "Can you get me a ranch check for three thousand dollars for the investigation report Richard ordered? I need to pay that."

"Hi, Craig. Sure I can do that. Do you want me to deliver it this afternoon? I could drop it off and pick up the report around 3:00."

"Ginny, I'm in a bad spot here. I have to be in court all afternoon and I promised Richard I would read the report and get back to him before I leave the office. The PI is asking for his money and it was due on delivery. I need to keep the report another day and talk with Richard late this afternoon. Is that okay with you? Can you deliver the check and we'll get the report to you tomorrow or the next day at the latest."

There was a slight hesitation. "Ok. I'll drop off a check at 3:00."

"Thank you, Ginny. Just give it to my secretary please."

Craig pulled the phone away from his ear and looked at the screen. There was an incoming call. He pushed the talk button.

"Where are you, Craig?" Bud Pinsky said.

"Mom's Café."

"Finish up and get over here. We need to settle something. I'll be in my office." The phone went dead. Craig raised his eyebrows, pulled the bacon out of the sandwich and took his first bite.

I'll get there when I get there. This iced tea is flat—they're not leaving the bag in long enough.

GINNY WROTE THE CHECK and sealed it in an envelope addressed to Craig Jamison and put it in her purse. She looked at Serena hunched over the computer. "Find anything yet?"

"No. Seems like most of the good jobs were locked up at end of the school year. Several say hiring is pending but not active until final budget figures are submitted at the July meetings. I think I'll move to Alaska. They need teachers there and the pay is really good."

"Oh, Serena," Ginny said, throwing her arm around her. "Don't even talk like that."

Serena got up, limped to the sink and poured a glass of water. "I'm so sore."

"You're gonna be sore until the bruises heal."

"Where you going?"

"Drop off a check at Craig's office, do a little shopping. I'll be back before supper." She picked up the keys and turned. "Need anything?"

Serena shook her head. "You have taken such good care of me."

"That's because we love you. See you soon."

THAD PERCY WAS SCANNING the galley prints for Thursday's paper checking every story for errors. Then he saw the Community Notes.

Why would the Columbus Dam suddenly decide to cancel their constant flow test?

He finished editing his article, picked up his note on the Columbus Dam and walked out the front door of the *Plattsmouth Journal* office. He dialed a number on his cell phone after making sure no one was in hearing distance.

"Loup Power District," a feminine voice answered.

"Is Charlie Wozniack there?"

"One moment please."

"Wozniack," the voice said.

"Charlie, this is Thad Percy. What's with the cancellation of the constant flow test?"

"Hi, Thad. How does a newspaper guy find out about that?"

"It's in our Community Notes where we report all the important stuff to our readers."

"Yeah—like what's for lunch at high school today, when the women's knitting club meets. That sort of important stuff."

"And when the river is gonna rise and fall."

"I don't know, Thad. I got a call from my Super saying to hold off. There was some sort of legal action filed that we had to respond to before we conducted it. That's all I know. When he says hold it—I hold it."

"Any idea who filed it?"

"None. You have bled me dry of any and all information I have retained this day."

"Poor guy. Hope you survive it."

"I will. Anything else? You're interrupting my important mission of watching water go through the units."

"No. Go back to sleep, Charlie. Sorry to have awakened you."

Thad shut his phone, holstered it, and turned toward the Court House. Even from a block away he could make out Craig Jamison striding into the 4th Street entrance. When Thad entered the building he took the stairs two at a time and walked into the district court a bit winded.

He approached the counter. "Molly—who would file a legal action to stop the Columbus Dam from doing a constant flow test?"

She shook her head. "Let's look." She thumbed through filings and pulled one out. "Appears Craig Jamison did so for a plaintiff named—Dixon Agribusiness."

"What's it ask for?"

"Hmm, let's see." She flipped the page, came back to the first page. "Claims potential damage to bank repairs in progress and requests delay until repairs completed." She held the paper out to Thad.

"Thank you, Molly."

HIS CAR WAS HOT INSIDE. He opened all the windows and turned on the air conditioning. He took Webster Boulevard out to Highway 75 and to the Platte River, maneuvered around to the old Beach Road and stopped on the bank. He got out leaving the car door open hoping the faint breeze might cool it off a little. The water was invisible until he got to the edge. He had seen it pretty dry before but not like this. From riverbank to riverbank there were sandbars. Little trickles of water, some looking greenish, traveled through the depressions between sandbars sometimes joining others to make a larger flow until that flow again divided on the slight prow of another sandbar. The bridge pilings, built to stand the flow of the river in flood stage looked like battleships beached on the sand.

Thad pulled out his phone and dialed Ginny Houston. Serena answered.

"This isn't Ginny. Is this Serena?"

"Hi, Thad. You two-timing me, calling Ginny?"

"Humph," Thad said. "This is official business. When I get ready to two-time you, you'll be the first to know it. And that will never happen."

"You're sweet, Thad. Ginny is in town."

"Say where she'd be?"

"Shopping is all. And to deliver a check to Craig Jamison's office." There was a pause. "Do you know where the guys are on the river?"

"They called yesterday near Columbus."

"That's what I needed to know. I'll call you back after I find Ginny—if I find her. If not, ask her to call me pronto…"

"Call her on her cell phone. You have that number?"

Thad checked. "Yes—I do."

SHERIFF PINSKY WAS PACING the floor when Craig Jamison walked in.

"Craig," Bud said, his face red and speaking louder than usual. "None of my people has seen the guys on the river. I need a plane to find them. They gotta be hiking the river, we've dried it up so much the carp are dying. Have you got funds to pay for a plane?"

"Let's not panic. I filed temporary restraining order against the release of water from the dam. They can't make it in time. Nobody can hike that 100 miles from Columbus to Plattsmouth on the river bottom dragging the canoe."

"What if they leave the canoe? They might make thirty miles a day. I've seen guys do it in the service."

"Those were twenty year olds. These guys are sixty."

"I don't give a damn. I want them nailed for trespassing if they're walking. I need a plane…"

"You said that; now hold it a minute… let me think." Craig walked over and looked out the window. "I'll ask Klete."

"Do it now, from here," Bud said and handed Craig the desk phone. "Please."

Craig took a deep breath; *that's a change for him.*

GINNY TOOK THAD'S PHONE call on aisle three at Thriftway.

"Ginny—can you get ahold of Richard and Seth?" Thad said.

"I think so. Why?"

"The whole story will come out in Thursday's paper but the short version is their environment is being manipulated to prevent them making it back in time."

Ginny thought a moment and grimaced. "They've got three days plus the rest of today. They should make that shouldn't they?"

"They could—if the river had any water in it."

"What?"

"Ginny, the river is being dried up. You couldn't float a copy of the *Journal* in the main channel today."

She lowered her head and thought a moment. "They can't make 100 miles walking, can they?"

Thad shook his head. "You have some sway with Loup Power don't you...the state wide dispatcher...what's his name? You dated him a few times in high school."

"Urzendowski. Vlad Urzendowski."

"You gotta call him and get him to release the water out of Lake Babcock. And I don't mean tomorrow—today."

"Ok. I'll do it right after I deliver a check to Jamison's office"

"Ginny—do it right now. Don't even check out first. Do it right now."

"All right. I'll call you when I'm done. Bye."

Thad dialed Charlie Wozniak's direct number. After five rings Charlie picked up.

"Wozniak."

"Charlie—Thad again."

"You don't have any other friends to call?"

"Look, I need some engineer information."

"Like what?"

"What is the maximum amount of water you can release?"

"If we're pushing all three turbines we can drop 4,800 cubic feet a second."

"What's that do for the river?"

"Well—given normal conditions it will raise the main channel of the Platte about a foot."

"How long does it take to get to the river once you release it?"

"About an hour."

"Now—after it hits the river how fast will it go and how long will it take the head to get to Plattsmouth?"

"It'll be running a little over three feet per second..."

"Damnit, Charlie. Give it to me in miles per hour."

Charlie smiled. "A little over two miles per hour."

"So how long for it to get to Plattsmouth?"

"Give or take about three days. It's 101 river miles."

"You know Vlad Urzendowski?"

"Of course."

"When he calls you, and if he calls you, will you implement an order from him pronto?"

Silence. "What are you getting me into here, Thad?"

"I'm asking you how long it would take you to implement his order?"

"I'm not comfortable answering that question for a newspaper-man, even if I've known you since your diaper days."

"Let me ask it in another way. You wouldn't question or delay such an order would you?"

Longer silence. "Why am I getting this itchy feeling in the back of my neck? This whole conversation is starting to turn my stomach. I'm gonna hang up now, Thad. Don't call back."

SHERIFF BUD PINSKY HAD to remove his gun belt to fit into the right seat of the Cessna 150. He rolled it up and put it behind the seat. Slung around his neck was a pair of Leica 10 power binoculars. He nodded to the pilot who pushed the throttle forward and the little plane jumped off the runway halfway down the strip.

"Head up the Platte toward Columbus," Pinsky said.

The pilot nodded, turned the yoke to the left and let the plane rise at 500 feet a minute.

Bud said: "Fly the south side." He lifted the binoculars and scanned the river. It was clear enough to see any human down there and where else could they be?

SETH STRETCHED LYING PARTWAY out of his sleeping bag. He was so sore he wasn't sure he could persuade his body to get out even though he was absolutely sure his bladder would explode if he delayed it another three minutes.

Richard woke up. "What time is it?"

"Time to get up. You damn farmers would sleep all day now that you got rid of your chickens."

"What does getting rid of chickens have to do with it?"

"Roosters. They're alarm clocks. Wake a man up before dawn."

"That is why we got rid of them. Farmer needs daylight to do work."

"That why all the equipment you buy comes with those big beautiful headlights and lights on the frame and back-up lights?"

"In case you are farming during daylight savings time."

"Shush," Seth let out through clenched teeth. He rolled over, got on his hands and knees and scooted to the door of the tent. He unzipped the mosquito netting, slipped his feet into his boots and walked like a scarecrow to the tree line where he disappeared behind a tree.

Richard could see Seth's shadow on the tent side as he did some loosening up stretches. "See any crops from over there?"

"Corn. You know, I'm thinking there's nothing but corn and soy beans from here to the Canadian border."

"Any animals?"

"Didn't see any."

Richard heard it first. There was a stretch in time when there was no noise but the sound of swallows and trickling water and then the first inclination of a motor noise. As it got louder he realized it was coming toward them.

The Cessna 150 banked to the left and dropped altitude, gliding down to a couple hundred feet off the ground as it slid by, Pinsky staring out the side window at the Barretts.

Pinsky turned toward the pilot. "Good enough for me. Let's get home."

The pilot nodded, pushed the throttle forward and like a departing goose its profile began to blend into the sky, the flight noise ebbed until Richard thought he still heard it but it was gone and only the residue of its passing reverberated.

Seth had stopped his calisthenics. "What the hell was that about?"

"I am not sure," Richard said. "But I think I recognized Bud Pinsky in that plane. Skip breakfast and get a move on."

In less than ten minutes their gear was stowed and they were moving the canoe across the sandbar to a likely looking patch of water.

"You know what day it is?" Seth said.

Richard nodded. "It is Tuesday." He could hear his brother's heavy breathing. They might have loaded the canoe somewhat heavier in the bow than the stern. Richard always hoped to settle the weight amidships, but it was not a scientific measurement. Like so much of this trip it was by guess and by gosh.

Seth dropped the bow into the water. "I think this will float us."

"Hop in." Richard shoved off and sat down for seven strokes before they hit the first sandbar of the day.

Seth stepped out and walked up the bank. He stood gazing down river. "I don't see any floating water nearby." He grabbed the gunwale, lifted the boat onto the sand, uncoiled the rope, slung it over his shoulder and leaned into it dragging the canoe across the drying sand. Richard could see small flecks of paint that the sand extracted from the boat for rights of passage.

The River

It was a river, not meant for travel by ATVs and four-wheel drive vehicles. It had tolerated airboats because they skimmed over the surface like water bugs and didn't leave tracks. Now they did. They left tracks where they nosed into a sandbar to have lunch, the guests talking loudly as they ate. It had never been almost dry until irrigation and power usage, combined with drought, soaked up all its flow. Some of its water was stored in stock ponds on ranches. More was in irrigation canals and lakes behind dams. It felt dismembered. It yearned to run full and collect its parts together, dreaming of the big rain that would make it a river again. The last one was talked about often. It had washed things clean—the bottom and the banks—and brought it all to the muddy Missouri there to donate it back to the sea from whence it came.

Can an old boyfriend help?

GINNY WAITED FOR THE dispatcher's office to answer the phone. On the sixth ring, a feminine voice said, "State Dispatcher's office."

"Hi," Ginny said. "This is Ginny Houston. Is Vlad available?"

"I'll see, Ms. Houston. May I tell him what this about?"

"I'd rather tell him myself, if you don't mind."

"Not at all Ms. Houston. Please hold." She punched the hold button, turned in her chair and looked through the open door. "Call on two, Chief. A Ginny Houston."

Vlad Urzendowski pushed his lower lip up over his upper, feeling the struggling sprouts of hair in his mustache. "I don't know a Ginny Houston."

"She was a Barrett before she married Donavon Houston."

"Ginny Barrett?" He smiled. "That's good news." He picked up the phone. "Ginny—by gawd it's been a long time."

"You remember me?"

"Remember you? Oh yes. You sound as sweet as ever. Are you as old as I am now?"

"Of course, silly. We age together."

"I always picture you in your high school cheerleader's outfit—un-aged like the rest of us."

"That's because you haven't seen me for twenty years."

"So why are you calling today?"

"Vlad—I need a favor as big as all outdoors. I gotta ask you to dump all the water from Lake Babcock you can into the Platte as soon as you can."

"Holy cow, Ginny. What for?"

"My brothers are on the Platte and they have to be in Plattsmouth by Friday. They're trying to canoe it but the river has dried up on them. If you could release the water they could ride it home. Could you do that?"

Vlad thought a moment. "Ginny—I can do it but I need more information than that."

"Here," she said. "Talk with Thad Percy. He's with the *Plattsmouth Journal*. He's written an article that will be in Thursday's paper." She handed her phone to Thad.

"Vlad—this is Thad."

"Sounds like a vaudeville show doesn't it—Vlad and Thad?"

"Yeah. Only this is serious business. Big time fraud, abuse of power, unlawful detainment, hindrance of free passage, and collusion between law enforcement, lawyers, and wealthy citizens for direct profit."

"Tell me how dumping water from Babcock will solve this entertaining problem?"

The turbines turn

AT 1:52 AM, WEDNESDAY MORNING, Charlie Wozniak got a written order to release water from Lake Babcock requiring the Columbus Dam to produce a constant flow. He recognized the signature on the order. He hadn't seen a written order from Vlad Urzendowski for two and a half years. The last direct written order for a constant flow had been to reduce the level of water in the lake so as to accommodate the huge amount of water coming in from the Loup River.

Well, Charlie reasoned, something is going on that I don't know about. Thad calls twice and Wally tells me to hold the test and now this. Go for the highest order I say. He pressed the buttons that opened the gates and little by little the noise level rose until the full 4,800 cubic feet of water per second cascaded down the penstock to the turbines, starting to reduce the 5,000 acre feet of water stored behind the dam.

The clock on the wall, which was synchronized with the atomic clock in Boulder, Colorado, read 1:55 am. Charlie entered the time, added his initials, put the order on the clipboard and sat back in the operator's chair.

Now—what the hell is this all about?

The flow reaches camp

SETH COULD TELL FROM Richard's breathing that he was not asleep as much as he tried to pretend he was. "You hurtin?"

"Yes." It was silent for a moment. "Everything hurts—even my eyes."

"Do you think we camouflaged our camp well enough?"

"We either did or we did not."

"Yeah, but I don't want those sons-a-bitches rooting us out in the middle of the night."

"Quit talking then."

A moment of silence. "Yeah—you're right."

Richard turned on his side. "I keep thinking I'll get a good night's sleep and feel better in the morning. But each day I wear out sooner."

Seth held his right hand above his head and massaged it with the other. "I hurt in places I've never hurt before."

"I have been thinking," Richard said. "We are not going to make it home in time."

Seth raised his head and looked at his brother. "We've got to."

"Got to and can do are two different things." Richard clasped his hands and stretched his arms to the top of the tent. This is Wednesday. We need to be home by sunset Friday. The way I feel there are no thirty mile days left in me."

"Let's dump the canoe and hike for it," Seth said.

"When is the last time you made thirty miles a day?"

"Never. But Richard, I don't have anything else but the ranch. If I don't get to stay there I'm busted. I've got no life left."

"You will have some cash from the distribution."

"Yeah—and after taxes how much? That's all I've known besides bumming around."

"Listen," Richard said. He rose up on one elbow. "Hear that?"

"Hear what?"

"That hissing sound. It is getting louder."

"Yeah—I kinda hear it."

"What time is it?"

Seth pushed the light button on his watch. "3:50."

"We need to get out of here." Richard groaned as he rolled over and slid from his ground pad.

They packed their gear in the canoe, each grabbed a rope from the bow and digging deep, they towed it farther up on the North bank, moving through the dark dodging trees and listening to the growl coming down the river.

"What the hell is it?" Seth said.

Richard shook his head. "Could be a flood from upriver. I do not want to be in it."

"Let's go higher." They lifted the canoe and walked through the stunted cedar trees across the dirt road.

"Is that a house over there?" Richard said.

"Appears to be a building of some sort. No lights."

"Stay clear of it."

They set the canoe down in a small cluster of trees, the noise from the river getting louder each moment.

Car lights shone on the dirt road fifty yards off to their side. They saw the lights go off, several car doors close, and hushed voices following a flashlight toward the river.

"Must be someone checking on the river," Seth said. "The Sheriff?"

Richard nodded. "Shhh." He motioned for Seth to move further in from the river after the lawmen had passed. They moved thirty yards to a cluster of three cedar trees in a shallow depression and laid down.

The flashlights were poking through the dark coming back toward the vehicles. Near the building they spread out. The nearest one came almost straight toward them.

"Found the canoe," he hollered.

"They there?"

The flashlight moved around the area. "Don't see 'em."

"They must be hiking it."

"Let's go down a couple more miles. We can get down to the river on Jensen's place."

The lights turned and met at the vehicle. Their voices carried in the cool morning air. "We gotta catch those sons-a-bitches."

Richard looked at Seth. He whispered, "That's Pinsky."

"I think so," Seth said.

"So that is why he flew over us. He is going to try his trespassing game again."

"We're trespassing now."

"I know that, Seth."

A vehicle started, turned around and left the way it came.

They went back to the canoe and walked to the riverbed. The noise got louder as they approached the bank.

"It could only be water," Richard said.

"From where?" Seth said.

"Who cares? Could be from a big rain in Wyoming or Colorado. See if we can get on it."

It was deafening. Sticks floated by in rafts and trees skidded along the bottom, tumbled and rolled peeling off limbs as they went by.

"We can't canoe in that," Seth said.

"We can in a few minutes as soon as the trash moves on."

Seth shook his head. "What'll happen to us if we turn over in that mess?"

"You will get a good scrubbing but you are not going to drown in a foot of water."

"Famous last words."

They watched the water clear up and fill the channel bank to bank, the noisy surge whizzing by looking dark and oily in the false light of pre-dawn. Richard studied the flow. It was steady now with some boiling up where sandbars were being ripped up and resettled.

He looked at Seth. "You ready?"

Seth took a deep breath and shook his head. "I'm as ready as I'll ever be."

They slid the canoe in bow first and Seth climbed in. Richard had but a moment to jump for the stern seat. He felt the torque as the water grabbed the bottom of the canoe and embraced it in its run for the sea.

"Move to the south shore—away from the Sheriff if he is there by now," Richard said. They paddled hard to cross the torrent of water. By maintaining a speed faster than the current, they steered the canoe where they wished and they bobbed along on clear water pushing a season of debris ahead of it.

"Whoopee," Seth hollered.

The first light broadened across the horizon turning the blue of night into a slight golden tinge across the flat land east of them. Just before the Platte took a hard right the current had hung roots and trees and sticks on each point of Jensen's land that stuck out into the river. The road on the north bank that Jensen had cut to get his equipment down to the river disappeared into the frothy water. Sitting on the bank was Sheriff Bud Pinsky, along with two deputies from the Platte County Sheriff's office.

Their paddling pushed the canoe faster than the water flow. Objects on the bank flashed by. In the growing light the river hazards became visible. For just a moment, the three brown clad officers sitting on the bank were visible. Richard blinked twice to see if his eyes were deceiving him before they whizzed by.

"That was him, wasn't it?" Seth said.

"I believe so."

"Stay to the left of this island coming up. Looks better there."

Richard steered to the left. "Think we can make it to Schuyler?"

Seth half turned in the seat and yelled above the roar of the water. "We'd better. That'll get us out of Platte County."

For more than a mile the two men dipped their paddles in unison, watching the water burbling on each side of the canoe as it plowed ahead leaving a wake in the fast running water. Small whirlpools opened on both sides and in front of them. In some, Seth could see the river bottom staring back. The blanket of water they traveled on was not thick but it stayed constant and the speed and turbulence began to feel like a carnival ride, like the horses on the merry-go-round at Popcorn Days. The canoe didn't touch the bottom. It skimmed over sandbars with a foot of water to spare and sped past floating trees caught in the water.

"How does one get out of this flood?" Richard said.

"We paddle out. You're wantin' food?"

"We haven't eaten yet today?"

"You're right." Seth looked on both sides of the river. "Stay on the right side of the river and we'll likely miss that Sheriff. There's an island coming up—you wanta go for it?"

"Yes."

The side of the canoe slid along the bank, the exposed roots bending and screeching against the fiberglass. Seth grabbed a root but before he could pull the canoe hard against the bank the current pushed the stern out and the canoe swapped ends, being forced by the rush of water.

Seth jumped out, bow rope in hand, and held the canoe tight against the bank while Richard plucked the food bag and stepped on shore.

"Ain't that by-gawd somethin'?" Seth said.

Richard shook his head. "I wonder who got that implemented?"

"Implemented? This is a friggin' miracle, that's what it is."

His brother easily attributed things to miracles and later forgot if they just happened in the natural course of events. He also thought some part of each miracle was implanted in individuals who believed in them. Personally, he would go with it either way.

What garbage reveals

"**WHAT IN THE LIVING** hell is wrong with those people?" Klete Dixon said. He circled the room, phone to his ear.

"Now, Klete. There was a mix-up between the dispatcher and our legal filing. He had not seen it and he authorized the release." Craig Jamison said.

"Can you stop it?"

"Not without a court order."

"Get one."

Craig shook his head. "It's not as easy as all that. There's the court calendar to consider…"

"…We had a legal filing. It should jump ahead of anything else."

"And it might, but I'm not guaranteeing it will…" Craig reached into his drawer and took out a mint. "…I'm an attorney, not a king. I can't make…"

"…Just get it done or you can kiss your senatorial quest goodbye. We'll be in court for a year if this gets out and it'll cost us a fortune."

Craig nodded his head.

We should have thought about that before we did it. But the dots would be hard to connect. Listen to Klete trying to come up with solutions to the current circumstances.

"…Call me when you get back from court." The phone line died with a clunk.

Craig stared out the window. It was earlier than he usually got to the office but Dixon's urgent call was not something he wanted to respond to at his house. He had built the office for confidentiality, covering the inside of the walls and door with cork and he could return Dixon's call before others in his office arrived. He brewed a cup of coffee in the break room and sat down to think.

There was a knock on his door. "Come in."

"Sorry, Mr. Jamison. Our regular janitor is sick so I came over to do the work before you open. I didn't realize you were here."

"That's ok."

The janitor emptied the wastebaskets, went into the break room and emptied the container into a plastic bag. Everything got dumped into the dumpster in the alley. The janitor closed the lid and hurried away to the next job.

Sitting in his car across the street, Thad Percy noticed two things. It was not the regular janitor and there was a light in Craig Jamison's office. *Too early for the office to be open.* He tried to recall if taking someone's garbage was illegal. A smile started on his face, he looked around and saw nobody, got out, locked his car, and walked across the street to the dumpster. He opened the lid and lifted the bag of trash out, letting the lid close with a whisper, and walked back to his car.

From his office window, Craig Jamison saw Thad Percy carrying a plastic bag to his car.

Must be his laundry.

Thad drove to his office, parked in the rear parking lot, locked the car doors and opened the bag. To his surprise he found that Craig was not a shredder. His trash, stored in a plastic bag, was a week's worth of everything he didn't want to save. Thad pulled out each paper, looked at it and started individual piles. He then picked up everything, put it back in the bag and locked it in the trunk of his car.

Chapter 21

GINNY HOUSTON AWOKE IN her own bed. She had almost forgotten what it was like to start a new day with her husband in her own house, where she had everything she needed to make the day work. She could hear Donavon talking to the kids and the scent of fresh coffee found its way down the hall. She smiled and got out of bed, put on a robe, brushed her hair and walked to the morning room.

Donavon looked up. "Thought we'd let you sleep in."

"That was kind of you." She poured a cup of coffee and smiled. "It's almost over, isn't it?"

"I hope so. I wasn't sure if you had filed for divorce or just liked living on the farm better."

"Oh, Donavon, you have just forgotten the demands of farm life." She sat, both elbows resting on the table. She set her cup down and counted off on her fingers. "Chickens fed, eggs collected, cow milked, cream separated, horses fed and turned out, stalls cleaned and dumped in manure spreader, hay spread for cows, animals checked for illness, hogs fed, fences fixed, irrigation gates opened and closed—it is an all day process, even with the new equipment which we had to learn to operate. The kids were a great help."

"When they due back?" Donavon said.

"Friday is the big day."

"Two more days. Anything I can do for you today?"

She shook her head. "I need to see if Serena found out anything about her job and how she made out at the ranch alone last night."

"Yeah—that was quite a blow."

"She'll make it. She's a bright lady and some school district will desperately need her."

"You don't think Richard is going to make an honest woman out of her before school starts?"

Ginny shook her head. "Who knows? That brother of mine drives me crazy sometimes. So methodical, so careful, so precise. Sometimes he lets life get ahead of him and then he's playing catch-up." She sipped the coffee. "It's hard to believe that he and Seth came from the same set of parents."

Donavon scratched his cheek. "I'm going to write an earnest money on the Jagger place this morning. I sure want that to go. It's a good deal for both parties and a good time for old man Jagger to let go. He's not up for the changes that are happening."

"Really?"

"He told me yesterday he'd like to convert to sustainable agriculture but he can't see his way through to it. The three or four years it would take would see him too old to be effective on the place. His kids have all moved to the cities, so this is a logical step."

"What's he going to do then?"

"He's got a reservation at Savannah Pines retirement home in Lincoln. He'll be close to his kids and the hospital."

"And plenty of old geezers to watch the football games with."

"Yeah—if he can still eat popcorn."

The phone rang and Donavon looked at the clock. "Who'd be calling this early?"

"Houston's," Ginny said. "Good morning, Thad. Are you going down to watch the water come through?"

She picked at her fingernail while she listened to him. "Are you sure?" A few more minutes of silence and then she said, "I'll be there in thirty minutes." She hung up the phone.

"Lordy, lordy, lordy. Thad has his hands on Jamison's trash."

"What's good about that?"

"Could be revealing."

Donavon's jaw dropped. "Good Lord, first we're combing solid waste containers and now office trash. What's to become of us?"

There is no report

IT TOOK GINNY THIRTY-FIVE minutes to arrive at the *Plattsmouth Journal* parking lot, lock her door and slide into the passenger seat of Thad's car. "Morning, Thad. What have you got?"

"The report Jamison was supposed to order for you that he thought he lost. It isn't in this weeks garbage," he held up the bag.

Ginny looked at the bag Thad held up. She shrugged her shoulders. "So—?"

"But here's the number for the PI in Omaha. Want to give them a call?"

She punched in their number and waited. A male voice answered.

"Good morning. This is Virginia Barrett Houston of the Barrett Ranch in Plattsmouth calling. Is Pat Dougherty there?"

"This is Pat Dougherty. How may I help you?"

"Mr. Dougherty, I am the sister of Richard and Seth Barrett and part owner of the Barrett ranch. Your company was hired by our attorney Craig Jamison to investigate the series of strange events that were happening to my brothers on their trip and the events here at the ranch. Have you finished that report yet?"

"Good morning Mrs. Houston. We were approached by Mr. Jamison to do a report but he didn't get back to us. We have not done a report."

Ginny frowned and clamped the phone between her shoulder and ear. "I delivered a check for $3,000 to Jamison's office for final payment of that report and expected to get a copy but he says he has lost it. I need a copy of that report. I'd be happy to pay for having it copied and delivered."

"Mrs. Houston—please understand. We did not get hired to do a report."

"There is no report?"

"Precisely."

She thought for a moment. "How long will you be there?"

"I'll be here all morning."

"Fine. I'll get back to you. Thank you." She closed the phone.

Thad looked at her. "I saw Jamison in his office not forty minutes ago."

"Let's go," she said.

Craig Jamison opened the door to Ginny's knock. "Well, good morning, Ginny, Thad," he nodded his head. "What brings you to town this early?"

"Good morning, Craig." She tilted her head. "We're here to see about the report that I paid for yesterday."

Craig shook his head. "I can't find it, Ginny. I think I mistakenly threw it out."

"I think we found it," she said. She turned to Thad who held up the plastic bag.

Craig's eyes went back and forth between them for a moment. "You stole my trash? That's a misdemeanor, taking unauthorized material." He lifted his head and stared down at them.

"It's trash, Jamison, and on public property—the alley."

Jamison held out his hand. "Please return that."

"I have no intention of doing so," Ginny said. "From what we have pieced together so far, there is no report. Pat Dougherty says you never contracted with him to do it."

Jamison sucked in his cheeks. His eye slits narrowed. "You better have some deep pockets, madam, if you think you can blackmail me."

"Oh—not blackmail. Something more serious than that. Mr. Jamison," Ginny said. "Let's call the investigator and order a copy of the report right now. They are waiting for our call." She punched in the numbers and held her phone out to him.

They could hear the phone ringing and a female voice answer but Craig did not put the phone to his ear.

"Hello? Hello?" After a moment the phone call disconnected.

"I'd like you both to leave my office. I'll deal with Richard and Seth when they return."

"It appears you are a part of the plan to see that they not return—on time."

"I have asked you to leave." He walked to the door and opened it. "This way."

Ginny looked at Thad, he nodded. "Thursday at noon, everyone in Plattsmouth will know about this, Craig."

Craig looked at the floor, one hand remaining on the doorknob of the open door.

Ginny followed Thad through the door, down the hall and out the front door.

"Now what?" she said.

Thad shrugged. "We wait."

"Oh, God. I hope the boys make it."

Ride the crest

CRAIG JAMISON CLOSED THE door to his law office and locked it. He thought for a minute, then called Sheriff Bud Pinsky's cell phone. Pinsky picked up right away.

"Sheriff Pinsky."

"Bud—this is Jamison. Any word on the operation."

"The sons-a-bitches just went by on the opposite side of the river. This river is moving right along."

Jamison sucked in his cheeks and lowered his head. "Damnit, Bud. You've got to make a trespass stop. This thing's getting out of hand."

"Yeah—well—I'm doin' my best."

"You don't understand…." Jamison looked at the phone for a moment then cradled it.

How could it come to this? You'd better sit down, Craig Jamison, and figure out the worst-case scenario. Then get busy.

RICHARD SHOUTED OVER THE howl of the water, "I need a break."

"We haven't got time for breaks," Seth said.

"Just fifteen minutes."

Seth nodded and pointed his paddle at a backwater where a creek emptied into the Platte. He switched sides with his paddle and drove for the low shore. They almost capsized when the bow struck the bank, then the current swamped the stern, swung it around and slammed it into the shore. They got out and tied the canoe to a log.

"This is something," Richard said eyeing the turbulent water.

Seth shook his head. "Reminds me of the flood of '49."

"It is staying within the banks."

"Kinda hard to do our farm and animal research whizzing past like this."

"We have learned enough."

Seth looked at him. "Think so? What sticks in your mind?"

"The first scene that plays is Filoh's hand at his throat and that snake hanging by the fangs. That is an ugly scene."

"Other than that. The animals and crops."

"There is a general concept in my mind but I am too tired, and hurt too much to delve into that right now. You ok with that?"

Seth nodded. "I'm with you." He bagged the jerky and raisins and stood up. "You ready to go surfing."

"Not only no, but hell no."

"Come on. Get up off your dead ass. We've gotta get past Fremont before sunset."

Richard looked up at Seth. "You really think we can make it?"

"I could do it on a horse. We can do it in this boat. Get up."

The rush of the water came back to him as soon as he stood up. Where had the noise been? Where had it gone while he sat?

The River

My life, as well as the life of other wild things, is not consistent. I some-times run full to the banks and over. That is when I clear out the debris that has accumulated within my boundaries. Many years ago, I filled the whole valley at times but I never dried up like I do now when the rains don't come for years. The farmers take me for irrigation and power companies put me in lakes for power, dropping me through turbines to create electricity. I am what I have become but I long for the old days when I ran free. Does not every wild thing? Today I am like an unbro-ken stallion on the Great Plains and the energy and drama are mine.

"Do we have any aspirin?" Richard said.

"Some in the kit bag. How many do'ya need?"

Richard downed the aspirin and stood with his head cocked. "Does it seem to you that the noise has diminished?"

"No," Seth said. He untied the knot and was rolling the bow rope up. "Seems the same to me." He got in the bow and picked up his paddle. "Let's go."

Every move tested Richard. He had forgotten how long it took for aspirin to work, but he was praying it was short. And Seth was acting like he was on some drug high, pushing everything faster and faster. His great grandfather had been young when he took on this task. It was probably just a usual type outing for him. His mother should have thought about that when she stuck it in the will. There were other ways he and Seth could have learned about the why and where of the homesteading.

"Come on, Richard. Paddle."

"I am."

"I mean hard. I aim to take a couple hours to see Martha when we get to Fremont."

So that was it. "You would jeopardize our timing just to see a girl?"

"Hey—she's not just a girl. She's my girl."

"That happened fast."

"A man's gotta move fast at my age. There aren't that many good ones."

"You are serious about this?"

"Serious as a heart attack."

Richard thought about it for a minute. "What if it is daylight when we get there?"

"Been timing it—it won't be." He dipped the paddle deep.

It seemed to Richard that Seth was getting stronger and more focused each mile they made. The river running seemed to push up and into him, like a trusted rival, one you could respect and still want to beat, one you shook hands with and looked in the eye and then tried every trick you knew to come out the winner.

"What are we going to do at North Bend?" Seth said.

"About what?" Richard yelled back.

"That damn sheriff."

"What about him?"

"We cross under a bridge there. He could have guys on both sides and if I remember right the channel splits and runs down both banks. The middle of the river is nothing but sandbars. He could nail us on either side."

"I WANT TWO MEN on each end of the Main Street Bridge," Sheriff Bud Pinsky said. "Now—I don't want any excuses. Wade in after them if you have to, but get 'em. I don't think there's enough water to let them float over that middle section, so it's a good chance they'll come down either side. Holler out if you see them so everyone's aware."

The deputies took up their stations. "Will we need the rifle?" one asked.

"No. These aren't desperados; they're farmers," the other answered.

"I sure don't enjoy the thought of wading in that tumultuous water."

The second deputy looked at him. "Where in the hell did you learn a big word like that?"

The first deputy shrugged. "School, I guess."

"Humph. "

"You think they'll be here before dark?"

"How the hell would I know? Shut-up now and keep your eyes peeled."

SETH PUT THE MAP back in his pack. "We'll wanta pull over to the right bank when we see the bridge."

"Aye, aye, Captain," Richard said.

Seth smiled. Just like his brother to want to know the chain of command on something like this. As if I know anything more about it than he does.

The bottom of the sun had flattened out on the horizon when the bridge came into sight. Both men paddled for the right shore.

"There's a lake about 1,000 feet from the bridge. If we portage over to that we can go around the bridge. Hand me the binoculars."

While Richard held the canoe tight to the shore, Seth scanned ahead. "They're there," he said. "Both ends."

Richard sat back and took a deep breath. "What now?"

"Plan B. Keep it quiet—we portage to the right. Little lake there." Seth stepped onto the bank. There was the noise of cloth against brush, the soft murmur of boot steps over the ground. The river noise drowned it out. They each slipped on their packs and lifted the canoe to their shoulders.

"They won't be looking for us on land," Seth said.

"I think that is what Paul Revere said, too," Richard threw in.

The dusk enveloped them, made them small and insignificant against the background of cottonwoods and only if someone was watching with expectations and intensity could they be seen. In 100 feet they crossed a road. Another 100 feet and they slipped the canoe into the small L-shaped lake and paddled both legs of it, reloaded their packs and canoe and hurried across highway 79 to the gravel pit, unoccupied this time of day.

Richard asked for a breather.

"Can't do it, Rich," Seth said shaking his head. He lowered the bow into the water of the sand pit. "Another short portage and we're around them. Come on. Suck it up."

Seth was supplying the energy, the electricity for the two of them, as if he was drawing energy from the situation and re-charging Richard's battery. Richard had stopped thinking now. Focusing his eyes in the twilight got harder. He'd have to see the doctor about those cataracts when he got home—if he got home. He was beginning to wonder if he had enough gas left to make it. Now—paddling on this rampaging water into the night just to make Fremont scared him. Since the Vietnam War he had arranged his life to avoid being scared. That's why he farmed and rode tractors instead of horses. Horses could damage you—tractors not likely.

They lifted the canoe out of the water and once again settled it on their shoulders.

"Take the road straight ahead," Seth said. "About four hundred yards to the river."

There were buildings and in the distance a dog barked but the only near sounds were boots on the road. They came to a concrete barricade at the end of the road, turned left and walked to the river's edge. Packs off and in the canoe, Richard jammed his paddle into the bank and shoved, scooting them out in the river using every trick they knew to keep the paddling quiet as they wetted the skin of the canoe and merged with the river headed for Fremont, fifteen miles away.

Seth did the calculation. If they could double the speed of the river with their paddling efforts they could get to Fremont early enough that he might by chance see Martha. Plus, they seriously needed a break. He wasn't sure how much more he could put out and, behind him, Richard was lagging. On the other hand, this water was not friendly, and if they capsized on a sandbar, or struck a buried tree in the dark it would be a chilling experience.

The leading edge hits Fremont

"CLOSE IT UP WHEN you leave, Martha." Doc Phillip grunted. He picked up his bag and slapped his Tilbury hat on. "I'm going to check on Watson's cow on my way home. See you in the morning."

"I might be a little late. Paul is taking me to the Spencer concert and then we're going to go out and watch the flood hit the Platte."

"What flood is that?"

"They let water out of Babcock Lake and it is supposed to hit here tonight. A bunch of us are going to go out to Dove's Cove to see it. Something different."

Doc rolled his eyes. "You haven't seen a flood before?"

"Oh sure, but not on a dry river bed."

THE CONCERT WAS OVER at 10:00. Paul suggested some beer and pizza before the river viewing. They met half of their party at Gambino's Pizza, ordered beer, and were halfway through their first pizza when Paul looked at the time, "We better get out there if we want to see the front of this thing."

Six cars peeled out of the parking lot headed for Dove's Cove where they lined up like cows at a fence line. It was warm. They shut off their dome lights, opened the doors and sat enjoying the food and drink. Every so often someone would call for quiet, thought he heard the water coming. It would turn out to be a false alarm.

But this time it was not. Car lights came on and they yelped and hollered and ran down to the bank. The front-end of the pulse of water was a mass of sticks and limbs and rocks that rolled under as the water behind it built up and pushed to break free and run full. And then it did. The noise decreased, the water cleared up and sped by with the occasional lone tree bouncing up and down like a tennis ball in the current.

"Hey—look at that," one of the party yelled and pointed to an object nearly upon them.

"What the hell is that?"

"Looks like a boat."

"There's a couple of guys in it."

"What the hell...."

Richard spun the line over his head twice then threw it to the closest man. "Grab ahold and hang on."

Paul grabbed the line and wrapped it around his hips. "Help me here." Two other guys grabbed the tail end of it.

Seth bent forward and jammed his paddle into the bank slowing the canoe. Their speed dragged the rope holders down the bank a few yards but they held on, laughing and stumbling over roots.

"That's a hot one," someone said.

Martha looked up just as Richard tried to step out of the canoe. The boat tipped and turned on its side. Seth and Richard, in slow motion, fell into the river and sank from sight. For a moment there was screaming on the bank until arms and legs surfaced and they clawed to stand up.

Richard moaned. The water ran through the shirt and down his back empting into his boots. His legs weighed a ton. He could not move against the current but stood atop two legs like concrete pillars sinking into the sand. Someone threw him a rope. He wrapped it around his wrist and they pulled until he tripped over the bank with half of him in the water. It was like they were dealing with a dead man, Richard's being unable to assist them because of the huge weight of water in his waders. Someone asked him to roll over and he pulled his waders off, showering him with Lake Babcock water. He looked up. Seth was hugging someone. A girl.

Seth didn't say anything, just hugged her. She ran her hand through his wet hair and then they kissed while the crowd whistled and yelled.

Paul was rolling up the rope he had thrown to Richard. "Who the hell is that?"

Richard smiled. "My little brother, Seth. Looks like he found his girl."

Paul shook his head. "I'll be damned, damned, and double damned."

"Don't take it so hard. He's worked for this."

"That's easy for you to say."

IN NORTH BEND THE deputies had waited five hours past the front of the floodwaters and neither group had anything to report. "Can you see anything?" Sheriff Bud Pinsky spoke into his phone.

"Barely see my hand in front of my face."

There was a pause. "Well hell, then. Come on in."

He scowled at his phone and dialed Craig Jamison's number. "You better answer, you son-of-a-bitch."

"This is Craig."

"Craig—Pinsky here. We missed them. I don't know where they went or if they're still up river but we didn't see them come through North Bend."

Craig thought a minute. "If they haven't gotten through North Bend, there is no way they can make it to town in time. I think we've won this one. Do you want me to let Klete know or just wait until tomorrow."

"Well—don't wake him up, but let him know as soon as you can."

"You coming back tonight?"

"Yeah. I'd like to sleep in my own bed for a little while at least. This merry-go-round has been stressful."

Craig nodded to himself. "I'm sure it has. I'll call Klete in the morning. If we need to meet we can do that tomorrow."

"Right."

MARTHA REACHED OUT AND took Paul's hand. "I'm sorry, Paul. This guy means a lot to me."

"I can see that. Where's that leave me?"

She shook her head. "I don't know at this moment. Give me time to sort things out, ok?"

Paul shrugged. "I guess. You need a ride back?"

"We'll get a cab. Thanks for tonight. I enjoyed it."

"Yeah—so did I. If it doesn't work out, let me know."

THE HOLIDAY INN EXPRESS night clerk looked up with an expression of disdain. "I'm not used to checking in people soaking wet."

"Have you got a dryer we can throw these clothes in?" Seth said.

"Are you checking in?"

"If you're quick about it."

"What's quick have to do with it?"

"We're in a hell of a hurry."

"The police after you?"

"We don't know that but we have a schedule to meet. We'll be out of here before daylight. Now, have you got a room or not?"

"How many will there be?"

Seth looked at Martha. She shook her head. "There'll be two—in one room. Separate beds."

Richard signed the register. "I paid the cab to take you home, Martha. He's waiting outside."

Martha turned to Seth. "Will I see you in the morning?"

"Honey," Seth began. "We'll be gone as soon as our clothes are dry.

"This isn't much of a reunion. I thought…"

"...I'll be back. We've got to get home tomorrow." He shook his head. "I've been doin' some good thinkin' about us. But this isn't the time."

DODGE COUNTY SHERIFF ORVILLE Ludington opened one eye. The red light was flashing on his phone. He reached over and took it off the cradle and settled it against his ear.

"Hate to bother you this early, Orville," his deputy said. "But I found something I think you ought to know about."

"Won't wait 'till morning?"

"Could. But I wouldn't want you cussing me out for not notifying you till then."

"What is it?"

"A canoe sitting down by Dove's Cove. Could be those Barrett brothers—either their bodies are in the flood water or they're on shore walkin' and talkin'."

"Is it upright?"

"Yup."

"Look damaged?"

"Nope."

"Any paddles or paraphernalia with it?"

"Don't see any."

"Hang tight. I'll get back to you."

"Yes, sir."

Sheriff Ludington sat up, looked at the pad beside his phone and dialed the number for Sheriff Bud Pinsky.

"Pinsky here."

"Bud, this is Orville Ludington. One of my deputies found a canoe just might belong to the Barrett Brothers."

"Did he arrest them?"

"Nope. Nobody in sight and no damage to the canoe."

"Find 'em and arrest 'em," Bud said.

"For what?"

"Trespassing. They've been trespassing for two hundred miles."

"Not in my county."

"Damnit it, Orville. You gotta hold 'em for me. Trespassing—vagrancy—shop lifting, I don't give a damn—just hold 'em." It was quiet on both ends for a second. "Hell—strip them down and arrest them for nudity on a public beach. I gotta make this happen, Orville.

My future is beginning to depend on it. I'm asking you please hold them until I get there."

Ludington thought about it. He looked around at his house in the dark, his wife asleep, or pretending to be, next to him. Pinsky's request was putting a pinch on his way of doing police business. He was supposed to be of service to the citizens of his county, not hinder people when they had broken no laws within his boundaries.

"Tell ya what," Pinsky said. "Tell your deputy to empty his gun through the bottom of the canoe and just walk away from it. Don't have to hold 'em. That work for you? You can blame it on vandals. Hell—nobody's gonna fight over a $300 canoe."

Ludington took a deep breath and let it out. "Call me when you get here."

"Thanks, Orville. I'll be there under two hours."

Sheriff Orville Ludington pushed the off button on the phone and held it in both hands. "This is crazy," he muttered. "Plumb crazy." He cradled the phone and lay back down. "Shoot holes in a canoe? Crazy."

DODGE COUNTY DEPUTY SHERIFF Roger Reynolds sat beside the canoe for two hours. His watch said 4:00 am—his usual time to stop at the Coffee Pot for a break and since nary a soul had come by after he reported finding the canoe to Sheriff Ludington, he felt comfortable leaving for thirty minutes. The seat in the patrol car felt more comfortable than the log he had been sitting on. He turned on the radio and headed for downtown.

He smiled at the waitress. "Marcie, how are you tonight?"

"Hi, Roger. Usual?"

"Yup."

"What's goin' on tonight?"

"Riding herd on a canoe. Big doin's—secret stuff. Can't let word out."

"Oh for gawd's sake, Roger. What's so dangerous about a canoe?"

"Nothin'. Sheriff just wants me to guard it is all. It's awful lonely down there."

"Down where?"

"Dove's Cove. You ever been down there at 4:00 in the morning?"

"Hell no. I work from midnight to eight."

"Oh yeah. Well I gotta get back to watch this desperado canoe. Never can tell when it might up and smack a Dodge County citizen."

"Good luck, Roger. I'm so proud of you."

"Marcie—you're full of it."

Roger's phone rang as he got in his cruiser. "Deputy Sheriff Reynolds," he said.

"Roger, this is Orville. I want you to empty your service pistol through the bottom of that canoe."

"You mean shoot holes through it?"

"Exactly."

"What the hell for?"

"Just do it. Then, Roger—?"

"Yes sir."

"Drive back to town and finish your regular patrol. When you write your report in the morning say you found an undamaged abandoned canoe at Dove's Cove, nobody around and no equipment. You assumed it broke loose upstream due to the release of water from Lake Babcock and was beached there by high water."

"Yes sir."

The phone clicked off. Roger holstered his cell phone and set his coffee in the holder.

What a crazy night. Shoot a canoe. Isn't even good target practice.

It took ten minutes to drive to Dove's Cove, park and take a sip of his coffee. He took his flashlight and walked toward where the canoe was tethered to a bush. He unsnapped the holster retension strap and drew his service revolver. A smile settled on his face as he sneaked up behind the bush and jumped out at the canoe, bright light flashing from his left hand, gun in his right.

The canoe was gone.

Roger looked to both sides, then all around.

Maybe he had the wrong tree. He walked up and down the bank for twenty yards in either direction. *That had to be the tree. Had to be. Canoes can't walk.*

THE WATER HAD SETTLED down to a constant flow, the banks full, all the debris pushed ahead of them for miles.

The cab had picked them up at 4:00 a.m. Seth had gotten their clothes from the motel dryer, they plucked an apple, a banana and

two sweet rolls along with two coffees from the kitchen, and arrived at
Dove's Cove at 4:20. They packed and slid the canoe into the water
at 4:26. By the time Deputy Sheriff Roger Reynolds came to shoot
the canoe they could hear the first crop duster take off from nearby
Werner Airport.

They set into a pattern of paddling hard where they could really
make a difference and resting for a minute to catch their breath before
starting again. The full moon helped their visability but the noise of
the water and the instability of the canoe kept them on edge.

"Get down on your knees," Richard shouted.

"Scared to. Might trap my feet," Seth said.

"It will stabilize us."

Seth got one knee down on the bottom, scooting his foot under
the seat. "Hurts my knees."

"Put your life jacket under them."

Seth looked up, dodged a tree moving slower than they were, got
the life jacket under his left knee and then his right knee. "Better."

He had to admit it was exhilarating moving along this fast on the
river. By his calculations they were making about four miles an hour,
much slower than a good runner could do and way slower than a
biker. But if it held, they would arrive at Fourmile Creek before dark.

DODGE COUNTY DEPUTY SHERIFF Roger Reynolds waited until
daylight to call Sheriff Orville Ludington. He wanted to make a clean
sweep of the area in the daylight. He did not want to call the Sheriff
and have him come down there and find the canoe in the morning,
un-shot.

"What?" Sheriff Ludington said.

"Sheriff, the canoe is gone," Deputy Reynolds said.

"You mean you shot it and it's gone?"

"No, sir. It's just gone. I came down to shoot it and it's gone."

"You looked everywhere?"

"I did."

"Reynolds—if I come down there and find that canoe you are in
big trouble."

"Yes, sir. But it's not here. I promise you that."

Sheriff Ludington chuckled. "Well—I'll just tell Pinsky it showed
up, rested a minute, and then took off."

"Well, it's not here."

"Ok, Reynolds, I believe you. Write in your report that it disappeared. I'll be down about 9 o'clock."

"Ok, Sheriff. I'm sorry."

"No big deal.

LUDINGTON DIDN'T KNOW WHETHER to call Sheriff Pinsky who was on his way to Fremont at this very minute, or let him arrive and break the news to him here. He bounced that thought around in his head while he poured his first cup of coffee. Pinsky would get mad either way and, at least in Fremont, they were in Dodge County where he was sheriff. He sat in his office doing paper work until he heard the cruiser pull up. He stood up and opened his office door.

"Morning, Bud. Want coffee?"

"Where you got 'em Orville?"

Orville shook his head. "They're not here."

"Not here?" Bud tensed. "Where the hell are they?"

"We don't know. My deputy went to shoot the canoe, at your request, and it was gone. We haven't seen anybody or the canoe since 4:30."

Bud sat down. He exhaled a deep breath and his chest sank. His belly stuck out. He took on the look of an older man with wrinkles showing up like magic to make a map across his upper checks and forehead. "I'll take that coffee now, Orville, if you please."

"I'm sorry, Bud, real sorry." He shook his head. "That's just the way it works sometimes."

"Ain't that the truth." Bud removed his hat, set it on the desk. "It surely is."

Orville poured a cup of coffee and set it in front of him and sat down at his desk. The two lawmen lifted their cups, sipped their coffee as steam rose towards the ceiling.

Connection dropped

GINNY HOUSTON AWAKENED AT dawn on Friday, June 30th 2014. She sat up in bed and let a smile creep across her face. This could be her last day operating the Barrett Ranch if the brothers made it back. Her back was sore. She lifted her hands palms up and looked at the calluses.

Will I ever be accepted into decent society again with hands like these? I'll have to soak them in lard a month to smooth them out again. Those guys better make it back. She would miss the day-to-day contact with the animals—she had given names to several of them and they responded to her voice. It felt good—warm—friendly. God knows how she'd feel if she had to slaughter one of them.

She could hear Donavon in the kitchen. She looked out over the yard into the hills that sloped toward the river. This was a great time of day until you had to do it every day, every day, every day. Then it began its wasting power and you felt you were no longer in control of your life. Something else had ascendency.

There was a knock on the door.

"Come in," she said.

Donavon entered with a tray of coffee and toast. Cinnamon toast, no less. "Thought you might like a starter on your last day as ranch manager."

She shook her head, the smile broadening. "Donavon—you're a gem. Thank you."

He sat on the side of the bed looking out the window. "Do you think they'll make it?"

"I hope so. You'd think they would call. They don't even respond to my calls anymore."

Donavon shrugged. "Maybe their batteries are dead."

"Yeah—could be." She sipped her coffee. "I trust Richard to figure out what to do and I swear to God that if anyone can get it done, Seth can."

"Well—it won't kill us if they don't. The ranch is gone, we've got a little money, we live our lives and remember we once owned part of the famous Barrett Ranch."

"True," she said. "It's just not our dream is it?"

"Not all dreams come true."

"Spoken like a true real estate broker."

"I've had my share."

"Indeed you have. And we have survived them over and over again."

He smiled. "You have been an accommodating woman—and wife."

"Accommodating? Is that the best you can do? How about wonderful or delightful or magnanimous?"

"You can throw those in, too."

There was a yell from downstairs. "Mom? Mom? Phone call from Uncle Richard."

She jumped out of bed, threw on a robe and disappeared through the door. She picked up the hall extension phone. "Richard?"

"Hi, Ginny. We are really rolling. Seth is with the canoe. I am borrowing a fireman's phone because ours are dead..."

"I wondered why you hadn't called."

"We could make it. We will need some help at Fourmile Creek. Get some guys with long ropes down there. We might be there before dark if nothing else happens."

"You're all right?"

"As good as we can be considering. I need to go while I can still move. Get at least four guys and ropes at Fourmile."

"OK, Richard. Our love to you and Seth." She added, "Where are you?"

The line was dead.

She cradled the phone. "Well," she said, "At least they're alive."

Donavon had brought the weekly *Plattsmouth Journal* on the breakfast tray, the paper folded to feature Thad Percy's article, face up.

"Oh my gawd—there it is," Ginny said. "There it is." She took a deep breath. "Right out there for the preacher and everyone to read."

Donavon raised his eyebrows. "Could start a whole new battle, but it sure explains a lot if it's true."

"Thad wouldn't write anything that wasn't true...do you think?"

"No. But he could be wrong and not know it."

She shook her head. "The paper wouldn't print it."

He shrugged. "They don't know everything either."

Ginny read some more. "Oh my gawd—oh my gawd...."

Plattsmouth Journal exposes conspiracy

KLETE DIXON HAD THE newspaper in one hand, his cell phone in the other. "I don't want either of you coming out here. We talk on the cell phone only."

"Craig," Klete said. "What can you do for damage control?"

Craig Jamison cleared his throat. "I can file a defamation suit against the *Journal* and Thad Percy and put a *les pendens* on both of them."

"If they don't make it back today, when does the ranch get deeded to Boys Town?"

"Thirty days," Craig said.

Klete thought a moment, took his feet off the desk. "What the hell went wrong with stopping them at Fremont, Bud?"

"They just lost them. They came and went and the deputies missed them."

"What a bunch of nincompoops." It was silent for a moment. "Bud, when's the next chance of stopping them?"

"We'll put some guys on the Highway 50 Bridge. They'll be in Cass County then."

"Put up a helicopter and find out where the hell they are. We need to know that. I'm counting on you two. Craig, keep the *Journal* article from derailing us, and you, Bud, get a legal hold on them. Now! Damnit, do your jobs."

THAD PERCY WAS ON his second cup of coffee at Mom's Café when Serena came in, got a coffee and sat across from him.

"Good article," She said. Don't know if you'll live through it, but it sure has the town buzzing."

A half smile broke on his face. "Humph...I don't think it is an executional offense. "

"You might not but what about them?"

"Serena, there hasn't been a killing in Plattsmouth for twenty-five years and I doubt there will be one now. Money is more important to them than blood."

"It could ruin all three of them."

"I doubt it. The public has had so much of this stuff. It'll be big news for a week or two and then fade away. The Sheriff may lose the next election and Craig might be sanctioned by the Bar Association, but I don't see Dixon paying any personal penalty."

Serena twisted her coffee cup on the table. "Then why did you write it?"

Thad looked out the window. "When I was in college I worked for the forest service one summer on a fire crew. If we caught a fire early, we could put it out before it got up a head of steam and really got rolling." He nodded. "That's what I see this doing. Putting out the fire before it gets so big you can't control it."

"Hmmm. Well—I hope you're right."

"Let's change subjects," Thad said. "How's the school teaching business going?"

"Well—I get my car out of the shop tomorrow. My doctor says I'm good as new with the exceptions of a few bruises. My school contract has not been signed yet as they haven't finalized their budget. So—in all I am available and ready if that counts for anything."

Thad smiled. "It does with me."

Serena put her hand on his. "You're sweet, Thad. I hope you find a gal that thinks as much of you as I do."

"I thought I had."

"Almost."

Thad's smile broadened. "Well—back to the salt mine. Gotta keep the citizens of Cass County current on stuff. "

"I gotta go too. Got shopping to finish."

SCOTT DIGNEY, GREASY COVERALLS and all, stepped across the threshold of Swede's barbershop, stopped and in one graceful move spun his hat at the rack in the corner. It missed the pegs but hit the top of the rack and stuck there. "Free hair cut," he said.

Swede shook his head. "Doesn't count. Needs to hit a peg."

"You've got more rules than a country club," Scott said. He picked up the *Plattsmouth Journal* and sat in the barber chair. "Make me look good."

"You'll have to talk to someone higher up the pay scale for that," Swede said. "I only deal with hair. You've got a lot more problems than that. Did you crash your plane or why so many bruises?"

"I'm rebuilding a motor and every nut is frozen on the damn thing. I've got bruises I haven't even found yet." He opened the paper. "Judas Priest—have you read this?"

"No. My customers get to read it first and if there's anything left of it by quitting time I take it home and read it."

Scott read out loud. "Cass County citizens are not used to conspiracies. Hardworking, loyal, friendly people look on the positive side of events and seldom are required to delve into the undercurrent of happenings in Plattsmouth and its surrounds. But there comes a time when actions by elected officials and prominent citizens in concert toward a united illegal goal, must be exposed and must be prosecuted."

Swede quit cutting. "It says that?"

"I read what it says."

"Who's he talking about?"

"Let me see…appears to be Craig Jamison, Klete Dixon, and, oh my gawd, Bud Pinsky. Could that be?"

"Lord Almighty. That'd be a three-some to draw to wouldn't it?"

"Get cutting, Swede. I've got to get back to the airport."

There was a police cruiser parked up against the building when Scott got back from town. He opened his office door to see Sheriff Bud Pinsky sitting in his chair drinking a cup of coffee.

"Morning, Scott," Pinsky said. "Got a chopper available?"

"Hi, Bud. Make yourself at home."

"I did, thanks. I need a chopper for an hour or two."

"What for?"

"I need to go up river a piece—forty, fifty miles. You got one or not?"

Scott nodded to a helicopter sitting on the tarmac. "I've got one but I don't want to fly it right now. It's been heating up and I need to get it in and fix it."

"Can't it make a hundred mile trip?"

"It might. I've never bailed out of a helicopter—have you?"

"I'm not in that business. I just need to slip up the river and come back."

"Looking for Barretts?"

Bud slipped his tongue over his gums. "Maybe. They've been trespassing all down the river. I need to teach them a lesson about that law."

"I'm sure nobody else has been trespassing," Scott said.

Bud glanced out the window, then back. "You gonna fly that thing or not?"

Scott shook his head. "Not safe."

"How about the Super Cub?"

"It's rented. I'm grounded today, Bud. Maybe tomorrow."

Bud put his lower lip between his teeth. "Tomorrow isn't a good day." He got up, put the cup in the sink. "Thanks anyway."

"You could wash it out," Scott said.

Bud stopped, looked at him and walked out letting the door slam shut.

In his cruiser, Bud called his office. "I want four guys on the Highway 50 Bridge from noon to midnight. Two on each end—get tall guys. You got that? Let me know who's going to be there and have them check with me when they get there. I'll be there shortly."

Chapter 22

RICHARD SLOWED DOWN. HE no longer could keep up the pace Seth had set. He could see it—he just couldn't keep up with it.

"Need a break, Seth," he hollered above the river noise.

Like a faint echo he heard Seth's reply. "Not now."

"Got to do it."

Seth turned around in his seat. "Richard," his face as stern as his brother had ever seen it. "There will be no stopping until we hit Fourmile Creek."

Richard shook his head. "I will never make it."

"Yes, you will."

"I can't take this any longer."

Seth's eyes narrowed. "You can take it as long as it lasts." He turned back to paddling.

Richard set the paddle across the gunwale, lowered his head. There were a few seconds when he thought he would vomit, that maybe clearing his stomach would wipe away the rest of the miles. Would bring them home. He focused on walking barefoot across the carpet in the library, sitting in his chair, washed and clean, a Scotch in his hand and a fire throwing warmth throughout the room. He pictured the deed to the ranch sitting on the side table, his mother's signature clear in the light of the setting sun. He lifted his head, took a deep breath and flexed his shoulders. Life was not a sprint—it was a marathon. He tightened his fingers on the grip. Marathon runners traveled twenty-six miles in three hours. The two of them could do it as brothers.

Seth turned around when the surge of Richard's paddle pushed them faster. He grinned.

So the old farmer has something left in him after all.

In sync, they reached their paddles out in front of them pulling back against the running water, small whirlpools trailing their blades. The bow lifted with each stroke, the weight shifting as they settled at the end, Richard giving a slight "J" movement to keep the canoe straight.

Seth began counting without thinking about it. Sixty strokes a minute. They would catch the front of the water flow at this pace and that wouldn't do. He was sure he would be able to see it and hear it if they got close.

As they approached the Highway 80 Bridge, Seth took the binoculars out and scanned both shores. "Don't see anybody."

"Look for police cars too."

"Yeah, I did. Just traffic."

"The river is half a mile wide—they would have a hell of a time getting to us at this speed."

"What I'm really worried about," Seth said. "Is Highway 50. The river narrows there and that could be their plan."

"They will have to be in the water to catch us, I think." Richard said.

"And they might be. But we're clear here—hit it."

"I am hitting it as much as I can hit it."

"You wanta sing?"

"No."

"Just a couple of verses. See how it works." Seth started it.

"Row, row, row your boat gently down the stream…"

Richard chuckled. If Seth had enough wind left in his sails to sing he just might have some too. "Merrily, merrily, merrily, life is but a dream," he finished it.

"Your verse has another merrily in it. Try four of them," Seth said.

"Merrily, merrily, merrily, merrily, life is but a dream."

"Good. Here we go. "Row, row, row your boat, gently down the stream."

"Merrily, merrily, merrily, merrily, life is but a dream."

On shore a small whitetail buck raised his head and stopped chewing. Ears forward, his gaze followed the strange floating thing with the sounds coming from it until it passed from view. He returned to browsing and only the river sounds brushed his ears, the unusual floating thing no longer a possible threat.

Richard opened the food sack, stuck a piece of jerky in his mouth, and handed Seth one. They split the last apple. Seth paddled his usual tempo with the apple in his teeth. Every fourth paddle, he would take a bite, move the apple out between his lips and chew the bite. They drank water, ate apple, and chewed jerky by paddle strokes. The teamwork invigorated them. Where before they were two guys working their way down a river, now they were a practiced team, paddle strokes synchronized at a steady sixty beats per minute. Every muscle had tuned in to paddle, lift, paddle; tighten, relax, tighten like a string on a bow; tighten to fling the arrow, relax as another arrow is notched.

Richard's mind wandered and he compared their paddling to his bailer that was a constant repeated motion: picking up the hay, compressing it, wrapping it, and spitting it out in the field; repeat. His head began to nod to the beat and river miles became nothing as the backache receded, the burn of blisters on his hands disappeared and his mind settled to a persistent level of pain that he could handle. *It won't hurt forever.*

In the bow of the canoe, Seth moved his legs in the cramped space. His butt was numb, taking the pain away from his hips. Used to sitting a horse, legs down, this stoking them out in front of him for hour after hour caused unusual pains to go up and down his body. The legs hurt and now his back muscles were tightening, just short of a spasm. The singing had helped take his mind off of it for a while, but they both got tired of the same ditty over and over and neither had the patience to teach the other some song he knew.

He recalled camp canoeing songs, stupid now fifty years later. But he remembered racing across Johnson Lake singing about their red canoe that went faster than the green ones. He had been in the bow seat in that canoe too. Always the bow, always out front, seeing things first. He flexed for one beat. It helped. He took a deep breath, held it, and tightened every muscle in his body. It gave him new life. He took a drink of water, swished it around his mouth, and swallowed. Another drink. He was ready for the final stretch. If they could get by Highway 50 Bridge, they could make it home.

Can you lasso a canoe?

SHERIFF BUD PINSKY HUNG a lasso from his shoulder. "I want two of you on the other side, one on each side of the bridge." He pointed with his long arm encased in a starched and straight-seamed shirt-sleeve. "One of you upstream about twenty yards and the other one downstream. Be ready with your ropes and be damn ready to wade out in that water. If you have any problems about that let me know right now." He stared at them. It was silent. "Ok, you know what to do. And leave your guns in the cruiser, we're not going to shoot these guys."

The group dispersed with a cruiser at each end of the Bridge. They put their gun belts in the trunk, locked it and found a good setting spot.

The radio crackled. "Pearson," Sheriff Pinsky said. "Turn off your damn rotating lights. You're advertising our presence."

"Oh—right," Pearson said. It seemed to quiet the scene and he adjusted his attitude about this stakeout. He was getting paid to sit beside the river for the afternoon. If he'd only brought his fishing pole. He opened the lasso, fixed a loop, spun it over his head three times and threw it at a washed up tree root. He missed. It had been a while since he was the steer-roping champion from Ord High School. He opened the loop and threw again. The rope settled over it dead center. He smiled. "That's more like it." For thirty minutes he cast at the root, changing his position every three throws. He'd have no problem laying a loop over one of those guys or over the bow of the canoe. He coiled his lasso, laid it beside the log and sat down.

"I THINK WE'RE SHAFTED," Seth said.

Richard drew up short. "Why?"

"If I'm remembering the river at the bridge correctly, the current swings close on the south end and turns to go right on the north end. That gives them two good shots at us."

"Maybe this flood will change that."

"Could. Gotta think on it."

Richard took a drink of water, drew in a deep breath and got in sync with Seth's paddle stroke again. In a way he liked riding the high water, it sure beat getting out and hauling the canoe across sandbar after sandbar. But lordy, lordy, was it getting painful.

"There's Louisville. I can see the recreation center," Seth said.

A tingle ran up Richard's scalp. "See any cops?"

"Yeah—on the north side. Pull over, I've got an idea."

Sheriff Bud Pinsky lowered the binoculars. "Here they come. They just stopped about a half-mile up river.

"Shall we get in?" one of the deputies asked.

"No—let 'em get a little closer. I'll tell you when."

Each deputy uncoiled his rope.

Pinsky raised the binoculars. "Here they come." He moved to the edge of the water and looked into it for the first time.

Damn—it's moving fast. Looks a couple feet deep right here. Must be the narrowing of the channel that's let it pile up.

When he looked up the canoe was 100 yards away.

"She's moving fast boys, let's get in there." Pinsky stuck his left foot in the water and was immediately knocked over. A deputy on each side lost his footing and fell. Two deputies were still standing. They moved toward the center of the channel as the canoe zipped toward them. Deputy Sheriff Pearson opened his loop, the rope humming over his head.

"Now," Seth yelled.

Richard and Seth stowed their paddles under the thwarts, grabbed the gunwales with both hands and tipped over to the right. The canoe capsized, its wet slippery bottom turned up.

It careened by Deputy Sheriff Pearson looking like a huge turtle, with only the bottom of the canoe visible. There was nothing to catch his rope. Sheriff Pinsky regained his feet, his dripping lasso hanging from one hand. "Throw it—throw it."

"There's nothing to catch," Pearson said.

"Throw it, Damnit..."

Pearson threw the rope. It slammed across the keel and slid off into the water as the canoe whizzed by.

Richard and Seth, their feet pointed downstream and their heads in the air pocket of the upturned canoe bounced off the bottom. They heard the rope hit. Inside it sounded like a whiplash. They were in a grinder, the water forging a new channel. Water ran out of their ears. Richard was surprised at the air trapped inside. He had agreed to wait for Seth's signal to right the canoe, but each bump of his legs on the river bottom drove a wedge of fear into his brain. The amplified noise inside terrified him. This was doing stuff, not thinking stuff.

"Up we go," Seth said. "Shove it up hard but hang on."

They pushed the right side up, breaking the suction the water had on the canoe. It settled half full beside them in the swirling water. They clung to the gunwales. Richard's paddle floated beside him. With one hand he grabbed it. They rounded the corner and rammed against a sandbar in the middle of the river.

Seth stood up. "Come on, come on," He pleaded.

Richard found his footing and jammed the paddle into the sandbar. Together they rolled the canoe over and drained it. They peeled off their waders and poured out the water.

"Feels good to stand up," Richard said.

Seth was looking at the scrambling deputies back up river. "Let's move. There they come."

Richard shook his head. "What's the score?"

"Barrett's two; Sheriff zero. Another ten, twelve miles and we win."

"You feel comfortable lightening our load?"

Seth smacked his forehead. "Hell yes—why didn't I think about that."

"There always has to be one thinker in the group."

"Yeah—well who thought about the canoe turnover?"

"That you did."

They untied the packs from the canoe, kept their water bottles, the small sack of jerky and raisins and threw everything else on the bank. Water dripping from their clothes, they launched off the sandbar, knelt on their life jackets and began pounding out sixty strokes a minute.

Steam rose from Seth's back. Richard smiled as he calculated the calorie burn they were getting. He had noticed his belt was at the last notch when he dropped his pants. It had been years since he had been at his college weight. Half the time he wondered if he could keep the weight off and the other half he thought about steak dinners with potatoes and gravy.

"WHO BROUGHT THE TOWELS?" Pinsky asked.

They all looked at each other.

"No towels?" Pinsky nodded then shook his head. "Go change clothes and get back to your regular duties. The parade is over for today."

Pinsky reached inside his cruiser and took his cell phone out of the glove compartment. He thought a minute before dialing. Would it be easier to tell this to Craig Jamison or Klete Dixon? He dialed the law offices of Craig Jamison. Hell—let him tell the mastermind.

"Hello, Craig. Pinsky here." He paused. "We missed them."

"What do you mean, you missed them?" Craig said.

"They got by us. Overturned their canoe and we had nothing to grab hold of."

"This isn't going to set well with Klete."

Pinsky looked down at the puddle he was making on the roadside. "I'm sure of that."

"You going to tell him?"

"I'd rather you did it. I'm in no shape to do it right now."

"If I were you I would stay out of sight for a few days. You know how he can be."

"Hell, Craig—it's only money here. We're not talking about drought or famine."

"That's what he lives for."

"Yeah—I know."

"Keep everything quiet and it'll go away in a week or two."

"I hope so."

"By the way, they've set the preliminary hearing for your sexual assault charge for next Wednesday. Stick around—we've got to spend some time guessing what the prosecution is going to ask."

Bud shook his head. "I hate the thought of that."

"You should have thought of that before you unzipped your pants."

"Don't go getting high and mighty on me, Craig. I've still got a few arrows in my quiver."

"Just a comment, Bud. I'll call you after I talk to Klete. I'm not looking forward to that call. Goodbye."

"THINK ABOUT IT," Seth said. "Do you think Filoh could have survived this part of the trip?"

"I don't know how he survived the riding part," Richard said.

"He'd have probably drowned when we turned the canoe over."

"He pulled me out of that flash flood pretty handily though."

"Different situation. He was standing up."

"How are you feeling?"

"I've got enough gas to get home. You?"

"Lead on, brother—lead on."

GINNY SET THE CREAM cheese kolackys on the granite to cool. "The boys love kolackys."

"Before or after Scotch?" Serena said.

"Both," she laughed.

"Do you really think they'll make it?" Serena said while she stuffed items in a picnic basket.

"Yup. Pack it for eight. It's gonna be a blast."

"We're having a party?"

"You bet. Right at the mouth of Fourmile Creek."

"What if it's dark?"

Ginny shook her head. "Won't make any difference. We'll stay there until midnight if that's what it takes."

"That's the deadline."

"Yes, Ma'am. Would you please hand me the powdered sugar?"

Dawson reached for a kolacky. Ginny caught his knuckles with a wooden spoon. "Ah ah."

"Come on, Mom. I'm starving."

"Eat something else. Grab an apple or a banana. These are for the party. You can stuff yourself tonight."

"Is it gonna be late?"

She shrugged. "Who knows, but I want to be down there by noon just in case."

Dawson screwed up his face. "What are we going to do down there for twelve hours?"

"You can do what we used to do when we went to Fourmile Creek. Play in the water, make sand castles, catch turtles, build a fire, and roast marshmallows."

"Aw, Mom, that's ok for Bucky and Valerie, but can't I stay here?"

"No, young man. You're coming with us. Get your gear."

"Can I bring my laptop?"

"If you keep track of it this time."

"Oh, Mom—I've only left it once. Is Dad going to be there?"

"Yes. He's on his way home now."

"Does he know he's going to miss the Newshour?"

"Of course, Dawson. Now quit being such a pain and get the stuff into the pickup. And don't forget the ropes to tie the canoe down."

"Do I get to open the gates?"

"You can switch off with Bucky for that chore."

"He's not strong enough to fasten the gate back up. He can't get the wire over the post."

"Well, he's getting close and one of these days he will. We need to let him grow up like you did. It took you a while if you remember back."

"I could do it when I was his age."

"Ok. Stop this nonsense and get the things loaded. Shoo—go."

CRAIG JAMISON LEFT HIS office through the back door, across the alley and over to the parking lot behind the Chrysler dealer. He unlocked the Cruiser, started it, and drove down the back road out Webster Boulevard to Klete Dixon's ranch.

He bit his lip as he idled along under the speed limit thinking of what to say and what Dixon's likely response would be to each statement he made. The end result, however, was simple. They, he and Sheriff Pinsky, had been unsuccessful in thwarting the Barrett's timetable enough to declare failure in meeting the dictates of Mae Barrett's will. Worst-case scenario? Dixon wouldn't get the ranch. Big deal. It wasn't a life or death issue. Maybe he couldn't bill Dixon for his time, but he'd survive. A small tingle went up the back of his neck when a picture of him in the $1,500 senator's chair in Lincoln passed through his thoughts. He'd have to wait this election out until the people forgot.

KLETE DIXON'S CHIN WAS almost to his chest. He sat in his office chair, turned to look out the French doors into the long green lawn that flowed to the pasture, his arms crossed over his chest. Yesterday's *Plattsmouth Journal* was on the desktop. Although it was just a little past noon, a glass of whisky sat untouched on a leather coaster next to the paper. Except for the slight rise and fall of his chest that gave evidence he was breathing, an onlooker would have thought he had stumbled in on a museum tableau. The ornate Regulator clock on the wall struck one o'clock. Dixon took a sip of whisky.

There was a way out of this. He had to figure out what it was, plan it, and execute it. Obviously, he could not count on Pinsky or Jamison. He would have to feed them to the wolves. Jamison would be the toughest. He could defend himself right up to the last minute and then change counsel and delay a lawsuit another six months. He could abandon Pinsky and let him sink with the sexual harassment suit—cut off his support Monday morning. Out of the corner of his eye he saw Jamison drive in and park his car.

He sighed and shook his head. Then a smile crept over his face. "So now it starts," he said. He stood up and unlocked the French doors as Jamison approached.

AT COLUMBUS DAM, DAVID O'Brian left a message for Charlie Wozniack to halt the constant flow at noon, Friday, June 30.

Wozniack smiled. The three turbines had functioned without a flaw and from reports clear down in North Bend, the rush of water had cleared the river of accumulated debris. He didn't like to think of the mush it would make when the Platte poured into the Missouri but that was the way with rivers. He looked at the clock and set about closing the steel gates that held back Lake Babcock waters. It was always a kick to see the spillway and the tailrace dry up. Like a race-horse at the end of the race, nervous, slowing down bit by bit, throw-ing its head into the air, dancing a little, until it slowed to a walk. Water was like that. It splashed and splattered, calmed down to a trickle until it was noiseless, having let its voice move ahead with the front of the tide.

He expected a call or two from the people who lived along the canal. Someone called every year to tell him something he already knew. He plucked the clipboard from the hook.

Constant flow ceased at 12:02 pm 30, June. He hung the clip-board up and walked over to look at the spillway.

THAD PERCY WALKED OUT of the offices of the Plattsmouth Journal, across the street and ordered his usual—a Monte Cristo sandwich and iced tea—at Mom's Café. He sat at the table he had shared with Serena weeks ago. An image of her sitting across from him came to mind and he let his daydream run unchecked. He had a small smile on his face when the waitress delivered his food.

Well—what the hell. There are other eligible females in town.

He took the first bite even though the fried Monte was hot.

THE LAST RAYS OF the sun glanced off Seth's back. "I see the bor-der of Dixon's ranch." He turned halfway around and smiled. "We're almost there."

Richard shook his head. "I think I can make it."

"You can. I know you can. Don't think about it. Just stay in sync with me."

Actually the pain had gone and with it his power. Power and strength were two different things. The power let him keep up the sixty strokes a minute and that was wasted. Gone. He had the strength to pull the paddle through the water but he was a fraction behind Seth on each paddle and soon he fell so far behind he needed to wait until the next paddle to synchronize again. The canoe was slowing down.

Richard waited a few minutes before he asked, "Can you see Fourmile?"

Seth shook his head, his paddling constant.

Richard imagined Seth's muscles contracting, relaxing, and could visualize the half on, half off intensity that allowed the French Voyageurs to paddle all day long with just brief stops. He didn't think his slowing down would hurt them. They were less than eight miles from home. What would it take? Another two hours? He could handle that. He could handle that with one arm tied behind his back. Energy surged through him. He dug into the slacking water.

The right shoulder is the one that hurt, a jolt lancing through the joint at every paddle, with every J stroke. He changed positions, tried to ease the pain. Finally he just settled on it, over-rode it, and pictured himself in the air-conditioned cabin of his tractor, turning the giant machine with one hand, the gift of power steering. Everything after this would be child's play. Maybe that was what their Mom had intended. She knew what it had been like for a hundred years. She wanted her boys to know the work and pain and sorrow that came with starting and building the estate they were to inherit. What better way than to have us follow Great Grandfather Melzer's path to ownership of the ranch; know the river intimately, choose the location with care, survive the trip. And Ginny. Let her know the day-to-day labor necessary to maintain the place; animals, crops, fences, contractors, irrigation—the whole enchilada.

"I'm gonna marry her," Seth said.

"What?"

"I'm gonna marry Martha."

"Does she know that?"

"She will soon."

"Let me know when so I can get showered and shaved."

Seth chuckled. "You'll get an invitation."

Richard closed his eyes. He could paddle without thinking about it now. It was ingrained in him. If he could manufacture something interesting enough to think about, he could over-ride the pain and keep up the count. Sometimes he didn't dip the paddle as deep as he should but then the river was falling now, the speed slowing. He looked at the sun hanging in the western sky. He judged it to be midafternoon and reached for the water bottle.

For the first time in two months Richard let himself actually dwell on an evening at home. Clean, fresh clothes, the warmth of the living room, and the oily, smoky, peaty fragrance of the Laphroaig Scotch rising from the glass in his hands. He always visualized himself with a smile on his face giving a slight nod to the urn on the mantle that held Mae Barrett's ashes. Now they were scattered on the river—possibly some under the canoe at this moment.

The River

I have lost track of the ashes. The earthly remains of Andrew Duncan Barrett, Rhonda Mae Barrett, and Filoh Smith were scattered on my banks. They and I have become one. And as I gave life to the Great Plains, so they derived life from me. The harness that scarred our backs, we share. And as they succeeded the Pawnee and Oto, so Richard and Seth and Virginia followed them, and Duncan and Bucky and Valerie will follow them. I am eternal. My blessings fall on generations throughout history.

IT WAS NEAR THE end of a day on the river and the pace increased. Seth had thought about it often. Was it the spurt end of their energy, draining the last they had, that pushed them faster, or the realization that the trip was almost over? Sometimes he thought the awareness that there was less than an hour to go before stopping led them to be more powerful, more persistent in their progress. It was cooler too. Sweat dried and irritated his armpits and the drying shirt scratched across his chest, stroke after stroke.

Duncan and Bucky, out on the mouth of Fourmile Creek, saw the canoe first. They shielded their eyes from the setting sun and could just make out the paddles moving stroke for stroke, the canoe moving toward the sandbar that Fourmile Creek had pushed and formed into the Platte.

"It's them," Bucky shouted. He jumped up and down on the wet sand. "It's them."

Seth turned toward Richard, a smile creasing his face. "Home."

Richard set the paddle across the gunwales. He straightened his back, let his eyes run along the bank of the Barrett Ranch, over to his family gathered on the delta of Fourmile Creek. His vision extended backward into time, and to the Old Testament phrase, *as all my fathers were.* And forward into time. He remembered for a moment ranchers past, and that he would grow too old for it in the end and that others would follow him, and that this piece of land would change hardly at all in a thousand years.

His chest filled, his eyes moistened. This was their land and Filoh was right—they could do better. They would do better.

They beached the canoe on the delta. It skidded to a stop in the mud and sand, for a moment, frozen in place, the water receding around it. Seth looked back at Richard, then stepped from the boat, stumbled, and hugged each family member as he wandered down the line.

Valerie smiled in her excitement. "Uncle Richard, we have kolackys…"

"…And whisky," Duncan said.

Richard smiled at the combination. Then he saw Serena and his smile broadened. He stood up, raised his head and walked to where she stood and stopped before her. "Miss Serena Baker?"

A smile visited her face and, in a coquettish tone she said, "Doctor Livingston, I presume?"

He pulled her to him in a hug that had the cousins giggling and pointing.

Richard shook his head. "I have missed you. A lot."

"Me too," she said.

He put a hand on each of her shoulders, held her arm's length, looked into her eyes and a serious mien furrowed his brow. He had not felt this sure of anything over the last twenty-five years. "Will you marry me?"

"When?"

"Today, tomorrow, Sunday?"

"Oh, Richard, Yes—I'll do that."

Seth shifted a kolacky to his left hand and patted his brother's shoulder. "Nothin' like a little river trip to get a man right with the world. Congratulations."

"A toast—a toast," Ginny shouted. "To the successful completion of the trip and welcoming my good friend, Serena, into the family.

Seth upended his Martinelli's Sparkling Cider. "Good to the last drop," he said.

Retribution

RICHARD CALLED THE OFFICES of Craig Jamison. He had read the *Journal* story, heard the family tales. It was a lot to digest. It was Saturday morning and he didn't expect Craig to be in, but he answered without the usual telephone business message.

"Craig Jamison."

"Craig—this is Richard Barrett."

"Welcome back, Richard. I heard you and Seth got in yesterday. Cut it pretty close didn't you?"

"We have some things to discuss with you. Would you be amenable to meet at 10:00 o'clock Monday at the law offices of John Sheldahl?"

"Now, Richard, there is no need for that. You can come to my office or I will come out to the ranch, whichever you prefer."

"The family has discussed it, Craig, and we prefer to have legal counsel when we talk with you next."

"You are stepping into a field of land mines, Richard. I would reconsider if I were you. Call me again Monday morning. Goodbye."

Richard set the phone down. "That was short and sweet."

Ginny and Seth sat waiting an explanation.

"He wants me to call him Monday morning. It looks like we are going to have a fight on our hands."

"So what," Seth said. "We've got the goods on all of them.

Richard stroked his chin. "Having the goods and proving them are two different things."

"Do we care?" Ginny said. She stood up, crossed her arms and walked behind the sofa. "The *Journal* article has exposed them. Let them sue the *Journal* if they think it's not true. We have the ranch. We've met the terms of the will."

"True," Richard said.

"We only need to make the report and we've finished the bargain. Let's get on with it and be done. Let the public supply the justice for those three."

"Yes, but we submit our report to Jamison. He has to certify it," Richard said.

"Let this hang over his head then, until it's done," Seth said.

"And what if he chooses not to certify it?"

"Then we take legal action. Fraud, collusion, dishonest broker. Now he knows we're talking to Sheldahl so let him stew in it over the weekend."

Ginny nodded. "I'm for that."

"Ok," Richard said. "We have agreed on Jamison." He crossed his legs and slid back in the chair.

How much more comfortable than the canoe seat.

"Now—what about Pinsky and Dixon?"

"Let them cook over the weekend as well," Seth said. "If we get the ranch we have nothing to gain from cooking their goose. Let the public cook 'em."

Ginny took a drink of water, coughed once. "Let the pot bubble awhile, maybe a week and see what comes of it. If we go about our normal business, others will, perhaps, take up the battle."

"We are all in agreement. Seth and I will write a rough draft of the report this afternoon. You can all read it and make comments and we will have it ready Monday morning."

"Make extra copies for Sheldahl, the court, each of us, and Jamison. He may try and lose his copy again," Ginny said.

AFTER LUNCH, RICHARD AND Seth sat down to construct the report.

"Read it again," Seth said.

"Starting May 1ˢᵗ the year of my death, or May 1ˢᵗ the following year," Richard said. "Seth and Richard will undertake a journey by foot, horseback, and canoe from the ranch to the junction of the North and South Platte River, using whichever means of transportation best suits that portion of the route. They are to stay on or as close to the river as possible going into towns only for provisions or assistance. They are not to use any motor or motorized vehicle to speed their journey and must complete this trip within sixty-one days."

"Shoot," Seth said. "We coulda used horses when the river dried up. Why didn't we think about that?"

Richard rubbed the side of his nose. "We were not thinking too well at that point." He continued.

After the reading, silence hung in the room like a shroud. Seth shook his head. "Didn't seem that hard when I heard it the first time."

Richard raised his eyebrows. "It is a lot easier to read it than to do it."

"Amen to that," Seth said.

"Well—let's begin."

"Wait, I need some coffee."

"Bring two. This is going to take a while."

BY MID-AFTERNOON THERE were coffee cups and saucers with kolacky crumbs sitting on the sofa table, the lights were on, and Richard, his head against the back of the sofa, appeared asleep. Seth was writing and the pen scratching the paper could be heard between the clicks of the clock on the mantle.

"Done," Seth said.

Richard lifted his head. "Did you get everything?"

"Yup." He flipped the pages on the legal pad, capped the pen and laid them on the sofa table. "Let Ginny proof it. I'm outta here."

"Where are you going?"

"Fremont."

"Martha is going to have the privilege?"

"Yes, sir."

"Drive carefully. It's a long time to spend the rest of your life in a wheelchair."

Seth shook his head. "Another Mom-ism."

Richard turned in his chair. "Before you go—did you check on the cattle?"

"You know," Seth said. "Ginny and the kids did an outstanding job. There was only one gate needed fixing and they only lost one heifer. Not bad."

"See you when?"

"Oh, I should be back tonight or tomorrow some time. Depends on how long I can stay awake and whether I get the right answers to my questions."

Richard smiled. "Good luck. But I think I know the answer."

Seth lifted his chin. "We'll see."

SUNDAY AFTERNOON GINNY STARTED typing the report. It was full of stuff the family had wondered about. She smiled and frowned as she typed it, checked for errors, and finished it by 3:00 pm. When Richard poured a Scotch, she handed him the printed sheets. He sat in the den, his reading glasses part way down his nose and read the report that Seth had written and Ginny had typed. He sipped his drink at intervals, and let the tiredness seep out through his eyes and face muscles, each joint in succession letting go until he felt like a skin bag that had corralled all the bones and muscles making up his body. He allowed the tiredness to take him. He set the Scotch down and watched with a smile as his eyelids closed and the colors changed. This is what he remembered. The report slipped to his lap.

Report of Platte River Expedition by
Richard and Seth Barrett, May & June 2014

It was the conclusion page that cornered their observations and gave the truncated report its thrust.

Crop and Animal Observations:

The majority of lands we observed produced a monoculture of corn and soybeans. There is a need to diversify like the Watson Ranch did. H.E. Watson established his ranch in 1888 and ended with 8,000 acres reaching from the Platte River on the south to the hills on the north. He raised wheat, rye, barley, corn, potatoes, sugar beets, squash, asparagus, and alfalfa. He built a barn that would hold 400 cows in 1900. Diversification can stave off the problems we are now having in regards to reduction of total crops and the application of increasingly larger amounts of fertilizer, herbicides, insecticides, and fungicides.

Farmers need to farm with all living things in mind: the land, water, air, bacteria, small animals, and on up to deer, including bees. The bottom line can't be the final answer when you are the stewards of the land. If you strive for the maximum bottom line at the degrading of your base (farm, water, air, critters) you miss the total picture and suffer in the long run.

Man has learned to plow so as not to allow topsoil to be blown away in dust storms, has learned to rotate crops to avoid depleting the soil. He can learn how to live with sustainable agriculture. We were most impressed with the need to return to sustainable agriculture as preached to us daily by Filoh Smith, a man who spent his entire adult life on a farm adjacent to the Barrett Ranch, and who died from a rattlesnake bite on this trip.

Richard and Seth were commissioned to determine why Adolph Melzer chose the land to homestead in 1845. Our conclusions:

1. The most water available being on Fourmile Creek and the Platte River.

2. The location is closest to metropolitan markets.

3. The location allows tapping into Nebraska markets and the three adjacent states of Iowa, Missouri, and Kansas.

4. It is closer to Omaha, Chicago, Kansas City, and Des Moines for shipping to major markets.

5. The location is protected from flat prairie wind-blasts.

6. The location provides deeper topsoil and more annual rainfall than western Nebraska.

7. The location is close to the mouth of the Platte
River and the Missouri River traffic and thus
was and is available for shipping commerce.

SERENA LOOKED IN ON him several times. He had not moved. A gentle whisper escaped his lips from time to time. It grew dark and the family ate dinner while Richard enjoyed the first comfortable sleep he had had in months.

MONDAY MORNING CHARLES SMYTH turned up at the ranch, a pad in his left hand and a plastic pocket protector in his shirt loaded with pens and pencils. Charles, a designer, walked with Seth down to Fourmile Creek. They were there an hour before they returned and Charles got in his car and drove back to town.

"What was that all about?" Richard said.

"Gonna build a house down on Fourmile if it's ok with you and Ginny."

"For you and Martha?"

"Yup."

"Why do I have to pull it out of you?" Richard said, shaking his head. "Give."

"Of course she agreed. How could she turn down a good looking feller like me?"

A smile crept over Richard's face. "Congratulations. I am proud of you."

"For what?"

"Making a fresh start. I sort of thought that might not be in your makeup anymore."

"Naw. She's anxious to meet my son in Florida and I'm building the house with the big dining room just like she wants it. We're excited." He pulled the top drawer of the breakfront open. "Where'd Mom keep that scrapbook of photos?"

"What do you need?"

"Your wedding photo. Martha wants to see what my first girlfriend looked like."

"Is that a good thing?"

Seth shrugged. "What do I know about it?"

"I think I would skip it."

"Why's that?"

"She will be looking at a teenage girl in the picture and thinking every morning when she looks in the mirror, that she is fifty and figures you are making mental and physical comparisons every five minutes."

Seth sat on the chair arm. He thought about it a moment. "You know—I think you're right for once."

"Once…"

"Yeah," Seth said nodding his head. "Just this once."

SERENA MOVED HER BELONGINGS from the upstairs bedroom to the master bedroom closet and unpacked the boxes she had stored over the garage and put their contents away.

Richard walked in. "Oh no—you're not moving in until after the ceremony."

She stood up. Put her hands on her hips. "Do you want me to sleep on the couch?"

"No, but I am not comfortable with us living in the same bedroom until—you know—until we are officially married."

Her head bobbed up and down a few seconds. "So your coming over to my place for the last five years was just for what?"

"One has nothing to do with the other."

"I think it does. Nobody around here thinks we are chaste."

Richard adjusted the throw over the bottom of the bed. "That is not the point."

"Pray tell, what is the point?"

"We are not married. That is the point. Married people live together."

Serena shook her head. She took her sweaters out of the top drawer and laid them in the box, then the socks and underwear. She closed the drawer, opened the closet and picked up hangers.

Richard laid his hand over hers. "I can't stand this." He hugged her. Her hand released the hangers and the clothes fell some on the bed, some on the floor. After a few minutes, he reached down, picked up the hangers, put them back on the rod and closed the door.

SHERIFF BUD PINSKY PACED the floor, a cup of coffee in hand. The dispatcher looked at him. "Bud—you're gonna wear a path in the carpet."

"I'm waitin' for a phone call."

"Gottcha, but you're turning the station into a nervous wreck. Take it outside. I'll call you when they call, ok?"

Pinsky opened the door and went into the alley. He lit a cigarette.

How long had he been on cigarettes and coffee? What would an eighty-year old Bud Pinsky look like after sixty years of nicotine and caffeine? Hell with what he'd look like—what would he feel like? That was more like it. And on a Sheriff's pension—if he kept his job after this Barrett affair—where could he live and how well could he live? If this had worked out like Dixon envisioned, he could have retired in a nice house on Johnson Lake, fished, drunk beer and enjoyed small town living. *Stop it! You've got two things to look at right now: Keeping your job and winning the next election. Focus, Damnit. Number one and number two. Focus.*

The rear door to the Sheriff's office opened. The dispatcher jerked his head up and Pinsky walked toward him, his heart racing, his skin becoming moist and clammy. "Phone," he said. "Randolph law office."

"I'll take it out here," Pinsky said. The dispatcher handed him the headset. He straightened his shoulders and stood as tall as he could get standing flat-footed on the asphalt where patrol cars had parked and leaked oil for thirty years.

"Bud, this is Randolph. Here's the deal the prosecutor is offering. Listen to it carefully before you answer. If you agree to plead guilty to attempted sexual assault, the judge is talking one-year probation. It would be over two years before the next election and if you kept your nose clean it would come off your record. The prosecutor is willing to drop the other charges—says they are too difficult to prove. But if you don't take this deal he'll combine the two and go for a jury trial and maximum sentencing.

"Now—I'm not going to tell you what to do but I will give you some suggestions you can ponder. I need an answer before 4:30 today. Does that work for you?"

"Take it," Bud said.

"What?"

"I said take it. Take the probation for a year."

It was silent a moment. "You're sure."

"Absolutely. Take it."

"Okay. I'll call you when it's over."

"Great. Thanks, Randolph."

"So far you're welcome. I think that is a good decision."

Sheriff Bud Pinsky hit the OFF button on the phone, crossed his arms. "That takes care of number one."

CRAIG JAMISON WAITED FOR someone to pick up the phone. He was on the fourth ring when a voice answered, "Cass County Democratic Headquarters."

"This is Craig Jamison. Is Spud there?"

"Just a minute, please."

"Hello, Craig. What can I do for you?" Spud Knowles said.

"I'm looking at my schedule and wanted to co-ordinate with you regarding my speech commitments over the next few months. I've started a fund raising com…"

"…Craig. Sorry for the interruption. The committee has decided to not back you for the senatorial seat due to the recent allegations. I'm sure when you clear them up they'll be happy to…"

"…You're saying I'm off the ticket?"

"At this moment, yes."

"And what moment do you expect me to be back on the ticket?"

It was silent. "I don't know. I'm sure when this is over…"

"…What's over? What are you talking about, Spud?"

"I'm sure you've read the *Journal*…"

"…Of course I read it. Those are false accusations. You mean the committee won't even let me talk with them before they shunt me aside?"

"That was their decision."

"Well, my gawd."

"You know them all. Why don't you call them and give them your side of the story. Maybe they can go along with it."

"Go along with it? Hell—I'm the best person they can have on that ticket."

"Tell them that, Craig. Was there anything else? I've got a meeting starting in two minutes."

Craig lowered his head. "No. No—that's all. Thanks, Spud."

"Anytime, Craig. Bye."

"Yes…goodbye." Craig cradled the phone.

GINNY HOUSTON POURED TWO thirds of a glass of Sterling Chardonnay before setting it down on the table that was within the booth Donavon had built. It would make it easier to get the kids fed and off to school in winter months He had built the back low enough that she could see the full backyard. Donavon was at work, the kids had gone to the Plattsmouth swimming pool, and she could sit for a few minutes, take deep breaths and relax for the first time in over two months.

Had it been that long? Longer, considering the couple of weeks the brothers had spent getting ready. The cattle, getting the kids used to doing tough grownup chores. And then having Serena there. And Bud Pinsky— my gawd—Bud Pinsky. What a circus that was. I'm happy about the court settlement. It wouldn't have done either of us any good to have him in prison. He is a good sheriff—if you are in the 99% of the people he doesn't want to screw or take advantage of. I can live with that. But I'll be aware to the max.

She sipped the wine, smacked her lips. It was too cold. She cupped the glass in her hands to warm it, lifted the bottle and looked at the label. Good year.

A turkey stepped out of the hedgerow and stalked at the edge of the lawn, picking at grasshoppers, being very alert. She smiled. "Goodbye, pheasants; hello turkeys." The world is always changing and the people with it. And the flora and fauna. Dick Reno had been right when he said "the only thing that is permanent is change." She had learned that in his real estate class and it had proven itself over and over. Mostly she was glad that she accepted it. She vowed to accept change as long as she was alive. And drink good wine too. She looked at her glass. This was very good wine.

KLETE DIXON WAS SITTING at the bar when Thad Percy came in and he motioned the reporter over. "Buy you a drink?"

Thad smiled. "After what I wrote?"

Klete smirked a bit and shrugged his shoulders. "You were doing your job."

"And you're okay with that?"

"Hell yes. You gotta step on everybody's toes sometime. What'll you have?"

Thad moved his tongue around inside his mouth. *Was this for real?*

"Tell you what," Thad said. "I'll buy my first drink. If we're still talking after that, I'll take you up on your offer."

Klete smirked. "Thad, I could buy and sell most of the people in this town. I won't miss $9. Let me have a good feeling by buying you a drink. After what you wrote about me, think how good it will make me feel to go home tonight knowing that I had bought you a drink. Hell—I'll buy you a whole bottle—or a case."

"Then how about a steak dinner?"

"Hell yes—that too."

"I'll have a martini—Boodles Gin, with a twist of lime. And the biggest filet mignon they have in the refrigerator."

This ought to be interesting.

"Now, that's a good order. Let's move to the booth over there." Klete picked up his glass and stood up. "Let me tell you," he said, "how I felt when I read that story you wrote. First of all, I was impressed with the quality of your writing and how you got the sequences so well laid out. Some of the facts were off a bit, but you got the family history correct. That's from you being immersed in the area, covering all the local stuff, and knowing all the people. That's good. That's good reporting."

Thad had sipped the drink before he remembered to squeeze the lime in it. He held it up and watched the oils move around in the glass. Reminded him of the lava lamps of the 60s.

Could you eat and drink with the enemy? Hell yeah—especially when he bought the steaks and booze. I don't have to take on his attributes or believe him but I could listen to him. I'm not going to escape seeing Klete Dixon around town and it didn't make him clean because the county pros-ecutor dropped all potential charges against him, but I'm not eating and drinking with an ex-criminal either. And listen to him justifying his every reported action. It's a hoot. Or is it the Martini hooting?

FOUR DAYS AFTER DELIVERING their report to Craig Jamison, the estate was settled and deed to the ranch and bill of sale to all of the personal property, including livestock was transferred from the estate to Richard Duncan Howard Barrett as to 40 % ownership; to Seth Andrew William Barrett as to 40 % ownership; and to Virginia Alexandria Mae Barrett Houston as to 20% ownership, as her own estate. At the first meeting of the new owners a motion was made and unanimously approved to contact James E. Horne, PhD, at the Kerr Center in Oklahoma and find out what the procedures were to convert from an industrial farming mentality to a sustainable agricultural mentality. If Filoh Smith could conceive of it, the Barrett Farm could do it.

"It is going to be a long process," Richard said.

"Yeah—but it'll be fun," Seth said.

"It's agreed then—we're unanimous on our first meeting. Hooray," Ginny said.

The River

The water slowed, then lowered inch by inch as the rush faded away like the last sounds of battle, a whisp of drums mixed with the musty odor of drying sand and mud that permeated the ozone charged air. The river sighed. Birds came back and perched on branches of trees that had made the journey, but short of the big river, had lodged in the sandbars. The water was clean now—the bottom visible. As the water level sank, sand feathered in layers like an ocean shore. It was quiet. The exuberant noise the release made had moved on with the rushing water. I have said my piece. Let us see what they do with it.

END

Anchorage, Alaska

Thank you for buying my books. Readers are driving the book market while accountants are driving the large publishing houses. The new way to garner attention for a book is to have readers go to public websites and write a short review, giving their opinion and feelings after reading the book.

I would appreciate it a lot if you could work your way to any or all of these websites and write your review. Be forthright and don't pull punches. Tell it like it is.

http://www.barnesandnoble.com/s/Jim-Misko?keyword
=Jim+Misko&store=book

https://www.goodreads.com/book/show/18600521-the-cut-of-pride

http://www.amazon.com/s/ref=nb_sb_noss_1?url=search-
alias%3Dstripbooks&field-keywords=Jim%20Misko

Double click on any of the sites above and proceed to write a review by clicking on the (#) of reviews on each site. That will open previous reviews and give you a page to write your review.

And you can let me and the world know about your review by posting it on facebook by clicking on the "f" at the end of the review.

May it go well with you.

James A. Misko
www.jimmisko.com
jim@jimmisko.com

Cover and interior book design by Frame25 Productions
www.frame25productions.com

Praise for:
For What He Could Become

"I was not expecting a full blown action and emotion packed, transporting reading experience. I could not put it down, and once the race started, did not. When I had finished…I reread it cover to cover. In forty years of fairly steady and broad based book devouring, I have seldom done that! You are in good company; Kipling, Faulkner, and Scott."

—Skip Lynar

"Great book!!!! Cathy got hold of it first and almost could not put it down until she finished it. She *never* reads a book. Then my turn. I didn't like it, I loved it. The story was so true to life and what I have seen so many times throughout Alaska. The race part was so perfect that I got cold, was elated, depressed, all the emotions one gets while actually running. It took me out on the trail again, especially the early years. Congratulations."

—Dick Mackey, Winner of the 1978 Iditarod, and author of *One Second to Glory*

"I stayed up till about 12:30 this morning…can't tell you how enjoyable the book is and am looking forward to your next. Found myself laughing in some parts and sniffling in others. Exhausted at the finish line pushing the dogs and Bill along all the way."

—Joyce Delgado

"I can see that old church where the natives stayed, walking to an early death. The effort the Gospel Mission gave to those people was incredible. In your novel the struggle of the Alaska native who leaves the village and subsistence lifestyle is clearly depicted. I sweat and bled and cried with him as he struggled to come back through the running of the Iditarod. An outstanding story."

—Don Jack

Praise for:
The Most Expensive Mistress in Jefferson County

"This is Great Stuff! I could not put this down in spite of having a business associate in town for two days."

—Mary Ann Shaughnessy Krum

"I tried, but I couldn't put it down. I ate lunch reading it, then scotch at 5:00, then dinner, alone at the dining room table with the lights full on, and finished it in bed. What a ride. Gimmie another one."

—Darry Gemmell

"Most entertaining, uplifting book I've read all year. Makes me wish he would write a novel a month. Having spent a good deal of my life in real estate, I can feel for the protagonist as he gets caught up in trying to close that large of a transaction, knowing he has every chip he owns in the deal. What a close one."

—Don Jack

"The characters were so real I could see, smell and feel each one and see inside their heads. Their emotions were mine. The humor had me laughing out loud while tears of tension and frustration welled in my eyes. The dialogue was faultless and kept the pages crackling. You have captured the essence of Native Americans with sensitivity and understanding. And you have given heart to a big business deal. Thanks for a great read."

—Jeanne Tallman

"Jim Misko's novels celebrate the spirit of adventure and the strength of perseverance."

—Irena Praitis, Author of *Branches* and *One Woman's Life*. Professor of Literature and Creative Writing at University of California State, Fullerton

Praise for:
The Cut of Pride

"Jim Misko's love of writing is evident in this richly detailed and closely observed account of the forces that hold a family replete with resentment, strength, weakness, and love in thrall to a life that leads inevitably to destruction."
—Lynn Schooler, author of *Walking Home, a traveler in the Alaska Wilderness*

"Jim Misko, in his new novel *The Cut of Pride*, does something that is really rare in modern literature; he writes about hard, brutal, unpleasant physical labor. And he does it with such vivid detail that the labor itself becomes one of the major entities in the story. His cast of complex, dysfunctional characters—owners and employees of a mink-raising farm in coastal Oregon—nearly destroys itself in its struggle with the endless, nasty toil. These are unforgettable characters, and their pride and distrust and bitterness make for grim drama. Like Hemingway, Steinbeck and Ruark, he writes close to the edge."
—James Alexander Thom, author of *Follow the River*

"'Nature is tough on the young,' observes Jeff Baker, the protagonist of Jim Misko's newest novel *The Cut of Pride*. In this gritty, evocative book, Misko looks unflinchingly at the harshest realities of running a mink farm on the Oregon coast. In doing so, he reveals the dirty underbelly that supports the glamour of mink coats and the violence that underlies so much of human existence. His characters sort through the work, the killing, and the fatigue to find the few factors of life that offer meaning. As they struggle with endless labor, each other, and their thoughts on living, they find friendship, pride, tragedy, and endurance. The characters, images, and emotions of this book will stay with a reader long after the novel ends."
—Irena Praitis, Professor of Literature and Creative Writing at California State University, Fullerton, author of *One Woman's Life*

Praise for:
As All My Fathers Were

"In this tough but tender story of two estranged brothers—and their event-filled trek down Nebraska's Platte River—Misko simultaneously paints a memorable portrait, as incisive as it is illuminating, of America's disappearing past and its increasingly conflicted future."

—Robert Masello, author of *The Romanov Cross*

"Jim Misko has done it again. *As All My Fathers Were* is a masterpiece. This novel has everything a reader searches for in pursuit of a fine book—strong characters, brilliant dialogue, exciting plot, tension that bounces off every page, conflict, high ideals and villainy. In addition, by the end of the book, the average reader is far better educated and informed of a real-life issue of which the vast majority is uninformed."

—Stephen Maitland-Lewis, Award-winning author of *Ambition* and *Emeralds Never Fade*

"*As All My Fathers Were* is highly recommended; it's a walk (or more accurately, a ride) down Memory Lane at the very same time as a bridge to the future. That's a tall order to fill, but Misko accomplishes it well and then some."

—Bryce Lambley, author of *Platte River Driftwood*

"This is Jim Misko's best book. What a read. Accurate because of his knowledge of the area. Misko's devoted followers should double as new readers finish the last page. The interplay of characters, both virtuous and villainous, is great as a major family calamity looms."

—Denis Bromley, friend, follower and fellow Scotch drinker

"A passion play for the New West, *As All My Fathers Were* gathers momentum the way a river grows, gathering substance with every bend and merging channel, and shines in its descriptive writing. This is Misko at his best."

—Lynn Schooler, author of *Heartbroke Bay*

"Jim Misko's *As All My Fathers Were*, set in 2014, with historical reference to the mid-1800s, the novel's core is the story of a deceased family matriarch, Mae Barrett, and her passion to convert their farming philosophy from one of "industrial methods" to "sustainable agriculture." Given this heady premise I can state the book still manages to achieve, at times, the momentum of an entertaining page-turner."

—John P. Hagen, author of *Play Away Please*

"Jim Misko in his new novel, *As All My Fathers Were*, has given us a novel and unique portrait of the Platte River country, as well as some interesting characters to conduct the reader on this journey. Well done, Jim."

—Dick Couch, author of *Act of Revenge* and *Always Faithful, Always Forward*

"*As All My Fathers Were* is a refreshingly unapologetic, environmental polemic—one with living characters and a pulse. But far more remarkable than the story of two Nebraska farmers on a quest to save their land, is its author: an 80-something self-described gun-toting political conservative. Jim Misko's condemnation of modern agribusiness bares an essential truth: Nature knows no politics, and we're all in this together. Off in the distance, you can hear Edward Abbey, Rachel Carson, and the Platte River itself applauding."

—Nick Jans, author of *A Wolf Called Romeo*

"If you want to know how the Platte River works, read James A. Misko's absorbing and rambunctious tale of Seth and Richard Barrett, who must complete a journey up the river from its confluence with the Missouri to its source near North Platte, Nebraska, and back if they are to inherit the family farm. In *As All My Fathers Were*, you'll learn the natural history of this once wild river that shaped the land and those who lived near it but in the past century has been broken by energy generation and the agricultural industry. Yet as Misko's novel bears witness, the Platte still has the power to inspire the imagination and fine literature."

—Lisa Knopp, author of *What the River Carries: Encounters with the Mississippi, Missouri, and Platte*